over the MOON

ROSEWOOD RIVER

USA Today **Bestselling Author**

Laura Pavlov

Entangled Publishing, LLC
644 Shrewsbury Commons Ave., STE 181
Shrewsbury, PA 17361
rights@entangledpublishing.com

Amara is an imprint of Entangled Publishing, LLC.
Visit our website at www.entangledpublishing.com.

Edited by Nicole McCurdy
Cover design by Hang Lee
Cover images by DrPAS/Shutterstock, omograf/Shutterstock,
Md Ashik Sarker/Shutterstock
Edge Design by Bree Archer
Edge image by Nongkran_ch/GettyImages
Interior design by Britt Marczak

ISBN 978-1-64937-975-7

Manufactured in the United States of America

First Edition July 2025

10 9 8 7 6 5 4 3 2 1

ALSO BY LAURA PAVLOV

Rosewood River

Steal My Heart
My Silver Lining
Over the Moon

Honey Mountain

Always Mine
Ever Mine
Make You Mine
Simply Mine
Only Mine

Magnolia Falls

Loving Romeo
Wild River
Forbidden King
Beating Heart
Finding Hayes

Cottonwood Cove

Into the Tide
Under the Stars
On the Shore
Before the Sunset
After the Storm

You walked into my life like you had always lived there,
Like my heart was a home built just for you.
a.r.asher

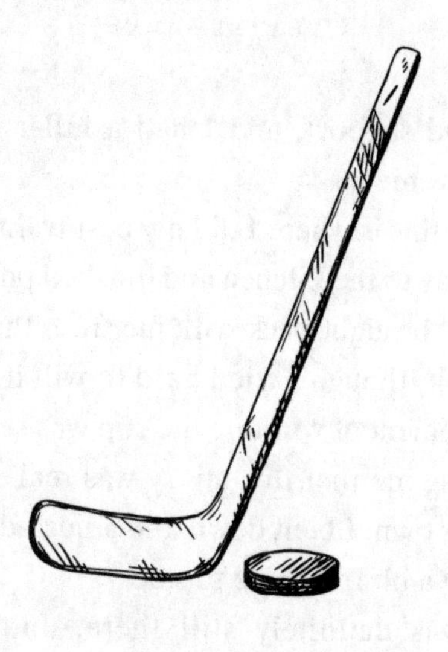

1
Clark

It had been one week since we won the Stanley Cup, and my days had been filled with interviews, celebrations, and doctor appointments. More celebrations than anything else, and I'd consumed more champagne than any one human should. But there was a time and a place for everything.

Work hard. Play hard.

To say that I was happy to be back in Rosewood River was an understatement. I'd be able to train at home for the next few months while I recovered from my MCL injury and get myself in game shape before the new season.

Home had always grounded me. It was the place where I focused best.

Surrounded by family, running trails, and the river. Less

distractions, good support, and I had a killer home gym that made it very convenient.

Bottom line, this is where I did my best training.

I made my way to the kitchen and finished putting away a few groceries that I'd brought back with me from the city. I was still limping a little bit, though I tried hard to will it away. And now that all the excitement of winning the cup was settling down, the reality was hitting me that this injury was real and wouldn't be going away on its own. I bent down and adjusted my knee brace, stretching my leg a bit from side to side.

The pain was definitely still there, and I grabbed an icepack and took a seat at the kitchen island, resting the ice on my knee as I propped my leg up. I glanced down when my phone vibrated, and Ryan Weston's name flashed across the screen. He was my teammate and one of my best friends. We just clicked from the first day we met at the start of last season. He was more like a brother; we just got one another. Weston played right wing, and I played center, so he and I liked to give one another shit about who could score more goals in a game. We worked well together, and it showed when we were on the ice.

"What's up, brother?" I said, reaching for my water bottle and taking a sip.

"Just seeing if you made it back home all right."

"Yep. Got in a little while ago, just getting unpacked and settled," I said, setting my water down on the island. "How are you feeling?"

He barked out a laugh. We've been going hard for the last few days as the Lions fans in San Francisco had come out to celebrate us and our win in full force. Last night, there was a big celebration downtown, and we enjoyed every minute.

"I've been chugging water all day. No more booze for me. I start training next week. How's the knee feeling?"

"It'll be fine," I said, blowing out a breath.

I was frustrated. I was coming off the best season of my life, playing for the team I've dreamed about playing for since I was a kid. And now I was fucking injured, at a time when I needed to push even harder. All eyes would be on me when the new season started. Hockey was my priority, and everything I've ever wanted was right here in my grasp. I just needed my knee to heal and then push harder than ever over the next few months. "It's not something I haven't dealt with before."

"Yeah, you've got this, dude. No doubt about it. And Coach has a full-time physical therapist coming to work with you," he said as he barked out a laugh. "And from what I just overheard, she's not all that happy about it."

Coach's daughter, Eloise Gable, had just been hired by the Lions as our full-time physical therapist, and Coach wanted me to work with her to get my knee healthy before the season started again in a few months.

I groaned. "Well, she's clearly not a fan of mine. She's snapped at me the two times I've actually spoken to her, and she glared at me last night when I poured that bottle of champagne over Coach Gable's head, along with everyone else on the team, but she seems specifically annoyed with me. What did you hear?"

"I went over to the training center this morning because I left my gym bag there, and she came storming out of Coach's office, then snapped something about seeing him in three months seeing as he banished her to Rosewood River." He howled in laughter. "I'm sorry to tell you, but I think we found the first woman who wants nothing to do with you, even if everyone else thinks you're the NHL's golden boy."

I rolled my eyes even though he couldn't see me. "She's acting like he sent her to the North fucking Pole. It's Rosewood River. Everyone loves it here. It's offensive that she's that worked up about it, and I sure as shit didn't request for her to come here."

"Hey, don't shoot the messenger." He chuckled. "You know I love Rosewood River. But good luck winning Eloise Gable over. I think you're already enemy number one."

I ran a hand down my face. "You seem to be enjoying this."

"Nah, you know I've got your back. I'm just not used to seeing a woman start out hating you like this. It might be kind of fun to watch." The sound of him clapping his hands together loudly had me pulling the phone away from my ear. "You've got your work cut out for you, brother."

"Listen, I'm just focused on getting this knee back on track and then pushing hard over the next three months. We're going to be on everyone's radar this coming season. Eloise Gable is the least of my worries. I'm not going to let her annoyance about being here be a distraction. I didn't demand she come here; Coach did. I'm happy to rehab my knee myself. I've done it before. If she doesn't want to be here, then so be it. I'm doing my thing."

"Dude, this might be more challenging than you think. I know she's Coach's daughter, but damn, she's smoking hot." He whistled. "So good luck with all of that."

"Please. I'm a professional athlete. I've handled worse. I'm not worried at all."

"All right, brother. You do have a one-track mind when it comes to hockey. And keeping your distance from Coach's daughter is probably not a bad idea," he said, his voice laced with humor. "And don't you have your big hometown Chadwick celebratory parade tomorrow?"

I chuckled, taking the icepack off my knee and making my

way to the freezer before placing it inside the door. "Something like that. When you grow up in a small town, they celebrate everything."

"We won the fucking Stanley Cup, dude!" he shouted. "You go own that shit tomorrow."

"I plan on it," I said. "And you're giving me a hard time when you've got some big party planned for you back home this weekend, don't you?"

"Yep. I'm leaving to head out in a little bit." He lived two hours outside the city in Brenswick, California, a town that was twice the size of Rosewood River. "I'm fairly certain I'm the first professional athlete to ever come out of Brenswick. So winning the cup is a big deal back home."

"As it should be." I smiled, still reveling in the fact that we actually pulled it off. "All right, drive safe. Text me later. We can commiserate when we start training on Monday."

"Count on it," he said. "We fucking did it, Chadwick. Let's enjoy this before we start the grind again."

"Yeah, we did, buddy. And I say we do it again next season."

He barked out a laugh. "Hell, yeah! Tell your fam I said hello, and we'll talk soon."

I told him to do the same before I ended the call.

A text came through as soon as I set my phone down on the counter.

Unknown Number: *Hello, Clark. It's Eloise Gable. I'll be in Rosewood River Sunday evening, and we'll start physical therapy and training on Monday. Just wanted to make sure you were aware of the situation.*

Me: *Hey, Eloise. I heard you're thrilled about relocating for the next few months.*

I chuckled, knowing that was going to irritate her, and for whatever reason, I enjoyed it.

I updated her contact info as I waited for her to respond.

Eloise: *I'm fine. It's my job. So, we're good to start working together Monday morning?*

Me: *If you come early, you could attend the parade they're throwing for me downtown tomorrow. I'm sure you'd love that.*

Reaching for my water bottle, I barked out a laugh because I knew that would be the last thing she'd want to do.

Eloise: *Well, Clark, I just found out I'm relocating for three months, and as much as I'd love to see you dance around on a float once again… I'll be packing for my move.*

Me: *I detect sarcasm.*

Eloise: *Nope, but I would appreciate it if you'd be careful moving around on that leg. I'm coming to help you heal, and it would be easier if you would get on board with that.*

Me: *It's called taking a minute to celebrate the biggest win of our lives.*

Eloise: *Well, I'm taking three months to get you ready for the season.*

Me: *This should be fun. <laughing face emoji>*

Eloise: *It's not about fun for me. This is my job. Text me the address to the gym, please.*

I let out a breath before sending her my home address,

unsure if she knew the gym we'd be training in was my own personal gym. But she'd figure that out quickly. She wasn't happy about coming here, and honestly, I wasn't thrilled about it either.

Hockey was my job, too. I took it very seriously. But we were allowed to celebrate for a few days before we got back to work.

The woman appeared to be very uptight and easily annoyed.

I saw the three little dots move across the screen before they disappeared.

She was done with the chitchat, and I wasn't surprised.

The pounding on my front door had me moving off the bar stool and heading that way.

"Open up, dickhead!" a familiar voice shouted from the other side of the door.

I tugged open the door to find my oldest brother, Bridger, standing there.

"What are you doing here?" I asked. "I thought we were meeting up tomorrow."

My entire family had been at every single playoff game, and it had been a battle, so there'd been seven games in total.

It meant a lot to me that they'd all been there.

Even my brother, Rafe, and his girlfriend, Lulu, who currently lived in Paris, had been there.

"I came to check on you," he said, moving past me as he held up a large bag of food from the Honey Biscuit Café. The smell of tangy barbecue had my stomach rumbling.

"Damn. I guess I am hungry."

"You look like shit. How's the knee?" Bridger asked.

"Thanks," I rolled my eyes at him as he pulled open the back door and set the food on the table there. "I haven't slept much this past week. It's been nonstop. Happy to be home."

The sun was just starting to go down, and my yard sat right on the river. Water splashed against the rocks, and the smell of pine and lavender flooded my senses.

We dropped to sit at the big wooden table on my patio, and he handed me my food and utensils. "You've been going hard through the playoffs and then celebrating just as hard. I assumed you'd be hungry, and I was just picking up dinner there."

"Thanks. This is great."

He studied me before taking the lid off his plate. "You worried about the knee?"

Bridger was a complete hardass by nature, but the dude had a soft side for his family, even if he tried hard to hide it.

"No. I've dealt with this before. I've got a full-time physical therapist moving here for three months to help me rehab it back to health, all while getting in shape for the new season." I scrubbed a hand down my face, knowing this was going to be a lot of work. I was up for it, but it wouldn't be easy.

"Good. I'm glad they're sending someone. And I'm glad you can do it from home." He picked up a giant beef rib and took a bite.

"Yeah, me too. But from what I've heard, she isn't happy about having to relocate here for the next few months."

"Well, you scored the winning goal at the Stanley Cup, I'm guessing you can call in a few favors."

It wasn't like that, though. I wasn't being an asshole about being here. I really was just a dude who liked being home.

"Nah, it's not like that. There are fewer distractions here, and I can get myself in shape and do what I need to do. There are no photographers trying to catch you doing something wrong. Fewer bars. Fewer distractions." I chuckled.

"I get that. So, you'll do your thing; it's what you do best." He shrugged. "And I'm sure you'll win your physical therapist over in no time."

I barked out a laugh. "That might be tougher than winning the cup."

He smirked. "You're Clark fucking Chadwick. You've got this."

I stretched my leg out on the bench seating and nodded.

I had my work cut out for me, and I doubted Eloise Gable was going to make it easy for me.

But he was right. I was up for the challenge.

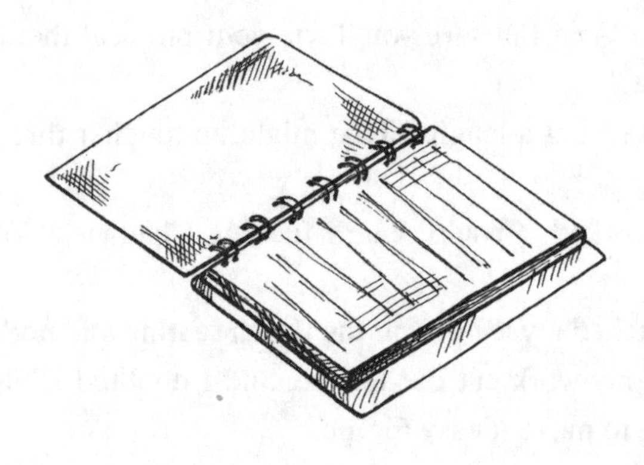

2

Eloise

"This is the cutest guesthouse I've ever seen," I said, as I glanced around the place. I rented the guest house from Emilia Taylor after finding the place on an online app for short-term rentals.

Wood floors, large white-paned windows looking out at the yard, and the most adorable cottage décor.

"Thank you, I just renovated it, so you're the first person to rent it out," Emilia said, as her cowboy boots clanked against the wood floor. She had the cutest style with her jean cutoff shorts and a cute white tee. "I figured it would be short-term tourists who would want it, so this is great for me that you're here for almost three months."

I was irritated that I had to relocate to accommodate a prima donna athlete, but as my father reminded me multiple times when I packed up to leave the city, this was my job, and I was lucky to have it.

Yes, I'd been hired by the San Francisco Lions as the team's physical therapist.

Yes, my father was the coach.

Yes, everyone assumed that's why I got the job.

But I was also extremely qualified, and I wouldn't have gotten this job if I hadn't been. My father may have gotten me in the door, but I had proven that I deserved to stay.

I attended one of the few universities that offered a dual degree program, allowing me to receive my doctorate in physical therapy and my master's in athletic training.

The team already had an athletic trainer, so I'd only been hired on as a physical therapist, but I was as qualified as one could get.

And from where I was sitting, Clark Chadwick was a diva.

He'd taken none of my advice thus far on the few interactions that we've had, and now I had to move to a little town and work one-on-one with him because he was ever so important to the Lions.

Yes, I also had my Ph.D. in sarcasm.

I couldn't stand an athlete who thought he was more important than anyone else on the team.

You know the saying… there's no I in team.

But interestingly enough, all the letters in the word *dick* happen to be in Chadwick.

Call it girl math… but I had this guy's number.

"Well, the team has offered to pay for three months' rent, but I'm hoping it doesn't take that long. I'm just here to work with one of our athletes."

"Is it Clark Chadwick? You mentioned you worked for the Lions, right?" she asked.

"Yes. I'm guessing you know him if you're from here?"

"I do. I grew up here. Everyone knows the Chadwicks. They have a big family. And Clark being a professional hockey player and winning the Stanley Cup is a big deal in Rosewood River," she said, pulling her long dark braid over her shoulder as she set the keys down on the counter. "You missed the big parade for him a few days ago."

"I heard about that. And yes, there is so much to celebrate." I shrugged, not wanting to praise the bastard any more than he already had been. He was on every news channel this week and several sports magazine covers, as he'd scored the winning goal for the Stanley Cup.

He was big news everywhere at the moment, so of course, his hometown was going to celebrate him.

"Yes, it's very exciting, and I'm glad that brought you here." She smiled. "Have you checked out downtown yet?"

"No. I just drove straight here. But I can't wait to go explore a little."

"Oh, there's so many cute shops and great places to eat. You'll have to stop by my flower shop."

"You own a flower shop?" I asked.

"I do. It's called Vintage Rose, and there's a boutique attached owned by a friend of mine."

"That sounds like my cup of tea," I said. "I'll definitely stop by."

"I just live in the main house on my own, so if you need anything, don't hesitate to come on over."

I was renting the little guest cottage behind her home. It was a charming white ranch house with black shutters, and the guesthouse was just a smaller version with the same aesthetic.

"I love the flower boxes you have on both houses. It's so charming," I said.

"Well, decorating is my love language." She chuckled. "I think it adds some nice curb appeal with that splash of color."

"It's amazing. And the décor in here is absolute perfection." I moved through the space, admiring all the details. White shiplap on the walls, a small white couch with pink floral throw pillows, and a crystal chandelier above. It looked like something out of a magazine.

"Thank you. My dad thought it was too girly, but I'm just fine if women are drawn to the place." She shrugged.

"I don't think you are going to ever have a hard time renting this place out." I stopped in the kitchen and gaped at how cute the turquoise-colored oven with bronze knobs was. There was a matching vintage refrigerator. It was the perfect pop of color with the white quartz countertops, white cabinets, and white subway tile backsplash. "This kitchen is dreamy."

"Ohhhh," she squealed. "This makes me so happy. You're really the first person to see the place all done, outside of my family, and they don't get very excited about home décor."

"Well, you killed it." I paused and looked at her. Emilia was definitely someone I would be friends with. We appeared to be about the same age, and I loved her style. She was petite with long dark hair and striking bright blue eyes. She was sweet and just gave off those friend vibes. "So, what do people our age do for fun around here?"

"Well, there's the river, which is in peak season right now. We've got great rafting, but it's also just a fun place to hang out on the weekends even if you don't want to take a death ride down the river. And then you've got Booze & Brews, which is where all the locals hang out on the weekends. Honey Biscuit Café has the best food in town—just avoid the mac and cheese because it's rich and can be a little tough on your stomach." She chuckled. "Anyway, probably TMI with that, but if you ever want to hang out, just let me know. I'd be happy to show you around."

"I'd love that. I don't know anyone here," I said.

"Well, you know Clark Chadwick, so you'll be in with the Chadwick family in no time. They're a tight bunch." Her cheeks pinked the slightest bit, which made me wonder if she was dating one of them.

"I don't know Clark at all. I've met him twice, and I wouldn't exactly say we hit it off. So, this job might be a little challenging."

Her eyes widened at my admission, and I prayed to God she wasn't dating one of the Chadwicks and I didn't just stick my foot in my mouth.

"He's actually really nice. They don't care much for me, so we're friendly, but just in passing."

"Oh, tell me more," I said, as I hopped up to sit on the counter.

Her head tipped back in laughter. "It's nothing exciting. My family owns the *Rosewood River Review*. I don't think the Chadwicks are fans of the newspaper."

"Really? Clark Chadwick is on the front page of almost every newspaper in the country right now, yet he has a problem with his small-town newspaper?"

"There is this anonymous column in the newspaper, and it's called the *Taylor Tea*. You know, they dish the tea." She shrugged, and her smile was forced as if she wasn't too pleased about it. "And the Chadwicks are a hot topic in this town. They are never fully named, but a lot of the articles appear to be about them."

"And they have a problem with it?"

"Apparently so. Or maybe they just don't like me… I don't know." She waved her hands, and her cheeks flushed once again. "The oldest brother, Bridger, just seems to despise me. The others sort of fake it, but Easton's and Rafe's girlfriends, Henley and Lulu, are really nice, and they come by the flower shop often. So at least they don't seem offended by me."

"I can't imagine anyone being offended by you," I said, and I meant it, because I had no doubt that Emilia Taylor was as genuine as they come. "And the oldest brother being that worked up about your parents owning a newspaper is ridiculous. Newspapers have been around since long before we were born. What is his deal?"

I was already annoyed with Clark Chadwick, but now they all sounded like a bunch of jackasses.

She shook her head, and her eyes were wide. "No, they're great. Really. Everyone loves the Chadwicks."

I certainly wasn't impressed.

"Well, you're my first friend in town, and I'm Team Emilia. I also happen to be a big reader, so I don't get offended by a local newspaper."

"Wait. Are you a *reader*-reader? Like a lover of books?" she asked, her voice going to a whisper. "What do you read?"

I fell forward with a laugh because she said it with such curiosity.

"I'm a big romance reader. Historical. Contemporary. Dark. Small-town. I even dabble in a little mafia here and there. How about you?"

A wide grin spread across her face. "I'm all about the romance genre. I've never met a romance I didn't like."

"Stop!" I shoved at her shoulder and chuckled. "We're going to be best friends, aren't we?"

"I think we are. And we can buddy read so we can talk about it while we read." She smiled so big it made me laugh.

"I would love that. I'm finishing up a small-town romance this week."

"Oh, I just finished this awesome football romance, so I'm ready to dive into something new."

"Okay, let's pick something to read together next."

"Yes! Count me in," she said. "I'll look at my TBR and run a few options by you."

"It's a deal," I said. "I love buddy reading. It's so much fun when you can discuss it with someone."

"Yes. It's the best. And how about we go to Booze & Brews this weekend, grab dinner and a drink, and talk about our favorite book boyfriends?" She waggled her brows.

"I would love that." I jumped down from the counter. "There's nothing better than finding new book besties."

"I totally agree." She chuckled. "Let me show you the rest of the place, and I'll help you bring your stuff in from your car."

"You're just winning me over more and more," I said, as I followed her to see the bedroom and bathroom. This house was perfect. And Emilia shared that the river was just a block away.

I was getting more on board with this move now that I'd made a friend and seen the place in person. The pictures were cute, but they didn't do it justice.

My only aggravation would be my reason for being here: Clark Chadwick.

And tomorrow we'd be starting PT and training.

Emilia and I spent the next hour and a half getting my car unloaded, and she'd even insisted I come over to her house for dinner.

It had been a full day.

When I finally got back to the guest cottage, I went to the bathroom to start a bath, and my phone vibrated on the counter.

Egomaniac Chadwick: *Hey. I'll see you tomorrow. Is 6:00 a.m. too early?*

I pulled out my notebook and wrote down the time beside his address. I've always been someone who liked to write everything down.

Notebooks were my thing.

So maybe I was slightly type A. It's what got me through college.

Hell, it's what got me through life thus far.

And why did I feel like he was testing me with the 6:00 a.m. question?

That was damn early. I figured we'd start at 8:00 a.m. But I wasn't going to be the weak link here.

Me: *I usually start at 5:30 a.m., but 6:00 a.m. works for me.*

I chuckled because I loved a salty comeback.

Egomaniac Chadwick: *Great. See you tomorrow.*

I switched over to my work notebook and took a look at my workout plans for Clark. I'd met with Randall Tallon, who was the athletic trainer for the Lions, to go over the conditioning that I'd focus on, and then we'd be doing physical therapy to heal and strengthen that knee. Randall would be working with every other athlete on the team, while the diva got all of my attention. My father was adamant that I come here and focus on Clark. He was their star player at the moment, and my father raved about the guy like he was some sort of god.

Ridiculous.

Yes, he had an amazing season. The best of his career.

But from where I was sitting, the man was reckless. He sustained an injury in the final game, yet he celebrated and partied as if he didn't have a care in the world.

But it wasn't my job to monitor his behavior.

It was my job to heal him and make sure he was in the best shape of his life when he returned to the city in a few months.

And that's exactly what I intended to do.

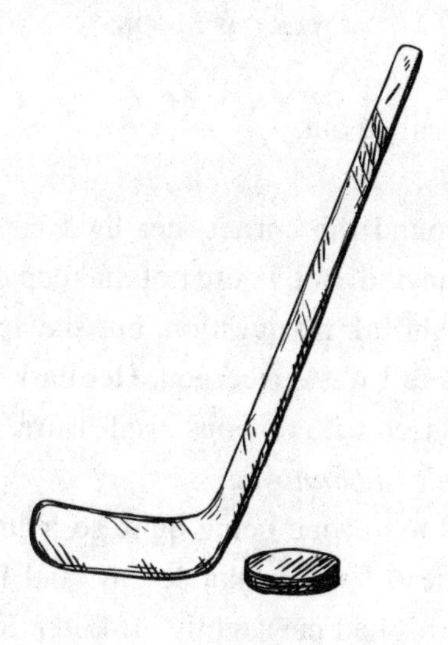

3

Clark

I was used to getting up and going for a run, but I knew running wasn't an option at the moment. Hopefully, in a week or two, I could get back out there. I wasn't sure how long this recovery would take. I've had issues with my MCL in the past, but this was definitely the most severe injury I've had to date.

I was a mellow dude in most aspects of my life, aside from hockey.

My job.

My profession.

My passion.

So I was feeling anxious about getting back into my routine.

There was a knock on the door, and I shouted for her to come in while I popped the last bite of banana into my mouth and slammed my protein shake.

"Hello?" she called out.

"I'm in here."

She came around the corner, her light brown hair pulled back in a long ponytail, not a stitch of makeup on her face. She was naturally beautiful, no question, but she appeared to have a big attitude where I was concerned. Her dark brown eyes met mine, and they blazed with obvious displeasure.

She was clearly still annoyed.

I wasn't used to anyone being quite so irritated with me, if I were being honest. I was a likable guy, and I got along with most people. So this had me slightly off-kilter. She was not only my physical therapist, but she was Coach Gable's daughter, and I loved the dude. I couldn't have his girl hating on me for the next few months.

She dropped the large duffle bag that she was carrying on her shoulder on the floor and folded her arms over her chest. She wore a black fitted tank top and black athletic shorts. They weren't showy in the slightest, yet they hugged her curves in the most distracting way.

"Who shit in your cornflakes?" I asked.

"Excuse me?"

"What's with the attitude? You've been here for all of two seconds."

She sighed. "I don't have an attitude. You're the one who felt the need to reference shit and cereal in one sentence. I haven't spoken yet."

"All right. Good morning, Eloise. Should I call you Eloise?"

She gaped at me. "What else would you call me?"

"I don't know. Aren't you a doctor? I thought maybe you'd want to be called Dr. Eloise." I smirked as I rinsed my blender cup in the sink and dried off my hands.

"Well, technically, if I were a medical doctor, I'd be Dr. Gable, not Dr. Eloise." She rolled her eyes. "But no, I'm not a physician. I have my Doctorate of Physical Therapy. So you can call me Eloise. No fancy title necessary."

"All right. Let's go to the gym, and we can get started." I reached for her duffle bag, and she slapped my hand away.

Literally, the woman slapped my hand.

"I've got it, Hotshot," she grunted, yanking the strap from my hand and making no attempt to hide her irritation.

For fuck's sake. What was her deal?

I moved in front of her down the hallway, pushing the door open to the gym. I invested a lot of money in my home gym, and it was one of my favorite rooms in the house, only second to the backyard that sat on the river, where I go for swims after my workouts when the weather permits.

She dropped her bag and turned in a slow circle, taking in all the equipment.

"This will do." She bent down to pull a few things out of her bag.

"This will do?" I said, not hiding my irritation now. This gym rivaled most professional gyms. Hockey was my livelihood, and keeping myself in shape was my job. So throw me a goddamn bone when it comes to my home gym. "Listen, I'm not sure what I've done to piss you off, but I'd like to just hash it out so we can get to work."

"I'm here to work." She pushed to stand, dropping a few straps and bands onto the floor and setting a stack of notebooks on the countertop beside her. "That's the reason I've relocated to *your hometown,* to focus solely on you."

There it is.

"That wasn't my choice. I am capable of training myself. I've done it my entire life."

"Oh, that's right. You're a hockey star, a physical therapist, and an athletic trainer," she said, arching a brow.

"I didn't say that. Don't put words in my mouth." I stepped forward, shoulders back, meeting her glare head-on. "I'm saying that I've always trained myself."

"So you don't need me here?"

I looked away for a few beats before turning back to meet her gaze. "Listen, it's obvious that you don't want to be here, and I get it. I know I need your help, and I didn't mean to imply anything differently. I came back home because it's where I train best. It's where my family is. It's quiet here, and I can focus. I did not know that your father was going to insist on you coming here. I figured I could just meet with a local PT and do the work here. I found out you were coming here a few days ago. I didn't ask him to uproot your life."

Her gaze softened. "I get it. This is home. But things are different for you now. You just scored the winning goal to win the Stanley Cup and you had the season of your life—so the game has changed, Chadwick. The stakes are higher, and everyone on the Lions team wants to make sure you heal correctly."

"And my goal is to recover and get into the best shape of my life for the upcoming season. This has always been the place where I do that best."

She nodded. "That's fair."

"So we can start fresh? And maybe it'll be another day before you hate me again?" I said, my voice all tease.

"Hate is a strong word. I'd go with despise or dislike." She chuckled as she reached for a few bands on the floor and pointed at the massage table on the left side of the gym as she walked in that direction. "Hop up. I want to check out your knee before we do anything."

I did as I was told and lay flat on my back as she removed the brace from my knee.

"So if you didn't hate me, what was the hostility about after the game?"

Her fingers moved along the outside of my knee, and she was quiet for several beats.

"The swelling has gone down, which is a good thing. Are you wearing the brace at night, as well?"

"No. I take it off when I sleep," I said.

"Let's wear it at night for now, until we get in a couple of sessions." She moved around the table, inspecting the other side of my knee. "You misread my frustration for hostility. You were reckless after the game, and I just can't get behind that."

I pushed to sit up, and her hand pressed down on my chest, and I fell back down on the table. "How was I reckless?"

"You didn't know what your injury was, and you refused the wheelchair. You were too busy popping champagne bottles and having a good time. I get it, you just won the Stanley Cup. So, sit in a damn wheelchair and drink your bubbly," she said, as her fingers traced over my knee and pressed down gently.

"I was fine on crutches. This isn't my first rodeo with an MCL injury," I said.

"I understand that you've had this injury before. I've read your file, Clark. But this is what I do for a living. I wouldn't attempt to tell you how to play hockey, so please don't tell me how to do my job. You're lucky that it was just an MCL tear, but we didn't know that at the time. And every time you tear the same ligament, it's even more challenging to rehab and strengthen it. So how about you listen to me while we're working together, so you don't make me moving here for three months a waste of my time."

She lifted my leg and slowly bent it until I resisted. She stretched my injured leg for the next few minutes, and it actually felt the best it had in a week.

I let her words resonate. I could feel her frustration, and I realized that I hadn't looked at this from her perspective. It could have been a more serious injury, and she was basically looking out for me, and I'd brushed her suggestion off without a thought.

"I'm sorry for being an ass. This wasn't a new injury for me, but you're right, it's more severe this time, and each time, it takes longer to recover. I should have at least heard you out," I said.

"It's fine. Let's just work on getting this leg stronger while getting you in shape for the season at the same time."

I nodded. I wouldn't say we were friendly yet, but at least she wasn't shooting daggers at me.

She worked on my leg for probably forty-five minutes, massaging and stretching, and then she explained that we would move to upper body strengthening and stabilizing. I walked over to my phone and turned on my playlist.

I worked out to music. Always. It was my thing.

She quirked a brow. "Does it need to be so loud?"

"Yes." I tried to hide my smile, because she was easy to get a rise out of, and I kind of enjoyed it. There was something about the way her dark eyes sparked when she narrowed her gaze at me.

"All right, I've got the workouts from Randall, and I've tailored them to get the max out of the workout without any strain to your knee." She jotted down a few things in a notebook and then discussed the workout with me.

Today was going to be upper body exercises. Most could be done without any strain on my knee. I put the brace back on, and she moved from each machine with me, taking endless notes.

After an hour of pushing hard on the machines, I tugged off my shirt because it was hot as fuck. I wiped my face, and I didn't miss the way her gaze moved down my chest and abs before snapping back up to look at me.

Interesting.

I smirked, knowing that she was enjoying the view, even if she was going to act like she hadn't noticed.

"So what's the deal with the blaring music?" she asked, not hiding the fact that it bothered her.

"It's my thing." I smirked before belting out the lyrics to "A Bar Song" along with Shaboozey. I swayed my hips back and forth to the beat as her cheeks pinked. "I like music, so you best get used to it, because I can't work out with it."

"And you need to dance and sing unusually loud while you work out, too?" she grumped.

"When I feel the need to dance, I fucking dance." I barked out a laugh as I waggled my brows at her. I reached for her hand and spun her around, trying to lighten the mood. She surprised me when she didn't pull back, and her head tipped back in laughter. I spun her a second time, and she shook her head, a wide grin on her face as the song came to an end.

"Okay, dance time is over," she said, feigning irritation, but I didn't miss the way her lips turned up in the corners. She gathered her notebooks and dropped them into her bag.

"So what's the deal with the notebooks?" I asked, before chugging an entire bottle of water.

"I always use notebooks. It's my thing, I guess," she said.

We continued through the workout, music blaring, and there wasn't a whole lot of talking, just Eloise telling me how to do the exercise in the safest way, as she hovered around and took notes.

"Do you take notes on all the athletes on the team?"

She paused with her pen in hand and glanced up at me. "Well, seeing as I literally just graduated and started this job and was immediately sent away for three months to work with only one athlete on the team, it's fair to say that all the notes are about you at this point."

"Wait, is this your first job?"

"I mean, it's not my first job in my life, if that's what you're asking. I waited tables all through college and I nannied in the summers, so obviously I've worked before now. But yes, I graduated in June from grad school. This isn't exactly how I thought I'd be spending the first few months employed at my new job, so I've got all my eggs in one basket here." She arched a brow at her own witty comment.

"Wow. No pressure. I'm guessing this means you need me to come back stronger than ever, huh?" I asked, my voice all tease, but I felt the weight of my words, even though I was good at hiding it.

Being a professional athlete came with an insurmountable amount of pressure, and in this moment, I realized Eloise had a similar kind of pressure.

"I'm quite sure you know how important it is that you come back strong. You live with that kind of pressure, and I'm experiencing it first-hand." She shrugged, turning back to her notes.

I hadn't seen anyone handwrite notes like this in a very long time.

"Well, we're on the same page. I want to come back stronger than ever for my own selfish reasons, so I'm as determined as you are to make that happen." I wiped my face off with a towel and reached for my sweaty tee that I'd removed. "I'm going to take a swim."

"Oh." She glanced down at her notebook. "Did Randall have that on your schedule? He didn't include a swim on my notes."

I chuckled. "No, Eloise. I actually have my own tricks of the trade that have always worked for me. And swimming in the river after a workout is always a good idea."

She followed me out of the gym, and I paused in the kitchen and grabbed a Gatorade, holding one up for her.

"I'm good. I have my water. Thank you, though." She cleared her throat. "So how far do you swim?"

"I go right off my dock, out a half mile and back. So a mile total." I finished chugging my drink and made my way toward the back door. "You're off the clock. I don't expect you to hang out and watch me swim. It's not a team-appointed workout."

"I, um, I need to stick around." She fumbled with her bag as she followed me outside.

I turned around to respond and she slammed into my chest. I steadied her shoulders.

"Shit. Are you okay?" I asked as her hands pressed against my bare chest to stop herself from face-planting into me. Her fingertips were soft and cool against my heated skin. I glanced down at her, as she stood a good foot shorter than me and her startled gaze collided with mine. We were both silent before she stepped back hastily and removed her hands from my chest.

"I'm fine. But I'm curious, would you ask Randall if he was okay if he slammed into you?"

"What?" I asked.

"You heard me. Don't treat me differently just because I'm a woman. Would you act like that with Randall?"

"I don't know. Randall wouldn't stick around to watch me swim. He would just leave. But I assume if he crashed into me, I'd ask if he was okay," I said, quirking a brow.

She shrugged. "I'm staying. This is what I'm here for. This is my job."

"Suit yourself." I smirked, even though I didn't mind her staying. She was passionate about her work, and I respected that. Most people would take the early out. "It'll take me a little bit if you want to wait inside. Unless you plan to swim beside me?" I sarcastic chuckle escaped my lips.

"Why do you say that like it's a joke? I was actually on the swim team in high school. I can swim a mile in my sleep, Hotshot."

Color me intrigued.

"Is that so?" I asked. "So are you coming?"

I had to push away every dirty joke that entered my mind.

That's what she said.

"I," she paused. "I don't have a swimsuit."

"Neither do I. This is a small town, and this side of the river is quiet. No one will be out there, and if they are, they'll be doing the same thing," I said, as I pulled my shorts down, leaving me in nothing but my briefs.

Her eyes widened as she stared at me, her gaze moving from my chest down to my… favorite hockey stick, who appeared to be responding to the way her gaze had tracked him.

"Tell me you've never swam in your underwear." I tilted my head and noted the way her cheeks pinked.

Damn. She was cute for an uptight physical therapist who took her job a little too seriously.

And that was coming from someone who took his job a little too seriously.

"Don't be ludicrous." She dropped her bag and tore her tank top over her head, exposing her pink sports bra. She kicked off her shoes and socks, putting them beside her tank top. She kept her shorts on, much to my disappointment, and stormed past me. "Of course, I've swum in my underwear. I wasn't born under a rock."

I barked out a laugh and followed her down to the dock. "When was the last time you did it?"

She whipped around, and I came to an abrupt stop before risking another crash and pissing her off. She repeated my question as if it were an outrageous question. "When was the last time *you* did it?"

"Yesterday," I said dryly. "You?"

She tipped her chin up defiantly with the hint of a smile that could have been easily missed. But I was a dude who paid attention. "It's been a little longer for me."

"I had a feeling you'd say that." I barked out a laugh. "Let's go, Weeze."

"It's Eloise," she snipped as she jogged to catch up.

"Nah. That name doesn't fit you, and it's too long. I like Weeze."

"I hate that name."

"Even more reason to use it." I chuckled before motioning for her to jump in first.

"Such a gentleman," she grumped as she dipped her toe in the water.

The sun was shining down on the ribbon-like water, making it appear a mix of blue, green, and yellow. The surrounding redwood trees provided a little bit of shade as we stood on the wood stationary dock at the edge of my property.

I arched a brow. "Having second thoughts?"

"In your dreams, Hotshot."

And she dove in like a professional diver being scored for entering the water without so much as a splash.

It was impressive.

I had a feeling Eloise Gable was as unpredictable as her mood swings toward me.

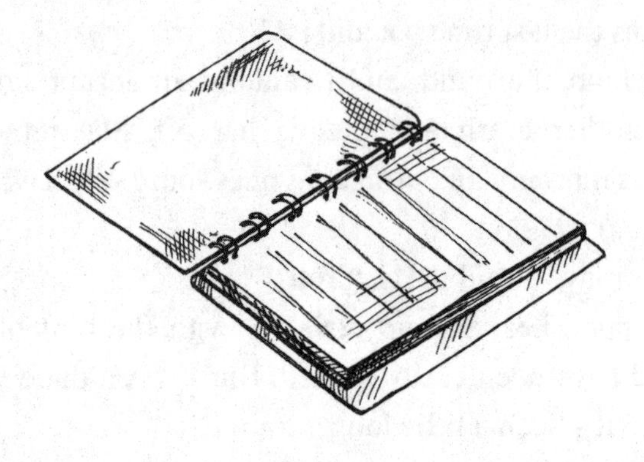

4

Eloise

"Damn. You basically skinny-dipped with Clark Chadwick. There are a lot of women who would pay good money to have that opportunity," Emilia said, as she dipped her french fry in ketchup.

"Well, I would have paid good money to get out of it," I said, and she laughed.

We were at the Honey Biscuit Café having dinner in downtown Rosewood River. It reminded me of the small town in Texas where I grew up, and I would be lying if I said I didn't sometimes crave small-town living.

"Are you the doctor here in town who came to help our local superstar get back on track?" an older man said as he approached the table.

"Hi, Oscar. This is Eloise Gable, and she's renting my guest cottage for a few months," Emilia said.

"Ahhh... the two musketeers. Eloise and Emilia, that's interesting." He quirked a brow.

"Well, we're fast friends, so there you go," she said.

"So, are you here for Chadwick? It's all everyone is talking about. Even the *Taylor Tea* knew you were coming." He arched a brow and turned to Emilia.

She told me about the anonymous column, and he was looking at her suspiciously.

"I wouldn't know," she said. "I actually don't work there, nor do I read that column."

"Is that so, *Emilia Taylor*?" He said her name like she was a suspect in a murder mystery.

"That is so, *Oscar Smith*." She mimicked him, and my head bounced back and forth between them.

"Well, you rented her your house, so you would have been the first to know that she was coming to Rosewood River." He smirked.

"I believe Clark Chadwick probably knew first. And we all know this is a nosy little town, so everyone knew she was coming." She turned to look at me. "Newcomers are big news in small towns."

"Wait, did I really make the *Taylor Tea*?" I gaped at them. "I've never been in the newspaper before."

"They can't name you, girlie. But they alluded to your arrival. A big, fancy doctor coming to fix our small-town hero," Oscar said, just as a woman walked up beside him and smacked him on the shoulder.

"Are you harassing these lovely ladies?" she said, before extending an arm. "I'm Edith, his better half."

"Hi. I'm Eloise. Nice to meet you."

"Pffftt... I thought *I* was *your* better half?" Oscar said. "And I'm not harassing them. I'm just inquiring about your favorite Chadwick."

"You say that about every single one of them," she scoffed. "Let's go. The kitchen is backed up, and they need some help."

"Keep us posted on the hockey star. He's the biggest thing to happen to Rosewood River since Nancy Prower got knocked up by her husband's brother," Oscar said, before his wife shoved him toward the kitchen.

"That's old news. Let's go," Edith said with a laugh.

"Wow. I guess you're right. The Chadwicks are a hot topic here." I rolled my eyes.

"Welcome to Rosewood River." She chuckled. "So tell me, how did the hockey star look in his briefs?"

I swatted her with my napkin. "I was not looking. I'm a professional. And trust me when I tell you he's not my type. The man sings too loudly, and he dances like he's working the room for tips. He's too smooth for his own good. He doesn't care what anyone thinks. He's literally a walking red flag. And you don't need to worry about me being tempted because I signed a contract as part of my employment agreement for the Lions about upholding the highest ethical standards. I'm certainly not going to lose my job because the man does a few pelvic thrusts while he's belting out a little Benson Boone."

"Oh, he's giving Travis Kelce energy. Not sure anyone would call that a red flag." She chuckled. "But you've clearly thought about this. Although, playing devil's advocate, you have to train with the man every day. You can't help but look. And what's your type if it's not Clark Chadwick?"

"I don't date hockey players. It's a hard line for me. My dad has been a hockey coach my entire life. I know the type all too well. Athletic, sexy, and way too cocky for their own good." I said. "My last boyfriend was a scientist. Quiet and humble is more my speed."

"Why'd you break up?"

"Well, he was a little *too* quiet and humble." I laughed. "And all he wanted to talk about was dinosaurs."

Her head tipped back in laughter. "That's better than my last boyfriend. All he wanted to talk about was himself. In his defense, he was his number one fan, so he couldn't get enough of the topic."

More laughter.

I realized in this moment that for the last few years, I've just been focused on school and getting past the next hurdle. I hadn't had a lot of time for lunch with friends or time to hang out.

This was the most fun I've had in a very long time.

Just talking and laughing and not stressing over exams or finals.

"Thanks for showing me around downtown. I was dreading coming to Rosewood River, but it's turned out pretty good so far," I admitted.

"Because you saw Clark Chadwick in his tighty-whities?" She covered her mouth to keep from laughing.

"No. That was the low point of my day," I lied, because it had been a while since me and Spencer had broken up. It didn't mean I liked the guy; he annoyed the hell out of me. But he looked good, and it was far from the low point of my day. "I'm just getting settled—meeting people who live here and finding my first friend in Rosewood River."

"I couldn't agree more." She smiled. "Hey, do you play pickleball?"

"I love pickleball, actually. We had a league in grad school. I played all the time."

"Great. You're coming with me to the Rosewood River Country Club this week. I just go on free play night, so there are no requirements. You can jump in when you feel like it and play when you want to."

"That sounds great."

"Do you work out with your prodigy just once a day?" she asked, as she reached for her iced tea.

"For these first two weeks or so. We just want to wait for that knee to heal a bit more. But yeah, we'll start two-a-day workouts here pretty soon."

Thoughts of Clark dancing around in his shorts with no shirt on, sweat glistening on his chest as he belted out the lyrics flashed through my mind, and I couldn't help the smile that crossed my face.

He was quite possibly the most entertaining man I'd ever met, even if he wasn't my type at all.

"You have a much more exciting job than I do. I don't get to see any hot men in their undies at the flower shop." She chuckled.

"Trust me. Cocky professional athletes are the last guys you want to see in their undies. They already know they look good. And you get to make people smile all day by handing them bouquets of blooms. That sounds dreamy."

"I do love it. It wasn't actually my plan to own a flower shop. I wanted to be an interior designer. I love it. I went to school on a full ride," Emilia said.

"And what happened?"

"My grandmother got sick, and this was her flower shop. My parents didn't think interior design was a real profession." She rolled her eyes. "So, they really pushed for me to take over

The Vintage Rose. The good news is that I still get to be creative there."

It infuriated me on her behalf that she wasn't encouraged to chase her dreams.

"Yeah, but you should have been able to do whatever you wanted to do. Do you have any siblings?"

"I have an older brother, Jacoby, but he lives in New York."

"They didn't want to guilt Jacoby into running the floral shop?" I asked, my voice teasing and trying to keep things light, though I didn't find it the slightest bit funny.

She laughed. "Jacoby is a lawyer in New York. He just recently made partner at some big firm. He's sort of the superstar of the family. I'm the 'daydreamer,' as my father calls me."

"You know, I think that's why I read so much. I never have time to daydream, so I'd take that as a compliment. I need to daydream more."

She shrugged. "Books are a form of escape, so that's probably your way of having a break from all the stresses in life, whether from school or work or the expectations we put on ourselves."

"Ain't that the truth. I've got a date tonight with a glass of wine, a hot bath, and a romance book."

"That's my kind of evening. But don't forget: Saturday, we're going to Booze & Brews, and we're going to line dance, have some drinks, and act like normal women in our late twenties," she said.

"Looking forward to a night out in Rosewood River."

"It's tourist season, so we might even find ourselves a handsome, grumpy, alpha hero looking to sweep a woman off her feet," she said.

"I'm in for the line dancing, but that's it. I'm here to work, and then I head back to the city. I've got no time for romance."

"I guess you'll just have to read a lot while you're here." She chuckled.

That's the only place I was interested in romance at the moment.

In the pages of a book.

• • •

"The training sounds like it's going well," Randall said, as I held my phone to my ear and walked toward Clark's house.

He lived less than two blocks from the guest cottage I was renting, and I was happy that I could walk there.

"Yes. I think the knee is healing well. But he's stubborn and keeps asking me when he can start running again."

"He's definitely someone who likes to push himself, which is both good and bad news. He's the hardest-working guy on the team, but he's stubborn about listening to his body. Hence the reason he did whatever it took to score that winning goal to win the Stanley Cup," he said.

"Agreed. But I'm on top of it. Are my daily notes helpful, or would you prefer I check in weekly with those?"

"I like seeing the daily results. That's working out well. As the trainer of this team, it's important that I am aware of what every single player is doing." He always made a point to mention that he was the trainer. I was more than aware.

"Then I will continue sending you progress notes daily."

"Great. How has your first week in Rosewood River been going?"

"It's going well. I train with Clark half the day, and then it leaves me some time to hike and explore. I think I'm going to try river rafting soon, and I'm playing pickleball this weekend," I said, wondering why I felt the need to let him know I was keeping busy.

"Yeah, it's a nice town. Lots of tourists in the summer, with the river there and all." He paused, and it sounded like he was sipping his coffee. "I just know that you probably don't have many friends there just yet, so be careful with Chadwick. You don't want to cross any lines while you're there. He's a charming guy and a bit of a ladies man."

I rolled my eyes at the audacity of this guy. I knew he felt threatened by me being hired by the team. My being dual certified as a PT and an athletic trainer had come up in a meeting, and the man was definitely on a power trip with me. It was clear he wanted to make sure I knew that he was in charge. He's already reminded me three times in the short time that I'd been hired that I answered to him and not my father.

"I assure you, I know how to behave like a professional. No need to worry."

I wondered if he'd been warned multiple times about not getting too close to the players—or if I was just being reminded constantly because I was a woman.

I was younger than him, as well.

"Well, that's why we're all forced to sign that contract." He chuckled, as if he wasn't trying to threaten me, when we both knew that he was. "All staff employed by the Lions must be held to a higher standard, ethically speaking."

I walked in on a very suspicious situation with Randall and his secretary, Talia, the first day I'd been hired. I found them together in the locker room after hours, and they appeared very nervous when I came in to find him.

Randall was a married man and much older than Talia, so perhaps he should take his own advice.

"I understood the contract when I signed it," I said, my voice lacking any emotion.

"Of course, you did. I'd expect nothing less from John's daughter." He laughed, but it sounded forced. "He's proud of you. Talks about you all the time. But it was a surprise when they agreed to hire you, you know, with your lack of experience. But just know that we can't allow for any favoritism, just because your daddy is the head coach."

I paused as I approached Clark's house.

My daddy?

I was twenty-seven years old. This man was acting like I was a child.

I ground my teeth, and my hands fisted as I continued walking, making a conscious effort to keep my voice even.

"It's not a secret that my father helped get me the interview, but I believe I've proven that I deserve to be here with my credentials and work ethic. I don't think they would have interviewed me three times and hired me if they weren't certain I was up for the job."

"Oh, yes. Of course, you are qualified. It's just that when I was going to school, they didn't offer shortcut programs with dual certification." More awkward laughter.

Please let this conversation end.

I counted down from ten to one, trying desperately to not lose my shit on this sexist, arrogant bastard.

"Well, it was a brutal and intense four-year program. But we don't need to debate that. I'm here at Clark's gym, and I need to get inside." I wasn't sure if Randall knew that his gym was at his home, and I certainly wasn't going to offer that up and allow him to question me even more.

I didn't choose to come here.

I was sent here, and I was doing my job.

"Sounds good. I'll expect a report later today with the results of today's workout."

"On it. Have a good day." I ended the call as quickly as possible and made my way to the front door, which was left open for me, so I waltzed into the house.

"What's up, Weeze?" he said, as a wide grin spread across his face. He stood there, wearing basketball shorts and no shirt, per usual. He had dark wavy hair and just the right amount of scruff peppered across his jaw. He was ridiculously tall, with broad shoulders and a tapered waste. My eyes betrayed me, scanning his body from his chest down to the deep V on display, where his shorts hung low on his hips. I hated that I found it impossible not to look.

Not to linger.

It made me irritated with both him and my lack of self-control.

"Stop calling me that ridiculous name." I huffed past him. We'd fallen into a routine these last few days, where he liked to annoy me, and I liked to let him know how irritated I was. "And how about we start with a shirt on, yeah?"

He chuckled as he followed me down the hallway to the gym, walking so close that I could feel his warm breath on the back of my neck.

"I was outside pulling some weeds this morning," he said. "It's already hot as hell."

Once we were in the gym, I turned around to face him. "You've already been landscaping this morning? Don't you have help with your yard? It's massive."

"I do. I have a guy. But I like being out there. I planted half of those trees in the backyard. Obviously, when I'm in season and living in the city, I can't keep up with it, but when I'm home,

I like to get my hands dirty," he said, and for whatever reason, Clark Chadwick talking about getting his hands dirty sounded hot as hell.

"Interesting. I wouldn't have guessed you a guy who enjoyed yard work." I pointed to the table, where we started each day so I could work on his knee.

He didn't put his shirt on, because he seemed to enjoy torturing me. Instead, he set his phone down on the bench beside him and started his playlist. Eminem was shouting through the speakers, and of course, Clark joined in, belting out the lyrics about Mom's spaghetti and only getting this one shot in life as he poked me a few times while he sang the damn song like he'd written it himself.

"Okay, let's focus please." I didn't want to tell him that I was a big Eminem fan, because it would give him too much pleasure that I approved of his music.

He just smirked at me as he was lying on the table, and his green eyes found mine. They were an unusual shade of light green, with pops of gold and amber and a dark brown rim around the edge. His lips twitched as he smiled. "Admit it, you like my music."

"It's fine."

"I think you like it, Weeze. And since when are you so concerned about my landscaper? You wondering what I do when we aren't together?" He winked.

"Pftt. Please. I never thought about it," I lied. I was a curious human just like most people. "It's just when you said you like to work in the yard, I guess I hadn't expected it."

"You grew up in a small town, didn't you?" he asked.

There was a fine line with athletes about how much you should share. What kind of friendship you could form while still keeping things professional but still connecting as you worked so close together. With Clark and I spending three months working together one-on-one, it would be odd if we didn't talk about our lives to some extent. I'd be spending four to five hours a day with the man, six days a week, for the next three months. So it would be normal to share a little bit with him.

"Yes. I lived in Windy Hill, Texas. It's a small town outside of Austin." I cleared my throat as I removed his brace and smiled because his knee was looking better each day as far as the inflammation. "Sleeping in the brace is helping. The swelling is coming down."

"That's all you, Weeze. You're working wonders on my body."

It's like the universe was completely tuned in to the man, because "Sexy and I Know It," by LMFAO started playing, and of course, the charming bastard moved to his seat and started dancing like a Chippendales dude at a bachelorette party.

His eyes found mine, and a wicked grin spread across his face as he started singing.

Did it just get hot in here?

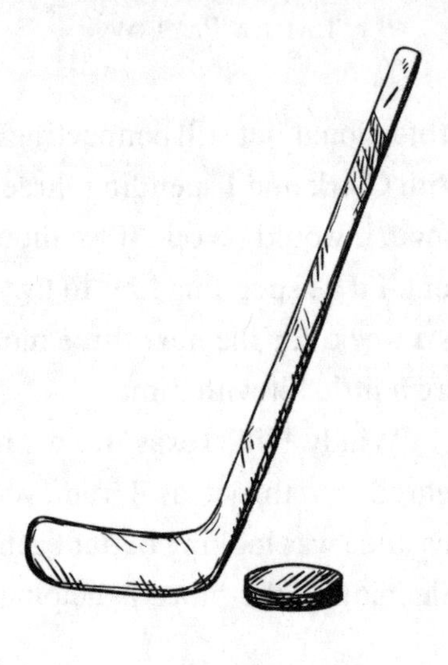

5
Clark

Easton: *Bring your A game, assholes. The Chad-Six ride tonight.*

My brother Easton was a complete lunatic when it came to pickleball. Our team, the Chad-Six, were the reigning champions at the Rosewood River Country Club, and though none of us really wanted to play anymore, we did it because it meant so much to the bastard.

Rafe: *I have jetlag, but apparently, I have no choice but to play fucking pickleball hours after a long flight.*

Rafe and Lulu had just arrived back in Rosewood River after living abroad in Paris.

Easton: *Correct. You signed up for the team. A commitment is a commitment.*

Bridger: *None of us signed up for this.*

Axel: *He's right. You forced us to play.*

Bridger: *And what are you talking about with the jetlag? You've been back in town for three days.*

Rafe: *Jetlag can last for weeks. Don't be a hater. And why does Archer get to have a sub?*

Archer: *Hey. Have a kid and then come cry me a river. You flew home from Paris. You probably ate a baguette and sipped champagne from your fancy pod.*

Me: *A baguette sounds fucking great right now. I'm exhausted from five hours of practice. But by all means, make an injured man play pickleball.*

Easton: *I plan on it. If you don't find a suitable sub, you've got to play.*

Me: *I found three replacements, and you said no to all of them.*

Easton: *Shall we revisit your choices…? Mrs. Dowden, a woman who is far too old to be a nanny, is who you asked to play pickleball. She can't even watch Melody while her father plays pickleball. It was an offensive choice.*

Archer: *I have to agree. She told me you offered her a hundred bucks to play. The woman can barely walk.*

Rafe: *That woman will do anything for a buck. Including guilting her boss into keeping her as his nanny when she barely gets around.*

Axel: *Wow. Mrs. Dowden was the first choice for pickleball? Clearly, you don't care if we defend our title. I can't wait to hear who else made the list.*

Bridger: *It better not have been Emilia Taylor. I will walk the fuck off that court.*

Here we go. My brother, Bridger, absolutely despised Emilia Taylor, as he was convinced she wrote the ridiculous column called the *Taylor Tea*. They often gossiped about our family, and he'd decided long ago that she was behind it, and his anger only grew each time the column was released.

Archer: *Your obsessive disdain for the poor girl is alarming.*

Me: *Agreed. Emilia is a freaking florist. She's harmless. And no, I didn't ask her to sub for me because I knew your irrational ass would throw a hissy fit.*

Bridger: *I don't throw fits. I walk off the court.*

Easton: *His second choice for a sub was Mom.*

Rafe: *Mom is a wonderful mother, an excellent cook, and no one recites the lyrics to Jelly Roll's music quite like Ellie Chadwick. But athletic, she is not.*

Easton: *She asked me if we won a jar of pickles after the tournament. <head exploding emoji>*

Axel: *Wow. Your candidates are very unusual. Who was the third choice?*

Me: *Janson Parker. He's athletic. Smart.*

Rafe: *The least reliable teenager on the planet. He flaked on shoveling snow for all of us.*

Easton: *Well, I almost went for it, but when I interviewed him, he told me that he could come tonight, "pending" his girlfriend doesn't get out of cheer practice early and want to "hang." I don't allow amateurs on the Chad-Six.*

Bridger: *You interviewed for a sub position?*

Archer: *<head exploding emoji>*

Axel: *I would expect nothing less. And for the record, this is not the same girlfriend from the snow shoveling debacle. He's got a new lady. I ran into them at the Green Basket.*

Easton: *I hate the Green Basket. Why do you still shop there?*

Me: *We all do. It's the only grocery store in town. I saw you there last week.*

Easton: *Correct. I'm not proud.*

Bridger: *We need to bring DoorDash to Rosewood River. I'd never have to leave the house or see anyone.*

Rafe: *I would suggest Janson for the job, but he'd never show up with the order.*

Archer: *The dude gets around. He's always got a girlfriend. He's become completely unreliable.*

Easton: *Hence why Clark needs to show up tonight.*

Me: *I can't run. My trainer will kick my ass.*

Easton: *Just stand there and use those long arms to hit the damn ball. Rafe, you're going to need to step it up as his partner.*

Rafe: *I'm exhausted, and the mac and cheese I had for lunch is not sitting so well.*

Me: *Dude. You're my partner, and you need to carry the team tonight. I can't run. I shouldn't even be going.*

Easton: *Suck it up, buttercup. Ball drops in an hour.*

Bridger: *It's pickleball, for fuck's sake.*

Easton: *Fastest growing sport in America, bitches. See you soon.*

When I pulled up at the Rosewood River Country Club for pickleball, I knew it was a bad idea. I would have to make a real effort to find a replacement for the next few weeks. I would be damned if I was going to fuck up my knee for a sport that didn't pay my bills.

When I made my way out to the court, it was a lot more crowded than usual.

"What's going on here?" I asked, as Easton dropped his bag on the bench.

"They started hosting a free play night for amateurs. Apparently, it's just for fun. Why the fuck would anyone be in a league that is just for fun? Who does anything for fun and not for a purpose?" he hissed.

"Um… most humans enjoy having fun," Henley said. "I think it's great that anyone can play at any skill level, and it's not structured as a tournament. There's less pressure."

"Says the collegiate tennis champion." Easton barked out a laugh. "You would not be playing pickleball if it weren't to win the gold at the end, baby."

"Easton," she said, as the corners of her lips turned up, "I did not sign up to play pickleball. You forced me to sub for Archer."

"And now I've got to play because Rafe doesn't think he can play every game," Lulu griped. "Hen and I could be inside sipping martinis instead of being yelled at on the court."

"I second that," Rafe said. "I would much rather be inside having a cocktail instead of being berated out here. Plus, there's a shitter in the dining room, so I wouldn't have to run for it if that mac n cheese decides to go medieval on my insides."

"Pull your shit together, people. Pun intended." Easton pointed at Rafe before turning to each of us. "You're a member of the Chad-Six. Check yourselves."

Laughter bellowed from everyone just as Bridger and Axel walked over.

"Pep talk?" Axel oozed sarcasm.

"Damn straight." Easton motioned to the courts. "Let's get after it."

"What's with all the people today?" Bridger grumped.

"Free play for anyone who has a pickleball racquet and no experience," Easton hissed.

"Chadwick, are you going to stand around and chat or come defend your title?" Barry Wilcox called out from court number three.

I rolled my eyes because the dude was a dick, and he loved to mess with Easton.

"What do you think you're doing?" a familiar voice shouted, and we all turned in her direction, a cocky grin on my face at the stormy look on hers.

This should be fun.

"Who in the hell is this?" Bridger snipped.

"This would be my trainer and physical therapist," I said, unable to hide my smile as Eloise stormed toward me.

Why was I happy to see her when she looked like she was ready to kick me in the balls?

"Chadwick, what do you think you're doing?" she hissed, as she stopped in front of me with her arms crossed over her chest.

Damn, she was pretty.

"I'm playing pickleball, Weeze." I arched a brow, as everyone just stood there, gaping at her.

"You are not." She yanked the racquet out of my hand.

"Excuse me. I'm Easton Chadwick, Clark's brother and captain of the Chad-Six. We are about to start a game, and he's part of this team," my brother said.

"Well, Easton Chadwick," her voice oozed sarcasm as she tipped her chin up and faced my brother directly, "Clark will not be playing pickleball. He's recovering from an MCL tear that he's working hard to repair, and playing pickleball is quite possibly the worst idea on the planet. I'm quite certain, as Easton's brother, that you would not find pickleball more important than his career as a professional athlete with the Lions, who happen to be the Stanley Cup champions."

Easton blinked a few times, and it was clear that she'd caught him off guard.

"He's not going to run. He's got long arms," Easton said, and even he didn't seem to believe his own bullshit.

"That's not realistic. I'm going to have to put my foot down."

"Put your foot down? You think this is your decision?" Easton huffed.

"Well, I was sent to live here for three months to help him heal," she said, flicking her thumb at me as I stood back and let my over-the-top physical therapist battle it out with my pickleball-obsessed brother. "And seeing as he's my only client, I need to make sure that happens. So yes, I believe it's my decision because in my professional opinion, this is a bad idea, and I think that your brother cares too much for his sport to argue this."

Easton narrowed his gaze and studied her before turning to look at me. "Be straight with me. Is this a bad idea?"

"It's a terrible idea," I said with a laugh. "I figured I'd try standing still, but it would never last, so I'll either reinjure myself or deal with the wrath of the Pickleball King."

He rolled his eyes before turning back to look at Eloise. "Well then, seeing as this is your job and all, I'm guessing you'll do whatever it takes to make sure Clark doesn't play."

"You'd be correct." She arched a brow, daring him to challenge her.

"Looks like you're subbing for Clark. You better not suck because I don't lose."

She looked to me for help, and I shrugged. "Trust me. If you don't want me to play, you're going to need to do this."

"I like this girl," Lulu said, moving beside me and extending a hand. "I'm Lulu Sonnet. My better half just ran to the bathroom once again, because he insisted on eating that damn mac 'n cheese again at the Honey Biscuit Café. So I'm first up with Clark. You and I can be partners." They shook hands, and Eloise quickly introduced herself.

"You best make sure she can hit the ball, Lu," Easton snipped.

"Take it down a notch, Chadwick. We're going to dominate." They jogged out to the court, and Easton led Henley over to their court.

"Your trainer is hot," Axel said with a smirk. "And she held her own with Easton, which is saying a lot."

"She's off-limits," I growled.

I wasn't sure why I felt so protective of her. Maybe it was because she was Coach Gable's daughter. Or maybe it was something else.

I wasn't sure.

He arched a brow. "Oh. Is that so?"

"Dude. She's my coach's daughter. Do. Not. Go. There." I held his gaze.

"I don't think it's your coach that I need to worry about." He barked out a laugh. "I'll grab our waters. Meet you on the court, Bridger."

"So, let me ask you something," Bridger said, staring across the courts to where the free play was happening.

"No, you can't date her."

"That wasn't my question. I don't ask for permission to date someone." He blew out a frustrated breath. "But why is your trainer here with the enemy? I saw her and Emilia playing together; I just didn't realize she was your trainer."

I followed his gaze to where Emilia Taylor was playing pickleball and literally missing every single ball that came her way. I prayed like hell that Eloise could play better than that, or Easton would lose his shit.

"She rents the guesthouse behind Emilia's house."

"So she's probably feeding Emilia information about us," he huffed.

I rolled my eyes. "She barely speaks to me. She has not asked for any family secrets."

"Just watch your back. Emilia probably brought her in to infiltrate the family," he grumped. "They may have known one another for years."

"Let me get this straight. You think that Eloise Gable went to physical therapy school and made sure her father got hired by the Lions as the head coach, all so that she could come to Rosewood River after I tore my MCL to get information about our family to print in the *Taylor Tea*?" I started laughing and couldn't stop, because my brother was ridiculous when it came to this shit.

He whacked my upper arm with his racquet like the dickhead he was, and I howled in pain, which he completely ignored. He used his two fingers, pointing them toward his eyes and then back to me, as if I wouldn't understand his next words. "Just keep your eye on her."

He jogged out to the court where Axel was bouncing the ball, and I turned my attention to where Lulu and Eloise were playing.

Eloise wore a pink tennis skirt and a white collared tank top. Her legs were lean and tan, and she was incredibly distracting. She stirred something in me that I knew I needed to stifle.

She was as off-limits as one gets.

I watched as she spiked the ball before high-fiving Lulu.

This was definitely not her first rodeo.

I sat back and enjoyed the show.

Eloise Gable had just stood up to my brother and took my place on the Chad-Six.

This girl was full of surprises.

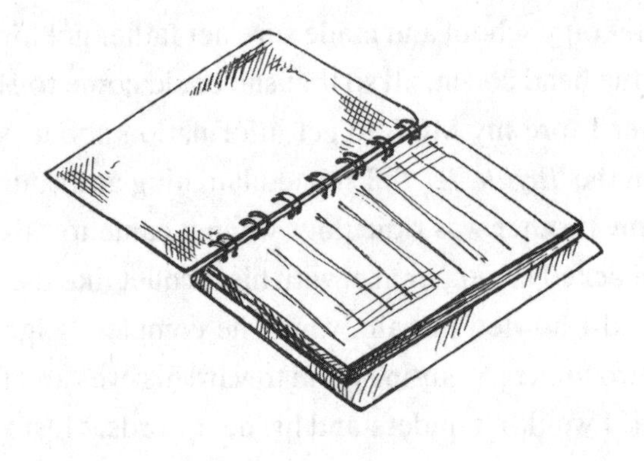

6

Eloise

We've been at Booze & Brews for the last hour, and I've already attempted to line dance a couple of times, though I've never had much rhythm. Emilia helped me the best she could, but I bowed out to go get a drink and take a break.

The bar was packed, and it was clearly a local hotspot. Country music boomed through the speakers, and I made my way to the large wood bar that made a giant square in the center of the space. My feet crunched against peanut shells as I moved, and I dabbed my fingers along my forehead, as I was sweating from all the energy I'd just exerted on the dance floor.

I met a few of Emilia's friends, and they were all nice, but I was ready to find a table and people-watch for a while.

I ordered a beer for both me and Emilia.

"Pickleball and line dancing. You're a woman of many talents," a familiar voice said, as he moved to stand beside me.

Clark Chadwick.

The smell of whiskey and cedarwood flooded my senses. He stood so close his finger grazed mine on the bartop.

Maybe it was the booze or maybe it was just the man himself.

His scent, his body heat, it did something to me.

Even when we were in the gym, this man had an air about him.

He oozed charm and was too sexy for his own good.

He nudged me with his shoulder, pulling me from my daze as I gaped at him.

I shook it off, chuckling a little, as if I just got lost in thought.

I needed to be a professional.

But being here outside of work, with country music playing and two beers in my system, it was obvious that talking to him was a bad idea.

A terrible idea.

Maybe the worst idea.

I thought the man looked good in his gym clothes and his briefs, but something about the way he looked tonight had my stomach fluttering. He wore dark jeans and worn-in cowboy boots. A white tee stretched across his muscled chest, and I licked my lips in response before clearing my throat and forcing myself to pull it together.

"Here you go." Jazzy, one of the bar owners and a friend of Emilia's, slid the two beers across to me, and I reached for some cash, but Clark handed her the money before I could get it out of my purse.

"Thank you, but you didn't need to do that," I said, as I turned around, my back pressed against the bar.

His eyes scanned me from head to toe, making no effort to hide his perusal. I've caught him doing it a few times at the gym in the mirror, but he'd never been this blatant.

Obviously, I wasn't the only one drinking tonight.

"It's the least I could do after you stepped up and took my place in pickleball." He thanked Jazzy when she handed him the glass of straight whiskey. "Don't judge. I don't drink during the season, and tomorrow is my one day off a week from training, so I'm indulging a little."

"I wasn't judging," I said, as my heart raced at his nearness.

Why was I nervous?

I worked with him six days a week.

I set my beer down on the bar top. I should stop drinking immediately.

"No? What were you doing then, Weeze?" His voice was smooth as silk, and the corners of his lips turned up.

My God. He was six foot four inches of pure man.

Broad shoulders, muscular arms, chiseled abs.

His light green eyes were flanked by long black lashes that most women would pay big money for.

And I only knew these specifics because I had all his stats as the team PT, not because I was constantly staring at him when he wasn't looking.

Okay, fine, sometimes I stared.

But his height was public record.

The rest was just—observation.

"Can I grab a water please?" I asked when Jazzy walked over and set another whiskey down for him.

His lips twitched as if he thought my request was humorous.

"I'm all about staying hydrated," I said, as I reached for the glass of water she set down and took a sip, sucking half of it down.

I needed to flush the alcohol out of my system immediately.

"You never can be too careful," he chuckled. "I tried to catch you after the pickleball game to thank you, but you ran out of there so quickly I didn't see you."

"I had to go get some things done. But thank you, I got your text." I shrugged.

"You just chose not to respond?" His voice was all tease.

"I was in a hurry and didn't know you were wanting a response." My teeth sank into my bottom lip.

I knew he wanted a response. He asked if I had fun. I just didn't think texting about things outside of work was a good idea.

"You're a pretty damn good pickleball player. You saved the day. Easton would have lost his shit if you'd sucked." He tipped his head back with a laugh.

"He's a little over the top, huh?" I shook my head in disbelief. "I mean, he really thought you should play? It's freaking pickleball."

I startled when his finger came over my lips. "Careful, Weeze, those are fighting words in the Chadwick family."

I sucked in a breath, and he pulled his finger from my lips.

"Well, my priority is you."

"So you do care," he said, a wicked grin on his face. "I knew it."

"It's my job. If you fail, I fail. And I have a lot at stake."

His gaze softened as if he felt bad for teasing me about it. "We both have a lot at stake."

"Correct. So how about you don't take silly risks that could cause us both a lot of grief."

"Fair enough." He clinked his whiskey glass against my water glass and tipped his head back. "For the record, I wasn't going to run on the court. I was going to prove a point to Easton that I couldn't stand still and win the damn game."

"But you shouldn't have even been out there. You might have turned the wrong way. It's just not a good idea to take risks right now."

"Maybe it's a good thing you're here then, huh?" He leaned close as the music piped through the speakers around us. The edge of his lips grazed the shell of my ear, and I shivered in response.

I guzzled the rest of my water and reached for the two beers. "Yes. I'm glad I'm here. For work. Just work. Love me some work. Yep. I'm a worker. Okay, I need to get this beer to Emilia. Thanks again for the drinks. I'll see you on Monday morning."

"I'll see you Monday morning." He winked.

The man was too smooth for his own damn good.

Too damn smooth.

Alarm bells were going off as I hurried across the bar to where Emilia was sitting, talking to a guy I didn't recognize.

"Hey," she said. "I was just going to come look for you."

"I'm here. Brought you this," I said, handing her the bottle.

"Thanks. This is Brett. We went to high school together."

I extended my hand. "Hi. I'm Eloise."

"Yes, you are," he said with a flirty smirk. He had blond hair and light blue eyes, and he oozed confidence.

"Oh, boy. Beware. This guy is the biggest flirt around," Emilia said.

"Hey, don't be a hater, Em. It's called being friendly." He flashed his smile at me, showing off his perfectly white teeth.

"Nice to meet you."

He raised his beer bottle and clinked it with mine. "It's definitely nice to meet you."

I chuckled, and my gaze moved across the bar to find Clark's eyes on me as he finished his whiskey.

Emilia turned to chat with some friends when they pulled up chairs at our table.

"So, you grew up here?" I asked Brett.

"I did. Left for college and law school and just moved back last year," he said.

"You missed home, huh?"

"My dad is battling cancer, so I wanted to be here." His gaze softened, and he looked away briefly, before forcing a smile when he turned back to me.

"I'm sorry to hear that. I'm guessing you two are close?"

"Yes. We have our moments." He chuckled. "But he's a good guy. And my mom isn't handling it well, so I knew coming home would help."

"How is he doing now?"

"He's actually doing a lot better. The chemo seems to be helping. We're just taking it one day at a time right now."

I nodded. "That's great news. I hope he continues to stay on this path to recovery."

I knew how tough it was to watch a family member suffer. My mom had battled cancer when I was young, and those last few months with her were still etched in my memories.

"Yeah, me too. So, where is home for you?" he asked.

"I currently live in San Francisco. I work for the San Francisco Lions."

"No shit. I'm guessing you're here for their star player, Clark Chadwick, huh?" he asked, and I didn't miss the way his jaw flexed at the mention of Clark.

"Yes. I'm the team physical therapist, but I'm also a certified athletic trainer, so I'm getting him ready for the season."

"Yeah, he sustained a pretty bad knee injury in that final game, right?"

"Well, for most, it would be brutal, but for Clark, it's more of a mild inconvenience." I chuckled.

"Ahhh… I see we're a big Clark Chadwick fan." He rolled his eyes.

"I'm his physical therapist and a member of the team, so I'm a fan of all of our players. But from the standpoint of rehabbing an injury, he's the kind of athlete you want to work with. He puts in the work and doesn't complain, which is a rarity most of the time." I chuckled, trying to make light of it. "I get the feeling you're not a fan?"

"Let's just say we have a history, and we don't speak anymore."

Interesting.

"It sounds like some small-town drama." I arched a brow.

"Yeah, you could call it that. But I have a beautiful woman sitting with me tonight, and the last thing I want to do is talk about Clark Chadwick."

I took a sip of my beer. "What would you like to talk about?"

"I want to hear about you. Where you grew up? If you have siblings? How long you're staying?" He paused, and the corners of his lips turned up. "If you'll have dinner with me tomorrow night?"

Like I said, the man oozed confidence.

He seemed nice enough, and he was a friend of Emilia's, so a little harmless flirting seemed fine.

"Very smooth."

"I like to think so." He smirked. "How about you dance with me, and then you can decide."

"I have two left feet. I've already embarrassed myself enough out there tonight," I said.

"I don't think that's the case. I couldn't take my eyes off you when you were out there."

"I find that hard to believe, unless you just enjoy watching disasters." I chuckled, just as a big body moved beside me.

"Sorry to interrupt," Clark said before turning to glare at Brett. What the hell could have happened that had them so bothered by one another? "Can I speak to you for a moment?"

"Yes. Of course," I said, before turning to Brett. "Just give me a minute, and I'll be back."

I followed Clark as he led me across the bar and outside, and I noticed the way his movements were still slightly stiff, which told me it was either the brace beneath his jeans or that he was still in pain. He turned around to face me.

"Be careful with that guy."

"Did you seriously call me out here to tell me that?" I asked, hands on my hips. The nerve of this man. Why did everyone feel the need to tell me who to avoid and how to behave? I wasn't a child.

"No, but it's worth saying. He's an asshole."

"Thanks for the information. He wasn't quite as unkind about you, but it's clear you aren't besties." I shook my head, making no attempt to hide my irritation. "I'm a big girl, Hotshot. You need not worry."

He looked away before shoving his hands in his pockets. "Fine."

"Fine. Was there something you wanted to talk to me about? Is your knee bothering you? Are you having issues?"

"No. I'm fine," he huffed. "I wanted to ask if you thought I could start running soon."

This is what was so urgent?

Something we'd already discussed numerous times.

"It's going to be a couple of weeks before you start running again. But swimming is a good alternative, and I'm fine with you doing that as often as you want."

"I thought you told me not to swim tomorrow," he said, quirking a brow.

"Well, yeah. You work out hard six days a week. Sunday is a rest day. Your body needs a full day to recover before we move into another challenging week."

He looked away, and I didn't miss the disappointment. "All right."

I chuckled. "Is resting that hard for you?"

"I don't know. I'm used to moving more. I just feel like I'm not doing enough cardio."

My chest squeezed at his words because I was a type A overachiever myself, so I understood that feeling all too well. Anytime I wasn't giving 100 percent, I felt like I was failing.

Clark was an interesting guy. He acted all cool and laid back, but his work ethic could challenge any athlete I'd ever worked with. He pushed himself until I forced him to stop most days.

"Listen, you're doing a lot right now. Five hours a day between physical therapy, weights and strength training, stretching, swimming, walking and cycling."

He nodded. "I like to get my heart rate going. Work up a sweat."

I'll bet you do, Clark Chadwick.

What. Was. Wrong. With. Me?

I pulled myself together, shaking off thoughts of how Clark might get his heart rate up when he's not in the gym.

I cleared my throat, scolding myself internally for my thoughts. "I get it. But I promise you, you are doing a lot as far as conditioning. It's still very early into training. We will slowly bring back cardio after a few weeks. You have to trust me on this."

"I trust you, Weeze."

There was something sweet and vulnerable in his words.

"Thank you. I know how much you want to get back to running, so I'll let you know as soon as I think you're ready. But when it happens, we are going to start slow."

"Slow is not really my thing," he said.

"Then I guess we won't run for a while longer."

"Fine. I'll start slow." He smiled, his eyes locked with mine with this ridiculously sexy smile on his face.

My mouth went dry. There was just something about this man.

Time to put some space there again.

"Okay, I'm going to go finish my drink and head home."

"Yeah, I'm heading home, too. Have a good night. Be safe." He smiled and crossed his arms over his chest.

"What are you waiting for?" I asked.

"For you to get your ass back inside. I'm not leaving you standing out here."

I tipped my head back in laughter. "Good night, Hotshot."

"See you Monday, Weeze." He didn't move. He actually waited until I pulled the door open and looked over my shoulder.

His eyes were still on me.

And maybe it was the alcohol coursing through my veins.

But I liked it.

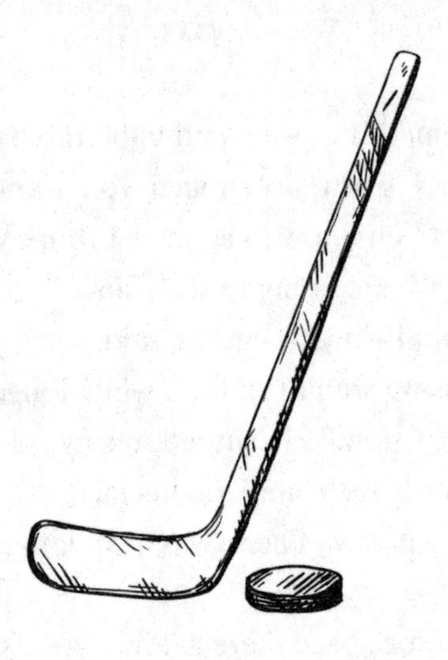

7

Clark

"It's been two and a half weeks," I said, as she massaged the area around my knee.

"Have you always been a stubborn ass? Or do you do this just with me?"

I barked out a laugh. "According to my mother, I was born this way."

"Clark."

"Eloise," he mimicked my serious tone.

I rolled my eyes. "One more week, and you and I will run a mile together. Slowly."

"I don't think you can keep up with me."

"I ran a 5:23 mile in high school. I assure you, I can keep up with you," she said, tucking the strand of hair that had broken free behind her ear.

"Ah, you were a track star. Is that why you write every single detail down in your notebook? Are you a stats junkie?"

I saw something pass through her gaze, and I could tell I struck a nerve. Every time I teased her about her notebook, she always went quiet.

I wanted to know what she was hiding. She had this tough exterior, and for whatever reason, I wanted to know what was beneath.

The woman intrigued me.

"I have my reasons," she huffed.

I sat up and studied her. "You know, I have to tell you everything I'm feeling all the time. My pain level. How I'm frustrated about the lack of cardio we're doing. But you don't share anything. That doesn't quite seem fair, Weeze."

"I'm the PT, and you're the athlete. You're supposed to tell me everything."

"It's pretty selfish." I tried to hide my smile. "I'm always giving, and you're just taking."

She swatted me with the towel sitting on the table. "I'm hardly taking. You mostly just complain about wanting to do more."

"Well, I have my reasons."

"Fine. If you want me to tell you something, then tell me why you're so freaking impatient about going for a run and stepping up your cardio. You're getting in fabulous workouts. What's the rush?"

I cleared my throat and thought it over. I spent a lot of time with this woman, and I trusted her to get me into the best shape possible. She hadn't steered me wrong thus far, and I was feeling stronger every day.

"I've been reading things online. A few articles that came

out were questioning if I'd be able to repeat the season that I had before sustaining this injury." I shrugged. "I don't normally let things get in my head. But you know, hockey is everything to me, and if I lost that, I don't know what I'd do."

I was my own worst enemy sometimes. Letting myself spend hours reading what sports analysts were saying about my chances of coming back and repeating what I'd done this season. It was easier when I was an underdog. When there were no expectations of me. When I would grind and push hard to prove who I was.

But now, I'd achieved everything I'd ever wanted, and I didn't want it to go away. So I was feeling the pressure of wanting something so badly and being terrified of it being ripped away from me. Achieving my dreams was both the best and the worst… because now I had to fight to keep them.

I was not going to let all the outside voices get in my head.

Eloise stared at me for the longest time before hopping up on the table and sitting beside me. "I get that. And this sport is not for the weak, that's for sure. It's what makes my job so challenging, because the injuries are endless. But you're probably the most resilient athlete I've ever worked with. I promise you, you are not losing anything. I think people are going to be very surprised with how strong you are when you return. You've done everything I've asked of you so far, aside from nagging me about running. But we're going to incorporate it back in after a month off, and we'll see how you do."

"Thanks. I didn't expect it to take this long. I'm ready to get back on the ice."

"Well, funny you should mention it. I booked us some ice time this afternoon," she said, her lips turning up in the corners.

"What? I thought you said no ice for a month."

I felt like a fucking kid at a candy store. I was itching to get back on the ice.

It's where I left every worry behind. Where I came alive most days.

I'd grown up skating and playing hockey, and it was a part of me.

"Don't get cocky. I'm going to skate with you. Nothing fancy, no pressure on your knee just yet. Just some casual ice time, all right?" she asked.

"Why'd you change your mind?"

It meant something to me that she'd take the time to arrange this. As if she knew that I needed it right now.

"I reached out to Everly Madden," she admitted, looking at me like she was prepared for me to be annoyed. She mentioned me scheduling a meeting with Everly, as she was our team psychologist. I've met with her a few times. She was also married to one of the greatest players to ever live, Hawk Madden, who'd also played for the Lions. She knew the sport. She knew the struggles that came with it. But I just wanted to run. I didn't need a therapist. "What did she say?"

"I wanted to ask if I was being too stringent about not letting you run. Some PTs would let you get back out there a little sooner, but I just don't want to set you back, you know? So I asked her advice."

"And?"

"She said to trust my gut on the running, but that a little ice time wouldn't hurt, as long as I was out there with you. She thought it might give you a little pep in your step." She chuckled.

"Pep in my step? Baby, I was born with pep in my step. You've seen my dance moves." I barked out a laugh and then turned to look at her. "Thanks for doing that. Getting on the ice will be nice."

"I'm still going to put you through hell this morning," she said, jumping down from the table.

"No, no, no. You don't get to have me spill my guts about my frustration and then not share anything with me. Come on, I told you my embarrassing shit. Tell me something. What's the story with the notebook?"

She rolled her eyes. "What is your obsession with the notebook? Why do you care?"

"I don't know, Weeze. But I'm curious. Maybe I have too much time on my hands because you won't let me run."

Her shoulders shook with laughter. "You're relentless."

"I've been called worse."

"Fine. The notebooks are sort of an anxiety thing for me, I think." She looked away before turning back. Her dark eyes locked with mine. "My mom fought cancer for over a year when I was young. I'd sit with her every day after school, and those last few months were brutal. She was on hospice, and you know, I didn't understand at the time, that the end was looming."

"How old were you?" I asked. My chest squeezed at the pain I saw in her gaze.

"Ten years old. And my dad had to continue working because we needed the insurance, so it was Mom and me for hours after school every day. And that's when the notebooks started. She'd have me write everything down for her. About things she wanted me to remember. Things she wanted me to hold on to. Some of it was her story, and some of it was her hopes and dreams for me." She let out a labored breath and looked away. "It just became a way of remembering her, keeping her close, I guess. Maybe it was a form of control for me. But it makes me feel comforted to write things down. Like they won't disappear if I do."

I pushed to my feet and wrapped my arms around her because it was the only thing I could think to do. I was pretty good at reading people, and whether she admitted it or not, I knew she needed it.

Her head rested on my chest, and I just held her there. It was a full-bodied hug, and her hair tickled my nose, but I didn't pull away.

I knew she didn't have siblings because her father bragged about his only child any chance he got.

"I think it's pretty cool that you shared that with her. And I forget shit all the time, so writing things down is a great idea."

She chuckled and pulled back. "Don't you dare get all sappy on me."

"It's a hug, relax. We can be friends, can't we?"

She stepped away, putting distance there. It's what she did often when we were working out and we'd share a laugh or say something that didn't have anything to do with hockey.

"Not really, Clark. We all signed that contract to be on the team, but it's different for me, you know? I'm a female working for a professional men's hockey team. My father is the coach, so people already assume that I got the job because of him. So, if anyone thought there was anything unprofessional going on, even a friendship, it would be me who was fired. You're the superstar. I'm replaceable."

Shit. I never thought of it like that.

"Well, that sucks. But I think you're being a little overly cautious. Randall and I are friends. The ethical contract is about being unprofessional in a romantic way. I'm friends with everyone on staff."

"We can be *friendly*. But actually being friends would be crossing a line."

"Well, you're friends with Lulu and Henley now. You're on the Chad-Six pickleball team." I barked out a laugh. "Like it or not, Weeze, we're friends."

She arched a brow before walking over to the mat where she would force me to do awkward stretches. "It's a professional friendship."

"Fine." I followed her to the mats. "But my mother is deeply offended that you haven't come to Sunday dinner yet. Henley and Lulu keep talking about you, and she knows you're helping me. She wants you to come this weekend."

She pointed for me to sit down on the floor, and then she dropped to her knees and reached for my leg.

Why the fuck did my dick respond every time she dropped to her knees?

It had been a while, and I definitely needed to get laid.

I've been so focused on my training, but the last time I'd been out at the bar, I considered going home with a woman I'd hooked up with before. She made it clear that she wanted it to happen. But something stopped me.

Maybe it was because I saw Eloise there, out on the dance floor, hands in the air with her head tipped back in laughter.

Maybe it was seeing her talking to Brett that got under my skin.

Maybe it was because I was spending all this time with my trainer.

She was getting in my head, in more ways than I wanted to admit.

"Yeah, Henley and Lulu asked me to go, but I just don't know if that would be weird of me to go to dinner at your family's house."

"It's weird that you haven't. Randall came to Rosewood

River last summer on vacation, and he came to dinner twice that week. Your father has come to Sunday dinner, as well. Stop being a stubborn ass. It's just dinner."

I groaned when she pulled my leg back, and I felt the pull in my quads.

"If it would make you feel better, I can skip dinner on Sunday if you want to go."

She let my leg relax and smirked. "Now who's being the stubborn ass?"

"All right. Twist my leg. I'll go to dinner, too."

"How gracious of you," she said.

"Are you still going out with that twat?" I asked, because Lulu and Henley had mentioned that Brett Lewis had taken her to dinner last weekend. I don't know why that bothered me so much. Obviously, I didn't care for the dude, but he wasn't a dangerous guy. We just had a falling out, and I thought he was a douchebag. But I had no claim on Eloise, so it didn't make sense that it bothered me this much.

Her eyes widened, and she ignored the question for a few beats.

"Twat? How very mature of you." She reached for my other leg and leaned forward, giving me a straight shot down her tank top. I looked away because she was worried that it was unethical to attend a Chadwick Sunday dinner, and I was hard as steel from being stretched and getting a shot of her tits, which were completely covered by a sports bra.

Pull your shit together, asshole.

"Just a friend making sure you're not making a huge mistake," I said.

"We went to dinner. He's a nice guy. I haven't gone out with him again, but he's asked." She smirked.

"Suit yourself. Don't say I didn't warn you."

"It would help if you told me what your issue is with him."

"Wouldn't that be crossing ethical boundaries?" I chuckled, and she led me through a few more torturous stretches as Zach Bryan's voice played through the speakers.

"Hardly. We're discussing a guy that I went out with. So clearly, we aren't interested in one another if we're talking about dating other people."

"Clearly," I said dryly. "And for the record, you're not my type."

"Good to know. You're not my type either." She chuckled. "Cocky athletes don't do it for me."

"Ahhh... you prefer douchebags over winners."

"Winners or weiners?" she said, as her head fell back in laughter, and it was cute as hell. She didn't relax all that often, and I could tell she was getting more comfortable with me.

"Who's the mature one now?" I asked, teasingly. "I'm not getting into it. I warned you, so do whatever you want with that information."

She pushed to stand, and I did the same before following her over to the circuit machines. I started with legs, grateful that my knee was getting stronger every day. I reached for my water bottle after the first set, and she snatched it and held it above her head.

"Tell me why you don't like him, Clark." She narrowed her gaze, holding the bottle out of my reach.

I always rose to the challenge, and I moved so fast she didn't see me coming. I grabbed the water bottle with one hand, snaking the other arm around her waist with the other.

Her body was flush against mine, and I smiled down at her. "You might be able to force me to hold off on running, but you can't withhold water from a man."

Her lips parted, her breaths coming hard and fast before she put her hands on my chest and pushed back, stepping away from me.

"Like I said, cocky athletes are not my thing. You're bigger and stronger, I get it." She huffed and turned around, giving me her back and stepping away.

Fuck. I was just kidding. I didn't mean to piss her off.

"Brett Lewis was my best friend, and he fucked my high school girlfriend when we all went away for college. They'd gone to the same school, and apparently, they'd been sneaking around behind my back most of the first semester. One weekend, I went there to surprise them both and found them in her dorm room looking awfully cozy. I confronted her, and she admitted it."

Eloise's mouth hung open.

"Wow. That is some shady business right there." She shook her head, and loud laughter bellowed from me.

Shady business.

That's one way to put it.

"She said some bullshit about being in love with both of us, and she couldn't handle the distance." I shrugged because it was water under the bridge. "She and I had run our course. We just had a long history, so I wouldn't have expected that kind of disrespect from her. But Brett, man… That one hurt. We were tight all our lives."

"So what did you do?"

"I told both of them that I was done with them. She cried, and he just stood there, looking dumbfounded, like he couldn't believe he was caught. And then he reached out two weeks later and came to see me. He told me he ended things with her because it was more about the chase, and they had nothing in common in the end."

"Noooooo. He betrayed his best friend, and it was just about the chase?"

"Yeah, I would have had more respect for them if they'd really been in love, and it went the distance. So I knocked his ass out, and we've never spoken again."

"He had it coming," she said, shaking her head with disgust.

"Like I said, the dude is an asshole."

"For the record, I wasn't going to go out with him again. The date wasn't great. He literally talked about you the entire time. He wanted to know how bad your injury was, and if you were dating, and how long you'd be in Rosewood River."

"Way to win a lady over on the first date," I said, not hiding my sarcasm. "So why the hell did you let me believe you were going out with him again?"

"I figured if I told you I was considering it, you'd tell me why you despised the guy."

"So you lied to me? Weeze, lying for information would definitely push the boundaries of the ethical contract." I chuckled.

Her lips turned up in the corners. "I stretched the truth."

"So, how much did you tell him about me?"

"Nothing. Nada. Zilch." She crossed her arms over her chest. "I'm quite the vault when it comes to being discreet."

"You're a damn good professional friend, Weeze." I chuckled.

"Right back at you, Hotshot," she said.

"Chicken Fried" by the Zac Brown Band started playing, and I leaned forward, singing the chorus right in her ear as she swatted me away.

"Get your butt over to the pull-up machine and get ready for those arms to start burning."

I've never enjoyed being tortured so much.

Eloise Gable could put my body through hell, and I'd just keep coming back for more.

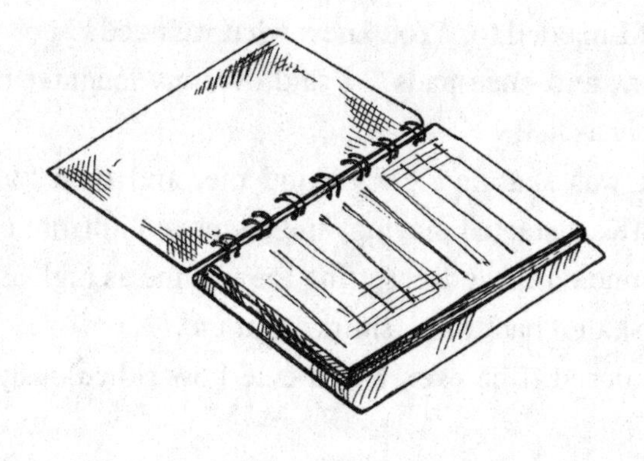

8

Eloise

I was glad that I'd spoken to Everly and booked some time on the ice for Clark. He lit up when I told him, and when we arrived at the ice rink, I could tell how anxious he was to get out there.

"You're not going to do anything crazy," I reminded him as I let go of the wall and moved to skate beside him.

"You don't want to race me, Weeze?"

"Not happening." I arched a brow and then nearly lost my balance because it had been a while since I'd put on a pair of skates.

Clark quickly moved behind me to steady me as I hurried toward the wall, grabbing on just before I made a fool of myself and fell. "It's just been a while. I'm fine, I promise."

He skated in front of me as I skated beside the wall so I could grab on if I needed to. "You know what we need?"

"Elbow and knee pads?" I said over my laughter because I was wobbly as hell.

Clark was skating right behind me, and then "Hey, Ya!" From OutKast started playing, and he moved in front of me. He set his phone on the ledge, setting the volume as high as it would go, as he skated backward, smirking at me.

I wondered if he even had a clue how ridiculously sexy he was.

Tousled hair. Green eyes. Broad shoulders. Plump lips.

It was unfair and infuriating all at the same time.

"Give me your hand," he said.

"No. I need to stay next to the wall."

"You either give me your hand, or I'm going to start doing some crazy hockey moves, and you won't be able to catch me to stop me." A wicked grin spread across his handsome face.

"Has anyone ever told you that you're a stubborn ass?" I hissed, reaching for his hand as I stumbled over my own feet.

"Many times." Before I knew what he was doing, he moved behind me, my back to his chest. His legs rested against the outside of mine, and his arms were wrapped around me just above my chest. My breath hitched in my throat, but I didn't pull away.

"You're helping me every day in the gym; let me do this for you. This will help you keep your balance. Just follow my strides," he said, as he spoke against my ear. His lips grazed my skin, and I nearly fell, but he chuckled and held me close. "Look forward, Weeze. I've got you."

That's the problem at the moment.

When the chorus played and we made our way around the

ice, he started swaying both of us to the beat. I couldn't help but laugh, and my body relaxed against his.

We continued skating this way, the songs changing on his playlist, and he'd change it up and pull back, moving us from side to side and around in a circle.

I was still laughing when the timer went off on my phone, and I realized our time was up.

"Time's up, Hotshot," I said, clearing my throat.

He led us to the wall, and I stepped off the ice, sitting down to take off my skates and put on my sandals, as he did the same.

"Thanks for that," he said. "Man, I needed some ice time."

"You really love what you do, don't you?" I asked, but I already knew the answer. This man oozed joy when he was out on the ice. Hell, even in the gym, pushing himself so hard he was soaking wet, he still had a big smile on his face.

"I really do." He reached for my skates and led us out of the rink. "How about you? Do you love what you do?"

"Well, it's still new, but I'm passionate about it. I'm excited when I wake up in the morning."

"Careful, Weeze. Sounds like you enjoy working with me, even if you don't want to admit it."

He was right. And this was all getting a little too flirtatious. I needed to make sure I kept my boundaries in place.

I was a professional after all.

"Don't get a big head. It's just that I enjoy helping people," I said, glancing down at my phone to see the time.

"You got to be somewhere? Do you want me to give you a ride home?" he asked, as we'd taken his truck from his house over here.

"No. I'm good. I've got a meeting with Randall, and I could use the walk after slipping around on the ice," I said, as we pushed outside, and he paused in the parking lot. "Good job today. I'll see you later."

I held my hand up and waved because I needed some distance there.

We were getting too close, and it was a big red flag.

And I steered clear of red flags.

• • •

My father and I had always done Sunday dinners, but dinner at the Chadwicks' was next level.

Dinner with my dad was conversations about hockey, school, and my grandparents.

But dinner at Clark's parents' house was quite possibly the most entertaining experience of my life.

The Chadwicks made you feel like you belonged there, and that wasn't a familiar feeling for me.

"I'm so happy you could join us," Ellie, Clark's mom, said. "We've heard so much about you."

"Thank you for having me." I passed the salad to Clark, who sat to my right. Lulu was on my left, and she handed me the basket of warm rolls.

"Your father must be awfully proud of you working with the team now," Keaton asked. He and Ellie were the kind of parents you saw on a TV sitcom. They were funny and sweet, and you could see how much they adored their children.

I'd met all the brothers, Easton, Bridger, and Rafe, as well as his cousin, Axel, at pickleball, and tonight was my first time meeting Axel's brother Archer, and his little girl, Melody. Lulu, Henley, and I had become fast friends. I've played pickleball with them four times now, and I had a lot of fun with both of them.

Isabelle and Carlisle were Archer and Axel's parents, and they lived next door.

This family could be on a reality show, because they were hilarious, and they played off one another so well.

"How close are you with Emilia Taylor?" Bridger grumped from across the table.

He was the toughest read in the bunch.

He didn't give much away, and he seemed pissed off most of the time.

"I love Emilia. I rent her guest cottage, and she's been a great friend since I moved to town."

"That's all I needed to know," he said, before glancing around the table as if he'd just proven his point.

Emilia had mentioned that he was particularly cold to her and that there were some issues with the Chadwicks regarding her parents' newspaper, but I didn't realize how serious this was.

Bridger's gaze found mine, looking at me like I just admitted I was best friends with Satan himself.

It pissed me off.

Emilia was kind to her core.

"Ignore him," Clark said. "He's got it in his head that Emilia has it out for us."

"It's not in my head—it's actually written in ink, genius," he snapped at his brother, and the table erupted in laughter.

"You don't even know that she has anything to do with it," Henley and Lulu said at the same time, and then turned and high-fived one another for it.

"Eloise." Bridger directed his question to me. "Let me ask you something."

"Okay." I cleared my throat and dabbed my mouth with my napkin.

Bring it on, Grumpy Smurf.

"Did you tell Emilia that you're training my brother? That he's been improving every day," he said, putting his hand up to stop me before I started to answer. "Specifically, did you mention that you and he went out on the ice for the first time this week?"

"I-I, er, yes? Emilia and I met for dinner after Clark and I had gone to the ice rink. Was it supposed to be a secret?"

"Nope. Just a fact. Thanks for clearing that up," he said, looking directly at Clark.

"Come on," Clark said. "There were several people at the ice skating rink. And everyone in town knows that I'm training with Eloise because she's living here full-time while she's training me. It's not a secret. You're reaching."

"What am I missing?" I asked hesitantly, directing my question to Lulu and Henley.

"The *Taylor Tea* wrote an article about Clark getting out on the ice for the first time yesterday. They made it sound like there was an issue because he was skating with his physical therapist, so they assumed something must be wrong." She shrugged. "But Emilia Taylor is not the only person who knew you were there."

"Oh, do we think that Old Man Moe, a man who can barely form a complete sentence, is writing a weekly column in the *Taylor Tea*?" Bridger hissed. "Come on, now. The man had his pants on inside out the last time I saw him. He's not savvy enough to pull this off."

"Old Man Moe runs the ice rink," Henley whispered, leaning over Lulu to fill me in.

"Emilia assured me that she is not involved in the family business. In fact, she has no idea who is writing that column," I said, reaching for my glass of wine because the man across the table looked like he might murder me.

"Oh, then, by all means, if Emilia doesn't admit that she's the devil, she must not be," he deadpanned, his voice void of all emotion.

"Bridger, you need to take it down about twenty notches. You're being rude." Keaton stared hard at his son.

Ellie smiled at me and then turned her attention to her eldest child. "Yes, you should listen to that song I sent you from Jelly Roll, "Dead End Road." It's about how you've got to stop living on a dead-end road."

"And you've got to stop quoting Jelly Roll to get your point across, Mom," Bridger grouched, and more laughs filled the room.

"Honey, I'm telling you, that man is deep in thought. The *Taylor Tea* is not something you can control. You need to quit living on that dead-end road, my love," Ellie said.

Rafe took a moment to contain his laughter as he wiped his mouth with his napkin. "I agree, brother. You need to let it go," Rafe said.

"Yeah. I really like Emilia. I just stopped by her shop and got a couple of bouquets for the house, and she's really great. I think you're misreading her." Lulu lifted her wineglass and took a sip.

"And she would be happy to sub on the Chad-Six anytime we need her," Henley said, softening her gaze as she looked at Bridger.

"I saw her play during free play, and I think we can pass on that offer." Easton shrugged before looking at me. "Sorry. No offense to her. I just like to win."

Axel barked out a laugh. "At the rate people are dropping from the Chad-Six, I wouldn't count her out."

"Well, if you all choose to wear blinders, be my guest. If she plays on our team, I will walk." Bridger spread some butter on a roll and set it down on Melody's plate.

"Thanks, Unc-ee," she said, which was damn cute coming out of that sweet girl's little mouth. "What's bwinders?"

"Blinders," Bridger said, surprising me with how patient he spoke to his niece. "It's when people show you who they are, and you choose not to see them."

"Doesn't Jelly Roll have a song about that, too?" Isabelle asked.

"What is the deal with Jelly Roll?" I leaned forward and whispered to Lulu and Henley.

"Ellie and Keaton went on tour for a few weeks with Jelly Roll. They followed him all over the US," Lulu said. "And Isabelle and Carlisle joined them in a few cities."

"They're superfans," Henley said over her laughter.

Keaton was still discussing the meaning behind the lyrics to a particular song, and Bridger looked displeased.

"Okay, can we move on from this ridiculous Emilia Taylor discussion? I get to start running in a few days, so cheers to that." Clark held up his beer bottle and clinked it against my wineglass, and everyone joined in.

"I think Eloise might be a little stronger player than you are on the court, so I'll leave it up to you guys to decide who plays," Easton said, reaching for another roll.

"It all comes back to pickleball." Rafe barked out a laugh.

"How do you assess who's a better player? I'm one of the strongest dudes out there," Clark said, and I chuckled at how defensive he was about it.

"It's not like he said I was a better hockey player," I said over my laughter.

"She's correct. Although, I haven't seen you play yet, Eloise." Easton winked at me. "Clark, you're good, but you tend to hit it out of bounds a lot. You use a little too much force. It's all about finessing it over the net."

Clark rolled his eyes and flipped Easton the bird.

"What's that mean, Unc-ee?" Melody asked, staring down at her own fingers now.

"Well played." Archer raised a brow at Clark. "Let's not teach her every horrid thing we've got in our arsenal all at once, yeah?"

More laughter.

Like I said, this family was entertaining.

We finished up dinner, and everyone helped clear the table. The guys all jumped in and did the dishes while Ellie and Isabelle got dessert on the table.

Once we finished up, I joined Lulu and Henley for a glass of wine out on the patio.

It meant a lot to me that they'd invited me here. I hadn't expected to feel so welcomed. So relaxed. My stomach hurt from how much I'd laughed.

And how much I'd eaten, too.

I finally understood why Clark wanted to be home while he recovered from his injury and trained for the new season. This family was warmth and kindness.

It was impossible to miss.

"Don't listen to Bridger about Emilia. I think she's great. Somewhere along the way, he just decided she's the one behind the column, and once he gets it in his head, it's hard to change his mind," Henley said.

"Agreed. He's being such a stubborn ass about it. I really like her, and I feel bad that she's being blamed for something she probably has nothing to do with." Lulu shook her head before continuing. "I mean, look at my family. If I was held accountable for all the crazy shit they do, no one would ever speak to me."

I chuckled. I liked these girls. It felt like I'd known them forever.

"I could just ask her directly. I mean, she's brought it up and talked about it, but I could just ask if it's her, right?" I said.

"Yeah, I mean, it's an anonymous column, so I'm assuming the author wants to have anonymity." Henley tapped her finger against her lips. "But she'd probably tell you the truth because you're friends."

"And what would you do if she admitted it to you? She would swear you to secrecy." Lulu laughed. "And does it really matter if it's her? I mean, they aren't writing horrible things."

"True. Although the column gossips about things you might not want talked about, like Emerson's fiancé cheating on her, and Easton briefly ditching me after our rafting accident. And they loved writing about you and your ex-rock star boyfriend." Henley nodded her head at Lulu. "It's not necessarily things we want discussed."

My head was spinning at all she just shared. "Emerson is their sister, right? Ellie mentioned her at dinner."

"Yes. She's married to Nash now, and they have the most amazing son. But she and her ex had been engaged, and he had an affair with her maid of honor," Lulu said, eyes wide. "It was a big scandal back then, according to Rafe. Her ex is a total douchebag. It's his loss."

"Wow. That's a lot," I said, leaning back and taking a sip of my wine. "And they can print whatever they want?"

"They don't fully name anyone, but they give enough hints that, in a small town, everyone knows who they're talking about. Like you were referenced as the new *lady trainer* in this week's column." Henley fell back in laughter.

"I do not think Emilia would call me that, because first off, it's slightly sexist. Why not just say the new trainer?" I insisted. "Would they say someone was a new *male trainer* if I were a man?"

"That's a fair point, but what if she's trying to throw everyone off her scent?" Lulu said. "That's what I would do. I'd make it seem like it's not me."

"Could it be you, Lu?" Henley asked, arching a brow before falling back in a fit of laughter.

"Girl! I wish it were me. I'd love to claim that shit. It's the highlight of my week, seeing what she has to report," Lulu said.

"I just don't know why Bridger is so convinced that Emilia is the one writing the column. She's pretty busy with the flower shop, and she's a part-time caretaker for her grandmother, as well," I said. She and I had grown close. I felt like I knew her pretty well in the few weeks since we'd met.

I knew a good person when I saw one. And Emilia Taylor was good people.

Clark and Bridger walked out onto the patio.

"You three look like you're conspiring," Clark said, and a jolt of awareness shot through me as his light green eyes found mine. A rush of flutters hit my stomach, and I tried desperately to ignore it.

"We're talking about the *Taylor Tea*," Lulu said, quirking a brow as she turned her attention to Bridger. "What if you found out that I was the one writing the column?"

He rolled his eyes. "Nice try. I have a gift for reading people. You'd never be able to keep a secret that big. Plus, you weren't living here when this column first came out."

"Touché," Lulu said, before reaching for her wineglass.

"Dude, does it really matter?" Clark groaned. "I don't really give a shit who writes it."

"Really, brother? This woman said that you might be done playing hockey because of your injury. That shit is not okay," Bridger hissed.

"But I'm not done. I'm practically back to 100 percent." Clark waggled his brows, and damn if the man wasn't sexy as hell. This is why, once again, alcohol and Clark Chadwick did not mix. "Right, Weeze?"

"I'd say you're 92 percent there." I chuckled.

"Loving the cute nickname," Lulu said, as she leaned close to my ear.

Yeah, me too.

9

Clark

"Damn, woman. It's not a race," I grunted, struggling to keep up with her as we came down the dirt trail near my house. The sun was beating down on us, and she'd been pushing the pace the whole time.

"I'm not the one who's racing. You keep trying to get one shoulder ahead of me," Eloise said, her words labored, as she was breathing heavily.

And let me tell you, a panting Eloise is sexy as hell.

"I'm used to running alone," I said, as we came to a stop in the back of the house.

We both bent over, hands on our knees, as we tried to catch our breath.

She wiped her forehead with the hem of her tank top, letting me see her toned abs before she let it fall back in place.

"So if you're running with someone, you have to lead?"

"Well, yeah. I mean, it's my nature." I chuckled. "I'm a professional athlete. I don't think it's a stretch that I like to win."

It was hot as hell this morning, which was not unusual for early August, but you usually got a reprieve this early in the morning.

"Fair enough." She glanced out at the river. I've gotten to know this woman over the last five weeks, and I knew exactly what she was thinking.

"You want to jump in?"

"We don't have time to go for a swim before today's workout. It's a long one," she said.

I tore my tee over my head and dropped my shorts, before kicking off my running shoes and socks.

She just stood there, gaping at me.

"You want to take a picture?" I teased. "It'll last longer."

She blinked a few times before putting her hands on her hips and tipping her chin up. "I was processing. I thought we were heading inside to the gym."

"I think we should take a quick dip and cool off before we start our workout. And that didn't look like processing, Weeze. That looked like fantasizing to me." I laughed because her cheeks flushed pink, and it was cute as hell.

"In your dreams, Hotshot. I've seen a million chiseled abs." She reached for the hem of her tank and tossed it on the ground before kicking off her running shoes.

"So my abs aren't anything special, huh?" I asked as she stormed past me, heading for the water.

"Nothing I haven't seen many times before," she called out over her shoulder, her long ponytail swooshing back and forth.

Her running shorts hugged her perfectly peach-shaped ass, and my mouth watered at the sight.

She dove off the deck, and I followed her as I cannonballed into the water.

“Damn you, Clark Chadwick!” she shouted, as she bounced around from the waves I made. “Can’t you just jump in like a normal person?”

I swam toward her, pushing the hair out of my face. “I’ve never been normal.”

“That’s the first thing you’ve said that I agree with this morning.” She chuckled.

“Such a smartass,” I said, moving closer.

Our knees bumped one another, her chest knocking into mine as she trod water to keep herself in place, whereas my feet easily found the bottom of the river.

“Well, it’s not like it’s the first time I’ve seen your abs. You find reasons every day to strip down.” Her teeth sank into her bottom lip to keep from laughing.

“Maybe I like stripping down in front of you,” I said, my hand brushing against hers beneath the cool water.

“Please. You like stripping down in front of anyone.” She pushed her hair away from her face as the sun shone down, causing pops of golden honey to dance in her dark gaze.

“Not true. I particularly like stripping down in front of you.” My voice was gruff now because being this close to the woman was getting to me.

Day after day.

Hour after hour.

We were always together, and I was struggling with it.

“Is that so?”

“That is so,” I said.

"And why is that?" She sighed as if she were preparing for a bullshit answer.

"Because I like seeing your cheeks flush. I like seeing the way your lips part when you're watching me. I like knowing you're as attracted to me as I am to you. I felt it that day out on the ice. The way your heart pounded in your chest." I've wanted to say it for a while now, but I knew she'd freak out.

At least out here in the water, she couldn't run away quite as quickly.

Her tongue swiped out across her bottom lip, and she looked away. "You can't talk to me like that, Clark."

"Am I wrong? Are you telling me you aren't attracted to me?"

She turned to look at me. Her gaze locked with mine. "I'm telling you that it doesn't matter. It's a no-go zone."

"Oh, you've named it, huh? I bet you wrote it in your notebook, too." My pinky finger wrapped around hers beneath the water.

"Clark," she whispered, her chest moving up and down quickly now.

"Eloise," I mimicked.

"I named it for a reason." She searched my gaze. "This is my job. I've worked hard to get here. I'm not throwing it away so I can scratch an itch."

Ouch. Tell me how you really feel.

"Scratch an itch? That's what you think this is?" I asked, my hand snaking around her waist as I tugged her closer. Her hands found my shoulders as she kept herself upright.

"I think you're a professional hockey player. I think women fall at your feet. And you're home for the summer, so it's a slow time for you, and I happen to be here."

"That's fucking offensive, Weeze," I said, but my body had a mind of its own.

My lips grazed along the line of her jaw, just as her legs wrapped around my waist.

"Your reputation precedes you," she whispered against my ear.

"Oh, yeah?" I pulled back. "Have you seen me out with a lot of women since I've been home? The only one who's gone on a date since you've gotten here is you."

Her gaze studied mine. "That's not how it is back in the city, from what I've heard."

"Maybe if you'd been in the city back then, things would have been different."

Her fingers moved to my hair. "Don't tease me, Clark. This can't go anywhere, and we both know it."

My hands moved to her hips as she rocked against me ever so slightly. "Doesn't stop me from wanting you, Weeze."

"I don't want you," she whispered, as her lips grazed mine, back and forth.

We stayed like that for what felt like hours but was probably less than a minute before she pulled back.

She shook her head and slid down my body before swimming to the dock and using the ladder to climb out of the water.

My gaze tracked every inch of her. The way her sports bra and shorts clung to her body, water droplets cascading down her golden skin and disappearing into the tiny space between her breasts. Her hair was wet and wavy, falling over her slim shoulders.

She turned around and studied me for a moment before speaking. Eyes guarded but watchful.

"Come on, Hotshot. Time to work out."

I groaned as I got out of the water, my dick hard as steel.

My trainer was completely unfazed now.

We gathered our clothes and walked toward the patio, where we each grabbed a beach towel and dried off the best we could before I led her into the house.

"I'm going to grab a quick shower," I said, clearing my throat because I was extremely uncomfortable at the moment.

She shook her head, eyes searching mine. "Really?"

"Really." I chuckled. "You know where the laundry room is. I've got clean clothes in there. You can grab a pair of boxers and a tee and throw your clothes in the dryer if you want. I'll be back in ten minutes."

"I can't believe you're showering before we work out," she said, lips pursed, as if she were completely baffled by the idea.

"I don't expect you to understand this, but you just had your legs wrapped around my waist, which means my dick is rock-hard. Have you ever tried to work out with an erection, Eloise?" I asked, and her eyes widened with surprise.

"Not that I can recall." She smirked.

"Well, it will make working out very difficult and slightly uncomfortable for both of us. So I'm going to take a quick shower and take care of business so we can get to work," I said, my voice gruff.

She tucked her lips between her teeth as her gaze moved down my body to where my dick was standing straight up, straining against the thin layer of my briefs.

"Sounds like a personal problem," she said with a chuckle, her cheeks flaming red.

"Sounds like an Eloise Gable problem." I arched a brow.

"Let me just tell you how this plays out, so you'll understand why what just happened can never happen again."

"Nothing happened. Hence my situation," I grunted, as my eyes moved down to where two hard peaks poked through her sports bra.

"What almost just happened." She looked down and then crossed her arms over her chest. "Let's say we acted on this brief little attraction, and then you decided to brag about it in the locker room—"

I cut her off. "This isn't fucking high school. Not that I'd have ever talked about anyone that way in a locker room back then either."

"You know what I mean. It gets mentioned to one person, and then guess what, Clark?"

"What?" I moved closer to her. This pull between us was not something I've ever experienced before.

"You're the star player. The professional athlete." She threw her hands in the air. "I'm the physical therapist. I'm the replaceable one. And I'm also the coach's daughter, so me getting fired because I acted on something frivolous—well, it would embarrass my father as well as put a big, fat blemish on my career. One that I just started."

"Clearly, you've thought about this." I arched a brow.

"It's not a joke to me. I'm the one who would be ruined by this. You would just be the playboy with another notch on your belt," she said on a huff.

"Notch on my belt?" I made no attempt to hide my irritation. "I don't know who you think I am, but that's not really my style. I don't disrespect women, and if you've noticed, I haven't been out womanizing in the time you've known me."

"You know what I mean," she said, tucking a piece of hair that escaped her ponytail behind her ear. "We both signed contracts. I take that very seriously. What happened out in the water was a mistake, and I don't think we should ever speak of it again. Nothing happened. It was nothing."

I nodded. "Got it."

"Go take a shower, and I'll get my clothes in the dryer. I'll meet you in the gym in twenty minutes."

"Yep," I said, before turning toward my room.

She was right. She was Coach Gable's daughter, and I respected the hell out of the man. I was extremely attracted to her, but I hadn't stopped to think about the consequences the way she had.

I respected the hell out of her, too. The last thing I'd ever want to do is cause her trouble. I knew how much this job meant to her, and I wouldn't be the one to get in the way of that.

So I'd figure this shit out.

I stripped out of my briefs and stood under the hot water, my forehead resting against the tiled wall as the water beat down on my back. I wrapped my hand around my throbbing cock and stroked up and down several times.

Thoughts of Eloise and her tight little body pressed against mine out in the water flooded my thoughts.

Her lips parting, inviting me in, as my mouth covered hers.

Our tongues tangling frantically as she grinded up and down my erection. I slipped my briefs down with ease, sliding her shorts to the side as she positioned herself above the tip of my dick.

"I need you inside me now, Clark," she whispered.

I shifted forward, and she took every inch of me.

She was tight and wet and perfect.

Fuuuuck.

I gripped her hips hard, sliding her up and down as I fucked her relentlessly.

She groaned, tightening around me, her nails digging into my shoulders.

She went right over the edge, crying out my name. I thrust one more time before I exploded with a grunt.

I continued fucking my hand as I came so hard my vision blurred.

It wasn't my first time getting off to thoughts of Eloise Gable.

Hell, it wasn't even my first time today, as I'd woken up with a boner, and she was my first thought.

But I needed to pull my shit together and shake this off.

She was right—it couldn't go anywhere.

And I needed to focus on getting into the best shape of my life.

I was a professional, after all.

I quickly got dressed and stopped in the kitchen, where I grabbed a protein shake and chugged it.

"Feeling better?" Eloise said from behind me, and I whipped around to find her standing there fully clothed.

Not even close.

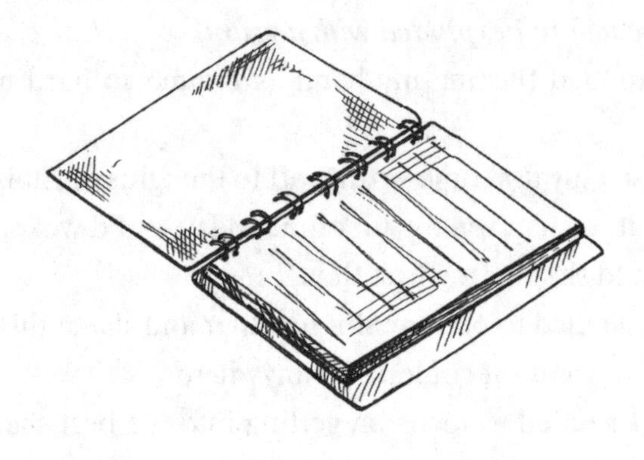

10

Eloise

"What is that?" I asked, tracking the notebook on the counter that had our names written in Sharpie across the top as I walked into his kitchen.

"I thought we could start keeping a notebook that we communicate in. You know, like texting but on paper." He chuckled as he pushed a protein shake in my direction.

Yes, Clark Chadwick was now concerned about my nutritional needs, and he'd convinced me to drink one of his fruity blended protein drinks every day when I arrived in the morning.

Sometimes we drank them after our runs, but today was a swim day, so we didn't run this morning.

"Thank you." I reached for the shake and took a sip before

turning my attention to the notebook. "Why would we communicate in a notebook?"

"Because it's your thing, Weeze," he said, as if it made perfectly good sense.

I flipped open the cover to see a note from him.

Weeze,

I'm feeling stronger than I've felt in a long time. I'm getting my stride back. I'd like more time on the ice and longer runs, but I will let you decide.

Professionally yours,
Clark Chadwick

I barked out a laugh. "Professionally yours?"

"Well, you're so concerned about making sure things are professional, so I was being respectful."

My stomach dipped at the way his green eyes took me in as he spoke.

"Very professional, Hotshot." I pulled the notebook from the counter and dropped it into my bag. "I'm glad you're feeling strong. I've noticed it, too. I was going to see if you wanted to get out on the ice today after our swim. And we can definitely increase your mileage this week. You're ready."

"Great. But I'd prefer you put it in the notebook." He winked before slamming the rest of his protein shake.

Damn, the man looked sexy, with his tousled hair falling over his forehead and his arms strained against his fitted white tee.

"Oh, now the notebook is your thing, too?"

"Listen," he said, as his gaze zoned in on where the straw sat between my lips as I sucked down a big gulp. "You spend five hours a day doing what I want, so I just thought we could incorporate a little bit of you into our days, too."

I finished off the shake and made my way around the kitchen island to the sink, where I rinsed my glass and loaded it into the dishwasher. We were so far past being professional with one another, I didn't know how to handle it. I'd already seen the man with an incredibly noticeable boner when we had our moment in the river. Hell, I couldn't get thoughts of what he'd done in the shower that day out of my head. This was a disaster. I was incredibly attracted to him, and it was getting more difficult to pretend I didn't like him. But the truth was, I couldn't like him. It wasn't even an option. I shook off the feeling and turned to look at him. "Okay. I like it. Maybe we'll argue less over things if we write them down and have time to respond. All while being very professional, of course."

He barked out a laugh and led me down the hallway toward the gym. "Always the professional, Weeze."

I rolled my eyes at the nickname, per usual, even though I didn't mind it at all. I've been called Elle and Lo over the years by friends, but no one had ever turned Eloise into Weeze, but somehow it was charming, coming from Clark.

He turned on the music, and we made our way through stretches. He was lying on the table on his back as I felt the area around his knee, doing gentle massage with one hand.

"The inflammation is nonexistent at this point," I said, my voice slightly dry as my free hand grazed his as it rested on the table.

"Yep. Thanks to you." His pinky finger hooked around mine, and I didn't pull away.

"You've done all the hard work." I continued tracing my fingers around his knee, even though there was no need to massage the area at this point.

"I think we've both worked hard. I mean, you gave up your

life in the city to be here with me. And now the real work starts. I'm finally feeling strong, and now I can push to take things to the next level," he said, his thumb stroking the inside of my palm.

Why wasn't I pulling away?

We formed a friendship over the last few weeks, and friends could share moments like this, right?

We still kept things very professional.

Outside the almost kiss that we never spoke of, even if I thought about it pretty much every night when I climbed into bed.

"Yep. Today, we start increasing the weights. And I'll even give you some freedom on the ice to open up when we get out there." I pulled my hand away and stepped back.

I was playing with fire, and I needed to be smart.

He sat forward. "I like the sound of that."

"Great. We're starting with pull-ups."

"My favorite," he said, making his way over to the pull-up bar as I followed. "But remember our deal. For every ten reps that I do, you have to do one."

I groaned. "Why did I ever agree to that deal? You have to do one hundred today, and as much as I hate to admit it, I don't think I can do ten pull-ups."

"If I can do a hundred, you can do ten, Weeze. I have five sets of twenty, so you can do two at a time in between my sets just like we did before."

"Fine," I grumped. "Get going."

I watched as he tore off his white tee and tossed it on the ground. His basketball shorts hung low on his hips.

Why was it difficult to catch my breath lately when he took his shirt off?

This damn man was occupying every one of my fantasies, even though I desperately wanted to think of anyone but him.

He got through the first set of twenty pull-ups with ease and motioned for me to jump up.

I positioned myself beneath the bar and jumped up, wrapping my hands around the cold metal bar and pulling my chin just above before dropping down. My arms shook as I got through the second one, and then I jumped down. He stood close, which I knew he was doing in case I stumbled on my way down.

He tried to help me the first time we started this ridiculous competition, and I shut him down. I may not be able to do one hundred pull-ups, but I was capable of hoisting myself up and dropping down when I finished.

We did this routine three more times, both guzzling water before the last set. Post Malone was blaring through the speakers, and I hoped it helped to hide the fact that I was completely out of breath. I could hold my own in the pool and on runs with him, but when it came to upper-body strength, I was weak in comparison.

I hated that.

Ten pull-ups were a challenge for me, even with breaks. And at the moment, my arms were burning, and I didn't think I had two more in me.

But I watched as Clark jumped up and grabbed the bar, his back covered in a layer of sweat as every chiseled muscle flexed.

Up and down.

He counted them out, and somehow, he even made counting sound sexy as hell.

"Ninety-eight," he said, his muscles flexing with every movement. "Ninety-nine. One hundred."

I shook my arms, begging them to give me two more so I didn't look as weak as I felt at the moment.

Clark wiped his forehead and pointed at the bar. "Last two, Weeze. You've got this."

I cleared my throat before jumping up and barely catching the bar. My arms were already shaking, and Clark moved right in front of me, where my body hung like a dense weight.

Dig deep, Eloise.

My arms shook so much, it was difficult to get my chin above the bar, but I did it.

"Nine," he said, standing so close I could feel his breath on my abdomen where my tank top rode up. "One more."

"Okay," I huffed, attempting to pull, but not going anywhere.

That's when two large hands gripped each side of my hips, and I startled.

"Let me help you," he said.

"No!" I squealed, trying to shake him off. "Because then you'll say I didn't finish them."

"Don't be a stubborn ass," he hissed, as he attempted to push me up.

My arms were on fire, but I wasn't ready to concede. So I did the only thing I could think of before falling to the floor in a heap.

My feet swung up, landing on his shoulders, just so I could catch my breath for a second and readjust my hands.

But the sexy jackass took it upon himself to pull my legs over his shoulders, his hands on my lower back.

Great. Now his face was pressed against my lower belly.

"What the hell are you doing?" I said, trying not to laugh because even though it was totally inappropriate, my arms weren't shaking anymore, and it was the much-needed break I'd been desperate for.

"I wasn't going to have you stand on my shoulders, Weeze. Your head would have hit the bar," he said with a chuckle.

I took a few beats to slow my breathing as he sang along to Morgan Wallen as if this were perfectly normal for me to be straddling his neck.

"Well, nothing about this feels professional," I huffed, as I readjusted my hands on the bar. "Okay, I've got it now."

"All right, do your thing. Go at your own pace," he said.

I started to lift up, but my arms felt like jello. I was just able to raise myself enough to put my groin directly in his face. "Oh my god! Back up, Chadwick!"

"Not going to let you fall, I've got you. And damn, you smell good, even when you're working out."

Was he referring to my vagina? Because that was currently right in front of his nose at the moment.

I pulled with everything I had, lifting myself just enough for my forehead to touch the bar before my arms gave out, and I tumbled down, crashing into Clark.

His loud laughter boomed as he caught me in the most awkward position.

One hand on my ass and the other on my rib cage, his large hand dangerously close to copping a feel of my breast.

He stayed perfectly still before sliding me against him and carefully maneuvering me to my feet.

"You okay?" he asked, his voice gruff.

"Yes. You can remove your hand from my ass now." I stepped back, arching a brow.

He held his hands up. "Couldn't really help the way you crashed into me."

His eyes zeroed in on my fitted tank top, and I glanced down to see my nipples hard enough to be noticeable through both my sports bra and my tank top.

I quickly crossed my arms over my chest and glanced down

as my eyes widened at the very noticeable tent in his shorts.

He casually followed my line of sight, appearing completely unfazed. “Hey, what do you expect? You just pressed that sweet pussy of yours against my face. I’m only human.”

My cheeks heated, and I quickly moved across the room to get my water as I processed his words.

“Sorry about that. That was a really bad plan.” I placed the cap back on the water bottle.

“I’m not complaining. I wouldn’t have minded if you stayed there for the rest of the workout.” He waggled his brows at me.

I chucked a towel at his face. “Let’s get back to work.”

He just laughed, and it should have been an uncomfortable moment.

But it wasn’t.

I’d grown comfortable with this man.

Oddly comfortable.

He got back to work, and we moved from one machine to the next.

When “The Man,” by Taylor Swift started playing, I quirked a brow.

“Are you a Swiftie now?” I asked with a laugh, because he knew I was, and he teased me about it several times.

“If you’re going to spend hours every day in here, you should have some music choices, too.” He wiped his face with the towel. “And this song reminds me of you. A woman living in a man’s world, trying to find her place and showing everyone what a badass she is.”

My breath hitched at his words.

This was a damn challenging business to break into not only as a woman, but as a young woman.

And hearing him say that meant something to me.

My lips turned up in the corners, I couldn't help myself. And then he did the most unexpected thing.

He started belting out the lyrics.

About the double standards women face.

It was sexy and charming… and sweet.

Yes, this beautiful, sexy, successful hockey player had a tender side.

And he was showing it to me.

My teeth sank into my bottom lip as I watched him.

He had zero ego about embarrassing himself, and I admired it.

The confidence. The swagger.

He had it in spades.

When the song came to an end, I sighed. "You'd make Taylor proud with that rendition."

"She's not the one I'm trying to impress." He winked.

Damn you, Clark Chadwick.

You're making it impossible to remain professional.

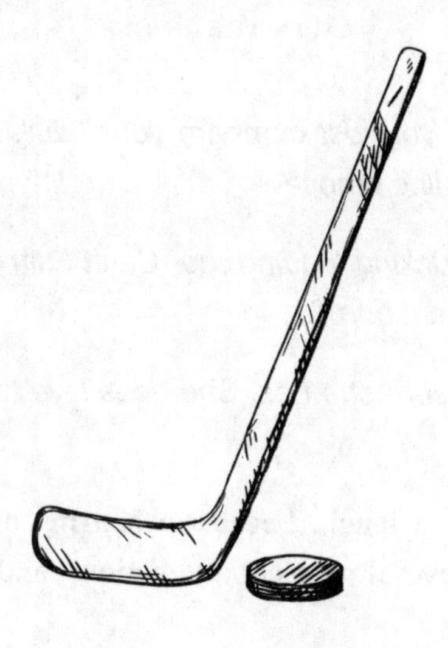

11
Clark

Rafe: *Holy shitballs. Pun intended. <poop emoji>*

Easton: *Is there an explanation coming? Or we just have to guess what you're talking about? <eyeroll emoji>*

Rafe: *Lulu ordered us a new toilet for our bathroom. It has all sorts of bells and whistles, starting with a heated seat.*

Axel: *It's August. Do you really need your ass heated when you take a dump?*

Rafe: *Dude, come over and sit on this seat. Having your ass receive a warm welcome when you show up to drop the kids off at the pool, so to speak, is as good as it gets.*

Easton: *Did you just compare your future kids to a turd? <head exploding emoji>*

Me: *You're fucking kidding me. Can't Lulu just smack that ass and make it burn?*

Archer: *I'm sure she has. She does love to cause our boy some pain.*

I barked out a laugh, because when my brother first met Lulu, they had several physical altercations, and he was slightly terrified of her.

Or so he claimed.

Bridger: *Are we talking about the shitter?*

Me: *Correct. Rafe likes his buns toasty.*

Bridger: *This is two minutes of my life I can never get back.*

Rafe: *The heated seat isn't even the best part.*

Archer: *I'm barely able to take a shit without Melody barreling into the bathroom to ask me for something. So please, tell me about your magical shitter.*

Rafe: *Buckle up, assholes. There are features you can't even imagine.*

Easton: *We're waiting with bated breath.*

Me: *I've never understood that saying.*

Bridger: *Because it's dumb.*

Easton: *There are no dumb answers. This is a safe space.*

Axel: *Did you shit glitter this morning, Rafe?*

Rafe: *There are water features. It has this little sprayer that cleans you up, and somehow, the aim is perfection. Like it just knows where you need it to go. And it shows the fuck up. Every. Single. Time.*

Bridger: *Are we talking about hosing your asshole?*

Archer: *Sounds like a car wash. You just pull up, and it gets the job done.*

Rafe: *All joking aside, it cleans the entire area, and then get this…*

Easton: *Did he just leave us hanging?*

Me: *Maybe he's having a moment with the toilet.*

Rafe: *Sorry, Lulu was asking me about the settings on the new toilet.*

Bridger: *That must be a riveting conversation.*

Axel: *Are you going to finish your toilet bragging? I need to get back to work.*

Rafe: *There's a blower.*

Axel: *Your toilet gives blowjobs? Sign me the fuck up.*

Archer: *I'm ordering a toilet for every room in the house as we speak.*

Me: *I haven't had sex in a few months. I'll be right over to borrow your shitter.*

Bridger: *I'm not getting my dick sucked by a toilet. I don't care how magical it is.*

Rafe: *For fuck's sake. It's a blow dryer. Not a blowjob, you filthy animals.*

Axel: *Damn. I was on my way over, but this changes things.*

Me: *Agreed. Who wants to have their ass blow-dried? <eyeroll emoji>*

Bridger: *The same dude who wanted it washed while he sat on a seat that cooked his ass.*

Rafe: *I'm telling you, it's the best thing I've tried since shaving my balls.*

Bridger: *Make it stop.*

Me: *Don't be a hater. I keep my balls groomed, as well.*

Easton: *Does the toilet shave your balls?*

Rafe: *No, asshole. Lulu does it.*

Bridger: *I'm out. I can't do this.*

Archer: *Who shaves Clark's balls?*

Me: *I do them myself. They are much more attractive when you clean them up.*

Archer: *I'm just a dude who wants to take a shit alone. Shaving my balls is not in the cards until Melody is in school full-time.*

Rafe: *If you had a nanny that wasn't a hundred and seven years old, she could watch your daughter while you shave your balls.*

Archer: *Go clean your asshole, asshole.*

Easton: *Did we gloss over the fact that Clark said he hasn't had sex in months?*

Axel: *I believe we "blew" right past that tidbit when we thought Rafe was getting a blowie from his toilet.*

Me: *It's not a big deal. Just a dry spell.*

Bridger: *I disagree.*

Me: *I thought you tapped out of this conversation.*

Bridger: *I'm done talking about Rafe's asshole.*

Rafe: *Let me ask you… does it have something to do with the fact that you're always with your coach's daughter?*

Easton: *I believe it does.*

Me: *Or the fact that I'm working out five to six hours a day and I'm fucking exhausted.*

Bridger: *Something going on there, brother?*

Me: *I mean, we spend a lot of time together. But she won't go there. It's a professional thing.*

Bridger: *You're a hockey star. Go find someone else.*

Me: *I tried.*

Easton: *And there it is. He likes her.*

Axel: *I think that's obvious. Did you see them at pickleball last night?*

Archer: *What happened at pickleball? I wasn't there.*

Rafe: *He just gapes at her the whole time like a lovesick puppy.*

Bridger: *It's uncomfortable to watch.*

Me: *Fuck off.*

Easton: *I didn't even notice. I just noticed her and Lulu dominating on the courts last night. So I prefer that Rafe and Clark just gape at their girls and let them work their magic.*

Me: *Eloise Gable is not my girl. She doesn't see me that way.*

Rafe: *She definitely likes you. I know these things.*

Bridger: *What is this conversation? I'd rather discuss the shitter again.*

Me: *Don't be an asshole.*

Bridger: *Then stop being a weak fucker. You like her. Do something about it.*

Archer: *You did score the winning goal at the Stanley Cup. This shouldn't be that hard.*

Rafe: *Come over and sit on my toilet, get a deep clean, and decide how to get the girl.*

Axel: *How did you ever get a girl like Lulu?*

Me: *It must be his shaved balls.*

Easton: *Or maybe it's his pristine asshole.*

Bridger: *I've reached my capacity for ridiculous conversations.*

Me: *I've got to get to the ice rink. See you at Sunday dinner.*

Several more texts came through, calling me a pussy and telling me to man up, but I tucked my phone into my gym bag and made my way out to the kitchen.

The notebook we wrote in every day was sitting on the counter. I didn't see her leave it this morning. She must have done it on her way out the door after our workout today.

She'd gone home to shower and do some errands, and I'd crashed for a few hours from pure exhaustion.

I opened the notebook and read our last few notes to one another from yesterday and today.

Weeze,

I'd like to request another pull-up competition. Happy to give you a hand when your arms get tired.

XX,
CC

I've fucked my hand in the shower more times than I could count since that little mishap. Her legs straddling my neck as I breathed her in.

Eloise Gable was equal parts sweet and sexy.

And I'd never been more attracted to a woman in my life.

Especially one who was determined to keep her distance.

We spent a lot of time together.

We formed a friendship.

We talked when we weren't together.

She came to Sunday dinners now, but always with Lulu and Henley. She'd talk to me, but she made it known that she was there as their guest.

My family loved her.

Hell, I was crazy about her.

This was uncharted territory for me.

Wanting a woman who didn't want me back?

I've never been in this situation.

I understood her hesitation as far as our jobs, but we weren't even in the city right now. Why overthink it?

I was all about having a good time.

No strings, no pressure.

The bigger issue is that I was uncomfortable. It had been a while, and I didn't want anyone else.

I'd gone to Booze and Brews with Axel and Bridger last week, and we received our fair share of attention from the women there.

Some that I'd had a good time with in the past.

But I couldn't fucking do it.

Maybe my body was just exhausted from the workouts, I didn't know.

But I knew that my hand was not going to keep me satisfied. I was a man who enjoyed spending time with a beautiful woman, making her laugh, and having a good time, and obviously, I appreciated good sex. I prided myself on always pleasing my lady, and I was very honest and upfront about the expectations of what I had to offer beforehand.

I wasn't a guy who promised things he didn't have to

give. And I knew that I had not time nor room in my life for anything more than a casual relationship at this point in my life.

My first love had always been hockey.

Sex was a close second.

But lately, I was off my game. Maybe it had something to do with coming off such a great season, that it had me questioning the rest of the areas of my life.

I'd accomplished what I'd always hoped for professionally.

But it almost felt like there was something missing, and I didn't know what that meant.

I quickly read through the rest of the notes.

Chadwick,

Get your mind out of the gutter. I just needed a place to rest while I regained my strength to finish the competition. That was a professional straddle.

Weeze

P.S. That was an impressive workout yesterday. Ice everything that hurts, and be ready to go again tomorrow.

Weeze,

Everything that hurts? That might be uncomfortable.

Thanks for pushing me today. Tomorrow, we hit the ice again, and then Sunday is an off day. Will you be at Sunday dinner?

XX,
CC

Chadwick,

Yes, today, we get to skate. You can open up and do your thing. I'll be watching from the sidelines because I trust you won't do anything stupid. And yes, Hen and Lu said I need to come to Sunday dinner because apparently, your mom makes the best lasagna. Is there anything that woman can't do?

XX,
Weeze

Weeze,

Good morning. I'm sure you're going to torture me today, being a Saturday and all. It's your thing. And I look forward to doing many stupid things in your presence. But I think you like watching me on the ice. And yes, her lasagna is the best, and she's amazing at all the things. Glad you're coming. Pun intended.

XX,
CC

Chadwick,

You have a one-track mind. Not giving that a response. Great workout today. See you at the rink this afternoon. And for the record, yes, I do like watching you on the ice. It's pretty magical. Don't get a big head. Maybe I just like hockey. LOL.

XX,
Weeze

I chuckled like a goddamn schoolgirl. And why? Because she liked watching me skate. Hell, most females liked watching hockey players on the ice. It didn't mean anything, and she'd made that clear.

I grabbed my keys and climbed into my truck, driving the short distance to the ice rink.

When I pulled up, I hopped out of my truck and jogged up the walkway. When I opened the door, my hands fisted at my sides.

Brett Lewis was standing there, talking to Eloise. He had his arm up resting on the wall above her, almost like he was caging her in.

The conversation looked intense.

And Eloise didn't look uncomfortable at all.

Brett fucking Lewis of all people.

Maybe she liked that fucker. Even though she knew I couldn't stand the dude.

It felt like a punch to the gut, which made no sense, because she owed me nothing.

We were friends.

Professional friends.

And as much as I teased her about it, flirting and going back and forth with her—she'd just showed me her hand.

She did not see me that way.

Because if she did, she wouldn't be getting cozy with my nemesis.

It was time to pull my head out of my ass.

Eloise Gable did not want me.

Not the way that I wanted her.

Maybe it was time I got the message.

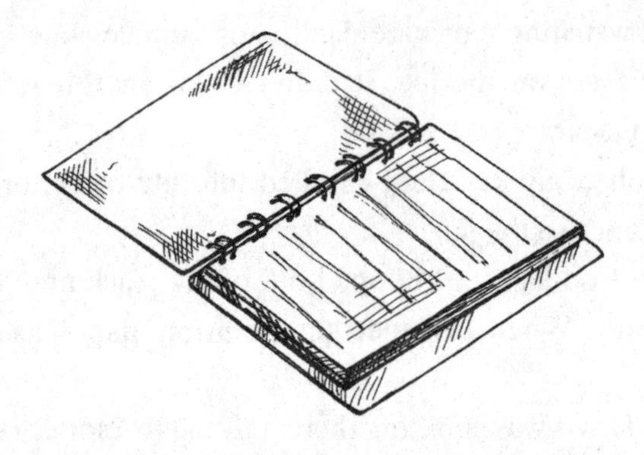

12

Eloise

"Take it easy, Chadwick," I called out from the bleachers where I sat watching him.

He was clearly in a mood because he barely acknowledged me when he walked into the ice rink, nor had he given me the time of day since we made our way to the ice.

I'd been surprised to see Brett here when I arrived. I didn't realize Moe, the man who ran this place, was his grandfather.

Brett had appeared a little down, and he ended up telling me that his father wasn't doing well.

I may not be a fan of Brett Lewis, but I empathized with what he was going through. Watching someone you love battle cancer was painful and emotional and exhausting.

I lived it, and it had shaped my life in a huge way.

Losing my mother at a young age was traumatic and devastating, but watching her suffer—that had stayed with me

"Oh, are you one of Clark's coaches?" a woman sitting a few seats away asked, and I turned to look at her. She was sitting with a friend and they appeared to be in their mid-twenties, both very attractive, and they were clearly here to watch Clark.

Why did that bother me?

He was one of the biggest names out there right now in professional hockey.

"I'm a physical therapist," I said, as I glanced back out at the ice at him.

"Oh, that's cool," she said. "I heard you were in town working with him. I'm Sasha, and this is Laney."

"Hey, I'm Eloise. It's nice to meet you."

"Nice to meet you, too," Laney said. "So you get to work with all the hockey players? That's a damn good job."

I chuckled. "Yeah, my dad is a coach, so I've been around the sport my whole life."

"You're so lucky. My dad is a surgeon, which sounds cool and all, but I think I'd prefer a hockey arena to a hospital," Sasha said with a laugh, and I didn't miss the way both of them kept returning their gaze to the ice.

"Are you guys Lions fans?" I asked, but I already knew the answer. They were here for him.

"We're big Clark Chadwick fans," Laney said with a laugh. "I've crushed on him since I was a senior in high school. He was a few grades ahead of me, and he's just a super nice guy, too. Well, I suppose you probably already know that."

Of course, I did. Clark was the whole package.

A ridiculously sexy hockey player and a really good man.

So why was I so irritated by the comment?

She liked him. He was single. They'd look great together.

"Yes. He's a great guy," I said, clearing my throat as I noticed him moving faster than normal down the ice. "I'm so sorry, can you excuse me for a minute?"

"Oh, of course. Nice to meet you," Sasha called out as I made my way down to the glass surrounding the ice.

"Hey, slow down out there!" I shouted, as he once again raced from one end to the other in an all-out sprint.

"I'm just skating, Eloise," he said, his voice light and laced with humor.

It caught me off guard because I couldn't remember him ever using my actual name.

I stormed around the side toward the entrance and made my way onto the ice just as he started making his way down to the other side.

Fast.

Faster than necessary.

This was just a time to skate around while he had the ice to himself. This was not the time to risk an injury.

It was ludicrous.

"Chadwick!" I shouted, my feet sliding from side to side as I tried to get closer. My tennis shoes were no match for the slick surface, and I looked up to see him skating toward me. His eyes were wide when he realized I was out there.

He skidded to a stop abruptly, shooting ice all over me.

I gaped at him, trying to wipe the shards of ice from my eyes, and he used his big hands and tucked my hair behind my ears.

"Are you all right?" he asked, before grabbing both of my shoulders to steady me. "I could have hurt you."

"You could have hurt yourself," I said, brushing the ice from my tank top before blowing out a breath. "I told you to slow down."

"You also told me I could open things up on the ice today." He moved back as if he wanted space from me.

Hey, that was my job to put space between us.

I stepped forward, not liking the distance. "I didn't say to go at full speed. You almost hit the wall a few minutes ago."

"I'm a hockey player, and this is how we skate." He chuckled, moving back a second time, making it clear this was not something that I was imagining.

"I know that, but you need to slow it down, at least for now," I said, hands on my hips because I knew how hard he'd worked, and I didn't want him going too fast just yet and risking another injury.

"Sure, Weeze. I can do that." He patted me on the head before crossing his arms over his chest, like a barrier between us.

What in the hell was going on? Why was he suddenly acting so weird to me?

"Time's up for your private skate, Chadwick," Moe shouted from the doorway, pulling us from our conversation. "We've got a bunch of kids here for a party that will be out in the next ten minutes."

"Thanks, buddy. I was just finishing up," Clark said.

"Hey, Chadwick. You want to go with us to Booze and Brews for happy hour?" Laney shouted from behind the glass.

He looked at me, and I saw something pass in his gaze, but I couldn't place it. He leaned down, his gaze locked on mine. "You want to go grab a drink? It is Saturday, after all. We're off tomorrow."

I looked up at Sasha and Laney, who were waiting patiently for an answer. "No, that's all right. I've got plans tonight. You should go have some fun."

Of course, I didn't have plans. But I had no desire to go watch Clark get fawned all over by two beautiful women

His gaze held mine, and he nodded. "Yeah?"

"Of course," I said with a nod. "Why wouldn't you?"

His gaze once again locked with mine before he turned to look at the two women. "Sounds good. Give me a minute to change out of my skates."

I didn't know why my hands fisted at my side or why my heart raced when he agreed to go with them. I just insisted he go, and now I was annoyed.

He should definitely go. There was no reason not to.

I attempted to make my way off the ice, but of course, my freaking feet had me walking like a newborn deer.

"Need some help?" he asked, as he quirked a brow, and I continued to try to move forward, even though I was basically staying in the same place but exerting a lot of energy to do so.

"No. I'm fine," I grumped.

"You're not fine," he said against my ear as he snaked a hand around my waist, my back to his chest, lifting me with ease as he glided me toward the opening to step off the ice.

My breath hitched as his lips grazed my earlobe before he set me down on my feet.

"Thank you. You didn't need to do that. I had it." I stepped out of the rink and glanced over my shoulder at him.

"Sure, you did," he said, the corners of his lips turning up the slightest bit, but it seemed forced. He was acting all cool and casual, but something was definitely off.

He sat down and took off his skates while I stood there, brushing off the rest of the ice shards on my tank top.

"You want to come with us, Eloise?" Sasha called out from a few feet away.

And before I could answer, he answered for me.

"Apparently, she's got a hot date," he said as he winked at

me, but there was an edge in his voice before he walked toward them and turned on the Chadwick charm. "So, you're stuck with just me, ladies."

And he walked off with them, not giving me so much as a second glance.

And it bothered me a lot more than it should.

• • •

Clark hadn't texted me since I saw him at the ice rink yesterday, which was a first.

We normally texted throughout the day, and I hadn't heard a word from him.

And it bothered me.

It really bothered me.

"I wish you could go with me," I said, as I sat on Emilia's couch.

"You couldn't pay me to go sit at a table with Bridger Chadwick. I ran into him at the diner this morning, and if looks could kill, I'd be three feet under." She held her hand up as if she were slicing her throat, and I chuckled.

"He is convinced you're writing that column, which, by the way, did you read it yesterday?"

She rolled her eyes. "No, but I heard about it."

I fell back in laughter. "I don't even know these people, and I'm invested. I'm guessing they were talking about the mailman because, according to the *Taylor Tea*, he delivered a lot more than the mail to his much younger lover."

Now Emilia was laughing, too. "Yes. Apparently, Harvey Lawson, our local mailman, who happens to look like George Clooney if you haven't run into him yet, has knocked up Cara Carmichael, who's twenty years his junior."

"Scandalous. But at least it wasn't about the Chadwicks this week, right?" I shrugged. "You would tell me if it was you, wouldn't you?"

She sighed. "Yes, which I assume goes against the code of being an anonymous reporter, but seeing as I'm a florist and not a reporter, I don't care. But I sound guilty when I continually insist it isn't me because then everyone assumes I'm staying loyal to my journalistic integrity. But I don't have any journalistic integrity because I'm not a journalist."

I leaned my head on her shoulder. "I believe you, Em. I'm sorry you have to deal with this."

"It's fine. Most people in town have known me my entire life, and they don't think it's me. Actually, the only one who's ice-cold to me about it is the grumpiest Chadwick." She chuckled. "So I just avoid him. I can't believe I used to have a crush on that guy. He's so rude, but he is hot in the broody, alpha sort of way."

"You had a crush on Grumpy Smurf?" I fell back in laughter. "And you just described a fabulous book boyfriend. We love a broody alpha."

"Yes. But we don't like a broody alpha who glares at you every time he sees you. We can live without that."

"I meant to tell you, Henley and Lulu saw the book I was reading, and they wanted to read it, too. How do you feel about starting our own little book club? We can meet when we all finish."

"Oh, I'd love that. Let's do it," she said.

"Okay, I'll set it up. I'm going to get going. They just texted that they are on their way. I'll see you later." I gave her a quick hug and stopped by the guesthouse to grab the bottle of wine I got to bring to dinner.

I walked the short distance to the Chadwicks' home, and my stomach was in knots because something seemed off with Clark. I checked my phone one more time, and he still hadn't responded to my text.

It was a ridiculous text of course, because I just wanted a reason to message him.

I asked if I left the notebook there, even though I already knew I'd left it there.

But he hadn't responded, which was unusual.

Before I even knocked, the door swung open, and Lulu and Henley were standing there smiling.

"We have a lot to discuss," Lulu said, pulling me inside.

"Yes, we're already addicted to the book. How have I not been reading romance all these years?" Henley said as they led the way inside. "I mean, this guy is one smoking-hot hockey player."

"Right? It's addicting. Emilia and I were thinking maybe the four of us could do a book club."

"Yes!" Lulu shouted, before bursting out in laughter. "Booze, brunch, and books. Let's make it our thing."

"I'm in," Henley said, just as we stepped into the kitchen.

I quickly assessed the room, noting that Clark was absent.

Was he avoiding me?

"Sweet Eloise, I'm so happy to see you," Ellie said, as I handed her the bottle of wine. She wrapped her arms around me and hugged me so tight, it made my chest squeeze.

This family was so warm and kind, and I've never felt so comfortable with people I'd only met a couple of weeks ago.

"Thank you so much for having me. I've heard your lasagna is the best." I squeezed her hand when she pulled back.

"Is Clark bragging about my lasagna?" She chuckled. "It's his favorite. Such a shame he's not going to be here. But I'll wrap some up and have one of you take it to him on your way home."

"Oh, is he sick?" This is something I should definitely know as his trainer.

"Well, he's been puking his brains out since yesterday," Bridger said, walking up beside me. "If it ends up in the *Taylor Tea*, I'll assume you passed the information on to your landlord."

I was still processing his words, but my mind was on Clark. Had he gone out with those women and partied too hard? Had he taken one of them home, or was he really sick? Why was I hoping that he was really sick and not lying in bed with another woman while they both suffered from hangovers? I was an awful person. I actually wanted him to have the flu.

"Her landlord?" Lulu said from behind me, pulling me from my thoughts. "Emilia is her friend. In fact, she's our friend, too. I like her. We're starting a book club."

He let out a loud breath before reaching for his beer bottle on the counter. "Then I'll expect all the family secrets to be printed every week."

"Hey, what if we test your theory? You know, we could say something that isn't true, and see if it gets printed," Henley said. "And then when it doesn't get printed, you can drop this vendetta against the poor girl."

"Oh, are we talking about Cara Carmichael?" Easton said, snatching a carrot stick off the vegetable platter sitting on the kitchen island.

"I wouldn't call Cara Carmichael a poor girl," Lulu said, as Rafe came up behind her and handed her a glass of Chardonnay. "Harvey Lawson is easy on the eyes, if you know what I mean."

"He sure is," Henley said over her laughter. "He could be George Clooney's doppelgänger."

"Please, he's not *that* good-looking," Easton and Rafe said at the same time before clinking their beer bottles together.

Keaton asked what I wanted to drink, and he left to get me a glass of wine.

Ellie leaned into the huddle we were standing in. "He really is that good-looking."

The room erupted in laughter, just as Axel and Archer walked into the kitchen with Melody. Their parents were out of town this weekend, so they weren't going to be at dinner.

"Why are they giggling, Daddy?" Melody asked, surprising me when she reached for me from her father's arms.

I scooped her into my arms, settling her on my hip, and she smiled, her little cherub cheeks round and pink. Her hair was tied up in two little buns at the top of her head. She was by far the cutest kid I'd ever met.

"They think Harvey Lawson is good-looking," Bridger grumped. "That dude always looks like he's up to something."

"Well, he is," Rafe said. "He's been busy knocking up Cara Carmichael."

"Isn't she good friends with Harvey's daughter?" Easton asked.

"You guys are a bunch of nosy hens," Ellie said, waving her hand around. "I've known Harvey for a long time, and it's good to see him settling down. He's a good guy."

"We're not the nosy hens," Easton said, holding his hands up and chuckling. "I didn't know about him and Cara. I read it in the paper."

"Correct. You can thank Emilia for sticking her nose where it doesn't belong once again," Bridger grumped.

"The flower girl, I love her," Melody said, clapping her hands together.

"You love getting your bouquet, don't you, angel face?" Archer said, winking at his daughter.

"He gets her pink roses every Saturday," Ellie whispered in my ear. "He's such a good dad."

"The flower girl?" Bridger grumped.

"She owns the flower shop where Archie gets her flowers," Rafe said, quirking a brow.

"Well, just don't tell her any secrets." Bridger slammed the rest of his beer, just as Ellie told everyone it was time to eat.

We all carried platters into the dining room, and I spent the next hour laughing harder than I had in a long time.

They talked about Rafe and Lulu's new toilet, which had the entire table roaring in laughter.

Then the conversation switched to the fact that Bridger had struggled to read the menu at the diner because the words were blurry, and his mother urged him to go to the eye doctor, for what was apparently not the first time.

"Fine, I'll go. But you know I have a weird thing about my eyeballs."

"What's wrong with your balls, Unc-ee?" Melody asked.

More laughter.

"He can't touch his balls. It gives him the creeps," Easton said.

"He said my toilet gave him the creeps, too, so he's clearly being dramatic," Rafe added over a mouthful of pasta, and Ellie shook her head and chuckled.

"Hey, I don't want to take a shower when I'm taking a poop. Sorry, Melody." Bridger reached for his water.

"Why did you apologize to Melody? It's my toilet." Rafe arched a brow.

"Because I said poop."

"Is poop a bad word now, too?" Axel asked.

"No. Everybody poops. Right, Daddy?" Melody said, as her little head fell back in a fit of giggles.

"Yep. They sure do." Archer smiled down at his daughter. "And you do know you can get glasses if you can't handle putting contacts in your eyes."

"You probably just need readers. It's not that big of a deal," Keaton insisted.

"Fine. I'll go this week," Bridger said, not hiding his irritation.

"Good. It's best to just get checked." Ellie pushed to stand. "I'll get dessert ready. And I'm going to pack up a to-go box for Clark. Who wants to drop it off at his house?"

"Oh, I'll take it to him. It's on my way home," I said, looking up to see Bridger studying me. No one else thought twice about it. It wasn't on the way home; it was in the other direction. But this town was small, and I didn't mind a longer walk home. "That way I can see if he's going to be up for practice tomorrow or not."

Because the truth was, I missed him.

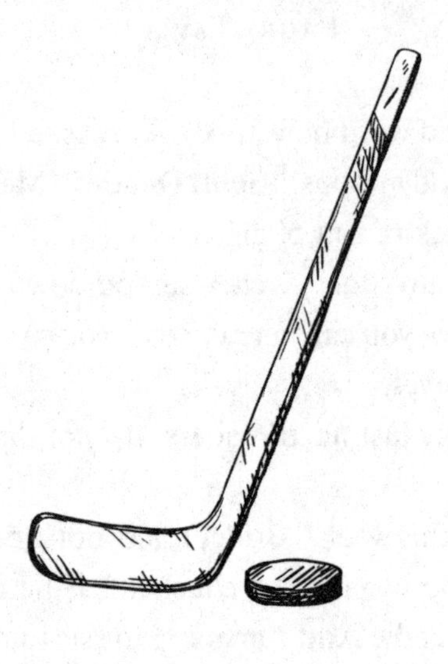

13

Clark

I vomited for almost twenty-four hours, and I'd finally fallen asleep for a bit this afternoon. I made my way to the kitchen and poured myself a glass of Gatorade and took a few sips, waiting to see if it would stay down. I still had the chills and a fever, and I was pretty miserable.

It was dark outside, so it was clearly well past dinner time. I glanced around for my phone, knowing my mother had probably called several times since we spoke this morning, and I'd told her I wouldn't make it tonight.

There was a knock on my door that I barely would have heard if it wasn't completely silent in the house. I padded down the dark hallway, flipping on a light as I reached for the door handle.

Eloise Gable stood on the other side, looking gorgeous, as usual.

I was too tired to be annoyed by how pretty she was.

"Hey, what are you doing here?" I asked. "What time is it?"

"It's 8:30, and I was just leaving your parents' house. Your mom packaged up some food for you, and I said I'd drop it off on my way home." She tucked her long brown hair behind her ear and avoided my gaze.

"My house is not on your way home," I said, feeling horrible but also happy to see her standing at my front door.

"Well, it is if you go the long way." She chuckled as she moved past me with the bag in her hand.

"You might not want to come in here. I've finally stopped puking, but I have a low-grade fever."

"Don't be silly," she said, as she set the bag on the counter and turned to look at me. "I never get sick. I have the strongest immune system one can have."

Now it was my turn to laugh. "All right, if you say so."

"Good. So how are you feeling?"

"Like shit."

She moved toward me, pushing up on her tiptoes, and placed the back of her hand on my forehead. "I don't think that's a low-grade fever. You're burning up."

"So, you are a doctor?" I smirked.

"Have you taken anything for your fever?"

"Nah. I just woke up right before you showed up. I'm actually feeling a lot better," I said.

Maybe that's because you're here.

She reached for my hand and guided me to the couch. "Lie down. Where's your medicine cabinet?"

I sat down, leaning forward to rub my head. "It's in my bathroom."

She disappeared down the hall and returned with ibuprofen and a glass of water. She also had a thermometer in her hand, and she ran her fingers through my hair, turning my head to the side, before pressing it into my ear. The little beep came, and she handed me the ibuprofen and the glass of water. "You've got a hundred and one-degree fever. You need to be taking both ibuprofen and Tylenol until this fever breaks. Lie down."

I did what she asked after I set the glass on the table. She found the blanket at the other end of the couch and draped it over me as she dropped to sit on the floor next to me.

"I'd call you bossy, but I'm too tired to argue with you."

She chuckled. "Good. Have you eaten anything?"

"No. I just stopped puking a few hours ago, and then I fell asleep."

"All right. Let's try to get some food in you," she said.

"Don't worry about me. I'll rally for practice tomorrow."

Her eyes widened. "You will not be working out tomorrow. I'm not here to help you in hopes that you can get in a workout. I'm not a tyrant."

"I don't ever miss workouts."

"Well, you're missing tomorrow, because I won't train you," she said, before pushing to stand and walking toward the kitchen.

I didn't argue.

I just lay there, listening to her move around my kitchen.

She returned with some toast and some cut-up banana. "Let's try this. Take a few bites, and we'll see how you feel."

I sat forward and reached for the plate as she took a seat beside me on the couch. I ate a few bites and groaned because it was damn good. "I'm starving, so that's a good sign."

"Yeah, but you want to take it slow."

"All right." I nodded. "Well, thank you for stopping by and for doing all this."

"I'm not leaving," she said, sounding offended.

"I wasn't kicking you out. I just figured you'd want to get home."

"Well, you figured wrong," she said, the corners of her lips turning up the slightest bit.

"I'll be fine for practice on Tuesday. You don't need to worry about it." I finished the second piece of toast.

"I'm not here as your trainer," she said, shaking her head as if the idea were appalling.

"I didn't mean to offend you," I said, scrubbing a hand down my face. I was exhausted. "I know how important your job is to you, that's all I meant. I'll be back on track in a day."

"My job is important to me, but as much as I've fought you on it, I consider you a friend." Her dark brown gaze searched mine. "I'm here as a friend, not a trainer."

"A *friend*-friend, or a professional friend?" I teased.

"A friend-friend." She arched a brow and sighed.

"Okay," I said, as I leaned back against the couch, my hand brushing against hers as she sat beside me. "How was Sunday dinner?"

"It was very entertaining." She chuckled. "Bridger made several digs at Emilia. I heard all about Rafe's toilet. And your mother recited the lyrics to her favorite song by Jelly Roll, per Lulu's insistence."

"'Save Me?'" I barked out a laugh. "She loves that fucking song."

"Well, I added it to my playlist because she was so passionate about the lyrics."

"Yeah. She's the best. She wanted to come over earlier, but I didn't want to get her sick. But here you are, huh?"

"Here I am."

"Such a good friend-friend. Nothing professional about this friendship," I said teasingly.

"I think so. Not that you can say the same, seeing as you didn't even respond to my texts earlier."

"I haven't been on my phone today," I said.

"Maybe you got sick at the bar last night with Sasha and Laney." She made no attempt to hide her irritation.

"Ahhh… that's what you think, huh?" I rubbed my temples, and I saw the concern in her gaze just as she insisted I lie back down, and she slipped down on the floor, sitting right in front of me.

"You seemed excited to go, and you were acting kind of weird to me, that's all," she said.

Was she kidding me right now?

"You sound a little jealous, Weeze."

"Jealous? No. I am so not jealous. Why would I be jealous? We're friends. But you did leave the ice rink with two hot women, and then you didn't answer my text. And you were acting a little distant, so I thought you were avoiding me when you weren't at Sunday dinner," she said, her arms flailing around. But she was showing me a vulnerable side that she rarely shared. "But then when I heard you were sick, I didn't care if you were avoiding me. I just wanted to make sure you were okay."

I scrubbed a hand over the back of my neck and groaned. I hated that she felt that way, but I was glad that she cared enough to be bothered by it. How fucked up is that?

"I really am sick."

"I can obviously see that. So did you have fun with Sasha and Laney?"

She was asking again.

Whether she wanted to admit it or not, she was clearly jealous.

"It was fine."

"Fine? Just fine? I'm sure it was more than fine," she said, her teeth sinking into her bottom lip.

"I didn't have fun. I went out with them because I wanted to make you jealous." I shrugged. "I had one drink, and I went home. Started puking shortly after."

"Really?" She arched a brow.

"I have no reason to lie. It's not like we're together." My pinky finger wrapped around hers. "You've just now agreed to be friends."

"So why did you want to make me jealous, then?" she asked, intertwining her fingers in mine.

"Because I saw you talking to that asshole, Brett, and I didn't like it."

"Why?" she whispered. "He was just there, and he opened up about his dad. His father is not doing well. I empathize with that, you know?"

Well now I felt like a dick. I might not be a fan of Brett's, but I wouldn't wish that on anyone, and I liked his father. "I'm sorry to hear that. And it was kind of you to speak to him about it."

"So you saw me talking to Brett, and then you left with Laney and Sasha to make me jealous? Why?"

"I don't know, Eloise. It's dumb. I guess I thought you liked him, and you just weren't telling me."

"And that bothered you?"

"It bothered me," I said, my gaze locking with hers.

"I don't like him."

"Good. He's an asshole, but I am sorry to hear about this dad. But at the end of the day, you deserve better."

She chuckled. "What do I deserve?"

"You deserve the best. You deserve everything you want, Eloise." I tucked the hair behind her ear, my thumb stroking her cheek as her gaze locked with mine. Her eyes were wide and trusting as I took in the dusting of freckles on the bridge of her nose. Her breaths were coming faster now, and it took all I had not to pull her onto my lap.

"I'm not used to you calling me by my actual name. You did it yesterday, and I thought you were annoyed with me." Her voice was just above a whisper.

"And I'm doing it today, and I'm definitely not annoyed with you." I chuckled, my gaze locked with hers. "I'm being serious with you. You deserve only the best."

"You're so much better than a professional friend, Clark Chadwick." She smiled, and I swear my fucking chest squeezed.

Even lying here with a fever, I wanted this woman.

I wanted her so bad I didn't know how to handle it.

"What if I'm a professional friend who wants to kiss you?" I stroked the inside of her palm with my thumb.

"That wouldn't be very professional." She smirked.

"I think you want to kiss me, too. I think that's why you got jealous yesterday. I think that's why you're here, because you like me, Weeze."

She sighed. "We've talked about this. It can't go anywhere, so why bother?"

"Then why are you here?"

"Because we're friends," she said, her tongue darting out to swipe along her bottom lip. "I wanted to make sure you were okay."

"Why is it so hard for you to admit that you like me?" I intertwined my fingers with hers.

"You know I like you. I'm not denying that."

"Then admit that you want to kiss me, too," I said, as I pressed my lips to the inside of her palm.

"You already know that I want to kiss you, but that doesn't change anything. It can't go anywhere."

"That's a ridiculous reason not to let this happen," I said, happy that she was finally admitting she felt the same way I did. "I mean, I'm assuming you've kissed other men before, right?"

I kissed the inside of her wrist.

"Obviously. I'm a grown woman." Her words were breathy.

"And they aren't here now. So just because you kiss someone doesn't mean you have to know where it's going. It's just a kiss."

"Fair point. And maybe we'll kiss and hate it," she said, sounding ridiculously hopeful that it would be awful, when I was fairly certain it wouldn't be.

"One can hope," I teased.

"Well, I can't kiss you now, you have a fever."

"I've been hot for you before today. Don't let a fever scare you off." I chuckled as my hand moved around the side of her neck.

She leaned closer, eyes falling closed as her lips were just a breath away.

"Oh, my god," she said, pulling back abruptly. "Oh, no!"

And she took off running down the hall.

I pushed to my feet. The ibuprofen clearly kicked in because I felt much better now.

I heard her heaving, and I groaned as I pushed the door open and found her hovered over the toilet.

"Clark, you can't be in here!" she shouted.

I reached for a washcloth in the vanity and rinsed it with cool water before wringing it out and folding it in half and placing it on the back of her neck beneath her hair. "Just relax. I come from a big family. I've seen plenty of vomit in my lifetime. Rafe has a sensitive stomach."

She heaved again, and I held her hair back.

We sat there with her puking and me crouched down behind, her rubbing her back.

After she continued to get sick over and over, it finally stopped.

"I cannot believe I just puked in front of you for thirty minutes after you were about to kiss me. I've definitely hit rock bottom," she said, a sad chuckle escaping as she flushed the toilet and then leaned over the sink and rinsed her mouth out several times before dropping to sit on the floor.

I dropped to sit beside her, pulling her into my chest and wrapping my arms around her. I pressed a soft kiss to the top of her head.

The fact that she let me see this vulnerable side of her, that she allowed me to stay and comfort her—it did something to me.

"I thought you were about to kiss me?" I laughed.

"Well, I told you it was a bad idea. We were cursed from the start."

"How are we cursed? Nothing happened… yet."

"We were about to kiss, and then I puked violently over and over. And now I don't even know if I can muster the energy to walk home. I'd say this was a bust." She groaned as she attempted to push to her feet and stumbled.

I caught her, quickly scooping her up in my arms and carrying her out of the bathroom.

"Why are you carrying me like a baby?" she said, and her voice sounded exhausted, like she had no fight in her at the moment.

I wasn't surprised. She was sick, and I was still coming out of this, so I knew how bad she must be feeling.

"You're not walking home. We're both sick. We can commiserate together." I carried her to my room and set her on the bed. "I've got a fever, and I can't drive you home, and you just had an *Exorcist*-worthy puking experience, and you're not going anywhere."

"Clark, I don't have the energy to laugh or to fight you right now," she said, her eyes barely staying open as she pulled her legs up and hugged them to her chest. "My stomach is cramping."

"I know it is, but I promise it'll pass soon." I climbed onto the bed facing her and stroked her hair. "Just breathe through it."

"I cannot believe we're lying in your bed, and we're both sick. This is not how I imagined this going," she whispered, before moaning and hugging her legs tighter.

"So you have been imagining it," I said, as her arms released her legs, and she relaxed. My free hand found hers, and our fingers intertwined.

"Yes, Clark. I've imagined it," she whispered.

I pulled her close to me and wrapped my arms around her.

"Me, too, Weeze."

Her breathing slowed, and her warm cheek rested against my chest.

And sleep took us both.

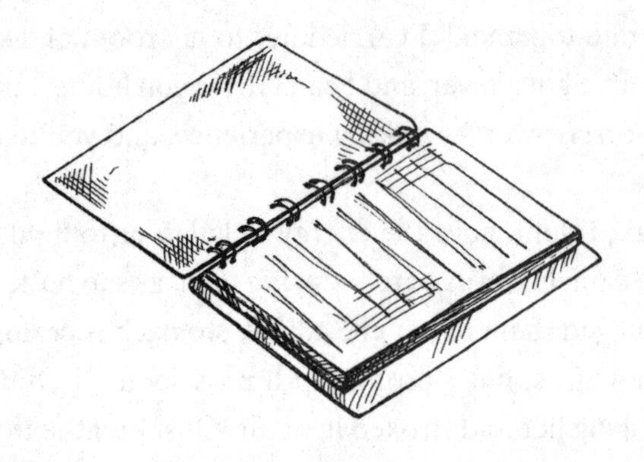

14

Eloise

I blinked my eyes open, startling when I glanced around, remembering that I wasn't in my bed.

The spot beside me was empty, but the covers were rumpled where he'd slept.

I lifted the covers to see that I was fully dressed, and memories of my head hanging over the toilet flashed in my mind.

I'd woken up in the middle of the night and vomited several more times.

Clark had gotten up with me, holding my hair up and comforting me.

And he stayed beside me through the vomiting and slept beside me the entire night.

He probably ran off this morning as flashbacks of me heaving all night had horrified him.

I covered my eyes with my hand and groaned. I've crossed so many professional lines at this point, yet we still hadn't kissed.

And that certainly wasn't going to happen now that he's seen me with my head in a toilet.

I heard footsteps coming down the hallway, as the wood floors creaked with each step. I tried to frantically pat my hair in place, tucking it behind my ears and brushing a hand over my black tank top.

I was grateful he had a spare toothbrush that I used in the middle of the night, and at least my breath smelled minty this morning.

He strode through the doorway with a pair of navy basketball shorts slung low on his hips, his muscled chest on full display.

"Good morning, Weeze. How are you feeling?" He walked to the side of the bed where I was lying and set down a glass of blue Gatorade and two pieces of toast.

I reached for the glass and took a long sip as my mouth was unusually dry.

I set it back down on the nightstand and glanced over at him as he sat down on the bed beside me.

"I feel a little horrified, but otherwise okay, I guess. I don't feel nauseous anymore, and the cramps are gone."

His lips turned up in the corners, as his back rested against the dark rustic wood headboard. "I mean, you were bragging about how you never get sick right before you projectile vomited like someone was extracting the devil from your body, so I'm sure it's a little horrifying."

I fell forward on a chuckle. "I literally haven't been sick in years. I blame you for breaking my streak."

"It's not like I've kissed you, so I don't know why I'm getting blamed," he said, his voice all tease.

"You're getting blamed because you had it first, and you made me do that damn pull-up competition, so I probably got your puking cooties from that."

He smiled, and then his sage green eyes softened. "I'm sorry for getting you sick."

"I'm just kidding. It's not your fault. And I appreciate you taking care of me last night. That was really sweet of you."

"I'm sweeter than I look." He waggled his brows, and my God, even after a night of tossing my cookies, I found the man so ridiculously sexy I had a hard time controlling myself. I wanted to run my fingers along the scruff on his jaw. I wanted to press my lips against his, just to see what they felt like. I squeezed my thighs together in response, begging my body to stop reacting to the man.

"You are, actually. I had you pegged as this womanizing playboy, and you appear to be the opposite."

"I'm not going to lie to you, Eloise," he said, his lips turning up in the corners. And why was it so sexy when he said my real name? Maybe it was his deep voice or the way his eyes were staring at my lips. "I've been with my fair share of women. But I've always been honest about the expectations. During the season, my focus is hockey, and I make it clear that I don't have much to give. Most women have been fine with that, and it's worked for me."

"I'm not built that way, Clark. I kind of wish I was at the moment," she said, her lips turning up the slightest bit. "But I know myself well enough to know that I'd want more."

"Maybe I'm not looking for just a one-night stand either. I want to get to know you," he said, his hand stroking my cheek.

"So what's different now?"

"Well, I'm sort of crazy about my coach's daughter," he said, putting his hands up when I started to interrupt, because he knew I was going to tell him it was a mistake. "And I don't know what it means. I know it's risky for you, and it's risky for me, as well."

"How so? The team will never cut you for an inappropriate relationship." I quirked a brow.

"Because I look up to your father, and I respect him. I also respect the hell out of you, so trust me, I've tried to push these feelings away. It just hasn't happened. And maybe we're better as friends, and we'll find that out quickly. But, I don't know, something tells me it's worth the risk. And I'm a man who trusts my gut."

He reached over on his nightstand, opening the top drawer, and pulling out our notebook. "I wrote you something because I know it's your thing."

I was still processing his words, but grateful for the distraction. My eyes moved to the notebook in my hands.

Hey Weeze,

We've spent weeks working out together and talking more than I've ever talked to anyone. I've seen you at your most vulnerable, with your head in a toilet and puke coming out of your nose. And yet, I'm not running away. I only want more.

I know you're scared, and I get it. We don't know what the future holds. But right now, I'd like to take you on a date. Just you and me. No gym. No work. No contracts or rules.

No one has to know, and it will be two non-professional friends on a date. Maybe it'll go nowhere, which would be easier for both of us. But I'd like to just try. One time.

What do you say?
CC

"You *had* to mention the puke coming out of my nose, didn't you?"

He barked out a laugh. "You're even cute when you're puking, Weeze."

I sucked in a long breath. "I'm not having sex with you. That will complicate things for me."

He nodded. "I understand that."

"Sex is probably just sex for you, but for me, it's just different. It's a vulnerable thing for me to share that with another person, and I won't apologize for it. Passion and attraction are great, but I need more from a partner."

"Tell me what you need," he said, his gaze studying mine as if what I was going to say was the most important thing in the world.

"It's an emotional connection for me. I need trust and loyalty when I'm with someone that way." I waved my hands around now, because I felt childish and embarrassed to have even brought this up.

He wasn't asking to have sex with me.

He just asked me on a date, and of course, I made it weird.

"I see your wheels spinning, and I think I know you well enough to guess that now you're thinking that I never asked you to have sex, and maybe I don't want that. I know how that brain of yours works, Eloise." He reached for my chin and turned my face up so I would meet his gaze. "I think about having sex with you every fucking day. It's torture being this close to you and not touching you. So take those doubts away and tell me your reasoning."

My breath hitched in my throat, and I shrugged. "I told you about how my mom and I kept notebooks those last few months of her life, and I saved every single one of them. They were filled with life advice, and some I didn't understand when I was young, so it has a different meaning now."

"That makes sense. You were young when she passed away,"

he said. His hand playing with mine as we sat facing one another. "What did she say?"

"Well, the one I always reference when I date someone is pretty basic. She said not to give my heart away unless I was completely over the moon about someone, and they felt the same way about me."

"She was giving you all her mama advice right there in your notebooks," he said, his gaze filled with empathy.

"Yep. And I haven't always taken it. The first guy I was ever with was my freshman year of college. I lost my virginity to him, and we dated for six months before we realized we had nothing in common. I think it was just this milestone I wanted to knock off my list." I sighed. "And then I dated a few people throughout college, but I never crossed that line again with sex, because it didn't feel right. And then I met Spencer in grad school, and he was the second guy I was ever with. I think I wanted to be in love so badly that I sort of convinced myself I was. And we were together for several years, and he's a great guy, but it just wasn't right. I've never felt the way my mom said I should feel, so maybe that's the problem. So at the end of the day, I'm just not super experienced sexually." I covered my face with my hand and groaned, because what was I doing? Why was I sharing all of this?

"Hey, you don't need to be embarrassed talking to me. We're friends first, Weeze. And I don't have a lot of female friends. I want to know this stuff. I think it's cool that you look at sex differently. I haven't had sex since before playoffs started, so weeks before you came to town, which is a long run for me," he said, wincing like I would find that offensive.

"Why do you think you haven't had sex?"

"I don't know, I just don't want anyone else." He shook his head as if it hadn't come out right. "That's not what I meant.

I don't expect sex from you. I know this is complicated, and knowing how you feel about it, I don't want you to think that's what I'm here for. I'm just being honest, because I don't want anyone else. I don't know what it means. I haven't been in a serious relationship since high school, and we know how that ended. I enjoy women. I enjoy sex. I guess I've just never been over the moon about anyone either." He chuckled.

"Do you have a pen?" I asked, as my teeth sank into my bottom lip.

I knew I was making a mistake crossing the line.

Putting myself out there.

Knowing this would end poorly.

Clark Chadwick was a hockey star. Women fell at his feet. He could have whoever he wanted. He didn't do relationships.

I was a relationship girl. I was inexperienced with sex. And I was not only his coach's daughter, but I worked for the same team he played for.

This was a line I shouldn't cross.

I knew it. He knew it.

But when he reached into his nightstand and handed me the pen, I didn't hesitate.

I turned the page in the notebook.

Good morning, Chadwick,

I appreciate you holding my hair back while I emptied my stomach into your toilet. When we are both back to normal and feeling well, I would like to go on a date with you. No gym. No work. No contracts. No sex.

XX,
Weeze

"I added just one rule at the end." I handed it to him, and he laughed.

"I can live with that."

"What if the kiss is awful?" I asked.

"Then we get off easy, no pun intended on that one." He smirked.

I shoved him in the chest and chuckled. "It would be great if the first kiss sucks. Then we would just be friends, and we'd stop thinking about it. And then you can go back to sleeping with random women, and I can find a guy who I'm over the moon for."

"Here's hoping the kiss sucks," he said with a wicked grin on his face as he held up his glass of blue Gatorade, and I reached for mine and clinked it against his. "So, today we rest. Tomorrow, pending you're feeling better because I feel back to normal today, we'll get back to our workout routine, and I'm taking you on a date after."

"Our date is tomorrow?"

"Yeah. I'd take you out today if you didn't have vomit breath." He barked out a laugh.

I placed a hand over my mouth and fell back on the pillow. "We've done everything backward. You know all my dirty secrets, and you've seen me praying to the porcelain gods, and we haven't even had our first kiss."

"I'm kidding. I've never met someone who brushed their teeth so aggressively after vomiting. But I've never discussed kissing someone so thoroughly before just doing it, so now I figure it shouldn't happen when you aren't feeling great. So, if you're better tomorrow, plan on it."

"Sounds like a plan." I pushed to my feet. "I'm feeling a lot better, but I need to go home, take a bath, and put on some clean clothes," I said, surprised that he looked disappointed that I was leaving.

"I'll give you a ride." He moved to stand.

"I can walk," I said, waving a hand in front of me. "You've done enough for me."

"You aren't used to anyone taking care of you, are you?" he asked, as he went to his dresser and pulled a tee out of the drawer, tugging it over his head.

I processed his words as I slipped on my shoes. "I'm just used to taking care of myself."

"Well, regardless of how our date goes, that changes now." His gaze locked with mine. "When you need anything, or you aren't feeling well, or someone at work gives you a hard time, you call me. I will drop everything for you, Weeze."

I swallowed hard, looking away because the intensity in his gaze nearly took my breath away. "Why?"

"Because you showed up for me when I needed you after the injury. I would have started running too soon. I would have reinjured myself, and you made sure I did things right. And I don't know, Eloise, at the end of the day, I just like you, so when you need me, you just have to say the word."

Damn you, Clark Chadwick.

I was still holding out hope that the first kiss would suck, and now the man goes and says the sweetest thing anyone has ever said to me.

I nodded. "Same. I'm always here if you need me."

"All right. Let's get you home."

The ride to my house was quiet. Almost as if we were both processing all that had happened.

Even though nothing physical had happened between us.

It felt like things had shifted.

He pulled into the driveway at Emilia's house, where the guest cottage sat at the end of the driveway.

"All right, get some rest. I'm counting on that date tomorrow." He winked.

"Practice first, Hotshot. And then you can kiss me after."

"Get ready to be knocked off your feet," he said, before coming around the truck and opening my door. I swung my legs out, and he stepped forward, his big hands finding each side of my hips as he lifted me down, sliding my body slowly against his before my feet hit the ground.

Our faces were so close that my nerves were jumping, and my stomach fluttered at the heat in his gaze. His lips were so close to mine I could feel his warm breath on my face.

"I'm hoping neither of us is knocked off our feet," I whispered.

"Yeah, that sure would be a lot easier."

I stepped back, holding my hand up and waving as I pulled my key out of my purse and pushed inside.

I said a silent mantra a couple of times just to settle my nerves.

Please let it be the worst kiss ever.

Please let it be the worst kiss ever.

Please let it be the worst kiss ever.

One could hope.

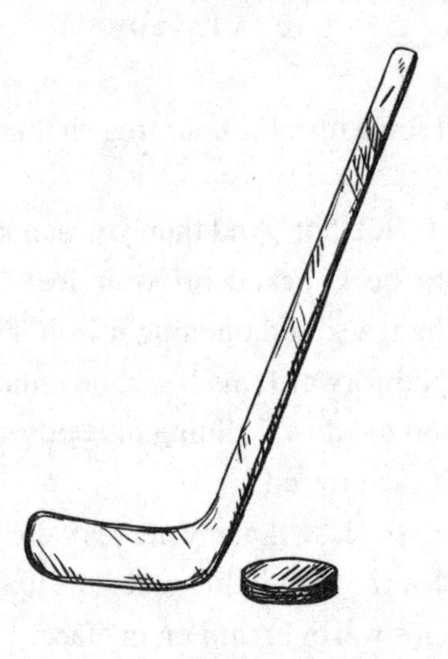

15

Clark

I was grateful that Eloise and I both felt better the following day, and I was well enough to get in a good workout, even if she insisted on going a little easy on me because I'd been down for forty-eight hours. I made up for it by playing loud club music and finally getting her to dance with me in the gym.

We're calling that a win.

And as much as I'd been focused on getting back to work, I only had one thing at the forefront of my thoughts—to impress the hell out of her.

She was far more concerned about where this would go than I was, if I were being honest.

I didn't let myself go too far in the future. We liked each

other. We were attracted to one another. I wanted to just see where it would go.

This wasn't about sex. This was something deeper, and I knew it in my gut.

If it were to turn into something that we didn't want to walk away from, then we'd cross that bridge when we came to it.

But I sure as hell wasn't going to say that to her and freak her out.

She was counting on this kiss sucking, and I was counting on kissing her until her lips ached.

I knew it wouldn't suck.

Though I knew she was right, and it would be a hell of a lot easier if the kiss was awful, and we just remained friends.

I just didn't think that would be the case.

But time would tell.

I pulled up at her house and jogged to the door.

I was fucking excited. I spent almost every single day with this woman, but I couldn't get enough of her. When she wasn't with me, I missed her.

It made no sense.

I talked to my mom this morning, and she helped me come up with a few ideas for the date. I've never wanted to impress someone the way I wanted to impress Eloise.

Of course, my mom loved being brought into it.

It was a first for me. I've never brought her into my dating life. But my mom was a hopeless romantic, and she and I both agreed that me making dinner at my house and eating out by the water was a good idea.

Simple yet romantic.

And then, of course, my brothers all inserted themselves, and Lulu and Henley got involved, so even though I was bringing

Eloise back to my house, I'd try to make it special.

She deserved that.

Even if this was a one-time thing and she didn't want it to go anywhere after tonight—the least I could do was make it nice for her.

I knocked on the door, and when she opened it, I had a hard time keeping my cool.

She wore a long blue dress that ended just above her ankles, with her favorite cowboy boots on beneath. Her hair fell in loose waves over her shoulders, and she was the most beautiful woman I'd ever laid eyes on.

I thought that the first time I saw her, and every day since.

"You look gorgeous," I said, reaching for her hand after she pulled her door closed behind her, and we walked to the truck.

"Thank you. I feel like I've lived in shorts and a tee since arriving in Rosewood River, so it was fun to get fixed up a little," she said, chuckling when I opened the passenger door and gripped her hips, lifting her up before setting her on the seat.

"Well, you look good in everything, Weeze, but this dress in particular is something."

"I figure if this is a one-time thing, we may as well have some fun with it," she said with a laugh.

I made my way back to the driver's side, trying not to be offended by the hope in her voice that this was a one-and-done.

We drove the short distance to my house.

Yes, I could have walked.

She could have walked.

But I wanted to show her that this date mattered to me.

"Oh, we're going to your house?"

"We are," I said, pulling into the garage and coming around to help her out.

"Good, I think it's better we don't make this a big deal. No sense being seen out in public together when we aren't in workout attire."

Buckle up, sweetheart. It's a big fucking deal.

"Sure," I said, reaching for the button on the garage door and smiling when I noted the sun just tucking behind the mountains.

I timed this perfectly.

"Oh, it smells so good," she said when we stepped inside.

"Yeah, I made some spaghetti sauce, but I wasn't sure if your stomach was ready for that, so we also have just noodles and butter," I said, making my way to the kitchen and lifting the lid on the sauce to smell the perfect mix of garlic and oregano.

"That was thoughtful," she said, moving to stand beside me as I heard her stomach rumble, and I barked out a laugh.

"Are you hungry?" I turned to face her, ready to kiss her right here. Right now.

But timing was everything.

Eloise was different.

Special.

I couldn't rush this. The last thing I wanted to do was to scare her off.

"Maybe I'm a thoughtful guy," I said, arching a brow before turning to place the bread in the oven. Something seemed a little off with her, almost like she was nervous, but I wasn't quite sure. "How about a glass of wine?"

"That sounds great."

I poured us each a glass of red and handed it to her. I held up my glass and waited for her to do the same. "Cheers to seeing where this goes."

"Put your glass down, Clark." Her voice was firm, and I internally groaned, because I knew she was going to put a stop to things right now. She couldn't get out of her own head with this.

I set my glass down, and she did the same. I prepared to hear all the reasons why this wouldn't work, because that was her MO.

But she shocked the shit out of me when she lunged forward, one hand on each side of my face, and her mouth crashed into mine.

My hand found the back of her neck before tangling in her hair, while the other moved behind her ass and scooped her up easily, setting her on the counter. Her legs opened, allowing me to stand between them, and our lips never lost contact. My tongue slipped inside and tangled with hers.

I groaned into her mouth as I tilted her head to the side and took the kiss deeper.

Her hands moved to my chest, pressing against me the slightest bit, and I pulled back to look at her.

Her dark, heated gaze told me everything I wanted to know.

She liked it as much as I did.

"Okay, glad we got that out of the way. Sorry for jumping the gun. I couldn't handle the anticipation anymore," she said, her words breathy.

"Don't ever apologize for kissing me. You can do that anytime you want." I winked, tucking her hair behind her ear.

"Thank you," she whispered. "Let's eat and sit with this for a little bit."

"Sounds good," I said, turning around to grab an oven mitt as I pulled the bread out and set it on the counter.

I dropped it into the basket, and she moved without me saying a word and added the dressing to the salad I made before giving it a little toss. "Let's take this outside."

"Oh, it's a great night to eat outside," she said.

I had the basket of bread in one hand and reached for the

bottle of wine and my glass, as well. Eloise had the salad bowl and her wineglass, and she followed me through the kitchen to the French doors that led to the backyard. When I pushed them open, I motioned for her to go first.

She took a few steps and then came to an abrupt stop.

"What is this?" She turned around to look at me, eyes wide, and a big smile on her face.

"You've never been out here at night with the lights on. It's pretty spectacular." I moved to the table and set everything down before taking the salad from her, as she was still mesmerized by the setup.

The table had flowers and candles and two place settings that were well-lit by the stands of lights that hung above the yard. The lights had always been here, as had the table, but I'd gotten a little help from Henley and Lulu with making it look like something you'd see in a magazine with what they did to the table.

"Clark," she said, her voice just above a whisper. "This is… unbelievable. It's so pretty. And what is that over there?"

She pointed at the large screen I put up in the yard this afternoon. I moved the outdoor couch over on the lawn, and we had blankets and pillows and a movie ready to go. I picked up some candy and popcorn for later, and she already told me her favorite movie was *How To Lose A Guy In Ten Days*, which seemed fitting, since she was hoping she'd be kicking my ass to the curb by tomorrow. I downloaded the movie on Prime, and we'd stream it after dinner.

"I thought we'd do a movie night after we eat." I cleared my throat, feeling slightly anxious because I'd never done anything close to this for a date before.

Maybe it was too much.

"And then I kissed you in the kitchen before we even started," she said, shaking her head like she'd done something wrong.

"I'm just glad you didn't kiss me and end the date because it sucked." I laughed.

"It was all right," she said, teasing, and her cheeks flushed pink.

"I don't know, Weeze. The way you were grinding up against me, I have a hunch you enjoyed it."

Her head fell back in laughter. "Well, I'm hoping you mess up the next kiss. I'm counting on it being awful, and you sort of ruined my hopes of that with the first try."

"That means there's a next one. I'll take it." I motioned to the table. "You sit, and I'll go grab the pasta."

I carried the rest of the food out, and just like always with this girl, we fell into comfortable conversation.

"You never told me why you fell in love with hockey," she asked, as she reached for her glass of wine.

"You're going to laugh at me when I tell you." I twirled my fork in the mound of pasta, getting a bite ready to go.

"I promise, I won't."

"Well, I'm the baby of five siblings and then you add in my two cousins who are also older. I guess all the other sports were taken. Football, baseball, basketball, swimming, tennis, golf," I laughed. "I think I wanted something that was just mine. My dad loved watching hockey when I was a kid, so I'd sit and watch with him, and then one day I told him I wanted to play. I was maybe nine years old then. And the first time I went out on the ice with a stick—man, I just knew that it was for me. That it was going to change my life."

"I love that," she said, as she listened intently like I was telling her the most important thing in the world. "Listening to you talk about it, I'd say you were over the moon for hockey."

I laughed. "I guess you could say that. So, why'd you choose physical therapy?"

"After my mom passed, it was just me and Dad. Hockey is his life, you know? So I started going on the road with him when I wasn't in school, and then I'd be with my grandparents when I couldn't travel with him. I'd already lost my mom, and I just missed him when he'd have to go to games. And I think when you lose a parent young, you just realize how precious life is. So I knew I wanted to do something in that field so I could be connected to him in a way. And I do love sports as a whole, seeing how far you can push your body—how to heal it after you get injured. I guess that was the lure."

"Your dad talks about you like you set the sun," I said.

"He's the best. He was so excited that the team agreed to hire a full-time PT, and when I got hired, he actually cried. It was the fourth time I've ever seen my father cry in my life."

"What were the first three?"

"My mother's funeral was the first, though I'm sure he cried the day she passed and many times during her illness, but he hid that from me. The second time was at my college graduation, and the third was my grad school graduation." She chuckled. "I think those milestones are hard for him because he knows my mother would have loved to be there."

I didn't stop and think before I pushed to my feet, picked up her chair with her sitting on it, and set it down right beside mine. Of course, she gaped at me, but I grabbed her wineglass and her plate and moved them over before sitting back down. "Sorry. You were too far away."

A smile spread clear across her pretty face.

"I love that you two are so close," I said.

"Yeah. That's why I have to be really careful, Clark." She

reached for my hand. "I like you. I like you more than I want to like you. But we only have a few more weeks here, and then we go back to reality. To a job I've worked really hard to get. And I know my dad went out on a limb to get me the interview. And embarrassing my father—it's just not an option."

"Hey, I promise you, this is fine. We're hanging out. It's not a big deal. We haven't done anything wrong." My hand moved to her neck, and I stroked her jaw with the pad of my thumb. "I think it would be weird if we went back to the city and we weren't friends. You've been here for two months already. Hell, your dad called me this morning and was asking about you, as if I know everything about you."

She nodded. "Yeah. I think he's aware that we're friends. But he wouldn't be okay if it were more than that. Not when I signed a contract. Not when we're talking about his star player. And don't even get me started on Randall. He reminds me daily about the ethical clause in the contract. It makes me paranoid, like he knows something. I feel like he's just waiting for me to fail."

I slipped my hand beneath her chair, pulling it even closer. "Randall can be an asshole, no doubt about it. But what does he know, Eloise? That we spend time together? That you spent the night at my house after you puked your brains out? He doesn't know anything."

She blew out a breath. "Maybe I'm afraid he can read my mind. It makes me feel guilty—the thoughts I have sometimes."

You and me, both.

"He can't read your mind, but I sure as shit wish I could."

Her head tipped back in a fit of laughter, and I scooped her up in my arms. "How about we go watch your favorite movie."

"You didn't?" she asked, and I assumed she thought I wouldn't remember.

"*How to Lose a Guy in Ten Days*, it's your favorite movie, right?"

"It is." She smirked as her fingers ran through my hair and down my neck. I walked over to the couch and set her down as I nuzzled my nose into her collarbone, making her head fall back in a fit of laughter. "But I thought you said that you'd never seen it, and romantic comedies aren't your favorite."

Maybe you're my favorite, Eloise Gable.

"I mean, I prefer something with a little more grit, but it's our first date, and I'm trying to be a gentleman." I waggled my brows as I sat beside her. "Plus, I think you're trying to run me off in a lot less than ten days, so maybe I can learn how to stick around a little longer."

Her gaze softened, and she climbed onto my lap. "If you played for any other team, I might just try to keep you for a little longer."

"I don't think I'd mind that at all, Weeze. But I just want you to enjoy right now. Can you do that?"

"I'm enjoying myself a lot tonight." She wrapped her arms around me, and I breathed her in. She smelled like a mix of lavender and honey, and I couldn't get enough.

"Yeah? Well, that's a good thing."

She pulled back to look at me. "It's a good thing at the moment. So let's just enjoy it."

I pulled her face toward mine, and I kissed her.

I kissed her like it was the first time.

And I kissed her like it was the last time.

I just hoped like hell it wasn't.

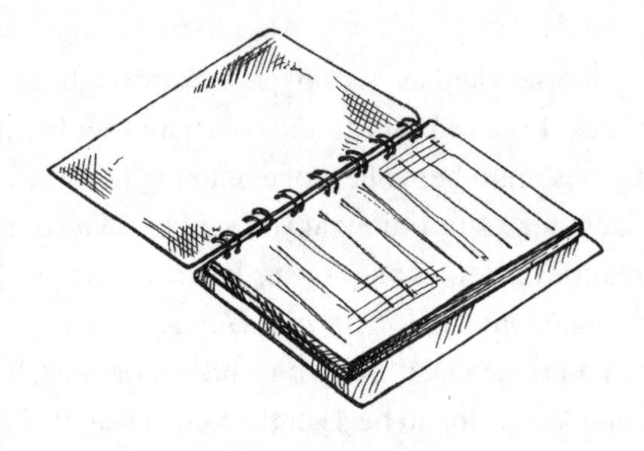

16

Eloise

"She's torturing this poor bastard," he griped, as we were wrapped around one another on the couch.

"It's all in the name of research," I said over my laughter. "And he hardly entered the relationship without his own ulterior motives."

"Oh, come on, she got that crazy-looking dog," he said over his laughter. "And the dude is still sticking around."

"Because he needs her to close his deal!" I shrieked, pushing up on my knees to look at him. We'd eaten a ton of candy because Clark had literally purchased enough for a party of twenty, and we had a giant bowl of popcorn, as well.

We made out until my lips literally ached, and I didn't want to stop but forced myself to.

This was quite possibly the most romantic date I'd ever been on. No one had ever gone to this kind of effort for me, and it meant a lot to me that he made it so special.

Why does the one guy I really like for the first time in a very long time, have to be completely off-limits?

Thanks a lot, universe, for making me spend three months with the sexiest man on the planet and then making him unattainable.

Clark moved fast, flipping me on my back and hovering above me. "She is writing about their relationship for the whole world to read. That's some cold shit right there."

He tickled me, and I laughed hysterically.

"He's just as guilty," I shouted over my laughter. "He's the one trying to close a deal!"

"Come on, let's watch the end, and then I'll walk you home."

"You don't want to drive? You didn't even have half a glass of wine," I said, moving to sit beside him as he pulled me onto his lap.

"I know. But it'll make the night last longer if I walk you home," he said, rubbing his scruff against my neck as he whispered in my ear. "I'm not ready for this night to end."

My chest squeezed at his words as he wrapped his arms around me, and we watched the end of the movie.

When the credits started rolling on the screen, I turned around to face him, as one leg fell on each side of his hips so I was straddling him. "You liked it, didn't you?"

"I liked watching it with you," he said.

"I want to kiss you one more time," I whispered.

"You don't have to ask." He leaned back against the couch as if he were giving me permission to take what I wanted.

I leaned down, and my lips found his. His large hand moved to the side of my neck as his fingers grazed the back of my head.

His other hand found my hip as I started grinding up against him.

I felt his erection grow long and hard beneath me, and it did something to me. I've never been so turned on in my life. It was beyond comprehension, and we were fully clothed. My dress was bunched up around my hips now, the fabric sliding against my sensitive nipples as the cool breeze bustled around us. He guided me up and down as his tongue slipped into my mouth.

My hands tugged at his hair, and he growled. I could feel his chest pounding against mine.

And our kiss grew more frantic, nipping and licking as I moved against him faster now.

Desperate for release.

I've never been so turned on in my life.

Lustful and needy.

He tilted my head to the side, groaning into my mouth as his tongue slipped in and out.

He paused only long enough to speak. "Use my cock, and come for me."

His voice was commanding and gruff, and I couldn't believe I was doing this right now.

But I did as he said, and I pressed harder against him, feeling every inch of him beneath me as he pulled back to look at me. His gaze heated, jaw locked and nostrils flared, as he grew thicker beneath me.

Faster.

Harder.

Bright lights exploded behind my eyes, and his name left my lips on a cry as I went over the edge.

Clark kept moving me up and down, letting me ride out every last bit of pleasure, as every inch of my body tingled.

And then everything slowed, and I opened my eyes and winced. "Sorry about that. Not sure what happened there."

He smiled, his desire-filled gaze locked with mine. "I'll tell you what happened. You stopped thinking so much and let yourself feel good. That was the sexiest thing I've ever seen."

"That's never happened to me," I said, feeling my cheeks heat.

"You've never come while making out with a man?" he asked, and I was mortified that we were talking about this now.

I shook my head and looked away before he reached for my chin and forced me to look at him.

"I've never, you know, finished with a man." I didn't want to remind him that there'd only been two.

He played with the ends of my hair, letting it run through his fingers, but his gaze turned stormy, eyes narrowing with disbelief. "Well, they're both dumbfucks if they didn't know how to please you. But I'm honored that I get to be your first orgasm, even if I didn't get to feel you come on my cock or my fingers or my lips."

My mouth fell open, and I leaned forward, burying my face in his neck. He just chuckled and stroked my back. "You don't need to be embarrassed. You can talk to me about anything. What just happened here was a good thing, Eloise. I fucking loved it. Seeing you let yourself go and fall apart. Sex is supposed to feel good."

"Okay." I sat back up before climbing off his lap. "I think I'd better get going before I dry-hump you into oblivion again."

He barked out a laugh, and when he stood, I saw his erection straining against his shorts. He followed my line of sight and looked down. "Does it turn you on to see what you do to me?"

My teeth sank into my bottom lip, and I raised one shoulder. "You do the same to me. But am I leaving you in a, er, bad situation?"

More laughter. "Nothing I can't handle. Let's get you home."

"Let me help you carry this in," I said, as we piled the leftover candy into the popcorn bowl. I grabbed our glasses, and we took it all to the kitchen. We'd already cleaned up from dinner a few hours ago.

The stars were out, and Clark pointed up at the shooting star moving across the sky.

The walk was filled with laughter about the movie, and then we shifted to discussing tomorrow's workout.

When we got to the door of the guest cottage, he paused, shoving his hands into his pockets, and there was something sweet and endearing about it. He was always such a confident guy, and it was nice to see him appear a little vulnerable. I'm sure Clark was used to dates ending with the woman in his bed.

"Thanks for coming tonight," he said, before chuckling. "Literally and figuratively."

I smacked him in the chest and laughed. "You're never going to let me live this down, are you?"

"Are you kidding? There's nothing to live down. It was fucking beautiful, Weeze."

I pulled out my key as I looked up at him. "Thank you for the best date I've ever been on. And thank you for making everything so special."

He smiled and took a step backward, off the front porch. "I'll see you in the morning. Get ready for a long run tomorrow."

"I'll be ready."

"All right, get inside," he said, his eyes still on me.

"Such a gentleman."

"You wouldn't be saying that if you could read my thoughts right now." He smirked. "Go. Get some sleep."

I waved and stepped inside and fell against the door, sliding down to the floor.

Holy hotness.

What the hell was that tonight?

He was sweet and romantic and sexy and bossy all at the same time.

And I was here for it.

There was a knock on the door, and I startled. Had he come back?

I looked through the peephole and laughed when I saw Emilia in her pajamas, standing on the front porch.

I pulled the door open and tugged her inside. "What are you doing here, Em? It's late."

"I was up reading, and the motion detectors turned on when you got home. I'm dying to know how it went." She plopped down on my couch. "By the looks of it, you did not hate the kiss the way you hoped you would. Or did the kiss not happen?"

"Oh, it happened." I filled her in on all the details, minus the embarrassing way I humped him like a horny teenager. But I told her that we made out multiple times, and we laughed, and we ate, and we even watched my favorite movie at the outdoor theatre he set up.

Her mouth hung open, and her eyes were wide. "This does not sound like a one-time kiss type of thing, Lo."

I loved that we had nicknames for one another now.

"I mean, where can it go? This is a temporary situation. When we go back to the city in a few weeks, everything will change." I shrugged, falling back onto the couch beside her. "Why does this have to be the one guy that I like?"

"So why not just enjoy it for a few weeks? Then you'll go back to San Francisco and you'll be distracted by work and life, and you can leave your small-town romance in the past."

I covered my face, feeling ridiculous about all of this. "I just… I don't know."

She pulled my hands away and arched a brow. "Tell me what you're worried about."

"I like him. More than I ever thought I would. And I don't want to get attached. I can't get attached. It's not an option."

"Hmmm... catching feelings would definitely complicate things. And what if he catches feelings? That could happen," she said. "What if you both caught feelings?"

"I would lose my job, Em. Not to mention I would embarrass my father in the process. I would have a hard time getting hired anywhere else if I were let go for inappropriate behavior by the first team that hired me. It's rule number one of being a woman in this business. I literally just started my job, and I'm falling for the hot hockey player that I'm working with. I'm a complete cliché. This is not good." I sighed.

"Okay, this is what we've got going for us..." She paused, and I laughed because I loved that she felt like she was in this with me. "He doesn't do relationships, so this could all fizzle out in a few days. Don't overthink it. He'll probably act weird tomorrow, which will annoy you, and we'll be laughing about this by next weekend."

"You're right. I don't even like hockey players normally. It's probably just a short-term attraction, and it'll pass. He could easily pretend nothing happened when I see him tomorrow. I mean, maybe he pulled out all the bells and whistles in hopes I'd sleep with him. He's probably disappointed with the way things went down, and he's going to be on to the next conquest. So, I'll just act normal tomorrow."

"Yes. And if that doesn't happen and you want to make out with the man a few more times before you go back to the city—no judgment. You're here for a few more weeks, and he's so freaking hot. No one would fault you," she said.

"That's where you're wrong. Everyone in my industry would fault me."

"Well, you're in Rosewood River, so no one's here. Think of it like this… What if you'd met him while you were on a vacation? And you'd had a hot fling. Then you got back to the city and found out that he was a new player on the team. You would be innocent because you didn't know. And it would be over by then, so no crime, no foul."

My head fell back in laughter. "But I do know that he's on the team, and I did it anyway."

"There's no witnesses. It's our secret."

"Well, here's hoping Bridger's wrong and you don't write about it in the *Taylor Tea*," I said, trying to hide my smile as we both started laughing.

"I actually wish I was clever enough to write that damn column. I'd use it to put Bridger Chadwick in his damn place." She shook her head and smiled. "Don't make it bigger than it is. Just enjoy the time you spend with Clark, and know that it'll have to change when you go back to the city. The season will start anyway, so things are going to be different no matter what happens between you two."

"Good point. I'll be working with all the athletes on the team once we get back. I like this idea. I'll just see how he acts tomorrow and go with it. It would be easier if he was a dick tomorrow because I would much rather be annoyed with him than attracted to him."

"Exactly. That would make life a lot easier. You'll have to text me tomorrow morning, or come by the flower shop after and fill me in. I'll be dying to know what happens." She pushed to her feet. "I better go get some sleep."

I gave her a hug. "Thanks for being such a good friend, Em."

"Of course. This is the most exciting thing to happen to me in a long time," she said over her laughter. "See you tomorrow."

I watched as she ran across the yard, and she waved from her doorway.

My phone rang, and I was surprised to see my father's name flash across the screen because it was late for him to be calling.

"Hey, Dad. It's late. Is everything okay?"

"Yes. Everything's fine, Els," he said. Just wanted to check in. I just got home from dinner with Wolf and Sebastian Wayburn."

There was something about my father's voice that always comforted me. He's always been my person. My safe place.

After my mom passed, it was me and Dad against the world in a way. The only two people who truly understood the other's pain.

"Oh, nice. How did that go?" I made my way down the little hallway to the bathroom and turned on the water in the tub.

Wolf Wayburn had been the one to interview me, but he shared that his brother was going to be taking over the day-to-day routine with the Lions, as he'd be stepping back to have more time with his family and take on some other ventures.

"It went great. They're excited for the new season. Sebastian is really going all in on the new position, and he's definitely invested in taking this team to another championship. Of course, everyone wants to know how Clark is doing. So it looks like we're taking a trip to Rosewood River next weekend," he said. "Sebastian wants to come see how Clark is doing and meet you, as well."

Oh, boy.

This was unexpected.

My mouth was slightly dry. "That's amazing. Who all is coming?"

"Me, Randall, and Sebastian."

So this was basically my worst nightmare.

I cleared my throat. "That's so great, Dad. How long will you be staying?"

"Sebastian is having rooms booked for all of us at the hotel in town, and we'll be there for two nights. You can show them how you train Clark and what you two have been up to."

Not sure you want me to show them everything we've been up to.

"I can't wait," I said, turning the bath water off and sprinkling in some bath salts, even though I knew in this moment it would take a lot more than bath salts to calm me down.

"I'll give you a call tomorrow with all the details. Miss you, Els."

"Miss you, too. See you in a couple of days," I said. "Love you."

"Love you."

I ended the call, got undressed, and sank into the water, stopping just at my neck.

I squeezed my eyes shut.

The universe was clearly bitch-slapping me in the face for my poor choices.

Message received.

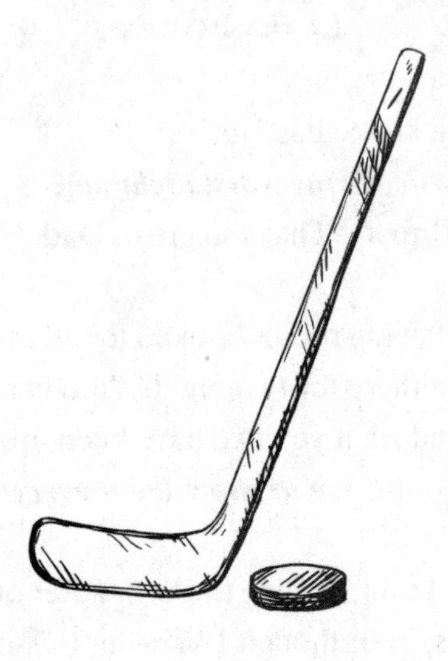

17

Clark

Easton: *Are we getting an update on the date, or is it still going?*

Axel: *I mean, he pulled out all the stops for this one.*

Archer: *You clearly like this girl. Has Clark ever liked anyone this much?*

Rafe: *Clark is a lover of hockey. And random women.*

Me: *Clark can hear you, assholes.*

Bridger: *He made a movie theater outside. That's very telling.*

Easton: *So… still going this morning?*

Me: *No. I walked her home. She's not like that.*

Axel: *Ouch. Did you get a kiss?*

Me: *A gentleman does not kiss and tell.*

Bridger: *Is there a gentleman on this group text?*

Easton: *<laughing face emoji>*

Easton: *Henley said there's a clause in the contract for the team about not crossing any professional lines. She works for the Lions. You're a player. I understand why she's hesitant.*

Archer: *So why go there at all?*

Rafe: *Because he likes her. Love does crazy shit to you. I moved to Paris for a few months, remember?*

Easton: *Love is a strong word. But so is a binding contract.*

Me: *No one is in love. She doesn't even like me most of the time.*

Bridger: *Yet you spent the day yesterday, preparing your backyard for a date?*

Rafe: *You can't really have input on this one, brother. Your idea of a romantic date is tater tots and hot dogs.*

Bridger: *Don't hate on the tots, dude.*

Archer: *You obviously like her if you're willing to even go there. There are lots of women out there who are allowed to date you. There's clearly something there, see as you are choosing the one you can't have.*

Axel: *The forbidden fruit. <apple emoji> <orange emoji> <lemon emoji>*

Rafe: *I have a new favorite fruit. The mango. It's spectacular.*

Me: *<head exploding emoji>*

Easton: *Maybe you go out a few times with her and you both realize you're better off as friends, and this is done before you head back to the city.*

Me: *Well, the city is coming to us. I got a call this morning. Coach Gable, our trainer Randall, and Sebastian Wayburn are all coming this weekend. It's going to spook the shit out of her.*

Archer: *And you?*

Me: *It's not the same for me.*

Easton: *He's not the one they will fire. This is pretty black and white. She's the new hire. She has a position where she can be replaced. She's also got the pressure of her father being the coach and causing a scandal for the team.*

Me: *Damn. You sound like Eloise. You've clearly thought about this.*

Easton: *I'm an attorney. I've read my fair share of contracts. This would fall on her. This is not an equal risk, so if you really like her, I suggest you remember that.*

Bridger: *I think scoring the winning goal at the Stanley Cup gives you some job security.*

Archer: *Could you just come forward? I mean, if it gets to that point and you really want to date her?*

Easton: *Sure. As long as she's fine with losing her job.*

Me: *We went on one date. It's too early to be having this conversation.*

Axel: *Why don't you come take the horses out for a ride? That's always been where you think best.*

Me: *Might take you up on that.*

Archer: *Just take it one day at a time. You'll figure it out. Mrs. Dowden just got here. I've got to make her and Melody some eggs real quick before I leave for work.*

Rafe: *<head exploding emoji>*

Axel: *I love that you have to cook for your nanny. Wake the fuck up, brother. Time to find someone new.*

Archer: *<middle finger emoji>*

Easton: *I've got a call in five minutes. Let us know how today goes, Clark.*

Bridger: *Well, Mom has tormented me into going to the fucking eye doctor. I'm sure they'll try to scam me out of a bunch of money, all in the name of vision.*

Me: *It's one of the five senses. It's kind of important.*

Bridger: *I only care about the two that count.*

Rafe: *Taste and smell?*

Easton: *I would say hearing and touch.*

Bridger: *Both wrong. My brain and my dick. They both work really well.*

Rafe: *Mic drop.*

Clark: *My dick is on edge from my newfound celibacy. It's been too long, and it's getting hard.*

Clark: *Pun intended. <eggplant emoji>*

Easton: *Dude.*

Rafe: *I guess it's time to decide if you're going to risk everything and date this girl.*

Bridger: *He doesn't want anyone else, so I think his dick better buckle up.*

Rafe: *The best things are worth the wait.*

Bridger: *I disagree. Many of the best things I have required very little wait.*

Easton: *Such as?*

Bridger: *Mom's cooking. The new fancy toilet I ordered, like Rafe's. I overnighted it, and I get it today. My current home closed in less than thirty days, no wait at all.*

Axel: *That's because you're rich as shit, and money talks.*

Bridger: *Add return on investment to the list. The stock I bought this week just doubled.*

Archer: *And the man still claims hotdogs are his favorite food. <eye roll emoji>*

Me: *Eloise just pulled up. This was not helpful at all.*

Easton: *Happy to help. Keep us posted.*

I made my way to the backyard, where I saw Eloise stretching for our run. I walked outside, wanting to feel her out.

See where her head was at.

I didn't know how she'd act today.

I didn't know if she'd spoken to her father yet, and if she was aware that all the higher-ups would be heading to Rosewood River in a few days.

I knew she would spiral.

Every time we took two steps forward, it seemed we took three steps back.

"Good morning," I said, closing the door behind me.

She was bent over at the waist, attempting to touch her toes, but her ass was on full display, and I tried hard not to stare.

But I failed.

Go figure. This woman was so far under my skin I couldn't see straight.

"Hey, how are you this morning?" she asked, pushing to stand and pulling her foot against her ass to stretch her quads.

"I'm good. How'd you sleep?" I asked. This was maybe the oddest conversation we'd had in a while.

Why were we making pleasantries?

We had a hard time pulling our lips apart just a few hours ago.

"I slept well, Clark. Have you heard from my father?" she asked, her chin tipped up as if she were preparing for my answer.

"I did hear from him this morning. I'm guessing you're not too happy about their visit?"

She narrowed her gaze. "Gee, let me think about this. My father, Randall—the man I answer to—and Sebastian, who happens to be an owner of the team I work for, are all coming here to see how it's going. Meanwhile, we're making out like teenagers and acting completely unprofessional. Yes, I'm thrilled they'll be visiting. Thrilled!" she shouted, making no attempt to hide her sarcasm. "The jig is up. I'm going to be fired and shamed and wear a scarlet A on my chest. No, it'll be a scarlet C, for Clark. The woman who couldn't even keep her job for a three-month stint with the big superstar."

"That's very sweet of you to call me a superstar," I said, trying not to laugh at how dramatic she was being.

"That's what you took from that statement? My ass is grass, Chadwick."

I believe my sister, Emerson, refers to this type of behavior as spiraling. And Eloise Gable was most definitely spiraling.

Normally, I'd run from this type of outburst, but I actually found it endearing.

The way she cared.

She was passionate and driven, and it was hot as hell.

And I wanted to fix it. Make everything okay for her.

"Your ass is not grass. We're not going to be making out in front of them. They have no idea what's going on here. They're coming to check on the progress. They want to make sure I've recovered from my injury and working hard. That's it. They aren't coming because they suspect something. They're coming because we just had a winning season and they want to do it again," I said, motioning for us to start our run, because the girl loved to stay on schedule, and we were already getting a later start than usual.

She was quiet after I responded, and I glanced over to see her deep in thought.

"Okay, that's a good point. No more funny business. This ends now. I appreciate the date. It was really great, and yes, you're a good kisser. But this cannot happen, and I need you to be on the same page as me with this," she said, her breaths coming a little faster now. "In fact, maybe you play it up this weekend. Act like I'm a tyrant of a trainer, and I'm pushing you too hard, and that's why you're stronger than ever. Yes, that's the plan. You can't stand me, but if you can toss in a few plugs that I'm good at my job, that would be helpful."

"You are good at your job," I said dryly. "I don't need to act like you are."

"Clark. You can't show them that you like me," she huffed. "You have to act like it's painful for you to admit that I'm good at my job because you can't stand me."

"Here's a question for you, Weeze," I said, as we turned down Main Street. Edith was standing outside the Honey Biscuit Café, adjusting the flower box, and she waved.

"Let's hear it," Eloise said as she panted.

"If we hadn't kissed last night, and we were just friends who were training together, I wouldn't have to despise you. You don't have to hate someone you aren't dating. It's too extreme. It's not my personality to be that irritated with someone I'm working with. It will seem unnatural."

"Says the hotshot hockey player. You don't have to worry about your reputation. I do. And trust me, if you're too nice to me, Randall will sniff it out. He'll think something is going on," she huffed as we picked up the pace. "The man totally has it out for me."

I swear, the more concerned she got, the harder she ran.

"What will he think is going on? In the few years I've known him, I have not been in a relationship," I said. "He won't think anything is going on."

"Oh, right, because you're just a playboy who likes a quick roll in the sheets," she snipped as if it were the most offensive thing she's ever heard.

"Well, if you want to put it that way, yes. That's what he thinks. And I was raised to be respectful to women, so I wouldn't be that hard on you, even if you pushed me. He knows I like to be pushed."

She let out a long breath as we ran down toward the river. "Okay, so how would you treat a woman that you had no interest in sleeping with?"

"The same way I'd treat a woman that I wanted to sleep with," I said, without hesitation. "I don't seek out women and change my personality because I want to have sex with them."

"Hmmmm... this is going to take some thought," she said when we crossed onto the trail along the river. "I think you just have to be indifferent. Like I'm a business associate."

"So let me get this straight. We've worked together six days a week, for a minimum of five hours a day for two months, and I'm going to treat you like a business associate? That's ridiculous," I said, pushing just a shoulder ahead of her because she was pissing me off now.

"Now you're annoyed because I'm trying to keep us out of trouble?"

"Correct. You're so worried about their visit, when nothing has even happened between us."

Now she pushed the slightest bit ahead of me, as if she wanted to lead. "Right. Because if you don't sleep with me, it means nothing happened? Are you forgetting the fact that I dry-humped you and had my first orgasm with a man? I am fairly certain that most people would find that unprofessional."

I barked out a laugh, even though I was breathing heavily.

"Yeah, I liked you a hell of a lot better when you were straddling me with your mouth on mine."

"So you like me better when I'm not speaking?" she asked, as if she were completely offended.

"When you're being irrational, yes," I hissed.

That was clearly not the right thing to say. She chose not to speak the rest of the run, even when I asked her random questions.

Silence.

Nothing.

Crickets.

So, I managed to piss her off because I didn't want to pretend that I hated her.

And this was all happening after the best date I've ever had.

Without question, this was the most complicated non-relationship I'd ever been in.

And I still wanted more.

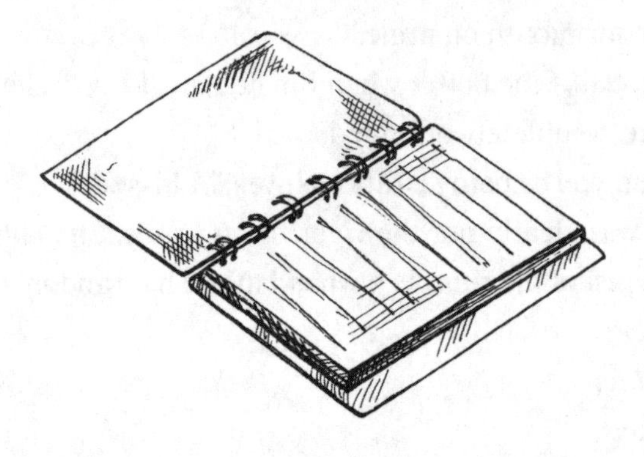

18

Eloise

Emilia, Henley, and Lulu had all come by the guesthouse for book club earlier, and they were hanging out while I got ready to go to dinner with my father, Randall, and Sebastian, and of course, Clark would be attending, as well.

We'd barely spoken this week. We went through the motions at practice, and we hadn't texted about anything outside of practice and workouts since Monday.

He wouldn't have to act like he didn't like me tonight; I managed to make him dislike me all on my own.

And it hurt like hell.

But I needed him to understand all that I had at stake, and he just didn't seem to realize the seriousness of the situation.

I filled the girls in throughout the week, as we all bonded

over this last small-town romance we read, and we'd grown close.

"So, you'll just act like the two of you are acquaintances?" Emilia asked.

"I guess so. I just needed him to act like I annoy him, you know, to throw everyone off the scent. But apparently, now I do annoy him, so it should be easy enough," I said, pulling my hair back into a loose chignon at the nape of my neck, while Lulu went through my makeup bag because she was much better at this stuff than I was, and she agreed to help me get ready.

"I think it might be more noticeable if Clark is cold to you because he's just not that kind of guy, you know?" Henley said, looking at me with a bit of concern. "He's the fun guy. The good time. He dances and sings and makes jokes and basically charms the hell out of everyone."

"I'm just worried because Randall is always making these comments about the contract and me being a professional. I feel like he wants to catch me doing something wrong. So I just need him to stop being suspicious." I shrugged as Lulu put her hand under my chin and studied my face.

"You have great bone structure," she said. "But I have to side with them. This is a risky plan. Clark's just not an asshole. But Randall, on the other hand, sounds like a real douche-weiner."

We all broke out in a fit of laughter at her choice of words.

"Well, Clark has adapted quickly to being an asshole the last few days," I said, feeling that lump in my throat form again.

Lulu bent down with the pink makeup sponge and started applying something beneath my eyes. I wasn't used to wearing much makeup, but I wanted to look like a professional tonight and not like I was here on vacation.

"El, I say this as your friend, okay?" Lulu said, as she continued blotting my face.

"Okay?" I said, but it came out more like a question.

"I think you're misreading him. And trust me, I was a big manhater for a long time before I met my goofy guy." She smiled and shook her head.

"Stay on point, Lu." Henley chuckled.

"Yes, right. Okay, so I think he's probably acting this way because you crushed him a little bit after the date." She held my chin between her thumb and pointer finger, turning it from side to side and praising her work. "Stunning."

"Crushed him? What? How did I crush him?"

"Listen, I'm not supposed to know this. Those Chadwick boys are like vaults with the things they share," she said. "But I heard Rafe on the phone with him the day after your date, and he was wounded. He said you didn't mention anything about that night, and you were adamant that it never happen again. And then I heard him mention that you asked him to act like he can't stand you in front of your father. He sounded pretty upset."

My chest squeezed at her words.

"That date was amazing, but what am I supposed to do? The owner of the team, the trainer I answer to, and my father are all coming to town. It's just a reminder that we shouldn't even go there. We'll be back in the city in three weeks. I can't date a player on the team—not that he even wants to date me. For him, this is just something he's having fun with. I'm not a casual girl. I've also worked really, really hard for my job, you know?" I swiped at the tear running down my cheek. "And my father went out on a limb to get me the interview. This would be really bad for him. I could never do that to him."

"Hey." Lulu bent down in front of me and smiled. "Trust me, I get it. I went through something similar a few months ago when I moved to Paris. I left the man I loved because I needed to do that for myself."

Henley moved beside me and squeezed my hand. "I totally understand your hesitation. It's a lot to risk for something that's very new and still unknown."

"And let's not forget that Clark doesn't even do relationships. So I'd humiliate my dad and lose my job and my reputation when he could easily kick me to the curb," I said.

"There's a lot at risk. But maybe you can tell him he doesn't have to hate you after they leave," Emilia said, as she sat on the bed, smiling at me. "He might have thought that you meant he has to act that way moving forward."

"Yeah. I kind of freaked out when I found out they were coming to town. I probably overreacted, and we should have just acted normal, like we were friends. I just got in my head, I think. But honestly, it's because of how much I like him. It freaks me out. I like him a lot. Too much," I finally said, feeling so vulnerable and anxious as the words left my mouth. "I thought I needed to overcompensate because I feel like everyone can tell how I feel."

"Listen, you are right to be concerned. You are a woman in a man's world professionally. I get it. You need to protect yourself. But I promise you, you can trust Clark. You can even tell him how you feel. Even though you can't go there, he'll understand. You are justified in not wanting to risk everything for something that might not go anywhere, but you can talk to Clark about this. You two can still be friends and not cross the line. I mean, you didn't sleep with the guy, so you're already stronger than most women who would have gone for it," Lulu said.

"I agree. You are strong and smart and fierce, Eloise Gable." Henley squeezed my hand. "And if you decide to go for it and keep it a secret, we support that, too."

"Gahhhh… I love my book besties," Emilia said over her laughter. "Girls rule, and boys drool."

Lulu shook her head and laughed. "I used to say *girls are cool, and boys are fools*."

"I do remember that phase." Henley chuckled. "Anyway, you've got this tonight. You have been training Clark for over two months, and even he says he's in the best shape of his life, and that's after coming off an injury. You're amazing at your job, and that's what tonight should be about."

"Yes. And Clark will follow your lead. So just go there and act like you normally do with him. Part of being good at your job is connecting with the athletes. He trusts you to train him, and that says a lot about your relationship right there," Emilia said.

I nodded. "Thank you. I feel much better."

"That's called a damn good bitch squad," Lulu said.

"It's girl squad. Not bitch squad." Henley gaped at her bestie.

"To-may-to. To-mot-to." Lulu shrugged and told me to close my eyes as she applied shadow to my lids.

I slipped into my black silk midi skirt and white blouse before sitting down on my bed to put on my favorite nude heels.

I glanced in the mirror, shocked by how different I looked all done up. My hair was pulled back, my makeup really defined my cheekbones, and my eyes looked twice as big. I applied some pink lipstick and puckered before making a popping sound that made everyone laugh.

"Damn, girl, you look like hot business Barbie," Lulu said.

Henley and Emilia both gushed over my look, and I thanked them all for being here for me today.

I'd been down in the dumps the last few days.

Clark was doing everything that I asked him to do, yet I wasn't happy about it.

I hated how distant he was being.

I hated that I hurt him.

I wouldn't have thought that possible, but hearing what Lulu said hit me hard.

Clark and I had a connection, whether we liked it or not.

And even though we couldn't act on it, it didn't mean I needed to be cruel.

I was so in my own head that I hadn't stopped to think about how it had made him feel.

I grabbed the notebook on my bed after the girls left, and I glanced through it. We hadn't written in it since our date, and I hated that. So I jotted down a note to him because I wanted to do it while I was all in my feelings. I'd give it to him at our next practice.

Chadwick,

I've been a real jerk. Fear took over, and I'm not proud of it. First, I want to thank you for the best date I've ever been on. I had so much fun, and you made me feel so special. I should have told you that the next morning.

I shouldn't have asked you to pretend to hate me. I was scared and insecure, and I messed up. I hope you can forgive me. Even though we can't do it again, I'm grateful for your friendship. You're the only guy friend I've ever had. Thanks for making me laugh every day, teaching me your dance moves, and being the best athlete on my first stint as a trainer/therapist. We're allowed to be friends. I just felt like everyone could read my feelings like an open book. It's hard not to act on them most days, so please understand that I'm just trying to do the right thing.

XO,
Weeze

I sighed as I tucked the notebook into my dresser drawer and grabbed my purse. We were meeting at Rosewood's. I hadn't been there, but apparently, it was not only the best steakhouse in Rosewood River, but people from all over the Bay Area traveled here just to eat there.

I got in my car and drove the short distance to the restaurant. My father had texted when he arrived an hour ago, and they were all dropping their bags at the hotel and then heading over to Rosewood's.

I opened the door, and my attention immediately moved to the loud laughter coming from the dining room. I'd know my father's laugh anywhere, but it was also Clark's laughter that was so familiar.

The hostess greeted me, and I took in the cherry wood décor and the rustic chandeliers hanging throughout the dining room.

"I see my party over there," I said.

"Great. They were just waiting for you to arrive." She led me to the table, even though I could clearly see them a few feet away.

"Thank you," I said to the hostess, and all four men pushed to their feet.

I hurried over to my father, catching Clark's eye over Dad's shoulder.

"Look at you, Ells. I missed you," Dad said.

"Missed you, too, Dad." I pulled back and made my way around the table, greeting the other men.

Randall's cheeks were flush, so it was clear he was a few cocktails deep. He pulled me in for a hug, which surprised me. He was in his fifties, close to my father's age, though Dad hadn't gone gray as Randall had.

I hadn't met Sebastian Wayburn yet, and he was a good-looking man, a few inches shorter than Clark, with dark hair and a dimple on his left cheek. I extended my hand for a quick handshake and then turned to Clark. I wasn't sure if we would hug or shake hands, but I didn't have time to decide.

He gave a curt nod, no hug or shaking of the hands. "Hello, Eloise."

And then he took his seat, which was on the other side of the round table from where I was sitting between my father and Sebastian Wayburn.

"We've been hearing how much you've been torturing our superstar," Sebastian chuckled, tossing me a wink.

"Well, it is my job. But he's done all the hard work, and it shows." I looked up and smiled at him, and he didn't so much as give me a glance.

Damn. He was really playing the part well.

"You should be proud, John," Clark said, as he turned his attention to my father. "She's all business. She pushes me hard and is probably the most professional trainer I've ever worked with. She makes you seem social, Randall." Clark barked out a laugh, and I hated that he was doing exactly what I asked him to do.

Note to self: When I spiral, I cannot be trusted.

"I think that means she takes her job seriously," Sebastian said. "That's exactly what the Lions team is about. Working hard. Pushing hard. Winning big."

"Thank you," I said, swallowing down the lump in my throat.

"Well, some of us like to have a little balance in life." Clark raised his beer, and his laugh sounded forced.

"Life is all about balance," Randall said. "Unless you work directly for me, and then I fully support being a workaholic. So you just keep doing what you're doing, Eloise."

"Pay him no attention," Sebastian chuckled. "We work hard so that we can also enjoy life."

I chuckled. "It's fine. I enjoy my job."

"Yeah, Chadwick was telling us how you've adapted the workouts to push his limits. But he also made it clear you will both be thrilled when you aren't stuck working together every day." Sebastian's lips turned up on one side. "Keep pushing him. We need him in his best shape."

"Well, she can only do so much during this part of the training, as she doesn't have the experience yet. The real work comes when he returns, because I show no mercy, and Chadwick knows that." Randall's words slurred the slightest bit.

"Well, I can't imagine him doing more than he's been doing since I arrived here. I'm sure you've all looked at the workouts I've been sharing each day, and it's just a reflection of the effort he puts in. He shows up every single day. I think he probably knows he could have trained himself this summer. I'm sure he's tired of being stuck with the babysitter," I said, trying to keep my voice light.

I looked up at Clark, and he glanced over at me, the move so quick it actually stung because he turned his attention back to my father.

The rest of the evening went exactly like this. Randall fawning all over Clark, my father sharing stories from last season about the way that Clark rose to the challenge, game after game, and Sebastian just taking it all in. He didn't say much in response to any of the conversation, aside from leaning in and cracking a few jokes just for me.

Everyone agreed that Clark's workouts had contributed to him returning for the new season in the best shape of his life. My father gave a little kudos to me, Sebastian gave a lot of kudos to me, and Randall didn't acknowledge me whatsoever. Clark stayed quiet on the topic and didn't say much. The cocktails flowed, though I didn't drink, as this was not the group I wanted to loosen up with. I noticed Clark wasn't drinking either, but the rest of the group was having a very good time, my father included.

"It's a good thing you aren't indulging tonight, Chadwick," I said, looking up at him as everyone listened intently. "I wouldn't want you to be hungover tomorrow. Monday is going to be the most grueling workout we've had yet. I suggest you rest up tomorrow."

He just stared at me, lacking all emotion. "Like I told you, gentlemen. This arrangement can't come to an end soon enough."

I startled at how cold he sounded, even though this was what I wanted. What I asked for.

Careful what you wish for.

Loud laughter bellowed around the table.

"Nice job," Randall called out from the other side of the table. "She's not too bad for a beginner, although working with one client is a lot easier than working with a ton of guys on the team. But she'll learn a lot once she shadows me back in the city."

My father patted my back as if he knew it was a backhanded compliment, and I looked up at Clark in hopes he would be looking back at me, but he wasn't. I did note the way his hand fisted on the table at Randall's words, but he didn't say anything.

"I'm looking forward to being back in the city with the team," I said, forcing the words from my mouth as I turned to my dad. "We can spend the day together tomorrow, right?"

"Yes. I think Randall and Sebastian are going to go see Clark's home gym setup tomorrow, and then we're all having Sunday dinner with Clark's family tomorrow night. Have you had a Chadwick family dinner yet?" Dad's voice was all tease, and I suddenly realized how wrong I'd been about all of this. He expected me to have gone to dinner. The Chadwicks were lovely people, and of course, they would extend the invite to someone living there for a few months while working with their son. But before I could answer, Clark jumped in.

"Nope. Working together for practice has proved to be plenty of time," Clark said with a laugh, and I didn't look at him this time.

I messed up, and I knew it.

"Oh, you're going to love it. Clark's mom is a fabulous cook, too," my father said. "And I'm hoping you and I can spend the day together while they're with Clark tomorrow, and then we'll head to dinner together."

"Sounds good," I said. "I've met a bunch of the Chadwicks in town; I just haven't been to dinner over there yet. But I could take you downtown and show you around."

I knew Clark had spoken to his family about not mentioning that I attended dinner there on Sundays because Henley had told me about it. I made him feel like he had to lie about everything.

"Actually, I don't need to see Clark's home gym, as it's just a temporary training facility for him. I came to make sure he was doing well, and clearly, he is. I also came here to meet our new physical therapist, and I've enjoyed chatting with you, Eloise. Would you both be okay if I tag along with you tomorrow instead, and go check out the downtown?"

I felt Clark's eyes on me for the first time tonight, and I looked up and saw the anger there.

"Of course, you're welcome to hang out with us," my father said, completely oblivious to the tension at the table.

"You afraid I'll challenge you to a workout, Sebastian?" Clark said, his tone light and playful, but I noted the way his jaw ticked as he looked at him.

"Nah. I just don't need to hear Randall talk about training plans anymore," Sebastian laughed. "I'd rather hear about the program Eloise has implemented for you this summer, as you've made it clear you're in the best shape of your life."

"Well, all of these workouts have been overseen by me," Randall snipped, holding his glass up for our server to bring him another.

"Well, Randall, I've been watching you train the team for the last eight weeks, so I'd like to see what Eloise has up her sleeve," he said, glancing at me and smiling.

"My girl is a rock star in her own right," my father said, his cheeks rosy from the three beers he'd had tonight.

"I don't doubt that for a second," Sebastian said, and if looks could kill, Clark Chadwick would end him right here at the table.

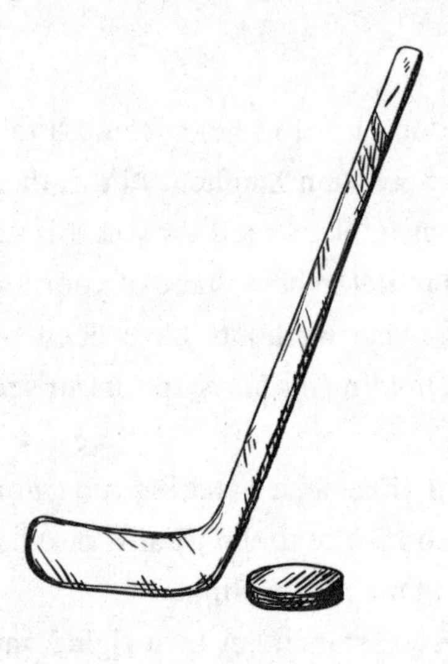

19

Clark

My blood was boiling over the bullshit dinner I attended. The fact that Eloise thought they would think we were having an inappropriate relationship, only to have the owner clearly hit on her all night, right in front of everyone.

I've never felt this kind of jealousy before.

Sebastian Wayburn was a rich kid, who was used to getting what he wanted.

And there was no doubt in my mind that he wanted Eloise.

The same woman that I wanted.

The same woman who asked me to pretend that I hated her tonight.

I ran a hand down my face in frustration as I took another long pull from my beer.

I hadn't had a cocktail at the restaurant because I wouldn't have been able to put on that ridiculous show at the table if I'd had any booze in me.

There was a light knock on the door, and I wasn't sure if I'd imagined it, until it came again.

It was nearly 11:00 p.m., so I definitely wasn't expecting company.

I pulled the door open, surprised to see Eloise on my doorstep, wearing that sexy-as-sin fitted skirt and blouse that dipped low enough to show a little bit of her white lace bra beneath it.

I'd taken every moment that she wasn't paying attention to me to look at her from across the table. The table where I had to sit, pretend to dislike her, and watch another man take his shot.

"Did you walk here alone?" I asked, my words coming out harsher than I meant them to.

"Yes. I just left my father at the hotel. It's Saturday night. There's a lot of people out downtown still, so I thought you might still be up."

I studied her. "Did you want to come in?"

She nodded. "Is that okay?"

"Of course, it is. You're the one with all the rules." I stepped back and motioned her inside. "Although I've got to say, coming to my house this late is much riskier than acting like we don't hate each other at dinner."

She moved past me, stopping once she got to the kitchen and turning around to face me. "I handled that wrong."

"You think?" I asked, folding my arms over my chest and making no attempt to hide my irritation.

"I wrote you back in the notebook, but I didn't have time to go back home and get it before I came here. So I just wanted to come tell you what I wrote in there today," she said, clearing her throat and suddenly appearing nervous.

"All right," I said, my tone softer now. I hated seeing her upset. "Tell me."

"Well, I don't think I want to tell you exactly what I wrote, because something hit me tonight while we were at dinner, so I think I'd rather tell you that." She stepped closer to me, and I shoved my hands into my pockets to stop myself from touching her.

"What hit you tonight, Weeze?" I asked, my gaze locked with hers.

I was exhausted, and I hadn't slept well in a few days. I hated this distance between us now.

"I should have thanked you for that date—the most amazing date." Her voice shook. "Because it meant everything to me."

"You thanked me that night. You don't need to thank me again," I said. "I'm not upset about you not thanking me for the date. I'm bothered that you want to act like it didn't happen."

"I know that it happened, and I wanted to say it to make sure you knew how much it meant to me." She sucked in a breath. "This is uncharted territory for me, Clark. And I'm scared about all of it."

"What are you afraid of?" I asked, fighting the urge to pull her close. If anything was going to happen, she was going to have to admit she wanted it to happen. "They don't suspect anything, Eloise. I think I did a pretty good job of convincing them we can't stand one another."

She shook her head rapidly, and I startled when I saw a tear roll down her cheek. "It's not about that. I'm scared of my feelings. I'm scared of how much I like you. I'm scared that you'll reject me. But then I'm scared that you won't, and that doesn't work either." She shrugged. "I'm scared that I think about you when I'm not with you. I'm scared that I asked you to pretend that you hated me, and now you actually might hate me."

"Weeze," I said, pulling her against me and wrapping my arms around her. "I could never hate you. I hate that the first woman I have real feelings for is the one woman I can't have."

She stiffened in my arms and then tipped her head back to look at me. "I think we should reconsider our options."

"Yeah? How so?"

"Well, I was thinking about it at the restaurant. I hated how far apart we sat. I hated that we've barely spoken this week. And I realized, sometimes, you have to take risks. And maybe we just take a risk. We see where this goes for the next three weeks while we're still here. We work hard at practice, and then if we want to spend time together privately, we can do it without anyone knowing it. Maybe this is the gift—being in this small town, where no one pays us any attention. My dad and Randall don't suspect anything, so let's see where this goes."

"Is that what you want?" I asked, tucking a piece of hair that broke free behind her ear.

She nodded. "It'll probably be a disaster, and we'll go back to the city knowing we at least let things play out. And if by chance we still like each other then, we'll cross that bridge when we get there."

I was stunned that she was saying this. It's everything I wanted to hear, but I never thought she'd actually allow herself to go there. "One day at a time. No pressure. Hell, if you want to just hang out as friends and spend time together, I'm fine with it."

"That's not what I want." She shrugged, her teeth sinking into that juicy bottom lip.

"What do you want, Eloise Gable?" I said, leaning down closer now. Her breaths came faster now.

"I'm feeling something I've never felt. And it might be dumb and risky, but I don't care. I want to spend the night with you. I want to spend the next three weeks with you. And I want to let myself enjoy this feeling. Even if it doesn't get to last forever, it's okay."

I reached behind her, palming her ass with one hand and lifting her off her feet, as her skirt bunched around her hips and her legs came around my waist.

"That's all I needed to hear." I tugged her face down and kissed her.

She pulled back, one hand on each side of my face. "Take me to your bedroom."

I searched her gaze. "There's no rush."

"We've got three weeks to do whatever we want, and we've wasted enough time already."

I nodded, pulling her mouth back down to mine as I walked down the hallway toward my bedroom. I set her down on the bed, hovering above her. "This is an unexpected turn of events."

"I couldn't stand how distant we were this week. Even if this can't go anywhere when we leave Rosewood River, I want to savor this. Whatever it is, I want to enjoy it right now. Life is short, and it hit me tonight that I've been being ridiculous."

"I can't argue with that." I smirked.

She swatted at my chest. "I was talking to my dad after dinner, and he was telling me that my mom would be so proud of the woman I've become, which of course, got me in all my feels. We talked about how much we miss her, and he said that it's okay to miss someone, even all these years later, because it means they impacted your life. Dad said that even though grieving her loss has been horrible, he'd rather have had an hour of wonderful, than a lifetime of just okay. I've had a lot of just okay, you know?"

"What are you saying? Are you over the moon for me, Eloise?" My voice was all tease as I ran the pad of my thumb over her bottom lip.

"Don't get cocky, Hotshot." She chuckled. "I'll say this… Not everything has to last forever to be worth doing it. So I'm going to try your whole *one-day-at-a-time* philosophy and just enjoy it. For once in my life, I don't want to overthink everything."

"Yeah? I like the sound of that."

I've always been a guy who believed in taking things one day at a time. Not overthinking everything. Yet, here I was, knowing one day would never be enough with this woman.

I already wanted more than one day.

Maybe even all of her days.

She raised her arms over her head for me to take her blouse off. I pulled back and found the hem of the silky white fabric and lifted it over her head.

"Damn, I've dreamed about these tits more times than I can count." My fingers traced over the thin white lace, and her nipples hardened beneath the tips of my fingers. I slipped one strap down her shoulder, my knuckles gliding across her silky skin as she arched her body up toward me. I leaned down, taking her hard peak between my lips, and she groaned. I flicked it with my tongue before slipping the other strap down her shoulder and moving to the other breast. Back and forth, over and over, as she squirmed beneath me.

I pulled back to look at her, her cheeks flush and lips parted.

"I could stay right here all night," I said, my voice gruff as she reached up and ran her fingers along the scruff of my jaw.

"I want you right now. No more waiting," she said.

"There's one thing I need to do first." I slid down her body, reaching behind her for the zipper on her skirt. "I want to taste you, beautiful."

Her eyes widened, and her breaths came faster. She gave me the slightest nod, but I could see the nerves there.

"Have you done this before?"

"I haven't. It's just never been… requested," she said, which made me chuckle. Because how the hell had no one ever gone down on her?

"Well, it's being requested now," I said. My voice was all tease as I pressed my erection against her. The thought of being the first man to bring her this kind of pleasure did something to me. "I want to make you feel good. Do you trust me?"

Her lips turned up in the corners. "I do."

I slowly slipped the skirt down her legs, stopping at her ankles and slipping off heels and tossing them on the floor. She was left in nothing but a pair of white lace panties, and her bra was pulled down just beneath her breasts.

I reached for the band of her panties, and she sucked in a breath as I slowly dragged them down her gorgeous legs. I reached behind her and unclasped her bra, removing the last strap of fabric covering her beautiful body.

I just stared down at her.

How many times had I imagined what was beneath her clothing?

"You're stunning," I said. "You just don't even know how many times I've thought about this."

"Tell me," she said, her voice trembling the slightest bit.

"Every fucking day, Eloise. Being close to you, talking to you, being lucky enough to be in your fucking presence—I don't take it for granted. And getting to touch you and taste you, I feel like the luckiest bastard on the planet," I said.

"I feel like the lucky one." She sighed. "But I don't like that I'm the only one who isn't dressed."

I reached behind me and yanked off my shirt. But I couldn't wait another second. I bent down and kissed the inside of her thigh, moving from one to the other. I kissed my way up her legs before burying my face between her thighs. I licked her from one end to the other.

Slowly at first.

I paused every once in a while to make sure she was okay.

She was definitely okay.

She was more than okay.

She writhed beneath me, rocking her hips over and over, as I teased her with my tongue and lips.

Sucking and licking and taking her just to the edge before pulling back.

I loved every little sound she made.

Her fingers tangled in my hair as she repeated the same words over and over, her voice just above a whisper. "Clark, please."

I loved hearing her beg for more, knowing that I was affecting her the way she affected me.

My dick strained against the zipper of my jeans, eager to be freed.

But I stayed right there.

I slipped one finger into her wet heat.

And then a second.

I sealed my lips over her clit and sucked as I pumped my fingers in and out.

Over and over.

Her body arched off the bed as she bucked wildly beneath me.

Her thighs tightened around my head, and I knew she was close.

I continued moving just as she cried out my name, and she went right over the edge.

I stayed right there, pumping in and out as she rode out every last bit of pleasure.

It was the sexiest thing I'd ever seen.

Seeing this woman vulnerable and needy.

I pulled back, smiling down at her. "That was worth the wait."

She was still catching her breath, and her arm moved to cover her chest. I pulled it away. "No. Now that I've seen you. Now that I've had a taste. There's no hiding anymore."

Her lips turned up in the corners, her eyes sated. "Okay. So let me see you, then."

I didn't hesitate. I unbuttoned my jeans and shoved them down my legs along with my briefs. My cock sprang free, making it obvious he's waited long enough.

Weeks.

Months.

And now minutes felt like torture.

I wrapped my hand around my erection and stroked it a few times. "This is what you do to me. I have never wanted anyone the way that I want you."

"I want you, too," she whispered, as she gaped at my dick like she was terrified of it.

"Is there a reason you're looking at me like that?" I asked.

"I just—er, I don't think it's going to fit."

I chuckled. "We'll go slow. If it hurts, we stop. There's no rush and no pressure."

"You know I don't like to concede," she said, teasingly. "Tell me you have a condom."

"I have a condom." I leaned forward and reached into the nightstand drawer pulling out the foil packet.

"I want to do it," she said, her voice sexy as hell as she took the foil packet from me.

She tore off the top before slowly removing the condom and carefully setting the scrap on the nightstand.

"Eloise." My voice was so gruff it startled me. "You can't say things like that and then move this slowly. You've got to roll that onto my cock because I'm about to lose it."

Her teeth sank into her bottom lip, and she quickly slid the latex over me. "Better?"

I quickly grabbed her hips, flipping her over as I rolled onto my back, adjusting her above me, with her legs falling to each side as she straddled me.

"Much better. You're going to set the pace. If it's too much, you just stop, all right?"

She nodded, pushing up onto her knees so the tip of my dick was lined up with her entrance. My large hands covered her tits before sliding down to her hips.

She moved down slowly, and I squeezed my eyes shut at the feel of her.

Tight and warm and wet.

So fucking tight I nearly stopped breathing.

She continued moving down, inch by inch.

I reached up, tangling my fingers in her hair as she leaned down, and I covered her mouth with mine.

I kissed her as she continued to slide down my cock.

It was the most erotic, sensual thing I'd ever experienced.

She groaned into my mouth as she took me all the way in, and then she stayed completely still, pulling back to look at me. She let out a few breaths as if she were adjusting to my size, and then she smiled. It was sexy as hell. Her fingers intertwined with mine, and she moved up ever so slowly, before coming back down.

Holy shit. Nothing had ever felt so good in my life.

Not sex with another woman.

Not scoring goals on the ice.

Nothing compared to this moment.

It was fair to say that I now understood what it meant to be over the moon.

Because I was all in on this girl.

And three weeks would never be enough.

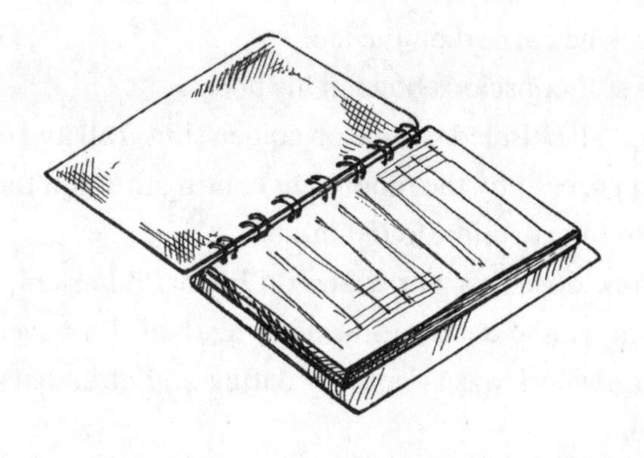

20
Eloise

I fell forward on top of his chest after we'd both gone over the edge within seconds of one another.

I've never experienced sex like this.

It had always been rather uneventful.

But this… this was everything I'd read about in the pages of my romance books. Something that I thought only existed in fiction.

But here I was, still coming down from the most epic orgasm of my life.

Clark wrapped his hand around my neck, fingers in my hair, as he kissed me hard. He then slipped me off of him and adjusted me to lie beside him while he pushed to his feet and walked to the bathroom.

I heard the toilet flush, and then he returned with all that big-dick energy he carried on the ice.

Not a self-conscious bone in his body.

He was all chiseled muscle on golden skin. Tall and confident. His green gaze, lit by the moonlight coming through the slivered opening in the curtains, found mine.

"So how does this work? Should I leave?" I asked, suddenly self-conscious about being naked in his bed. I'd never had sex with a man who I wasn't actively dating and already calling my boyfriend.

This was different.

This was a secret.

An attraction we had agreed to give in to.

And I had zero regrets. But I also didn't know how the protocol for this type of arrangement worked.

Would I do the walk of shame now? I wasn't complaining because my body was still on a high.

I knew when I arrived here tonight that I wanted this.

I wanted him.

This hockey superstar who could have anyone.

A man I worked with and could never be seen with.

So, I'd take whatever came with that. At least for the next few weeks.

He barked out a laugh and slipped back into bed, pulling me onto his chest. "Don't be ridiculous. Why would you leave?"

"Well, we just had sex after we agreed we wouldn't go there before completely changing lanes tonight. So this is kind of our dirty little secret, and I'm fine with it. But I just figure you usually have sex and then get the hell out of there."

"Eloise," he said, looking down at me.

"Yes?"

"I'm not sure where you got your information about me, but I'm certainly not a guy who bangs a woman and then ducks out."

"You told me you haven't had a relationship since high school," I reminded him.

"Correct. Meaning I haven't been going home for Christmas to meet anyone's parents. But it's not quite as abrupt as you seem to think." He shrugged. "Plus, you're different. We're friends first. And now we're lovers, and I'd keep you tied to my bed if you'd let me."

I rolled onto my belly, pushing up onto my elbows and smiling at him. "Well, that's not happening. Plus, we've got another day with everyone in town tomorrow."

"Speaking of tomorrow, that was a dick move by Sebastian. He was totally hitting on you in front of me," Clark said, making no attempt to hide his irritation.

"He was not," I said over a fit of laughter. "He thinks you hate me, and I think he felt sorry for me."

"So let me get this straight." He rolled me onto my back and hovered above me. "You insisted that I pretend to despise you, and now the billionaire team owner takes that as his opening to date you? I'd say I got the short end of the stick, but my stick feels like he won tonight." He winked, and I smacked his chest.

"You have an impressive hockey stick, Clark Chadwick. No doubt about it."

"I mean, I don't want to brag, but you just experienced a Stanley Cup hockey stick, Weeze. I think Sebastian has small-dick energy."

"Clark." I arched a brow.

"Yes."

"I'm not interested in Sebastian." I put my finger against his lips when he started to interrupt. "If you hadn't been so distant tonight, I might not have realized how much I missed you. So it all led us to this moment, right?"

"Fair enough. So how do we handle tomorrow?"

"I'll be with my dad and Sebastian during the day, and you'll have Randall with you. And then we'll meet you at Sunday dinner."

"I'll make sure my family acts like you've never been there. It'll be fun. And I can keep my eye on the billionaire. But he better not make a move when you're showing him around downtown."

"I love that you think he's going to make a move with my father there. Do you always get jealous with women you sleep with?" I asked, teasing.

But his gaze shifted, turning serious. "No, Eloise. And you are not just *some* woman that I'm sleeping with."

I ran my fingers along the scruff of his jaw, the way I'd been dying to do for weeks. "Who am I, then? Your physical therapist? Your trainer? Your coach's daughter? Your dirty secret?" I said, my voice light and playful because we both knew what this was.

"I don't see it that way." He lifted one shoulder, his smile sweet. "You're my friend and my lover. Are you planning to sleep with anyone else while we're in Rosewood River?"

"I mean, I haven't slept with anyone in over a year. I don't see me taking on another lover in the next three weeks, so no." I chuckled.

"Then I guess that makes you my woman for now, doesn't it?" He nipped at my ear, and I squealed. "Say it. For now, you're mine."

"Fine, you big Neanderthal. For now, I'm yours."

"Was that so difficult?"

"Painfully so." I chuckled. "And how about you say it? For now, you're mine."

"For now, I'm yours." He smiled down at me. "I'm just glad you're not running out the door."

"Nah. You and your magic hockey stick can keep me for three weeks," I said.

"Ah, I love that even you admit I have a magic penis."

"You're a man of many talents."

He reached beneath my arms and shifted me to lie on his chest again, our heads on the same pillow. "We better get some sleep. I'll need my energy to act like I can't stand you tomorrow, all while making sure Sebastian doesn't hit on my woman."

My woman.

Why did I like hearing him say that so much?

"Go to sleep, Hotshot."

He wrapped his arms around me tighter, and I listened to the sound of his breathing.

I was surprised at how much I liked sleeping with his arms wrapped around me, the sound of his heartbeat soothing me to sleep.

Even when I knew I shouldn't get used to it, I didn't care.

And sleep took us both.

• • •

"I can see this town has grown on you," my father said, as we sat at the Honey Biscuit Café.

"Yes, I really love it here." It surprised me how much I've enjoyed my time in Rosewood River after pouting that I had to spend three months away from the city. Obviously, Clark had a lot to do with it, but honestly, this town was easy to love. The people. The river. The mountains. All of it.

Everyone in town that we ran into stopped us to meet my

father and Sebastian. It was just that kind of place.

"I'm impressed that you packed up your life and came here all for one client," Sebastian said. "It shows how committed you are to your job."

I hadn't been given a choice, but I wasn't going to bring that up.

He knew how this worked.

"I'm grateful for the opportunity to work with the Lions," I said.

"We're lucky to have you." He winked.

"Honestly, I wasn't sure if they'd extend the interview, seeing as I'm the coach and all, but having you on the Lions with me is more than I ever could have hoped for," Dad said.

My chest squeezed at his words because I felt the same way.

"Of course, we'd interview your daughter. And from what I was told, she was by far, the best candidate, and they interviewed nearly a dozen applicants. You were the standout," Sebastian said.

"That is so kind of you to say. I'm so happy to be part of this organization, and I'm looking forward to another winning season."

"Count on it," Sebastian said, as he and my father started discussing a player they were interested in drafting.

I glanced down at my phone to see a text from Clark.

Hotshot: *We made it down the river, but I swear, Randall did nothing to help.*

Hotshot: *Has Moneybags asked you out yet?*

Me: *Don't be a baby. It's a good upper arm workout for you. And no. Of course not. It's not like that, and we're with my father, you jealous Neanderthal.*

Hotshot: *It's Sunday. I believe you told me I'm supposed to rest on Sunday.*

Me: *Well, a little time on the water won't kill you. <laughing face emoji>*

Hotshot: *I survived.*

Me: *I'm glad you made it down safely.*

Hotshot: *Me, too. Are you having fun?*

Me: *Yes. You?*

Hotshot: *Not really. <laughing face emoji>*

Hotshot: *I'd much rather have my face buried in your <cat emoji>*

I quickly pulled the phone down on my lap as my cheeks heated.

Me: *Clark Chadwick. No. You can't say that.*

Hotshot: *Eloise Gable. I said it.*

Me: *You're insane.*

Hotshot: *You fucking love it.*

Me: *I kind of do. <heart eyes emoji>*

Me: *But I'm sitting at a table with my father, so I cannot be sexting you. <head exploding emoji>*

Hotshot: *Got it. But just know that my <hockey stick emoji> is crazy about your <cat emoji>*

Me: *<head exploding emoji>*

I tucked my phone into my purse when our pancakes arrived, and we spent the next hour talking about the upcoming season, the travel schedule, and the dynamics with some new players that were coming on board.

After we finished up, Oscar stopped by our table and drilled them like he worked for the CIA.

Were they here for Clark Chadwick?

Did my father have anything to do with me getting hired by the Lions?

How did Sebastian feel about being born into a family that had enough money to buy a professional hockey team?

Would they kick Clark to the curb if he wasn't healed the way they hoped?

Was I the only female employee on the Lions team?

Thankfully, Edith came over and put a stop to the questions, and we made our way out of there. We walked downtown and stopped by The Vintage Rose so I could introduce them to Emilia.

"It's great to meet you. Thank you for renting out your guesthouse to Eloise on such short notice," my father said.

"It worked out great for me. I got the place rented and made the most amazing friend in the process," Emilia gushed.

"Yeah, she's pretty special," Sebastian said, his smile reaching his eyes. I'd quickly deduced that he was a flirt by nature.

I didn't miss the way Emilia watched him and then looked at me with an arched brow.

He's hot.

I gave her a look that said, *Not interested.*

She gave me one back that said, *I know, but he's still hot.*

I filled her in this morning on the events of last night, and of course, she was thrilled about me and Clark finally admitting how we felt, and enjoying the moment without overthinking the future.

I chuckled as Sebastian's comment went right over my father's head.

"She sure is," Emilia said. "So what do you guys have planned for the rest of the day?"

"I'm going to take them around downtown and then down to the river. We have dinner at the Chadwicks' tonight, so we've got a full day." I chuckled.

"Ohhhh, dinner at the Chadwicks'. That'll be fun."

"You know them?" Sebastian asked curiously.

Emilia's head tipped back with a laugh. "Everyone knows them. It's a small town, and they're a big family."

"So will you be joining us for dinner, as well?" My father asked.

"No. I don't know them that well," she said, her cheeks flushing as she said it.

I was definitely going to talk to Bridger about lightening up with Emilia. Lulu and Henley had invited her to dinner last week, but she thought it would cause an issue with Bridger, so she turned them down, even though I'd all but begged her to come.

"Oh, got it. And Eloise is only going because we're here?" my father said.

"Yes. I've gotten to know a bunch of the Chadwicks just from being here for the last few months, but it's not like I'm hanging out with his family outside of work," I said defensively, wondering why I felt the need to even say this much.

No one was suspicious. This was all in my head.

"I get that," Sebastian said as he studied me. "I'm sure you see Chadwick more than you want to with the workout schedule. Your time off should be your time off."

Oh, Sebastian. If you only knew how much of Clark Chadwick I've actually seen on my time off.

I had a flashback of him striding toward me, completely naked, with a sexy grin on his face.

I felt my cheeks heat at the thought and glanced over to find Emilia smiling at me, as if she knew exactly where my mind had gone.

But luckily, she was the only one who seemed to notice.

We just had to get through tonight, and we'd be out of the woods.

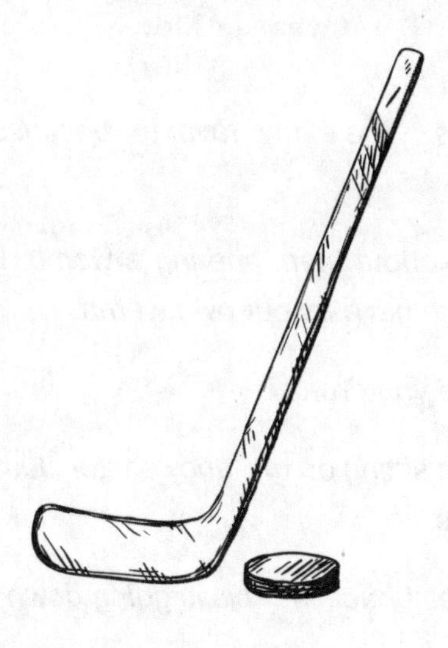

21

Clark

Easton: *I'm proposing to Henley next weekend. Emerson, Nash, and Cutler will be coming in to town for it. Clear your schedules for Saturday evening. More details to come soon.*

Bridger: *Whatever happened to just taking a knee on a walk?*

Rafe: *Did you tell Emerson first?*

Easton: *You were all with me when I got the ring several weeks ago. I just decided to do it this weekend, so yes, I talked to her this morning.*

Archer: *It's that twin bullshit. They always favor each other.*

Easton: *Yes. She's my favorite because she isn't an asshole.*

Rafe: *It's all about them sharing a womb. Don't punish us because Mom gave us our own womb.*

Bridger: *Are you drunk?*

Rafe: *No. I'm sitting on my fancy shitter. Just doing the petty twin theatrics.*

Easton: *Reel it back in. This is going down this weekend.*

Axel: *Congrats. Are we doing a grand gesture?*

Me: *Of course, he is. He's a fucking Chadwick.*

Rafe: *Go big or go home.*

Bridger: *Go home.*

Easton: *Well, I'm doing it at your stables, Bridger. So we'll be transforming the space.*

Bridger: *Yet you told your womb-sharing twin first?*

Easton: *Correct.*

Rafe: *I'm glad I'm not the only one who sees it. <laughing face emoji>*

Easton: *See you tonight at dinner. Are we still acting like Eloise is a new friend? <eyeroll emoji>*

Me: *Yes. Just talk less and listen more.*

Bridger: *I want that on a shirt.*

Rafe: *That's a shirt I wouldn't wear. I was born to play this part. I'll act like I've barely met her.*

Me: *Don't overplay it. Just be cool.*

Bridger: *Good luck with that.*

Easton: *I was born cool.*

Axel: *There are a lot of players to control on this chessboard of yours, Clark. I don't understand why you can't just say you're friends.*

Archer: *Aren't they friends?*

Rafe: *I'm getting lover vibes. I think he's holding out.*

Easton: *Agreed. I think the hockey stick has left the building.*

Axel: *You think so?*

Easton: *I saw him this morning. He had a little more swagger in his step. <winky face emoji>*

Archer: *Dry spell is over?*

Me: *I don't kiss and tell.*

Rafe: *That's the same thing as saying you did the deed, brother. Because if there was nothing to tell, you wouldn't have to say that.*

Bridger: *What happened to talking less?*

Me: *Maybe you can all say you got a bad case of laryngitis tonight and stay home.*

Easton: *Stop worrying. We've got this.*

I arrived at the house with Randall, and my family was already talking his ear off. They'd met him many times, along with Coach Gable. But they had never met Sebastian, as he was newly taking over the day-to-day operations for the Lions.

The doorbell rang, and my father went to answer the door. He walked in and made an over-the-top announcement, completely off-script from what I told him to say.

"Look who we have here. We've all met Coach Gable, but we've not yet met Sebastian Wayburn nor Coach Gable's daughter, Eloise. Is it Eloise, am I saying it correctly? Whenever I meet people for the *first time*, I'm terrible with names," my father said, looking at me like he just earned an Academy Award.

He'd most likely win a Razzie Award for this performance.

For fuck's sake.

She already shared that she'd met most of my family during her time here. They didn't need to act like strangers. All they were told was to not make it obvious that she came to Sunday dinner every week.

"Yes, you can call me Eloise. Nice to see you all." She cleared her throat, clearly uncomfortable with how over-the-top my father had been. Sebastian made his way around the group, shaking hands and shmoozing, and I wanted to hate the dude, but it was only because I knew he wanted my woman.

My woman.

I'd never had a thought like that in my life.

"I've got the best whiskey in Rosewood River for everyone to sample," Easton said, giving me a look like I had nothing to worry about. By the way he was pouring the whiskey, it was clear that he planned to get everyone drunk so they wouldn't remember any of this anyway.

Easton, Henley, Rafe, and Lulu passed out glasses of expensive bourbon, and I stuck to water because I sure as hell wasn't going to get shitfaced in front of my coach, trainer, and owner of the team. I noticed Eloise had also passed on the whiskey and opted for a glass of wine.

"Come on," Sebastian said, nudging her with his shoulder before tipping his head back. "You can have a few whiskeys with me, can't you?"

Motherfucker.

He was going to pull this shit in my parents' home?

He wore a navy polo shirt and green plaid pants, which pissed me the hell off. The preppy fucker reeked of money and education. He probably played golf and chess and met his old fraternity brothers in the Hamptons once a year for vacation.

"Sebastian, I've got to tell you, those plaid pants are a whole vibe. I think I'm definitely going to get a pair," Rafe, the kiss-ass bastard said.

"You've got a good eye. According to my mother, they are all the rage on the East Coast," the cocky bastard said, as he winked at Eloise because the fucker was sticking to her like glue. "I'm a bit of a mama's boy."

Easton came around with the bottle to refill their glasses. Sebastian tipped his head back a second time, along with every member of my family, and chuckled. "This is my kind of Sunday dinner."

"Ours, too, Sebastian. Meeting you for the first time, and of course, meeting Coach Gable's daughter—what was your name again, Elander?" my father asked, and I closed my eyes and internally groaned at how awkward he was making this.

Bridger shot me a look like I shouldn't worry because he was stepping in. "It's Eloise, Dad. Word on the street is that you live in the rental property owned by the anonymous author of the *Taylor Tea*?"

And that helped the situation how?

"Oh, Emilia, your landlord, is an author and a florist?" Coach Gable asked.

"No. She's not an author. She's a florist. And yes, I live in her guesthouse," Eloise said, arching a brow at my brother.

"Interesting. I guess we'll see if this visit gets mentioned next Saturday. I'm sure she knows about your comings and goings, which will make writing about our family very easy."

For fuck's sake.

"It's time for dinner," my mother said, wincing at me as if she wanted to make this better.

"Great," Easton called out. "Get your glasses filled on the way to the table."

"This is like a college party tonight," Archer said against my ear, keeping his voice low. "I'm glad I walked here."

I groaned and made my way over to Easton after everyone found their seats at the table. "You don't need to get them so wasted that they won't be able to walk back to the hotel."

"Hey, I'm your best shot at coming out of this in one piece. The old man is pouring it on far too thick, and Bridger has a one-track mind. You can thank me later." Easton tipped his head back and downed his drink.

I'd never been so grateful that Melody was not here.

Aunt Isabelle and Uncle Carlisle had taken her to see Isabelle's sister for the weekend.

We sat down, and Rafe insisted we all raise our glasses once all the food was set down in the middle of the table. Easton took that moment to refill Sebastian's, Coach Gable's, and Randall's glasses because they were shooting the shots back as quickly as he could fill them. My parents were meeting them shot for shot, and I just watched as this shitshow unfolded.

Of course, the dickhead Sebastian found a way to score the seat next to Eloise. The dude couldn't take his eyes off of her.

"To all of our new friends," Rafe said before my father interrupted.

"Miss Eloise is a new friend," Dad said, words already slurring, and I silently begged him to stop talking.

"Are we ever going to eat dinner?" Bridger grumped under his breath.

"Anyway," Rafe said, looking around the table. "It's a Chadwick tradition to finish the bottle of whiskey and break bread when we gather for the first time with loved ones, new and old." He winked at me as if he were saving the day.

We had no such tradition, and he was making this dinner awkward as fuck.

Eloise shot Lulu a look of panic, and she quickly squeezed my brother's arm. "Beautiful sermon, Father. Let's eat," Lulu said.

Laughter erupted around the table as I passed the chicken to Archer.

Platters moved from one person to the next as Randall asked for a refill. Easton poured the last of the bottle for him and opened a second.

This party could hold its own with any college party I'd ever attended.

And I was the only sober one at the table. Eloise was on her second glass of wine, and everyone else was elbow-deep in bourbon, and their words were slurring.

My father tipped his head back and emptied his glass before turning to Eloise. "Tell us, young lady, who we've never met before, what is it that you do for our son?"

Easton fell forward in laughter. "Why are you talking like you're in a Shakespearean production?"

I shoved the basket of rolls at Bridger, keeping my voice low. "Hand these to Dad and tell him to eat some bread."

"Your father has gotten more thoughtful with his words since attending all those Jelly Roll concerts," my mother said proudly.

Sebastian held his glass up for yet another refill and then spoke. "Eloise is our team physical therapist with a dual certification as an athletic trainer. She's quite an impressive woman. And beautiful, as well."

Are you fucking kidding me right now?

I wasn't allowed to admit I was actually dating her because we worked for the same organization, yet the owner can blatantly hit on her at Sunday dinner in front of everyone.

"Thank you," she said, clearing her throat as her gaze found mine, and she looked very uncomfortable.

"Well, athletic trainer is a title that comes with years of experience," Randall interrupted before reaching for the bottle from Easton and filling his own glass. "And she is not the athletic trainer on this team. She's a newbie, and we'll see how it goes."

The nerve of this fucking guy. It took everything in me not to stand up and tell him to shut the fuck up.

"Actually," Coach Gable said, directing his attention to Randall. "It's a title that comes with her degree. She is both a certified PT and AT."

"And very beautiful, as well," drunk Sebastian said with a wink.

"I wouldn't know. I've never seen her before," my father added, and I pushed to my feet and made my way to his end of the table. I reached into the basket that my brother had passed him and pulled out two dinner rolls.

"For the love of God. Eat some bread, Dad." I gave him a pointed look.

"Yes, my loved ones. Break bread and be merry," Rafe said, holding his arms out.

Had everyone lost their fucking minds?

Eloise, Henley, and Lulu started laughing, and they didn't stop.

Everyone at the table gaped at them before joining in.

"I don't even know what we're laughing at, but I'm having a great time," Randall said.

The booze continued to flow, and I did my best to encourage everyone to eat.

I had a migraine because I was watching Richie Rich hit on my woman, and it was pissing me off.

My mother broke out in her favorite song, "Save Me," by Jelly Roll, and my father sang backup. They were completely off-key, yet everyone at the table watched as if they were seeing Jelly Roll perform live and in person at the dinner table.

I excused myself and went to the bathroom, needing a minute of quiet.

There was a knock on the door, and I cracked it open to see Eloise standing there. Cheeks flushed, goofy smile, and absolutely stunning.

"Lulu and Henley have Sebastian trapped in a long story, and I wanted to check on you," she whispered. "No one else is paying any attention. They are too enthralled in the live concert."

I tugged her into the bathroom, pressing her back against the door, before leaning down and kissing her.

"Fuck. I've been wanting to do that all day," I said, after I pulled back.

"I've been wanting you to do it all day, you sexy beast of a man." She poked me in the chest a few times as her words slurred.

"You're a little tipsy, huh?" I smiled down at her.

"Just a little. I'm not used to having three glasses of wine in one sitting." She shrugged. "I wanted to sit next to you, but Sebastian motioned for me to take the seat beside him."

"That preppy bastard is hanging all over you. I can't stand him or his plaid pants," I hissed, and her head fell back in laughter.

"I like you, Clark Chadwick."

"I like you, too," I said, leaning down to kiss her again.

There was a knock on the door. "Mayday! Mayday!"

I groaned at the sound of Lulu's voice, reaching for the door and cracking it open. "You beckoned?"

"I know Eloise is in there, but we're losing Sebastian. He keeps saying he has to go to the bathroom. Henley is trying to hold him off. Your mother is on her second set, and Bridger is getting very impatient about having dessert. Easton is refilling drinks to people who shouldn't be served, and Rafe thinks he's a minister now," Lulu whisper-hissed.

"Fuck." I stepped back as Lulu pushed inside. "What's the plan?"

"You leave me in here with Eloise. You go and make it look like you're coming from a different bathroom and just go back to the table."

"Got it," I said, winking at Eloise. "Thanks, Lu."

"Of course. I left my Superwoman cape at the table. Get out there." She peeked out the door and waved me on.

I didn't see Sebastian coming, so I headed for the kitchen and gaped at the scene before me. Bridger was sitting on a bar stool at the kitchen island, with a large chocolate cake and a fork. He looked up mid-bite.

"They're never serving this shit, and I'm done waiting." He shrugged before shoving the fork into his mouth.

I reached for a fork in the silverware drawer and pulled up the stool beside him. "I'm done with this night."

"Yeah, that's how I feel most days. Welcome to my life," he said.

I barked out a laugh as Rafe's voice carried into the kitchen. "Thank you all for breaking bread and singing Jelly Roll songs. It's been a night to remember of memories being made with both new friends and old friends. Mom, take it away!"

"He's encouraging this?" I said.

"He sure as shit is. But guess what, brother?" Bridger said, keeping his voice low as he forked another bite of chocolate cake.

"What?"

"No one is suspicious that you're in a relationship with your physical therapist, aside from your family. So, it looks like this shitshow did it's job."

I nodded and took another bite. "It's not a relationship. We're just seeing where it goes."

"Well, I think you two are going to an awful lot of trouble for something casual." He arched a brow. "So I'd start figuring this shit out soon because you head back to the city in a few weeks."

I've never felt this way about any woman before, that much was clear. But I didn't know how to handle all these feelings without scaring her off or causing her a whole lot of problems at work.

This was complicated, and we both knew it.

I blew out a breath and nodded. "Yeah. Shit's about to get real."

"Well, you better figure out what to do about it real soon, then," he said over a mouthful of cake.

But I didn't know how to make this work in the real world.

And I knew Eloise was right. This would all fall on her.

And I sure as hell would never be okay with that.

So, we had three weeks to figure out if this was something worth risking a whole lot for.

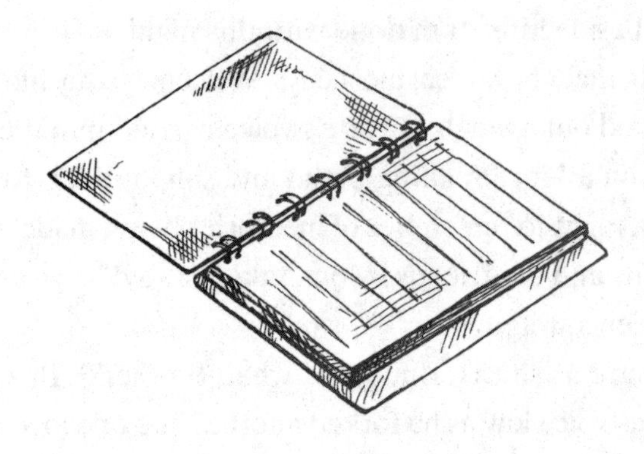

22

Eloise

"You cheated!" I shrieked, as I reached for the edge of the dock and pushed the hair out of my face.

"Don't be a sore loser, Weeze."

Damn, the sexy bastard even managed to be attractive when he was irritating me.

"You took off before me." I feigned irritation.

He reached for my hips beneath the water and pulled me close. Being a tall man worked to his advantage in the river because he could stand with ease, while I had to tread water to stay afloat. My legs came around his waist, my arms around his neck.

"Listen, a bet's a bet. So I get to choose something I want you to do." He smiled.

When Clark Chadwick smiled at me, I felt like I was the only girl in the world. Like he only had eyes for me.

I mean, we were alone out in the water with no one around, so technically, there was no one else to look at in the moment.

But I felt it even when we were out in public or at Sunday dinner or at Booze and Brews with a group of people. Even though we kept our relationship private, Clark's gaze would always find mine. And he'd smile like we had this secret that no one else was privy to.

Because we had this secret that no one else was privy to.

Well, sort of.

I confided in Emilia, Henley, and Lulu. I'm sure Rafe's brothers had a clue that there was something going on.

We've spent every night together over the last ten days—ever since we agreed to just enjoy this time together.

"Please, no pull-ups. My arms are still sore from the last challenge," I said.

His grin widened, water droplets falling from his hair down his face, and his green eyes glistened with pops of gold as the sun shined down on him.

"No pull-ups, Weeze," he said, his voice deep and gruff. He walked forward, and my back bumped into the dock. He glanced around and then looked back at me. "We're all alone out here. It'd be a shame not to take advantage of that."

My chest raced at his words. "What do you have in mind?"

"Put your hands on the edge of the dock and hold on."

I reached up, finding the groove between the slats of wood and locking my fingers there. He stepped back, raised my legs, and hooked them over his shoulders. And before I could even speak, he pushed my bikini bottoms to the side and buried his face there.

I was in the midst of my sexual awakening with this man.

I'd gone from never having an orgasm during sex, to having multiple orgasms a day now. He explored every inch of my body and made me feel things I never knew possible.

I nervously glanced around, making sure no one was there. He lived on a large lot, and his neighbors were set pretty far apart.

He looked up as if he knew exactly where my mind was. "Baby, relax. I wouldn't let anyone else get a glimpse of your beautiful pussy. I've got you. No one is coming—well, aside from you."

I nodded, and my stomach fluttered with his words.

We were crossing so many lines that I couldn't keep track of all the ways I'd broken the ethical contract.

But I let my eyes fall closed as my body floated in the warm water, with the feel of his tongue on me.

He had magic lips. A magic tongue. He knew just where to touch me. How to make me feel good.

I was panting shamelessly as my hips bucked wildly, and I wanted to reach for his head, but I was holding on to the dock.

It was erotic and sexy, and I was lost in the moment.

His lips sucked hard on my clit, just as a finger slipped inside me, and then another. He pumped faster now, and every inch of me started to tingle. White lights shattered behind my eyelids as I exploded on a gasp.

"Clark," I cried. "Yes. Oh my god."

He stayed right there, letting me ride out every single bit of pleasure.

My neck strained against the wood dock as my body went limp.

Clark pulled back, his mouth wet with my release and a sexy-as-sin smile on his face. He adjusted my swimsuit bottoms and moved me down to his waist, and I sat forward and tangled my hands in his hair before leaning down and kissing him.

His tongue slipped between my lips, and we sat beneath the sun, the warm water all around us, making out like teenagers.

I couldn't get enough of this man.

I've never cared for sex before. It had always been sort of uneventful and fast. But this was the opposite.

My body was drawn to his in a way I couldn't explain.

This connection was intense and undeniable.

Like there was no option but to be attached to him when he was near.

When we were in public, it had grown painful to keep my distance.

He pulled back to look at me. "Goddamn, I want to be inside you right now."

I ran my nails along his scalp. "Yeah?"

"Yeah. You're so fucking beautiful, Eloise." His voice was just above a whisper.

"I'm on the pill. I've never been with a man without a condom." My tongue swiped out along my bottom lip.

His eyes widened. "I've never not used a condom either. I've also been tested, and I'm clean."

"I want to feel you. All of you," I said, my gaze locked with his.

"Are you sure?"

I nodded, my teeth sinking into my bottom lip.

This relationship was undefined.

There was a looming expiration date.

Yet this was the man I was willing to go all in on.

It felt right. He felt right.

Maybe it was infatuation or lust, but I wanted this.

I wanted him.

"Hold on to my shoulders," he said before his hands left my hips. He must have pushed his swim trunks down because I felt his skin against mine. He untied the two bows on each side of my hips and pulled off my bottoms, tossing them onto the dock. He walked forward, turning so his back pressed against the wood, and then he lifted me just enough to settle me above the tip of his dick, his hands back on each side of my hips.

"Take your top off," he commanded, and it was sexy as hell. "I want to see your tits bouncing when I fuck you bare."

I untied my top and tossed it onto the dock beside my bottoms. His lips came down over each of my nipples, and I gasped at the feel of his mouth there.

I slid down, slowly at first.

Taking him in and loving the way he felt.

The water, the sunlight, his mouth on me, while he filled me inch by glorious inch.

My head fell back on a gasp once he was all the way in, as it always took a few seconds to adjust to his size.

He shifted me so I moved me up and down his shaft, and his head tipped back to look at me.

My fingernails dug into his shoulders as my gaze locked with his.

"You feel so fucking good, baby. So fucking good." His voice was gruff. "Nothing has ever felt this good."

My breaths were coming hard and fast, and my body trembled as he pumped into me over and over.

Every inch of my body tingled in a way I'd never experienced.

I gasped as the most powerful orgasm ripped through me, just as Clark groaned in pleasure, and we tumbled into oblivion together.

And I wished like hell that we could stay right here in this moment forever.

. . .

"Guess who made the *Taylor Tea* today?" Lulu said, as we sat at the Honey Biscuit Café sipping mimosas as she leaned in and whispered. "At least it's safe to say that no one suspects anything about you and Clark."

"What? *I'm* in the *Taylor Tea*? For what?"

"Ugh," Emilia groaned. "I'm sure Bridger will blame me for writing this one, too."

"Read it to us. I haven't seen it yet," Henley said, glancing over her shoulder at the paper in Lulu's hands.

"My pleasure. I live for this small-town pick-me-up." Lulu cleared her throat. "*Hey there, Roses. It's been a busy week in Rosewood River. On top of our favorite silver fox knocking up his much younger lady friend and the two of them going public with their relationship, Booze and Brews had a sold-out line dancing night this week, and the Honey Biscuit Café had an hour-long wait just to get a seat despite the fact that they still haven't updated their menu, per many requests.*" Lulu's head fell back on a chuckle. "Shots fired."

"This is so good. Continue," I said.

She cleared her throat and waggled her brows before looking back down. "I digress. *We had some out-of-towners here to see Rosewood River's favorite hockey star this past weekend. Were they here to see if he is really healing as well as he claims he is? Or is there more to the story? What some observed was one particular man who seemed awfully interested in our newbie visitor, who's just here to train our superstar for a few months. But she showed him around town, and the good-looking billionaire looked as smitten as a kitten.*" Lulu paused and raised a brow. "It's not Clark they're referring to."

"Don't leave us hanging, go on," Henley said, her eyes wide with curiosity.

"*Maybe the sports healer will get tired of running alongside her sweaty athletes, and she'll run off with the wealthy prince and live happily ever after,*" Lulu said dramatically.

"Ack! Why do they print this crap?" Emilia grumped. "I'm sorry, Ells."

"You don't have anything to be sorry for. You didn't write it." I sipped my bubbly. "Well, it makes sense why Oscar snipped at me when I came in. I'm sure he didn't appreciate the dig about the menu." Emilia laughed.

"Well, then he should take it up with your parents, not you," Henley said. "And the good news is, no one suspects anything with you and Clark."

"Yeah. That's a relief. But also, it's super awkward that they'd insinuate that about Sebastian. He's the owner of the team that I work for. Talk about a power imbalance right there." I shook my head in disbelief. "I don't know why everyone thinks he was interested in me that way. Clark has been over-the-top ridiculous about it, and now this. I didn't get that vibe from him. I think he's just a super flirty guy."

"Girl," Lulu said, as she set her mimosa down and quirked a brow. "That man might be flirty by nature, but he was definitely looking at you like he wanted to see you naked."

The table erupted in laughter.

"I noticed it when you came by the flower shop. He just stared at you when you were talking to me," Emilia said.

"I could feel Clark's irritation during dinner. I mean, even though I had whiskey oozing out my pores because I drank so much, I noticed all of it. And Sebastian Wayburn is definitely interested in you, and it's not in a professional way." Henley waggled her brows.

"Well, I didn't notice it, and hopefully, I don't see him very often when we go back."

"Speaking of that… You're down to ten days until you guys head back to the city. How is this all going to play out?" Lulu asked.

I fidgeted with my napkin.

"I just don't know. I thought it would fizzle. I actually hoped we would not be into it and lose interest, if I'm being honest. But it hasn't. It's good. No, it's great. It's the worst-case scenario." I covered my eyes with my hand because the stress was definitely getting to me.

"Why is it the worst-case scenario? You like him. He likes you. You can keep it between the two of you and just see where it goes." Emilia squeezed my hand.

"I didn't expect to like him this much," I whispered. "And there is no way this works when we leave here. I cannot date a player on the team."

"Listen, I went through something similar with Rafe. I moved to Paris, and we called it done. We couldn't date and live on opposite sides of the world. Yet here we are. It all somehow worked out," Lulu said, her eyes filled with empathy.

"But you guys made it work because he moved to be with you, and then eventually, you both came back here." I shrugged. "We live in the same city. We work for the same team. I would lose my job, which would mean disappointing my father and moving to a new city for a new job, if anyone would even hire me after a scandal like this. Clark's name is one of the biggest names in professional hockey right now. This would be big news. My reputation as a professional in this industry would be ruined."

"Why couldn't you fall for an unknown, unimpressive player?" Emilia teased.

"I mean, the owner of the team is clearly hitting on you. How would that be okay and this be a problem?" Henley asked.

"I don't think he was actually hitting on me. But that wouldn't be okay either," I said.

"I'm sure he'd make it okay and bend the rules if he wanted to. He owns the team. He makes the rules." Lulu arched a brow. "Maybe they could do that for you and Clark."

I shook my head. "I don't think so. It would be bad, and we both know it. I feel like a black cloud is hanging over my head, reminding me that there is an expiration date soon. And I'm not ready for it to end."

"Listen, speaking as someone who had a workplace romance with my mentor, at a company owned by my father, it will all work out the way it's meant to. Just enjoy these last few days, and when you go back, you can keep it a secret for a few months and see how things are once you're back in the city. Back in your regular lives. If the feelings are still there, then you come up with a plan," Henley said.

"That's a good idea. And Clark might just want to call it done when we leave here. He's got his superfans back in the city, and he'll be getting a lot of attention. He might be over this quickly." I reached for my drink because I needed a distraction.

The thought made me sick to my stomach.

I knew in my gut that this wouldn't end well.

And my heart ached at the thought because I never wanted it to end.

23
Clark

"I love coming to Uncle Clark's house because that's where I get my big muscles. The ladies love the muscles," Cutler said, and I barked out a laugh.

My nephew was one of the cutest kids I'd ever met; the only one that matched him on cuteness was Melody.

"Do I gots the muscles, Unc-ee?" Melody asked, looking down at her arms.

"Eloise is the physical therapist. She would be the one to ask about your muscles," I said, as the four of us sat at my kitchen table eating cupcakes.

Melody was on Eloise's lap, and Cutler was sitting in the chair beside me. Tonight was the night that Easton was proposing to Henley, so Emerson, Nash, and Cutler were in town under the ruse of being here for the annual Rosewood River Pumpkin Patch opening this weekend.

"Lolo, do I gots the big muscles?" she asked.

"You both do," Eloise said, stroking the hair back from Melody's face. Archer had to work today, and Emerson and my mother had gone shopping with Henley to keep her distracted.

Easton, Lulu, Rafe, and Nash were setting up whatever surprise Easton had planned for Henley tonight. He hadn't shared the details, just told us to meet at Bridger's barn at 7:00 p.m. I was just happy that I got to have the kids with me today.

"You really do," Eloise said as Melody took a bite of her cupcake.

"Eloise, are you Uncle Clark's girl?" Cutler asked, and I barked out a laugh because Eloise looked panicked about the question.

"Relax. He doesn't work for the press. He's my nephew." I rumpled the top of his head. "Weeze is my friend, and we like to spend time together, so if that makes her my girl, then so be it."

"Well, if you're Uncle Clark's girl, then you're my girl, too. And that means you can call me Beefcake. That's what my family calls me."

"I heard about your handle from Lulu and Henley. That's a very cool name," she said, smiling at him.

"Oh, man, Lulu and Henley are my girls, too. Do you have a handle?"

"I call her Weeze. It's short for Eloise." I chuckled.

"Easy, breezy Weezy," Cutler said before he whistled.

"She's my Lolo." Melody snuggled against Eloise, her chubby little hand resting on her shoulder.

"I like that name, Mel. It's a good one." Cutler looked up at Eloise. "Man, your girl is real pretty, Uncle Clark."

"She sure is," I said. "And she's real smart and funny, and she thinks she can swim faster than me."

"What is this? An episode of *The Bachelor*? I'm sitting right here. And for the record, Beefcake, I can swim faster than him if we actually start at the same time," she said.

"Oh, man, Weezy is throwing the shade." Cutler's head fell back in laughter. "I think I'd put my money on her."

"What are you, a gambler now, Beefcake? And you just jumped ship just because she's pretty." I barked out a laugh.

"Maybe he jumped ship because he recognizes a winning horse when he sees one." Eloise arched a brow.

"I love horsies," Melody said.

"Yeah, that's why I thought we'd take you out to Uncle Axel's ranch and go for a ride this afternoon," I said.

"Do you ride, Weezy?" Cutler asked.

"I do. I love riding."

"Me, too. That's why I wore my cowboy boots today," my nephew said. "And Mel can ride with Uncle Clark."

"Yep. We'll take the horses out for a little bit, and then it'll be time to see what Easton has planned for us."

We finished up our cupcakes and made our way over to Axel's house, as it was a short walk. I scooped up Melody, and Cutler slipped his hand into Eloise's because he was a smart little dude, and we made our way out to Axel's ranch.

Once we were all saddled up, and I settled Melody on the horse right in front of me, keeping one arm wrapped around her, we took off for the river.

Eloise was laughing at Cutler, as he was pouring on the charm, and I just took it all in. I knew there was a lot of unknowns right now. I knew everything would change when we left Rosewood River next week.

But for whatever reason, this moment right here, felt like a glimpse into our future.

I'd never say it aloud because it would freak Eloise out, and my brothers would give me shit for thinking this way.

But when I glanced over my shoulder, seeing her head tipped back in laughter, with the sun shining down above us, and Cutler riding beside her, I swear she looked like forever.

And I've never known what forever looked like, so that was quite a strong revelation.

Maybe I was just feeling this type of way because my brother was getting engaged tonight.

Maybe it was because I knew everything was about to change, and I wasn't sure how to feel about it.

Or maybe it was because I was in love with the one girl I couldn't have.

But I've never shied away from a challenge. And I sure as shit wouldn't start now.

I just needed to figure out a way to make it work.

• • •

"I can't believe Uncle E is proposing, and we get to watch," Cutler whispered to his mama, and she smiled down at him.

Man, my sister was made for motherhood. She's been everything Nash and Cutler were missing, and seeing them become a family together was pretty amazing to watch.

Eloise was part of the family after months of being around us, and meeting my sister, Emerson, made it official. The Chadwick family not only approved, but they loved her. I hadn't shared all the details of our relationship with everyone—obviously, my brothers and my sister knew we were more than friends. I assumed my parents and my aunt and uncle figured out that there was more going on here than we'd shared.

But they hadn't pressed, because I think everyone understood that it was complicated.

Emilia arrived, and Eloise waved her over to where we were standing, and they both went on and on about how good the barn looked. Twinkle lights covered every beam overhead, and hay bales were placed all around the large barn, with bouquets of pink flowers and framed pictures of Easton and Henley sitting on every surface. Easton was going all out. There was a table with donuts and chocolate milk, because that was their thing, and he'd planned a big barbecue after he proposed that Easton was having catered in Bridger's backyard.

Eloise smiled up at me. "This is stunning, isn't it?"

"It is. He's doing it right." I winked at her.

I wanted to pull her into my arms, but we were careful about how we acted in public, so I stopped myself. Our hands brushed, and my pinky finger wrapped around hers.

My mom walked over, hugging all three of us as she clapped her hands together. "I can't believe he's proposing, and we get to be here for it."

"Yeah, this is pretty cool." I nodded.

"It sure is," Mom said, before turning to look at Eloise. "You've only got one week left before you all head back to the city. I know you said you wanted me to teach you how to make my lasagna, so you just tell me what day works for you this week, and I'll get everything set up."

"Thank you. I would love that so much. I swear, I dream about it. It is the best lasagna I've ever had," Eloise said, and she didn't pull her hand away from where mine was connected to hers.

It meant something to me, the way she and my mom got along. The effort that Eloise made to get to know them. The way my family had welcomed her in as if she were already part of the family.

It spoke volumes.

"She has been talking about this lasagna for weeks," Emilia said with a laugh.

"Well, that makes me awfully happy. I would love nothing more than to share this with you. I'm available every afternoon, so you just text me and let me know what day you want to come over."

She nodded, just as the door flew open, and Lulu and Rafe walked in, with Henley's father, mother, and stepfather behind them. My mom hurried over to greet them.

"It's game time, people!" Lulu said, glancing around and smiling as if she was pleased with how good it all looked now that the sun was going down, and the lights were shining on the space from overhead. "They are on their way here."

She filled us in on how it would play out. Easton had told Henley that he was taking her to dinner, when Bridger had phoned them that he had an issue at the barn and needed Easton's help real quick.

"Those are Henley's parents, right?" Eloise whispered to me.

"Yep. Her mom and stepfather flew in from Paris to be here, and her father lives in the city," I said, leaning close to her ear and breathing her in.

Lavender and honey had become my kryptonite.

"That's amazing that they are here for this special moment," she said. "She's going to be so surprised."

Rafe walked over and held up his hand to show us where

he'd gotten several splinters because his girlfriend had him on a ladder all day hanging lights. Lulu laughed hysterically at his theatrics.

"I'm the one she made drag these bales of hay in here, and my back is killing me," Bridger grumped. He turned his attention to Emilia. "I would appreciate that tidbit being left out of your gossip rag, as I'm sure the engagement will be announced in the next issue."

Emilia glanced at Eloise and shrugged. "I don't know how many times I can tell him that it's not me."

Bridger walked closer, crossing his arms over his chest. "An awful lot has been written about us these last few months, and with this cozy friendship you two have going on, I'm guessing you have a lot more information than usual. Eloise has no idea who she's confiding in."

I was about to step in because he was being an asshole, but my mother came sauntering over and shot him a warning look.

"Bridger Chadwick," Mom said, her voice calm and cool. "Emilia was invited here as a guest, and you're being rude."

Mom didn't get angry often, but when she did, you knew it.

He held his hands up in defense. "Fine. I've said all I need to say."

"I told you that he wouldn't want me to be here," Emilia whispered to Eloise, but my mother and I heard her.

"Lulu and I both insisted you come because Henley would want you here." Eloise took her hand and squeezed it.

"Pay him no attention. He gets this way about things, and I'm really sorry. He's always been protective of our family, but he is being incredibly rude, and it's unacceptable. I'll speak to him." Mom smiled at her. "I'm really happy you're here, Emilia. We all are."

I've gotten to know Emilia a lot better over the last few months, which was ironic, considering we've lived in the same town together our entire lives. But she's always been a little on the shy side, and stand-offish with us, and now I was certain Bridger had a lot to do with that. He could be an intimidating guy. But he was a really good man beneath that layer of broody asshole.

The dude would walk through fire for any of us.

But for whatever reason, this ridiculous column had gotten under his skin, and he was determined to expose the author.

"Hey." Lulu snapped her fingers to get our attention and then looked directly at Bridger. "The people in this barn are the people that Henley and Easton would want to share this special moment with. So, lose the attitude."

Bridger smirked as if the whole thing was hilarious before walking away.

Emilia's shoulders noticeably relaxed after he was gone.

"They're about to pull in the driveway," Lulu said as she stared down at her phone where she was tracking their location. "No more talking. I'll look through the crack and hold up my fingers when they're coming in, and we can all shout surprise."

Everyone nodded in agreement, and we stood there in silence. Rafe was bouncing up and down as if he couldn't wait one more minute for them to get there. Bridger was pacing around the barn because that's what he did when he was nervous. Emerson was leaning against Nash, my dad stood beside her, and Cutler was holding Melody's hand and staring at the door like they were waiting for Santa to arrive.

Lulu raised her hand. Holding up three fingers.

And then two fingers.

And then the door pulled open as she held one finger in the air.

"Surprise!" everyone shouted at once.

Henley startled, her eyes wide as she took in the group. "What is going on?"

Easton was already down on one knee when she turned around. She had her hands over her face, and on instinct, my fingers intertwined with Eloise's.

"Hey, Princess," he said, and you could hear a pin drop in the room. "I brought all of our friends and family here so they could be part of this moment with us."

Henley nodded as tears streamed down her face.

"I stopped believing in forever a long time ago, and I was good with it for many years. And then this beautiful woman sets off the alarm at the office and drops a cup of scalding-hot coffee on me and turns my world upside down," he said, and the room erupted in laughter.

Henley swiped at her face and smiled down at him. "Not the most romantic meet-cute, but I wouldn't change one single thing."

"Me either, baby. And I want forever with you. I want to work on cases with you, ride horses, play pickleball, and go out on the river together," he said, pausing to look over at us as more laughter followed.

My brother had dealt with some serious trauma and loss in his past, and the first time he took Henley on the river, it did not go so well.

"Hey, I'm better now," he muttered, turning his attention back to Henley.

"I want to raise kids and travel and grow old with you sitting on our front porch, eating donuts, and watching the sun rise and set. You, Henley Holloway, brought me back to life, and I want to keep living it with you right beside me," he said.

"Ask me," she whispered.

"Will you marry me, Princess?"

"You had me at donuts. That's a hard yes." She fell forward as he wrapped his arms around her and kissed her.

We all cheered.

Even Bridger couldn't hide the grin on his face.

Eloise looked up at me and smiled, her eyes wet with emotion. "That was beautiful."

"Yeah, it was," I said, leaning close to her ear. "And so are you."

Now I just have to figure out how to keep her.

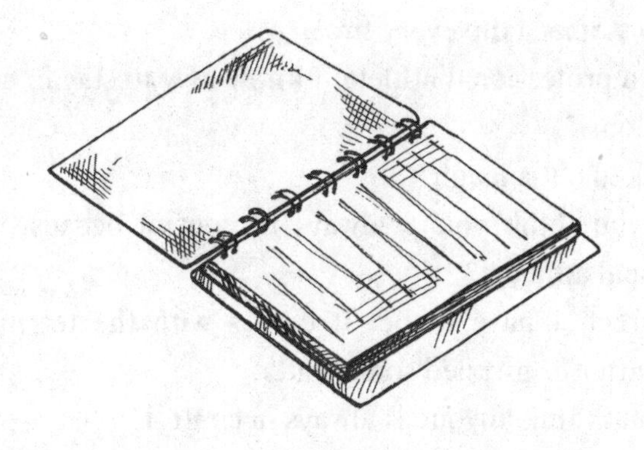

24

Eloise

"It's not going to be that easy to pull off," I said, as he reached for his water bottle.

"You worry too much, Weeze. We'll be fine."

We've had the conversation several times already. We were heading back to the city tomorrow, and everything was going to change.

He knew it.

I knew it.

But neither of us was ready for it.

"You will not be able to kiss me whenever you feel like it once we're back there. You can't just show up at my apartment because, for all you know, a reporter will catch you. We're going to have to be very sly."

His lips turned up in the corners, this lazy, sexy smile that made my stomach dip every time.

"I'm a professional athlete. I know how to stay in control of my emotions."

I barked out a laugh.

"So you think you're always in control because you're a professional athlete?"

"Correct. I have to be. It comes with the territory." He smirked after he guzzled some water.

"I don't think anyone is always in control."

"We can agree to disagree on this one. I can handle it. The question is, can you?" he asked.

"Well, I'm clearly nervous about it, which is why I'm talking it through. But I guess I am not always in control." I arched a brow.

"Follow my lead. We've got this." He reached up and wrapped one hand around the pull-up bar, all cocky and sure of himself.

"All right. Let's test your theory, Hotshot." I moved closer, licking my lips slowly. "Put your other hand on that bar, and don't let go."

"Not a problem." He raised the other hand, gripping the bar with ease.

I ran my finger down his bare chest before stopping at the waistband of his shorts. He sucked in a breath as I moved my way around him, my finger tracing a line to his back and up to his shoulders.

"It must be so nice to always be in control," I said, pushing up on my tiptoes to whisper in his ear.

He chuckled, but the sound was slightly more strained than normal, so I knew I was getting to him. I came back around to his front side, tipping my head back and looking up at him.

"What are you up to, baby?" he asked, his voice gruff.

I dropped down on my knees, running my hands up his legs.

If you'd asked me three months ago if I'd ever have the confidence to do something like this with a man, I'd have laughed.

But I felt empowered and strong, knowing the way that I affected him.

This beautiful, sexy, incredible man.

"I think the question is, what are you *up to*, Clark?" I purred, as I tugged his shorts and briefs down in one swift move.

His dick sprang free, ready for a good time, as always.

His hand came down and stroked my head.

I snapped my eyes up to him. "Hands on the bar, Chadwick. You said you're always in control, so we're going to test that. You don't get to touch me. I do all the touching."

He sucked in a breath and nodded before wrapping his hand back around the bar. "Yes, ma'am."

My fingers gripped his thick erection and stroked a few times as his legs flexed in response, and his breathing picked up.

"It's all about control, right?" I said, my voice breathy as my tongue circled the tip of his dick, and he hissed out a breath. "Don't let go of that bar, baby."

My lips covered him, and I leaned down, going as far as I could without gagging.

"Fuck, Eloise," he groaned.

"Oh, you like this?" I asked, tipping my head back and smiling up at him. His tongue slid along his bottom lip, and he nodded.

I gripped the bottom of his thick cock and stroked a few times as my mouth covered him once again, slowly at first. When he started panting and bucking into my mouth, I moved faster.

Over and over.

My hand was wrapped around his muscled thigh, and I could feel him flexing in response as I took him deeper.

Taunting and teasing.

Bringing him right to the edge before pulling back.

"Fuck. I'm close, baby," His hand came over my head as a warning that he was about to lose control. I pushed it away and stayed right there.

He pumped into me once more.

Twice.

A guttural sound escaped his lips as warm liquid filled my mouth, and I swallowed it down as he continued riding out every last bit of pleasure.

I loved making him feel good, just the way he always knew how to make me feel good.

And then I looked up at him and wiped my mouth with the back of my hand.

"Can I let go now?" he asked, a sated look in his eyes as he watched me.

I nodded, and he reached down and pulled up his briefs and shorts. Before I could process what he was doing, he reached beneath my arms and pulled me up so my legs wrapped around his waist, and he hugged me close.

"I guess I'm not in control when it comes to you," he whispered against my ear, and I smiled.

"That's okay. Neither am I."

And that was the truth.

• • •

"This is much easier than I expected," I said to Ellie as I jotted down the baking instructions in my notebook.

"Yeah, I've made it so many times I could do it in my sleep

now." She chuckled. "And I love that you write it down in a notebook because I have all my recipes written on notecards, as well."

I filled her in on how it was something that I started doing with my mom before she passed away. Ellie listened intently, and instead of doing what most people did, which was to say how sorry they were and how awful that must have been, she did the opposite.

"Okay, the lasagna is in the oven, so let's refill our sun tea, and I've got some delicious cookies for us. Why don't we sit at the table and chat? I want to know everything about your beautiful mama."

I slipped into the corner banquette with a bunch of pretty throw pillows and reached for the glass of tea after she refilled it.

"Thank you so much," I said, just as she set down a plate of oatmeal chocolate chip cookies. "Ahhh… these are my favorite."

"I remembered you said that the first time you came to Sunday dinner, and I put it in the vault." She tapped the side of her temple. "It was all in hopes that one day I'd get you all to myself for a chat."

My chest squeezed at her words.

Ellie Chadwick was the kind of mom people dreamed about. She was funny and sweet, she could cook and bake, her home looked like something out of a magazine, and she took no shit from her kids.

"That was really sweet of you. Thank you so much. You've made me want to learn how to cook." I chuckled. "I literally know how to make grilled cheese sandwiches and spaghetti."

"Well, I learned how to cook as an adult. I didn't know how to do most of this stuff in my twenties." She reached for a cookie, and I did the same. "So tell me about your mom."

"Well, she was brilliant. She was a professor of literature, and she loved to write, as well. She and my father met in college. He was a hockey player back then, and she was an English literature major. She's the reason I love to read, because she had a huge collection of books, and of course, I devoured everything from the romance genre." I chuckled.

"I'm a big reader, too. We'll have to swap recommendations," she said, and I felt my cheeks heat because I doubted Ellie read the steamy books I loved.

She must have noticed my discomfort because her lips turned up in the corners.

"You don't need to worry about anything being too steamy for me. I read it all," she said with a chuckle. "So, you're mama loved to read and to write. Tell me more about her."

We spent the next hour talking about some of my favorite memories with my mother. The Sunday walks we'd always take and our summer camping trips that I still remembered so vividly. I told her about the last few months with her, how brutal it was, and how I was with her when she passed.

She wrapped her arms around me and hugged me tight. "I know how hard that must have been to have to watch her suffer. There is no right or wrong way to grieve. It's just something that you have to deal with the best you can. It can get better at times, and then a memory can slap you right in the face."

I pulled back and swiped at the single tear streaming down my face. "You sound like you know a thing or two about grief."

She nodded. "My sister had a complicated delivery with her first child, and she died shortly after she gave birth. She and I were more than sisters; we were best friends. We talked every day, multiple times, most days." She shook her head, her eyes glossy as she spoke of her sister.

"Oh, my gosh, I'm so sorry, Ellie," I said with disbelief. "And was her baby okay?"

A wide grin spread across her face. "Yes. You know him well."

I searched her gaze with confusion.

"Bridger is my sister's baby boy. Her name was Bridget, and her husband named him Bridger to honor her." She let out a long sigh.

"I had no idea," I said.

"Yeah, it's not really talked about. I mean, we adopted him when I was pregnant with Rafe. His father just couldn't keep it together, and he really spiraled after Bridget's passing. We tried to support him the best we could. He and Bridger never went back to their home after they left the hospital, and they came to live with Keaton and me. But unfortunately, Bridger's father got caught up in drugs and alcohol and did not want to be saved. He asked us to adopt their son, which we did happily. Bridger already felt like ours in many ways, just as my kids would have felt to Bridget."

"What happened to his biological father?" I asked. "Did he ever come out of it?"

"I wish I could say there was a happy ending to his story, but there isn't. The grief just took him down, and he abused his body terribly. His liver failed, and his body shut down, but he just kept drinking. He passed when Bridger was in middle school."

"I'm so sorry. That's horrible. Did Bridger know him?"

"Not really. His father moved out when Bridger was too young to remember him, and they met two times after that, but he doesn't remember him at all. Bridger has a lot of resentment about it, but I do think that's the reason he's so fiercely protective of his family. It's his way of showing his loyalty, I think. But I am going to talk to him about the way he spoke to Emilia. That wasn't okay, and I will be letting him know that again."

I squeezed her hand. "You're such an amazing mom."

"It's the greatest job in the world. I remember the day Bridger came home from the hospital. I was grieving so deeply, but that little boy healed me. I consider him my firstborn. Where his father, Duncan, shut down after he lost his wife, I found hope and love in that little bundle of joy. He saved my life in a way, because there were moments when I thought my heart had stopped beating after she passed, but then he'd scream at the top of his lungs for a bottle, and I'd remember that I was still here. That there was still a reason to keep moving forward."

I nodded. "I can only imagine. You were dealing with this tremendous loss, but then there was life and joy in this little baby that came out of a horrible situation."

"Exactly. So, one thing I've learned during this life that I've lived thus far," she said, taking another bite of her cookie as she thought about her next words, "is that life is filled with ups and downs, love and loss, joy and sorrow. So you've got to treasure the time you have. Tell the people you love how you feel."

I nodded. "That's very true."

"So, you and Clark seem to be getting along very well," she said, as she waggled her brows.

My head tipped back in laughter. I wasn't sure how much she knew, as Clark said he had avoided her questions about it, but he thought she probably knew because she had a great instinct when it came to her children. "We do get along well. I wasn't super thrilled about coming to Rosewood River when my father said I would be moving here for three months, but it's been full of surprises."

Clark Chadwick had been the biggest surprise of all.

"I can imagine you weren't thrilled, not knowing anyone at the time. But look at you now. You feel like a local." She chuckled. "I know this is complicated, sweetheart, but I've learned that the best things in life are not without complications."

I nodded. "I've worked really hard to get here, you know? I'm just starting out. I'm lucky that I was able to graduate from all my years of schooling debt-free, thanks to my father and a few scholarships. But I have no savings at this point in my life, so I not only want this job to work out, but I need it to."

She squeezed my hand as if she understood. "And you shouldn't have to give that up because of the way you feel about someone."

"Unfortunately, the league won't see it that way. I'm an employee, not a player. The rules are a bit different for me."

"And you're a woman in a male-dominated profession. That can't be easy," she said, her eyes filled with empathy.

"Yes. I feel like Randall is just waiting for me to mess up. Every time we speak on the phone, I just get this vibe that he wants me to fail. So I'm going to have a lot of eyes on me when we return to preseason training next week."

"Trust your gut. If you feel that, there's probably a reason." She reached for another cookie and pushed the plate toward me, and I grabbed one more.

"It's not something I can talk to my dad about because he's the coach, and I don't want to put him in an awkward position. So it's going to be challenging because he's always been my sounding board," I said, as that sad truth settled in my chest like a heavy weight. I only had one parent. And now he was basically my superior on a professional level. So that father-daughter dynamic that we'd always had was going to be a little more complicated now that I worked for the team.

Her gaze softened. "I had a really hard time after I lost my sister because she'd always been my person when it came to talking things out. And yes, Keaton is a wonderful husband, but he's also a man, and he likes to get to the point faster than I do." She chuckled, and my head fell back in a fit of giggles before she continued. "So, if you need a good listener, I would be so happy to be there for you. You just let me know."

I imagined this is what it would have been like if my mother were still here. I could talk to her about these things, and she'd just listen and help guide me.

My chest ached.

I longed for something my mother, and I had both been robbed of.

My father had always stepped up for me.

But I couldn't imagine breaking the news to him that I'd fallen in love with his star player.

Because the reality was, I was in love with a man I knew I couldn't keep.

And it was weighing heavily on me.

"I might just take you up on that," I said.

"I hope you do, sweetheart. Because now that we've had some time with you, you're stuck with us. We aren't going anywhere."

My heart raced at her words.

I wondered if that could be true.

If there'd be a way to not only keep Clark, but to keep his entire family.

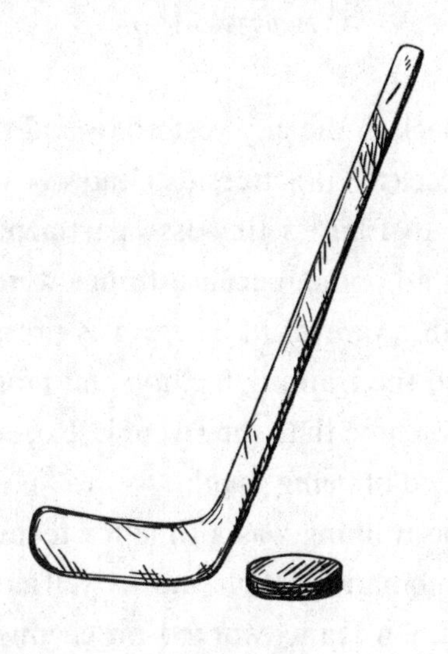

25

Clark

When I signed my two-year contract with the Lions before last season, it was all with the hopes that this would be my long-term home. After having a kickass first season, our team won the Stanley Cup my first year on the roster, but I still had one more season before I could negotiate a new contract.

A contract that was predicted to be a much more impressive package than what I'd originally signed.

I had the season of my life this last year, which was why it was so important to me to come back stronger than ever this season.

And now, I wasn't so sure that my place on this team would be my long game anymore.

Eloise Gable had changed the game for me.

We arrived back in the city yesterday, and this was our first official day of preseason practice, also known as training camp.

I snuck over to Eloise's tiny-ass apartment last night in a baseball cap and a hoodie, because things were different here, and we were both aware of it. There was press and paparazzi constantly around the training facility, and more people would be paying attention here than they were in Rosewood River, and my girl was terrified of being caught.

But preseason training was a time for teams to experiment with different combinations of players, as well as strategizing new plays. This was when teams worked on chemistry and formed deeper relationships.

Real friendships.

We were already there in a lot of ways, but there were three new guys on the team this season and a few who still preferred to keep to themselves, so this was an opportunity to build on those strengths even more.

We played preseason games to test out different roles and tweak some positions, and then Coach would make adjustments before the regular season began.

But this time was all about teamwork and bonding and all the other things that go into being part of a winning team.

"Holy shit, Chadwick. You were not joking about working your ass off this summer," Weston said, as I dropped down from the pull-up bar, music blaring in the background.

"Yeah, our boy definitely did not spend his summer floating in the lazy river back home." Walter Wizowski barked out a laugh. "You're definitely looking even stronger than last year."

We called him Wizz, and he was our goalie, and after last season, many considered him the best goalie in the league.

"Let's see how he does on the ice before we give him a big

head," Sebastian said, as he stood next to Randall and Coach Gable. He must have just walked in because he hadn't been here a few minutes ago.

The dude was inserting himself in conversations he didn't belong in. If my teammates wanted to comment on the work I'd put in over the last three months, he should be happy to see it.

That's what training camp was all about.

But this fucker and I clearly didn't like one another.

"I think they're referring to my big muscles, Sebastian, not my ego." I kept my tone light, and he chuckled.

Weston laughed, completely missing the tension between us, which I was happy about. I needed to keep my feelings about this dude in check. He was technically my boss, as well as Eloise's boss.

It was possible that this was a one-way irritation and that he didn't have a fucking clue that he was rubbing me wrong, because he didn't know Eloise and I were together.

"Let's just keep our heads down and keep working," Randall said. "You best bring you're A game out on the ice today, boys."

"Stick Season," by Noah Kahan began playing, and Weston and I started belting out the lyrics, while the rest of the guys pretended they didn't want to join in.

"You two better hope you bring your hockey moves out on the ice today and not your dance moves," Pete "Lefty" Levine said over his laughter. His nickname came from playing left wing, and the dude was a badass as well as being our team captain.

Randall and Coach turned their attention to the new rookies as I wiped my face with a towel.

"Don't you worry about our moves. We'll be just fine," I said as I waggled my brows.

"What's the deal with Randall being such a dick all the time?" Wizz said, keeping his voice low.

"I don't think he likes that Coach's daughter is more qualified than him," Weston said, tipping his head back and sucking down some water. "He's been making some backhanded comments about her when Coach isn't around."

"Like what?" I asked, my voice coming out harsher than I meant it to.

"Yeah, I've heard it, too. He said she only got the gig because of her father." Lefty leaned in, voice low. "He definitely feels threatened by her."

"Well, it's not Randall's job to tell us to bring our A game. We always bring our fucking A game. And he's being an insecure little pussy griping about Eloise coming on board. Looks like she's worked wonders on Chadwick," Wizz said.

"Agreed. If Coach wants to ride our ass, that's his job. But Randall has been out of control lately. You're lucky you were back in Rosewood River these last few months because he's been more of an asshole than usual lately," Weston said. He and I talked every couple of days, so he'd been filling me in about Randall while I was gone. I just hadn't realized how bad it was.

My blood was boiling that he was talking shit about Eloise behind her back. It was completely unprofessional and disrespectful. Coach Gable would have his ass if he found out about it.

"All right, let's take a break, grab some food, and then meet on the ice at 1:00 p.m. Talia ordered lunch, and it's ready for you in the team room," Coach Gable said, referring to Randall's assistant who handled all the training camp meals and activities. There was a rumor that she and Randall were having an affair, yet the dude never stopped reminding Eloise about the ethical clause in her contract.

It pissed me the hell off.

I glanced around to see where Eloise was, but she hadn't returned since she'd gone off to check out Tyler Cane's ankle injury. He played center with me, and he was a beast on the ice. Go figure that the dude rolled his ankle teaching his little girl how to ride a two-wheeler. We'd all given him shit this morning when we saw it wrapped, and he admitted he tripped over a pothole in the road. Eloise insisted he come get it checked out, and she hadn't come back yet.

We made our way toward the team room, and I said I'd meet the guys in there. I turned down the hallway toward Eloise's office, knowing I could make up a reasonable excuse about wanting to check in regarding my MCL injury without making anyone suspicious.

When I turned the corner, I heard Sebastian's voice before I saw him.

Sebastian fucking Wayburn.

"It was completely unnecessary, but thank you," Eloise said. "Do you get all the new employees flowers?"

"Only the smart, pretty employees." He chuckled, and my blood boiled as I paused outside the door for a few seconds before turning in the doorway and knocking on the open door.

"Hey, I hope I'm not interrupting anything," I lied.

Sebastian stood on the opposite side of her desk with a cocky grin on his face, where an outrageously large floral arrangement sat on her desk.

"No, of course not. Just welcoming our new employee to the team." He winked at her.

"Wow, Sebastian, I don't recall receiving any flowers when I signed with the team." I forced a chuckle as I arched a brow.

"I wasn't running the show when you signed last year." He turned to face me and smirked. "Gift-giving is my love language."

"I can see that. Nice touch. I'm sure the new rookies will be thrilled to receive the personal touch you're bringing to the team," I said.

He barked out a laugh as if I was playing around with him and not completely appalled.

He. Was. Hitting. On. Her.

On my woman.

My fucking woman.

And I couldn't do a goddamn thing about it.

Eloise cleared her throat and turned her attention to me, her gaze softening when I looked at him. "Thank you for stopping by, Clark. I wanted to get an update on that knee of yours after this morning's workout."

"I'm a man of my word," I said, as Sebastian walked toward the door.

"Yes. We've got to make sure our star player doesn't get hurt," Sebastian said. "I'll stop by to finish our conversation later, Eloise."

She nodded just before he walked out of the office.

I dropped to sit in the chair across from her, even though it took everything I had in me not to lock the door and kiss her senseless.

I didn't like this. The sneaking around. The lying. The not being able to claim her and let everyone know that she was mine.

"Hey," she said, as she opened her top desk drawer and pulled out our notebook. "How was practice?"

She wrote something down and passed it to me.

I read the short note.

I'm sorry about that. The flowers arrived, and he showed up shortly after. I promise you, it's harmless.

I nodded and played along with the conversation just in case he was lingering out in the hallway. "Practice was good. Everything feels fine, and I'm looking forward to getting out on the ice this afternoon."

I jotted down a quick note back to her.

You have nothing to apologize for. I don't like that fucker.

She chuckled when I passed it back, and she read what I'd written before tucking the notebook back into her desk. "I'll be there. Looking forward to seeing everyone out on the ice today."

"Glad you'll be out there. You'll get to see us in action."

"Well, you're definitely ready, but I appreciate you giving me updates. Let's touch base after the scrimmage, all right?"

"Absolutely," I said. Her tongue swiped out along her bottom lip, and I groaned internally, giving her a warning look. She laughed, shaking her head as if she hadn't realized what she was doing to me.

"I'll see you later, Clark."

I pushed to my feet and mouthed the words, *count on it,* before holding up my hand and leaving her office.

I made my way to the team room, where everyone was sitting around on the couches and chairs, chowing down on sub sandwiches. I grabbed a plate and joined my boys, where Weston motioned to the empty seat beside him.

"You good?" he asked, obviously wondering where I'd gone.

"Yeah. All good. I just stopped by to see Eloise to give her an update on my knee. She just wants me to check in these first few weeks to make sure everything is still feeling good with us pushing hard during training camp."

He nodded, his gaze narrowing the slightest bit. "She not only healed you, she got you in good shape this summer. You weren't kidding when you said she's a badass trainer, as well."

"Yep. She followed Randall's workouts, as she respects the fact that he's the team trainer, but she tailored them for me, getting me into shape while allowing my knee to recover properly." I reached for my water. "So what do you think of the new rookies?"

"They've got potential. With Bear and Stitch retiring, we need to bring in some strong defensive players."

"For sure," Wizz said. "I was at Bear's house this weekend. I took Layla to his son's birthday party. The dude was already sporting a beer belly." Wizz had a little girl who was the same age as Bear's son.

We all shared a laugh. Robby Baroni, also known as Bear, was one of the best defensive players I'd ever had the honor of playing with. He and Wizz had come up in the league together, and they were tight. I was bummed that I'd only gotten one season with him, but grateful that we shared that Stanley Cup win together. He considered retiring the year before, and to say he was happy he pushed one more year to go on to win the cup was an understatement.

"Hey, he's earned the right to sport a beer belly," I said with a laugh.

I called over the two rookies, who were looking awkward as fuck sitting by themselves, and they came to join us. I remembered my rookie season well, and having older dudes who took me under their wings made all the difference.

They were both coming straight out of high school, so they were young. I researched them both, and they were each a standout in their own right.

They told us about where they moved from, and both seemed to have followed the team closely, so they were aware of our positions and the team stats, which, considering we won the cup last season, wasn't a surprise.

Everyone was watching us.

We listened and talked about the training and what they should expect. We gave them a little shit about how young they were, which came with the territory. But they were definitely more relaxed when we finished lunch. I gave them a few tips for the scrimmage, and they listened intently.

And then we suited up and got ready to get out on the ice.

When we made our way to the arena, I saw a few of the players' wives with their kids, sitting low in the bleachers. We encouraged family to come out during training camp. We'd have a few games where we opened it to the public, but today was our first day on the ice, and Coach wanted to keep it small.

My eyes found Eloise immediately, as they always did. Her father sat beside her, with Randall on his other side. Her lips turned up in the corners the slightest bit just as a big body blocked my view, and Sebastian fucking Wayburn moved to sit beside her.

Weston slammed into me on the ice, shoving me forward and leaning close enough so only I'd hear him. "You don't want to show your hand, brother, at least not with an audience."

I gave him a look that said I had no idea what he was talking about, and he gave me one back that said, *nice try, asshole.*

That didn't take long.

I chuckled before turning my focus to the scrimmage that was about to start.

My hand wrapped around my stick, and I tapped it against the ice a few times.

I glanced back one last time at the stands, my gaze locking with Eloise as I tuned everyone else out.

Hockey had always been my first love.

But it sure as hell wasn't my only love anymore.

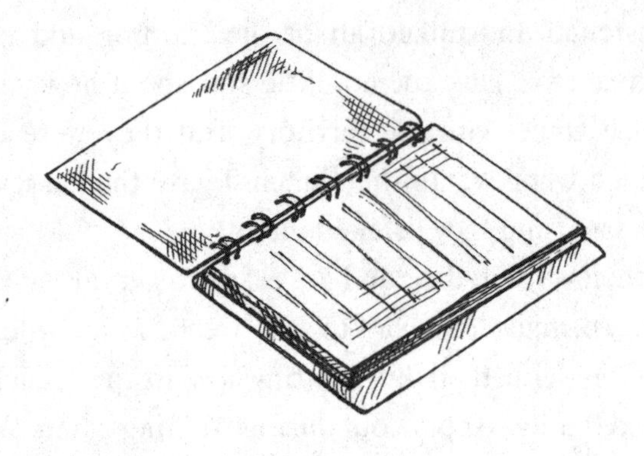

26

Eloise

It had been a week since we'd returned to the city, and we were falling into a rhythm. Clark spent every night at my apartment because I felt less likely to be caught at my place. His apartment was in a big, fancy high-rise, and two other players lived in the same building.

So far, we'd been able to keep things professional at work, and then we'd spend our evenings wrapped around one another.

But it was a struggle spending my days with the man I was crazy about and having to hide those feelings.

The toughest part was not sharing any of this with my father.

Clark's family knew about us. He thought Ryan Weston had also picked up on something, yet I was completely hiding a big part of my life from my dad.

He and I had always been open with one another. We've never had secrets, and I felt extremely guilty about it.

But involving him would be selfish.

If he knew and kept our secret, it could cost him his job.

I'd be putting him in a terrible position.

Yet it pained me to keep something so important from him.

I pushed the thought away and smiled at the beautiful man beside me.

"Why is your bed so comfortable?" His voice was all tease as he pulled me onto his chest and kissed the top of my head. "It's like a cloud in here."

"It's the sheets and the bedding. They're extra cozy," I said, tipping my head back as he leaned down and kissed me.

"You're extra cozy, baby." His fingers interlaced with mine, and he rolled me onto my back and looked down at me. "God, you're so fucking beautiful."

My breath hitched in my throat, and I blinked a few times because I've never felt this way about anyone. This connection was so powerful and all-consuming.

My teeth sank into my bottom lip, and I smiled before tugging him down to kiss me again.

My alarm startled me when it went off on the nightstand, and Clark pulled back and reached for my phone. He turned it off and set it back down on the nightstand, his fingers tracing over my nipples as his sleepy gaze took me in.

"We've got to get up," I whispered. "But I don't want to."

"How about we take a shower together this morning?" he said, scooping me up out of bed and tossing me over his shoulder.

I laughed and smacked his ass. "You know you don't need to carry me. I do have legs that work."

He set me down on the counter in the bathroom and turned on the shower before turning around to face me. We were both buck naked, and I didn't have a self-conscious bone in my body around this man anymore. He made me feel like the most beautiful woman in the world, and I loved how comfortable we were together now. He placed one hand on each side of me on the counter and leaned forward. "What if I like carrying you around?"

"Well then, I can't argue with that. Take me to the shower, Hotshot." I held up my arms and chuckled when he scooped me up. "And then I'll make you pancakes for breakfast."

"Deal."

He set me down under the warm water. There were moments like this with Clark that made me very aware that this was something special. Something bigger than a job or a contract. I pushed the feeling away every time I thought about it because I didn't want to get ahead of myself.

He poured the shampoo into his hands and turned me around, my back to his front. His large hands massaged my head, and he tilted it back just slightly so that I wouldn't get soap in my eyes. His fingers moved along my scalp, and I groaned. We already had sex this morning, and here I was, getting all turned on again when we didn't have time for more than a quick shower and breakfast. He rinsed my hair and turned me around, and we took turns washing one another's bodies. It was intimate and sweet, and I loved that he always stepped out of the shower first and grabbed a towel to wrap me up. We hurried to dry off, and I quickly slipped into my robe and brushed out my hair, adding some product and letting it air dry while we made breakfast together.

It was the routine we'd fallen into since we returned. I flipped the pancakes, while he pulled out the syrup and made us some coffee. My head tipped back with a laugh when he pulled me onto his lap. This was his thing. He wanted to be touching all the time, and I loved it so much. When we were at work, it wasn't an option. But behind closed doors, it was a completely different story.

We shared one plate of pancakes piled high, and I poured syrup over them and cut the first bite, holding the fork out to him. We took turns eating, sipping our coffee, and talking.

"Do you think we'll ever run out of things to say?" I asked, turning on his lap so I could see his handsome face.

"No." He shrugged. "Because I went a long time before I met you, and I want to know everything."

I sucked in a breath. That was the thing with Clark. He was so genuine, and he just said what he thought and didn't hold back.

"I want to know everything, too, Hotshot."

My phone vibrated, and he chuckled when he looked down to see the text from my dad, along with the time. He pushed me up and set me on my feet.

"We'll have to save that thought for dinner tonight."

He leaned down and kissed me, and I wished we could stay right here forever.

...

The day had gone by in a blur, and I was catching up on emails now.

There was a knock on my office door, and I glanced at my calendar to make sure I hadn't forgotten a meeting, but there was nothing scheduled.

"Come in," I called out.

"Hey, you got a minute?" Sebastian Wayburn asked.

I nodded. "Of course."

He strolled in, closing the door behind him.

He took the seat across from me. "How's it going?"

"It's going. Just typing in some notes for a few of the athletes I met with this morning. What's up?" I asked.

He leaned back in the chair, crossing his feet at the ankles.

"Is Chadwick being nicer to you now that you're not only training him?" he asked, and I felt bad that we'd made him think Clark didn't like me.

"Yes. We're all good now. I'd even say he's friendly to me." I cleared my throat because I was uncomfortable about being dishonest about all of this.

"Glad to hear it. And Randall, is he treating you well?" There was an edge in his voice, but I couldn't quite read it.

"Yes. He's fine." I kept my answer short because he wasn't fine. He was constantly picking at me, and it was obvious he didn't want me here.

"All right. I wanted to talk to you about a few observations I noticed in the scrimmage yesterday and thought you, me, and your father could grab dinner tonight so it's not quite so formal." An easy grin spread across his face. He was a good-looking man, and he exuded confidence.

"Oh, er, yes," I said, clearing my throat and looking back at my computer screen. "Let me check my calendar."

"Sure. I know it's last minute. I just need to get out of this place sometimes and thought a nice restaurant would be a more comfortable meeting place."

I already knew that I didn't have anything on the calendar because I was making Clark his mom's famous lasagna tonight. "Yes, looks like I'm free for dinner."

"Great. I already discussed it with your father, and he's free, as well. I'll send you over the time and place." He pushed to his feet.

Sebastian Wayburn was my boss. I couldn't exactly turn him down and say that I was making dinner for his star player instead.

"Sounds good."

He closed the door, and I quickly dialed my father's extension.

"This is John," he said when he answered his phone, which always made me laugh.

"It's your private extension, Dad, so of course, it's you." I chuckled.

"Well, I like people to know they're getting who they're looking for." His voice was all tease. "What's up, Ells bells? Did Sebastian tell you he wanted to speak to us both tonight over dinner?"

"Yes. What do you think that's about?" I asked, chewing on the edge of my thumbnail.

"He said he wanted to discuss some things he observed at the scrimmage. But he also seems to have some concerns about Randall, and I'm not sure what that's about."

"I did wonder why Randall wasn't included in the dinner, but hopefully, it's nothing serious." I cleared my throat.

"He's definitely been more on edge since this last season ended. I mean, it comes with the territory. There's more pressure coming off a winning season when all eyes are on us now. But he's the last guy who should be feeling it, as the players and the coaching staff are typically the people who feel that pressure." He paused, and I could tell he was taking a sip of his coffee because my father drank four to five cups of strong black coffee every day before noon. I didn't know how the man got any sleep at night.

"You seem fine," I said, teasing.

"Yeah, you know I love what I do. Coming off a winning season doesn't make me feel pressure; it makes me feel excited to do it again." He chuckled.

"You definitely handle pressure better than most," I said, because it was true. My father was a strong man. He never complained. He just did whatever he needed to do for the people in his life.

"I was actually hoping to have dinner with you on our own this week. You've seemed a little distant since you got back to the city, and I wanted to make sure everything is going all right. I've always been able to tell when you've got something on your mind, and it seems like maybe you do."

"Yes. I'm good. You don't need to worry about me." I sighed.

"You're the only person I ever worry about. And you don't need to be stoic with me. You know that, right? If there's something bothering you, you can talk to me, Ells."

I closed my eyes for a moment, a flashback from many years ago when I was drowning in grief after losing my mother, and my father forced me to talk about it. He dragged me out of bed and insisted I eat something after days of being down with what I thought was the flu. He said those exact words.

"You can talk to me, Ells."

But this was different. If he knew about my relationship with Clark, it would bring him into an already sticky situation.

"I know that. Everything is fine." I let out a long breath. My stomach wrenched, and I chewed on the corner of my lip. The guilt over lying to my father was taking a toll.

"All right, well I'll see you tonight. Looking forward to spending some time with my girl."

I smiled even though he couldn't see me. "Thanks, Dad."

"Of course. See you later."

There was another knock on the door just as I ended the call.

"Come in."

Clark strode in like he owned the place, closing the door behind him, and all I felt was relief.

His sage green eyes had a way of soothing me.

"Hey," he said, studying me for a moment and standing in front of my desk. "You okay?"

I moved around the desk, brushing past him as I walked to the door and locked it. I turned back toward him, his arms open and ready, and I walked right into them. He wrapped his arms around me, and I breathed him in.

Cedarwood and mint.

"Tell me what's going on," he said, his voice low and deep.

"This is just—harder than I thought it would be."

He held me there, resting his chin on top of my head. "I know."

"I have to have dinner tonight with Sebastian and my father."

He stilled at my words. "Who set it up? Your dad?"

I pulled back to look at him. "Sebastian set it up, but he did ask my father first. I'm sorry, I know we had plans."

"Hey." He stroked the hair away from my face. "You don't need to apologize. It's just a shit situation. But I'm telling you, the dude is interested in you. I can't confront him because he doesn't know we're together, so I can't blame the dude for wanting you—because of course, he fucking does. He doesn't know you're taken."

I groaned. "He doesn't want me. It's not like that. But all of these secrets are making things messy. I don't like it."

"I know. This isn't sustainable, Weeze."

My eyes widened at his words. Was he already throwing in the towel? "What does that mean? You're already over it?"

I took a step back, and he frowned. "Of course, fucking not."

He moved closer, wrapping a hand around my waist and tugging me against him.

"What options do we have?"

"I'm working on it," he said before he dipped his head down and kissed me.

I was so stressed out that I didn't even care that I was now kissing him in my office. He tilted my head, taking the kiss deeper. Both of us were frantic and needy.

He pulled back suddenly, staring down at me, his tongue sliding along his bottom lip.

"Look at me," he said, his voice deep and commanding as my gaze locked with his. "I fucking love you. So whatever it takes to be together, I'm willing to do it. This isn't a fling for me, Eloise. This isn't something that I need to wait and see where it goes anymore. I want it to go the whole way. I want you. All of you."

My heart raced, and my eyes welled with emotion. I blinked several times as the first tear broke free. "I love you, too. I love you so much, and I don't know what to do."

"Don't worry, baby. I'll figure it out, okay?"

I loved Clark more than I loved my job, but should I have to give up my career to be with the man I love?

"Okay." I swiped at the tear rolling down my cheek.

"No more tears. I'll figure this out. I promise." He used the pad of his thumb to swipe the excess liquid away. "Loving me shouldn't make you cry."

"I'm just nervous about what to do, you know? I feel sick about lying to my dad. I feel like Randall is suspicious because he's constantly asking me questions about you." I blew out a breath.

"You locked the door, right?"

I narrowed my gaze. "Yes."

And without a word, he dropped to his knees, looking up at me with those beautiful green eyes. He pushed my skirt up around my waist and slipped my panties down my legs, helping me to raise each foot as he slipped them off.

"Spread those pretty thighs for me, baby. Let me make you feel good."

My breaths were coming hard and fast. Was I really doing this? I pushed each foot farther from the other.

"Good girl. Now put your hands on your desk to brace yourself," he said before he buried his face between my thighs. He pulled each leg over his shoulders, my black stilettos resting against his back, and his tongue swiped across my most sensitive area as I gasped.

He pulled his head back, a wicked grin on his face. "You need to keep quiet, baby. Can you do that?"

I nodded, my teeth sinking into my bottom lip.

He licked and sucked as his hands gripped my ass, and he held me close. My head fell back as my body melted into him.

His lips.

His tongue.

Tasting and teasing me in every way.

I leaned against the desk and tangled my hands in his hair, tugging him closer as I ground against him.

Wanting more.

Needing more.

"Clark," I whispered. "This feels—"

I lost my words as his tongue slipped inside me, and his thumb moved to my clit, knowing just what I needed.

My hands and feet tingled as bright lights skyrocketed behind my eyes, and the most powerful orgasm ripped through my entire body.

I used my hand to cover my mouth as I rode out every last bit of pleasure.

The sensation felt like it would never stop.

And I didn't care.

Neither did Clark.

He stayed right there until my breathing slowed.

He pulled back, setting my feet on the ground and looking up at me, his lips wet with my pleasure.

"I could die a happy man right here with my head buried between those beautiful thighs."

I couldn't speak; my feelings for him were overwhelming.

Powerful.

All-consuming.

He raised each of my feet, slipping my panties back on and adjusting my skirt, before pushing to his feet. I reached over my desk and found our notebook. I quickly wrote out the only words that mattered.

I love you, Clark Chadwick.

"I love you, too, baby. And that's all that really matters," he whispered against my ear.

I just hoped like hell that he was right.

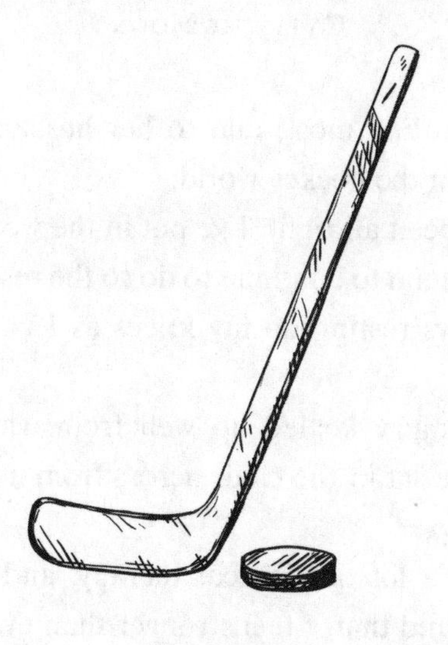

27
Clark

"I'm sure you're feeling the pressure after this past season," Everly said. She was the team psychologist, but she only worked part-time now, as she lived back in Honey Mountain with her husband, Hawk Madden, who happened to be one of the best players to ever live. He was a sportscaster now, so he didn't work directly with the Lions anymore, as he'd been offered a big, fat contract to be a commentator on all the games. But he visited the team a few times last year, pumping us up and talking to each of us individually before the final game. *Once a Lion, always a Lion.* Everly always came out during training camp and preseason, and then she'd been here during the playoffs, as well. They hired another psychologist to come aboard full-time, but everyone wanted to work with Everly because she understood the game better than most, due to her husband being such a prominent part of the hockey world.

"So far, it's been all right. I've put in the work the last three months, and I intend to continue to do so the rest of the season," I said, my elbows resting on my knees as I clasped my hands together.

"And that injury healed up well from what I've heard?" she asked, as she sat in the chair across from me, her notebook resting on her lap.

"Yep. I did a lot of physical therapy, and Eloise tailored my training around that. I feel stronger than ever. Physically, at least."

She studied me for a moment before nodding. "How is it going with your teammates? Is everyone getting along?"

"Yeah, I'm lucky to have guys who feel more like brothers than teammates." I shrugged.

"That's how it should be. That's what makes a team strong. And you're probably very adaptable, coming from such a large family." She chuckled. We bonded over that last year because Everly was one of five, just as I was.

"Yes. My siblings have trained me well to get along with others." I smirked. "My oldest brother missed the memo on that."

She tipped her back with a laugh. "I get that."

"Can I ask you something?" I said, trying to find a way to ask her a question about something that could be perceived as too personal.

"Of course," she smiled. "I'm an open book."

"When you first came to work for the Lions, were you already dating Hawk?" I asked, letting out a long breath. "And if that is none of my business, you can just say that."

"I'm guessing you're asking that for a reason?" she said, the corners of her lips turning up.

"Maybe." I scrubbed a hand down my face. "It's complicated."

Her gaze softened. "First off, anything you say in this room is confidential."

"What if it's something that breaks my contract? Or someone else's contract? Wouldn't you be knowingly keeping something from the team? I don't want to put you in a bad position." I blew out a breath. I needed to talk to someone who understood this situation. My family wanted to understand, but they also thought it was ridiculous that we were two consenting adults, and we couldn't just be open about our relationship. They didn't understand the dynamics.

Everly Madden would understand the situation probably better than anyone.

"I mean, if you murder someone and you confess to me, you'd be putting me in a bad position." She chuckled. "A personal relationship is very different. But we can discuss this without getting specific, if that makes you feel better."

"All right. I appreciate it."

"Okay, so Hawk and I had a past. We grew up together. The Wayburns weren't aware of that when they hired me to work with their star player. I thought I could handle it, but it turns out, all those feelings were still there, though I fought it so hard." She smiled. "I had a lot more concerns than Hawk did, I can tell you that. As a woman in this field, especially a position that is replaceable, it was terrifying to risk everything I'd worked for. There was no guarantee that our relationship would make it once we returned to the real world here, back in the city. And with Hawk being as famous as he was, I just didn't know how it would all play out."

"So what did you do?"

"Well, the short version is that it all eventually worked out. But not without a lot of stress, which is tough on a new relationship. We kept it a secret, and then I considered going elsewhere. But in the end, there are relationships that happen in the workplace. You've met my sister, Dylan. She's the chief legal for the team, and her last name is now Wayburn." She arched a brow and shrugged.

"I knew Dylan was married to Wolf, but I assumed she joined the team after they were married."

"Nope. They worked closely together, and they fell in love, and it was explosive and stressful and passionate all at the same time." She shrugged. "But at the end of the day, they were able to make it work because they are professional at the office and husband and wife when they go home."

"He also owns the team, so I'm sure the rules can be bent for the owner," I said, arching a brow, because we both knew that was the truth.

"Hawk wasn't the owner of the team when we were dating," she reminded me. "He was a player, and I was the team psychologist."

"I'm guessing he had a lot of clout," I said. "Being the rock star that he is."

"He did. And I'm sure that helped. But I ultimately made the choice to stay. I had other offers. I'm sure your..." She paused, tapping her chin. "Your special friend has other opportunities, but if this is where she wants to be, I suggest you both fight for it. You're a very valuable player, Clark. And I believe you're a free agent after this season, right?"

"Correct." I studied her.

"Trust me when I tell you, this team will do whatever it takes to keep you. You are not only a valuable player who scored the winning goal to win the Stanley Cup, but the players love you, Coach Gable loves you, you stay out of trouble, and you aren't in the press, so you're kind of the golden boy of this team. Remember that if anyone is—unreasonable," she said. "Because I'll tell you something that I've learned after being married for a long time to a professional athlete, raising our children, and living our life outside of all of this." She waved her hands around.

"What?"

"This was just a piece of our life. Yes, I still work for the team part-time because I love the Lions, and it allows me to get out of the house and have a career of my own while still being a mother. A huge part of Hawk's life is still hockey, and he loves it—but not the way that he loves us. This team, this sport, it enriches our life. But my husband, our relationship, our family—*that is our life.* It's way bigger than hockey, so at the end of the day, if someone tells you that you can't love the person you love, they can suck it," she said.

I barked out a laugh. "They can suck it. The best words I've ever heard from the famed Everly Madden, sports psychologist extraordinaire."

She smiled. "Life is short. I learned that at a very young age when I lost my mother. And after Hawk came back into my life, I realized how important love is. If you're lucky enough to find it, you should always fight for it. The question is, is she worth it?"

"Yes. Without a doubt," I said, no hesitation at all.

"Well, then remember, she has a lot more to lose than you do. Her job, her reputation, and if I'm reading the situation correctly, and it's who I think it is, it also complicates things for her father."

I nodded, knowing everything she was saying was true. "Correct."

"You're the one who has the most power in the situation. It isn't fair, but it is what it is. Hopefully, it doesn't come down to that. But you could always remind the Wayburns that they've had several office relationships on this team that have gone the distance and caused no drama to the organization. I think that ethics clause is in there to protect teams from lawsuits when there are inappropriate relationships, which, from what I've heard from the rumors around here, there is some of that going on, as well. But a consensual, loving relationship, those aren't threats to the team from where I'm sitting. But I'm also just the team psychologist." She chuckled. "Sebastian and Wolf are good men. Reasonable men. You can talk to them. They consider the players on this team part of their family. They would hear you out."

I blew out a breath. "This is all good to know. I'll talk to—" I paused before saying her name, just to be safe. "I'll talk to my special friend about these options."

Her head tipped back in laughter. "You do that. And just know that I'm here if you or she want to talk. And consider talking to Sebastian and Wolf. It might be better than being outed by someone else."

That was a fair point, but I didn't know if Eloise would consider it.

"Man, I can't tell you how much this helps. I hadn't realized we had options. You know, I haven't been in a relationship in many years, since high school really, so this was all new for me when we were back in Rosewood River. We didn't want to cause a big uproar by saying anything, but the truth is, I love her. She loves me. We want to be together. She only helps my career, as she understands the sport and the training as well as I do. And working for the same team, it should be a good thing."

"I agree." She shook her head. "I think those contracts need to be rewritten. They're old and dated, and there are always exceptions to every rule."

I nodded. "Thanks, Everly. This really helped so much."

There was a knock on the door, and she smiled. "That's my husband coming now because he knows I'm talking to you, and he's a big fan."

My jaw hit the ground. I met Hawk Madden last season a couple of times, but I didn't think he knew who I was. "You're kidding me."

"I kid you not." She walked to the door and pulled it open. "Don't go all fangirl over the guy, baby."

Hawk dipped her back and kissed her.

"I only fangirl over my wife," he said. Then he pulled back and looked over at me. "And maybe I'll fangirl a little over Clark Chadwick."

I pushed to my feet and extended an arm. "Good to see you, Mr. Madden. I'm a huge fan. I know I told you that last year, but I was a little starstruck when I saw you."

"You'd better call me Hawk. I don't answer to Mr. Madden unless I dislike you." He tugged me in for a hug. The guy was a big teddy bear. "Clark, my man, that was some season you had last year. And that final game, you came into your own. From what I've heard from Wolf, you put in the work this summer, and you're coming back stronger than ever."

"Yes, sir. That's the plan." I nodded. "I'm honored that you noticed my games last season, and I hope to make the Lions real proud this season."

"I'd say you're well on your way to doing so." He clapped me on the shoulder. "And did my wife give you some wise advice?"

"She really did. It helped more than I can say. She's damn good at her job."

"She's the best. If you're lucky enough to find a woman who makes you a better man—you best hold on tight, Clark," he said, as he wrapped his arms around his wife and leaned down to kiss her cheek.

I planned to do exactly that.

"Such a sweet talker." Everly winked. "Love you, Hawky player."

"Love you, Mrs. Madden."

"All right, I'll leave you two to it," I said. My voice was all tease.

"Think about what I said," Everly said as she smiled up at me. "I'm here if you need support or just an ear."

I walked out of her office, and my phone vibrated several times in my back pocket, so I leaned down to read the text message from my sister.

Emerson: *Hey, superstar. Cutler and I are looking forward to seeing you soon. I texted Eloise to let her know, as well. Can't wait to see you both. I know it's tough right now, but I promise, you'll get through it.*

Me: *Working on it. Can't wait to see you both.*

My sister knew what was going on, and she was always the voice of reason. My brothers tried, but they would just call me a dickhead and tell me to figure my shit out. Emerson was different. She listened. She was logical and reasonable and understood the seriousness of the situation.

And it was definitely time to figure this shit out.

I loved Eloise.

She loved me.

And anyone who had a problem with it could suck it.

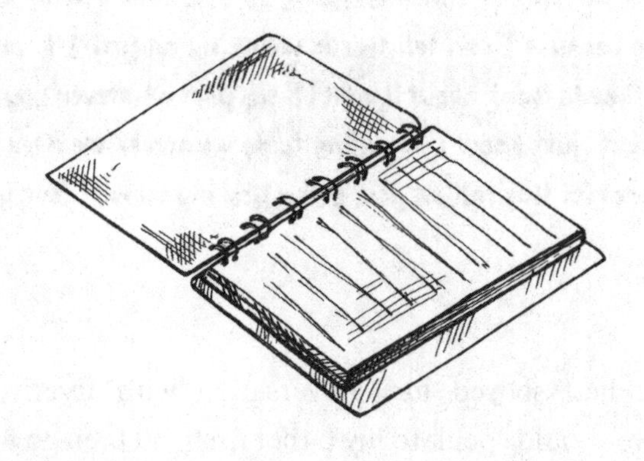

28

Eloise

My dinner with Sebastian and my father had been uneventful, and he definitely wasn't hitting on me. He was just a friendly guy, who was new to the team, and I think he was trying to make some connections and form relationships of his own.

I smiled when I saw the notebook from Clark on my desk when I walked into my office. I slipped it into his gym bag yesterday, and even though we spent every night together, we continued writing in this notebook and passing it back and forth, which I actually loved.

Hey, Beautiful,

Loved waking up with you this morning, but mostly loved showering with that beautiful body wrapped around mine.

I think we should consider going to HR and getting ahead of this because I can tell this is weighing on you. I know you want time to think about it, and I'll support whatever you want to do, but just know I'm willing to do whatever we need to do. I will not let this fall on you, I give you my word. I love you.

XX,
CC

Clark had shared his conversation with Everly, and he thought we should speak to my father first and then go to Human Resources. I understood the reasoning; I just wasn't sure it was a good idea to risk it. They could easily fire me right then and there and then let him ride out his contract for the rest of the season, then not sign him once he becomes a free agent.

They could make us an example.

And yes, I would be devastated to lose my job, humiliated and embarrassed. But if this fell on Clark, as well, how would he deal with that? This was his dream team to play for. He loved his teammates, he and my father were so close, and his heart was here with the Lions. His family lived just outside the city and attended all his home games.

That would all change.

We'd probably end up moving to different cities, and then where would that leave us?

There was so much to lose, and I was terrified to start that ball in motion.

I stared down at his note and started writing him back when a knock on the door had me looking up.

"Come in," I called out.

Randall stepped into my office and moved to sit in the chair across from me. "You got a minute?"

"Yes, of course," I said, noting the way his eyes moved to the notebook. I quickly closed it and slipped it into my top desk drawer before pushing it closed.

"What's that you're working on?" he asked.

"Oh, I just take notes on the progress of the athletes. I document everything in the portal for you to see, but I like handwritten notes for my own personal system."

He nodded. "Never heard of that. It seems kind of silly to me, but if it works for you, I guess you should keep doing it."

He had a way of always putting me on the defensive, but I didn't bite this time. "What can I do for you?"

"I heard that Ryan Weston was asking you for some tips on cardio training during the preseason. Something that you did with Chadwick that wasn't part of my training plan?"

My shoulders stiffened at his tone, and my heart raced as I tried to act unaffected. "He was asking about the cardio that Clark did, as he integrated both road runs and distance swims in the river over the past three months," I said, tilting my head to the side. "Did Ryan come to you about this? I'm confused as to why you're making it sound like I did something questionable. I recorded all of Clark's workouts—the workouts that you requested as well as the addition of his cardio training. That was something he added, not me. I just advised on how not to overdo one over the other and how to build up mileage and speed," I said.

He leaned forward. "I have ears everywhere, Eloise. And let's just be clear, I am the team trainer. I know your father is the coach, and nepotism got you here, but it won't keep you here. You best stay in your lane. I'll advise the players on their training. You just focus on bandaging their injuries, okay?"

I was stunned at how he was speaking to me. I never felt very welcomed by Randall, but this made me feel like we were at war.

Like we were on opposing teams.

"I haven't offered any training advice to anyone. Ryan asked me about Clark's cardio this summer because he said he'd like to increase his cardio during the off-season next summer. I just shared what he'd done as far as building up his runs and swims over a period of time. Clark himself was standing there, and he offered the information, as well. It was not in any way undermining what you do as team trainer. I would never do that. I respect the training plan you have in place."

"As you should. I've been doing this a hell of a lot longer than you have," he snipped. "And don't go running to your daddy about this. If you want to play with the big boys, then you better pull up your big-girl pants and handle it like a man."

Was this guy for real?

I mean, he was a walking HR violation.

"Listen, Randall, I'm not the enemy. I am happy to be here, and I'm grateful for the opportunity. But don't be mistaken, I am more than qualified for the position I'm currently in. I may have gotten my foot in the door because my father works for the team, but I'm here because I'm good at my job. I'm passionate about what I do, and I don't appreciate you undermining my ability, nor do I appreciate the sexist comments you just made. I don't need to '*handle it like a man*.' I just need to handle it like a grown adult, which I'm happy to do."

"Well, don't get all worked up now. I'm just having a real talk with you. It's what we do here. Real talk, Eloise. Man to man—or I guess you'd call it, adult to adult?" He chuckled, and it was arrogant and laced with sarcasm. "You're in the big leagues now, kiddo. You've got to get a thicker skin."

My phone alarm went off, and I was extremely relieved to have a reason to end this conversation. I turned it off and looked up at him. "I have a PT appointment I need to get to. Are we done here?"

"Sure." He pushed to his feet when I stood. "Hey, how was that dinner with Sebastian? You two seem to be getting awfully cozy. You just want to be careful about rumors starting around here. Once they get going, they can take on a life of their own."

This freaking guy.

I narrowed my gaze and squared my shoulders as I stood in front of him. "Sebastian requested to go to dinner with both me and my father to discuss some things that he noticed at the scrimmage. No one is getting cozy, although, from the rumors that I've heard swirling around, you might want to worry about your own issues before making something up about me. But thanks for the warning. Everything you've said today has been noted, Randall." My voice came out harsher than I meant it to, and I wasn't mad about it.

He could be a prick to me if it made him feel better. I wasn't fragile, nor did I expect special treatment. I could take it. He was technically my boss, and I could handle whatever he wanted to throw at me. But I wouldn't be accused of doing something that I wasn't doing, nor would I be threatened by a guy who knew nothing about me.

His face turned a shade of red, and I noticed the way his hands fisted at his sides before he chuckled and narrowed his gaze.

"And you didn't think the team trainer should be included?" He quirked a brow, and I saw the accusation right there in his cold gaze. "Be careful, Eloise. You're playing a dangerous game."

"It wasn't my dinner. I didn't plan it. I was just invited. I'm not trying to play any games. I assumed you two had a dinner of your own."

"Well, you know what they say about making assumptions, Eloise. It makes an ass out of you and me," he hissed.

"I'd say you're handling that part just fine on your own." I moved toward the door and then paused and turned around. "How did you even hear about the dinner? About my conversation with Ryan Weston? It seems like you're keeping pretty intense tabs on me."

My heart raced. Was he having me followed? Did he know about Clark coming to my condo every night?

"It's my job to keep tabs on everyone that works with my players. So, I'd make sure you stay in your lane, and we won't have a problem."

"Sounds like we already do have a problem, and I have been in my lane the whole time." I yanked the door open. "So now I'm going to go do my job, if you're all right with that?"

"I've got athletes waiting for me, as well. Good talk." He chuckled as he stepped in front of me and walked out the door.

I was still stunned as I made my way to the PT room. I worked with several athletes over the next few hours and shook off the conversation with Randall.

He was clearly threatened, but I would just keep my head down and do my job and hope he eventually stopped worrying about what I was doing and focused on his own job.

I made my way to the training room with Benjamin Adams. He was the starting right defenseman. He wanted to show me the way he was doing the leg press to make sure he wasn't putting any strain on his Achilles muscle.

All the guys were just finishing up their strength workout, and the music was booming. "The Humpty Dance" by Digital Underground was playing through the speakers, and all the guys were in a circle around Clark, who was singing all the lyrics like he'd written the song himself. Weston and Wizz were dancing around like fools, and the other guys watched with big smiles on their faces. Benjamin's head fell back in laughter as he stood beside me, watching. When the song came to an end, my gaze locked with Clark's, and he winked.

It was difficult not to stare, as he was wearing nothing but a pair of sweatshorts. His chest glistened with sweat, and the muscles in his arms flexed as he reached for his water.

I could feel someone's eyes boring into the side of my face, and I looked over to see Randall watching me.

I hoped he missed that little interaction, although he just accused me of being inappropriate with Sebastian, so hopefully Clark wasn't even on his radar.

I walked over to him to let him know why I was there and asked if he'd like to observe Benjamin on the machines, as well, just to make sure we were on the same page.

"Yes. Thank you," he said, and relief flooded that maybe this awkwardness would go away quickly.

We both stood and watched as the group of guys around us cracked a few jokes and finished their workout.

"Hey, Doc, why don't you join us for happy hour in a little bit at the Lion's Gate across the street," Weston said, wiping his face with a towel. "It's tradition to celebrate the end of training camp."

"Yeah, Randall and your dad are coming. It's tradition." Wizz chugged from his water bottle.

Clark stayed quiet, and I noted the way Randall watched him before turning to me. "You should come. It's team bonding, and you're part of the team, *Doc*." Randall accentuated the nickname.

I forced a smile. "Sounds good. I'll be there."

Randall's phone vibrated, and he glanced at the screen and then walked out of the gym.

"All right, let's go grab a shower so we don't close the place down with our stench," Clark said with a laugh before turning his attention to me. "See you there, Weeze."

I left the training room and went to meet my father, who was just ending a call.

"Please tell me that you're going to the Lion's Gate," I said, as I stood in his doorway. "I just got invited, and I'm not going unless you go."

He barked out a laugh. "It's a team thing. You're going. Sebastian is going, too, which is new, because Wolf never went when he was running the show. But I think Sebastian wants to be more involved than his brother was."

I closed the door and sat down in the chair across from him. "Randall knows that we went to dinner with Sebastian, and he seemed pretty offended that he wasn't included."

Dad arched a brow. "That's not really our problem. That's between them."

"Well, I think he thinks I should have said something. He is my boss, after all."

"Randall is old-school. He's stuck in his ways and can be an arrogant prick, so most people tolerate him," he said, keeping his voice low. "But he's one of those guys who always keep score of what everyone else is doing, you know? So I'm not surprised he found out about the dinner."

That's the understatement of the year.

"How do you think he even found out about the dinner?" I asked, trying to keep my voice steady and unaffected. I did not want my father to know that Randall and I weren't exactly getting along. But I was concerned that he seemed to be keeping tabs on me, and I wanted to know if this was normal behavior for him.

My father sighed as if he wasn't sure he wanted to say more. But then he leaned forward, his voice quieter than usual. "I'm fairly certain Randall is having an affair with Talia, his assistant. It's none of my business, and I don't want to get involved in other people's private lives. But he appears to be off lately, and maybe he's just paranoid that people are talking about it."

"Okay," I said, studying him because he clearly had more to say.

"I think he gets a lot of information from her. He's that guy, you know, the kind of guy who likes to have something on everyone around him. So just keep your head down and stay out of his hair."

"I thought they had the strict rule about the ethics clause in our contracts?" I asked, because it was fairly hypocritical of Randall to be calling everyone else out when he himself was having an extramarital affair.

"They do. But Randall grew up with Duke Wayburn, who passed the torch down to his son, Wolf, before they passed it to his younger son, Sebastian. So Randall knows he has that friendship in his pocket, which is why I think Sebastian isn't a big fan of his." He shrugged. "But keep all of this in the vault. It comes with the territory, Ells Bells. Office politics are not something new. Just be aware, and don't give him anything to use against you. That's how I've survived all these years." He chuckled, and my stomach twisted in knots.

Because if he found out about me and Clark, he would most definitely use it against me.

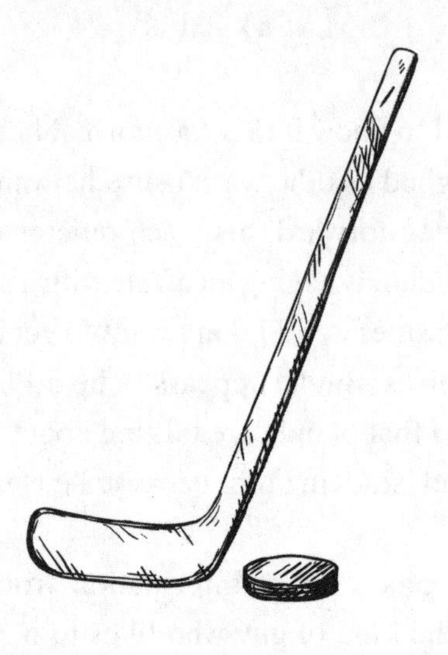

29
Clark

After our night out at the Lion's Gate, Eloise definitely felt like part of the team. The guys loved her. I just sat back and let her impress the shit out of everyone.

She was witty as hell, knew as much about hockey as we did, and took no shit.

But now, she was on everyone's radar.

"Chadwick, are you going to put the good word in with Doc for me?" Adams said, a ridiculous smirk on his face.

I already told them that she was off-limits. I had a feeling they were able to read between the lines, knowing there was more to it than just her being Coach's daughter. It was obvious we were close, just by the way we interacted.

I rolled up my towel and snapped it against his leg. We just finished practice and showered. “No interoffice fraternizing, dickhead.”

Weston howled in laughter. “Wolf met his wife working here, so that rule is slightly flawed.”

“Didn’t Everly Madden marry Hawk after joining the team?” Drew Parsons, one of the new rookies, asked. He was blending well with the team. So was the other rookie, Scotty Barton.

“I don’t care. You can’t date her,” I said, looking at each of them, letting them know I wasn’t kidding around.

“Awww… man,” Adams said, reaching into his pocket and slapping a twenty-dollar bill in Wizz’s hand. “You were fucking right. He’s a little too protective.”

“Fuck off. We’re friends.” I turned my back to them, pulling my hoodie over my head so I wouldn’t have to look at them.

“Then let’s go out tonight. Andrea has some friends in town, and they want to meet you,” Weston said. Andrea was a woman he’s had an on-and-off relationship with for years.

“Can’t do it tonight. I’ve got plans.”

He smirked. “You’ve had plans every night since you came back from Rosewood River.”

I shook my head. “Just focused on the season.”

“Dude, just know, we’ve got your back. You do your thing, all right?” He clapped me on the shoulder.

“Wait, if they’re just friends, does that mean I can ask her out?” Scotty asked as his lips turned up in the corners. “I’m a rookie. I’m only here for the year unless a miracle happens. I’d switch teams for a girl like Eloise.”

I picked up my dirty socks and threw them in his face as he ran around, laughing like an asshole.

“You’re barely out of high school, Barton. She’s a bit out of your league.” I chuckled.

“I’m kidding! I’m kidding!” He held his hands up. “I just

wanted to make sure that twenty dollars was justified. But for the record, the ladies love this baby face."

I flipped him the bird as all the guys howled in laughter.

"Hey, remember, my sister and nephew are coming into town tonight. So let's put on a good show for the little guy tomorrow, 'cause he's coming to watch us."

"Beefcake will be in the house!" Weston said, cupping his hands together to make his words louder.

"Is his name seriously Beefcake?" Parsons asked.

"It's his handle. He's one cool cat," I said. "And the little dude loves hockey, so let's show him a good time."

"He's the coolest kid I've ever met," Weston said. "He came to a few games last season."

"I'm sort of partial to that little angel, Melody," Lefty said. "She was cute as hell, the way she wanted me to carry her all around."

"That's because your beard was grown out, and she thought you were Santa." Weston chuckled, dodging the shoe Lefty chucked at him.

"Hey, the ladies love my beard. It's an added bonus when I take them on a trip to pleasure town." He waggled his brows, and laughter erupted.

"That is more information than I ever wanted to know about you and your overgrown beard." I barked out a laugh. I held my hand up and high-fived the guys before draping my gym bag over my shoulder and making my way out to my truck.

I sent a text to Eloise. I hated that I couldn't just go pick her up and drive her to my place. I didn't think sneaking around would be a big deal, but I was wrong.

I hadn't been in a relationship in a very long time. This was something special, and I wanted to share it.

Wanted to be open about it.

Me: *Hey, Weeze. I'm heading home. Emerson and Cutler are already there, if you want to head over.*

Weeze: *<screenshot of her and Cutler>*

Weeze: *Emerson called me an hour ago to say she was here, so I put on a baseball cap, some big sunglasses, and came over. She's got dinner in the oven, so it'll be ready when you get here.*

Me: *Sounds good. See you soon. Love you.*

Weeze: *Love you more. <heart emoji>*

I drove the short distance to my place, parked underground, and took the elevator up to my floor.

When I pushed the door open, Cutler was already sprinting toward me. "Uncle Clark is in the hizzle!"

I couldn't help but laugh, because this kid was hilarious without even trying. I bent down and wrapped him up in a hug. "Hey, Beefcake. I'm glad you're here, buddy."

"Are you kidding? I can't wait to watch you on the ice tomorrow. I know the Lions are going to win the Stanley Cup again this year."

"We're going to give it our best shot, that's for sure." I pushed to stand just as Emerson walked over and hugged me.

"Nice to see you, brother."

"Yeah, I'm glad you guys could get away. I wish Nash could have come," I said.

"He's bummed he couldn't make it, but he's glad we could sneak away. He knows how much Cutler wanted to see you out on the ice, and I just thought you and Eloise could use some support." She smiled at me, and I could feel her concern.

Eloise came out of the kitchen, and I rushed her, dipping her back and kissing her hard. I hadn't seen her since this morning, and I'd missed her.

I missed a woman I'd seen just this morning.

That was a new one for me.

"Missed you, baby," I said, when I pulled back, her cheeks flushed as her lips turned up in the corners.

"Missed you, too, Hotshot."

Cutler's head tipped back in a fit of giggles. "Man, my uncle's got it bad for his girl."

"Damn straight, Beefcake." I shot him a wink as Eloise smacked my ass and chuckled.

"Come on, you're probably starving, and dinner's ready," my sister said.

We took our seats at the dining room table, and Emerson and Eloise carried the chicken and potatoes out and set them down. The salad and bread were already out, and I took the seat beside Eloise while Cutler and Emerson took the chairs across from us.

"This looks great. Thanks so much for cooking. I would have been happy to get takeout," I said, as I piled food on my plate.

"I know. But I love cooking, and I thought you both might want a home-cooked meal after working all day."

"And we made you unicorn Krispies," Cutler said over a mouthful of potatoes. My sister chuckled and arched a brow to remind him to finish chewing before he spoke, but he just gave her this corny smile, and she was putty in his hands.

"What are unicorn Krispies?" Eloise asked, as she scooped some salad onto her plate.

"Only the best treats in the whole wide world. Did you know my mama is the best baker and the best doctor, too?" he asked.

Emerson was a pediatrician back in Magnolia Falls, and baking was her favorite hobby when she wasn't working or with her boys.

"I did know that," I said. "I've known her my whole life."

That earned me a laugh and a high-five across the table from my nephew.

"Man, Uncle Clark, I like seeing all the tall buildings from your place."

My condo had nice views of the city, and the sun was just starting to go down, so everything below would be lit up soon. It hit me that it was the first time Eloise had ever been to my place.

The woman I loved had never been to my home, which was wrong in a million different ways.

"Yeah? It's pretty cool seeing the whole city from up here. What do you think, Weeze? You've never been here."

She smiled, and her hand found mine beneath the table. "It's gorgeous."

"What? Eloise has never been to my uncle's house. Why? You're his girl, right?"

Emerson arched a brow at Eloise and me as if to say, *good luck explaining this mess to him*.

"Well, I've seen it on FaceTime many times, but Uncle Clark usually comes to my home." Eloise shrugged.

"Oh. Can you see the city from your house, too?" he asked, before forking some chicken and popping it into his mouth.

"No. My place is small." She chuckled. "But Uncle Clark is sort of famous here in the city, so we just wanted to be careful about people seeing us together, and that's more likely to happen if we're at his home."

"Oh, boy." Emerson raised a brow as she leaned back in her chair and reached for her glass of wine. "That's going to open up a whole lot of questions."

"My uncle is a hockey superstar for sure," Cutler said, setting his fork down as his little brows cinched together. "But superstars can be seen with their girls. My uncle Romeo is a famous boxer. He was the champ in his last fight. And he loves Aunt Demi, and the whole world knows it. You don't want the whole world to know about you two?"

I glanced over at Eloise, and all I saw was sadness in her eyes as she took in his words.

"I do want the whole world to know it, buddy. But it's a little complicated." I reached for my water and squeezed her hand.

"Oh, I know about that," Cutler chuckled and shook his head. "All of my uncles are complicated people."

We all laughed at that, and I shrugged. "We're trying to figure it out, little man."

"I remember when my mama almost moved away, and me and my pops were going to be real sad without her." He looked up at my sister like she set the sun. "Do you remember that, Mama?"

"I do, my love," she said.

"Man, my pops was being so silly."

"What happened?" Eloise asked.

"I almost took a job on the other side of the country back then. Nash and I just weren't sure what to do." She shrugged.

"But me and my pops realized that it didn't matter where we lived." He laughed and shook his head. "We were a family, and that's all that really mattered, right, Mama?" he asked.

"Exactly. So, I was at a hospital that I thought was my dream job, and I was miserable without my boys. Then there was a knock at the door, and there they were, standing there with their suitcases." Her eyes were wet with emotion at the memory.

Eloise had her hand on her chest as she listened intently.

"We told her that we go where she goes," Cutler said. "But Mama missed Magnolia Falls, and she's the best doctor there, so she wanted to go back home. But I get to come to the city to see my uncle Clark now."

"Wow. That's the sweetest thing I've ever heard," Eloise said.

"So why can't all the people see you two together?" he asked, his gaze bouncing between us.

I was going to give him some bullshit short, kid version, but my girl jumped in.

"So, I work for the Lions, too, and we aren't allowed to date people we work with." Eloise shrugged. "I would most likely lose my job if they found out that we were together, and Uncle Clark could get kicked off the team next year if they found out."

Cutler's eyes were wide as he listened. "Oh. That's not fair. That's not fair at all."

"I agree," Emerson said, her gaze empathetic.

"That's really silly, though, isn't it?" my nephew asked, but he didn't wait for an answer. "Because you can't help who you love, right? And it's not your fault you found the person you love at work. You spend a lot of time there, so I think it's a real silly rule."

I barked out a laugh. "I think it's a real silly rule, too."

"So nobody that works for the team likes each other that way?" he asked, and the question was so innocent and genuine that it made my chest squeeze. This little seven-year-old boy wanted to fix this situation for us.

"Well, there are two couples there that fell in love and got married. But one of them owns the team, and the other one is probably the best player to ever live," I said, trying to make sense of it all myself.

His mouth fell open. "What? This is great. My uncle is one of the best players to ever live. And other people didn't lose their jobs before you. So what are you waiting for?"

Emerson fell forward in laughter, and Eloise and I did the same.

"Wish it were that simple, Beefcake. But Weeze is new to the team, and her dad's the coach, so it's a little messy," I said.

"We don't want to cause any problems or get into trouble, you know?" Eloise shrugged.

"I don't think you're causing any problems. Don't you love each other?" he asked. "It sure seems like you do."

"Very much," Eloise and I said at the same time, which caused a wide grin to spread across his face.

"That's all that matters. You're a family now. And my pops says sometimes rules are meant to be broken. This seems like a good reason to break the rules." He reached for his glass of milk, setting it down as a milk mustache settled on his lip.

"Yeah, Beefcake. This does seem like a good reason to break the rules." I winked.

This kid was onto something.

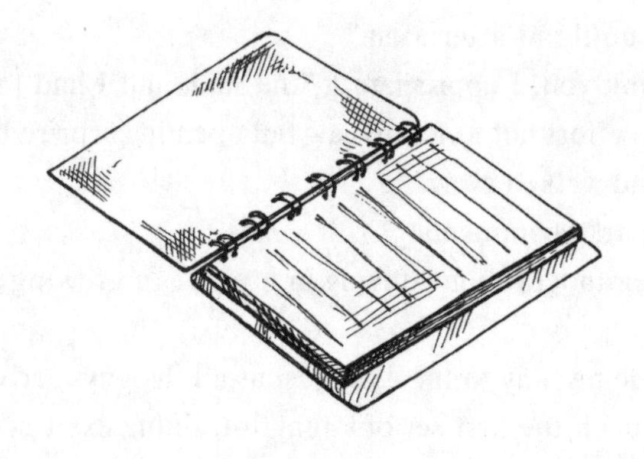

30
Eloise

I spent the night at Clark's for the first time last night, and I didn't feel anxious about it. Spending time with Emerson and Cutler helped me to see things more clearly.

I was starting to think that coming forward about our relationship might be the best thing to do. Sneaking around wasn't really in my nature.

And keeping this from my father made me feel physically ill.

I just needed to figure out the best way to do it.

I was sitting at my desk, the door open, when Randall poked his head in. "Hey, can you oversee the workout this morning? Something came up."

He was unusually pleasant, which was a nice surprise.

"Of course. I'd be happy to. I don't have anyone on my schedule until this afternoon."

"Thank you. I appreciate it," he said, and I had to make a conscious effort not to let my jaw fall open in surprise before he turned and walked away.

No snarky comments.

No reminders about staying in my lane or growing a thicker skin.

I made my way to the gym, just as all the guys arrived. I led them through the first set of strength-training exercises as they belted out the lyrics to "Mr. Brightside" by The Killers as it piped through the speakers.

"Is it just me, or is it much more pleasant having Doc here instead of the grump?" Weston said, and laughter erupted around the gym.

Clark's gaze found mine, and he smiled, and my stomach fluttered in response.

This man affected me in ways I couldn't explain.

"I couldn't have said it better," Lefty said, tossing me a wink before clapping Clark on the shoulder as they switched machines with one another.

"Stay focused on the workout, please," I said, trying to appear serious when I was fighting back a laugh.

"Doc is all business!" Wizz said. "I dig it."

They took a break to drink some water between sets, and Weston was the first to start the questions. "What was Coach like as a dad? Was he a hardass?"

"Nope. He was kind of a softy with me, aside from expecting me to work hard at school."

"Are you serious?" Adams bellowed. "That dude scares the shit out of me when I'm on the ice. He shows no mercy."

Now it was my turn to laugh. "He's supposed to be that way when he's at work. But at home, he was just—a really good dad."

Lefty scratched at his scruffy beard. "Damn. I'm going to stop talking shit behind his back. I never pictured him at home. The man haunts my dreams when he's shooting me those daggers to get my head in the game."

More laughter.

"Well, anyone who can scare the shit out of Lefty should win coach of the year. It's his job to get your ass moving," Clark said as he motioned toward the machines. "We need to get one more set in before we get out on the ice. Beefcake is expecting a good showing, so let's get this done."

I sat there with my notebook, writing down the workout they completed to upload into the portal later for Randall.

Once they finished their last set, they went to grab some lunch that Talia had brought in for them before they headed out to the ice.

Clark and I were in the back of the group, and after they turned one way, he pulled me down a little hallway in the opposite direction and pushed me up against the wall and kissed me. When he pulled back, he stroked the hair away from my face.

"Hey, Weeze," he said.

"Hi." I sighed, as I ran my fingers over his scruff. "You're getting a little bold, huh?"

"No one is around, and I needed to kiss you."

This man had a way of stealing my breath by simply existing.

I was this weird mix of elated and terrified when it came to my feelings for him.

I've never felt this way about anyone before. I wished I could just enjoy it and be in the moment, but the fact that it was a secret and that there was a lot at risk for both of us made it so complicated.

"Yeah?"

"That's my favorite part about knowing you're mine," he said, his green eyes locked with mine. "That I get to kiss you whenever I want to. But there's so much more I want to do with you, Eloise."

"What do you want to do?" I whispered.

"I want to take you to dinner. I want to pump your gas for you and hold your hand in public. I want to send flowers to you at work and take you to lunch in the middle of the day. And I want the whole fucking world to know that you're mine."

My breath caught in my throat, and my teeth sank into my bottom lip. "I like the sound of that. We just need to figure out how to do this."

He nodded. "Agreed. Even Cutler thinks the whole thing is ridiculous."

I chuckled. "He's a smart kid."

"I know you're nervous, but we'll figure it out. I won't let this fall on you."

"Randall is looking for a reason for me to leave, and apparently, he's good friends with Duke Wayburn. So giving him anything against me is not going to fair well for me. And what if they turn this on you, and you get cut from the team after this season for violating the contract?" I blew out a breath. "This is our reality, Clark. Are you sure you wouldn't resent me if you didn't get to play for the team that you love? We would be forcing their hand. They'd have to do something."

He scrubbed a hand down his face. "I'm not letting this fall on you."

"Listen, we don't have to decide this right now. You go grab some food, and I'll meet you out on the ice, okay? Let's give Beefcake a good show," I said.

"Count on it, baby." He leaned down and kissed me. "Love you."

"Love you," I said, as he leaned closer, and all I wanted to do was get lost in this man.

But this wasn't the time or the place.

I pressed my hands against his chest, my words breathy. "Go, Hotshot."

His lips turned up in the corners and he took a step back. "See you soon."

I went back to my office, ate my salad at my desk, and typed in the workout from today for Randall, along with some notes about their progress.

I met Emerson and Cutler out on the bleachers and took the seat beside them. My dad came over and said hello, as he'd met them at a couple of games last season.

My father took his place down by the ice. I stayed seated beside Emerson, and Cutler stood when the guys came out onto the ice. I scanned the room and noticed Sebastian was here, but I was most surprised that Randall hadn't shown up. He must have something going on today because he never missed practice or time on the ice.

The next hour was spent rotating players as they took turns scoring. Clark definitely stood out, and after both of his goals, he held his arm up and waved at Cutler.

His gaze always found mine.

Clark took off his skates and came over to see Beefcake and Emerson before he hit the showers. They had to head home today as Cutler had to get back to school, and Emerson needed to get back to work. It was a short trip, but I was grateful I got to spend some quality time with them.

"Listen, I want you to call me if you need to talk, okay?" Emerson whispered so only I would hear her. "It's going to all work out. You just need to have faith in that. But I know it's uncomfortable right now, and I hate this for you. For both of you."

I nodded. "Thank you so much. I've loved having this time with you guys. Drive safely, and text me when you get home, okay?"

I gave her a hug and then bent down and wrapped my arms around Cutler. "Love you, Beefcake."

"I love you, Eloise Gable. You're my girl. Don't you forget that," he said, tossing me a wink.

This kid had more charm in his pinky finger than most grown men had in their whole bodies.

I chuckled and waved goodbye as Clark walked them to their car.

I headed back to my office to finish up a few things before I made my way home for the day. I spent the next hour checking emails and getting caught up on some admin tasks.

Just as I was shutting down my computer, my desk phone rang.

"Hello," I said.

"Eloise, this is Sebastian. I need to see you in my office right now, please. It's urgent."

He wasn't his normal, friendly self, which immediately put me on edge.

"Um, sure. I'll be right there."

He ended the call abruptly, and I reached for my purse and made my way to the admin offices one floor above mine.

I'd never gone to his office before, but I knew it was two doors down from my father's. When I opened the door, a woman sitting behind a large cherry wood desk looked up at me.

"Hi, Eloise, they're expecting you." She pushed to her feet and led me to a closed door before knocking and pushing it open.

They're expecting you. As in more than one person.

My stomach tightened immediately when I saw Sebastian, my father, Randall, and Scarlett, the head of Human Resources all sitting there.

The door closed behind me, and I stood there awkwardly, my father's gaze locked with mine.

I saw the hurt in his eyes.

The disappointment.

He knew. They knew.

A pit settled deep in my stomach, and I clasped my hands together to try to stop them from trembling.

Sebastian motioned for me to take the only open seat, between my father and Randall.

"Eloise, we've had something brought to our attention, something that is against team policy and cause for immediate termination if so proven. We'd like to hear from you if this is true, and Scarlett is here as the human resource representative. Your father was called in as he is the coach of this team, and he'll have to be involved in how this affects his player. The fact that you're his daughter involves him in a unique way." Sebastian's words were not delivered with any anger, and I saw no judgment in his eyes.

I couldn't say the same for everyone else.

There was a lot of mixed emotions in this room.

Excitement radiated from Randall. The man had never shown any sort of joy, yet in this moment, he exuded it.

Scarlett appeared uncomfortable, but I couldn't tell if it was with me or just the fact that she'd been dragged in here.

And my father—he was impossible to read. He looked almost wounded, and I felt a crack in my heart before he even spoke a word. I tried to swallow over the thick lump in my throat, but it was difficult.

"Which is why nepotism is always a bad idea in the workplace," Randall said, as he glared at me, making my stomach wrench even more.

"Well, you knowing my father your entire life didn't hurt when you applied for this position all those years ago." Sebastian arched a brow as I fidgeted with my hands and stared at my father, who wouldn't look back at me.

"I was more than qualified for the position as team trainer," Randall hissed.

"And Eloise is well qualified for the position as physical therapist, as well as trainer, with her dual certification," Sebastian countered.

Randall handed everyone a thick stapled packet, and I looked over, recognizing the handwriting and realizing that it was a copy of the notes that Clark and I had written to one another. It felt as if the blood drained from my body.

How did Randall get this?

Had he gone through my desk?

Had he read what we'd written?

This was a violation in the worst way. Our private thoughts and feelings were handed out for everyone to read.

It was reprehensible.

"So I've already read you the most incriminating letters that Eloise and Clark have exchanged in their little love letter of a notebook, but I made copies of every entry for you all to have."

No.

Nooooo.

My face heated, and my stomach twisted so violently, I thought I was going to be sick.

I couldn't breathe.

They all had copies of our most intimate words.

I wanted to run out of the room and never look back.

But I did this. I knew what I was doing was wrong, and I did it anyway.

I looked up, and I saw something pass across Sebastian's gaze. Maybe it was empathy, or maybe it was pity.

I couldn't look at anyone else.

"You've read enough from the notebook to us already, Randall," Scarlett said, and maybe I was having an out-of-body experience, but her tone appeared to be laced with irritation. "I don't need to read everything they wrote to one another. It's a complete invasion of privacy."

Scarlett tossed her packet onto the desk and folded her arms over her chest.

I glanced at my father, and he wasn't moving.

He wasn't speaking.

He just stared down at his hands, the packet resting on his lap.

"Agreed." Sebastian set his packet down and cleared his throat. "And you found this notebook because it was left in the training room, is that correct?"

"Yes. Not that it really matters where it was found," Randall snipped. "It's such a blatant violation of the contract, I don't even know where to start."

"It wasn't left in the training room. It was in my desk drawer," I said, unsure how I even found the words to speak because I was beyond humiliated.

Mortified.

Embarrassed.

And everything in between.

But I sure as hell did not leave that notebook in the training room. He'd gone looking for it.

Sebastian scrubbed a hand down his face. "Is this notebook something that you and Clark Chadwick shared? Are you having an affair with a player on this team?"

"Yes," I whispered, my bottom lip shaking so badly now I couldn't say more.

"Of course, she is. They're having a torrid affair. She has crossed the line with our most valuable player, only months after being hired by this organization. Who knows who else she's sleeping with on the team at this point," Randall said, and everything after happened in a blur.

My father dropped his packet on the floor as he lunged at Randall, gripping him by the shirt and slamming him into the closest wall. "You shut your fucking mouth when you speak about my daughter."

Sebastian was on his feet, pulling them apart. I jumped up and reached for my father, but he stepped back and put his arms up, still unable to look at me.

"John, sit down now." Sebastian's voice was low and even as he dragged Randall's chair over to where he stood. "Randall, stay over here."

He picked up his phone and dialed what I assumed was his assistant, asking her to send security over before ending the call.

"I'm being punished for protecting this team?" Randall hissed. "She clearly doesn't care about this team because she could get Clark cut after this season for this behavior. Yet, I'm the bad guy?"

"Randall, you need to stop talking, now," Sebastian hissed. "Eloise, I have to speak to my brother and our legal department, and Scarlett and I will discuss our options here. Right now, I'm going to ask you to take leave until I figure out how to handle this situation." He pushed to his feet and moved to the door.

When he pulled it open, there was a large man on the other side, and his eyes found mine, showing no emotion at all.

"Security is going to escort you to your office to get your things, and make sure you go straight to your car. Do not stop to speak to anyone. I'll be in touch," Sebastian said.

I blinked several times, as the humiliation was almost too much. I did not want to cry in front of everyone. I knew it was what Randall wanted, and I was going to do everything in my power not to give him the satisfaction.

"You're treating her like a goddamn criminal!" my father snapped, and my breath caught in my throat.

"John, I need to figure out how to handle the situation. I can't do that with you and Randall physically fighting. I did not go looking for this. I'm as caught off guard as you are at the moment. But right now, Eloise is in violation of her contract, and I'm simply asking her to take leave until we figure out how to move forward. I think that is the only fair option at the moment," Sebastian said.

"And Chadwick?" my father asked. "Are you bringing him in here, or does he just get a slap on the hand?"

"That's how this works, John," Randall said. "Your daughter is having an affair with our most valuable player at the moment. She could cost him his career because she couldn't keep her legs closed."

"How fucking dare you!" Dad shouted, and he was back on his feet.

Tears streamed down my face, and I put my hand on my father's shoulder. This was so much worse than I ever could have imagined.

"I'm so sorry," I croaked.

"Eloise, you're excused, and I will reach out when we have more information about how we will proceed." Sebastian turned to face me, and I nodded.

I walked out the door, swiping at my face.

The ride down on the elevator was completely silent, and I'd never felt so disgusted with myself in my life.

"Here you go." The large man beside me pulled a handkerchief from his suit pocket and handed it to me. "I'm Bullet, by the way."

Seriously? I was too overwhelmed to process the fact that I was being escorted to my office and out of the building by a man named Bullet.

"Thank you," I said, as a sob escaped.

I did my best to pull it together as we walked the short distance to my office where I grabbed my notebook from my desk, even though there were already copies of everything in it printed. I doubted I'd ever be back here, so I wasn't going to leave it here.

I snatched my purse off the desk and followed Bullet down the hallway toward the exit.

"You all right, Doc?" I heard a familiar voice from behind me and turned to see Weston watching me with concern.

"No stopping," Bullet said, his voice low.

I nodded and kept moving. The large man escorted me to my car, and once I slipped inside, I offered him his handkerchief back.

The slightest chuckle escaped. "You can keep it. Get home safely."

He shut my door, and I pulled out of the parking lot and drove about a block before I pulled over and the dam opened.

I sobbed until I had no tears left in me.

And when I walked into my apartment, I knew that everything had changed.

There was no fixing this now.

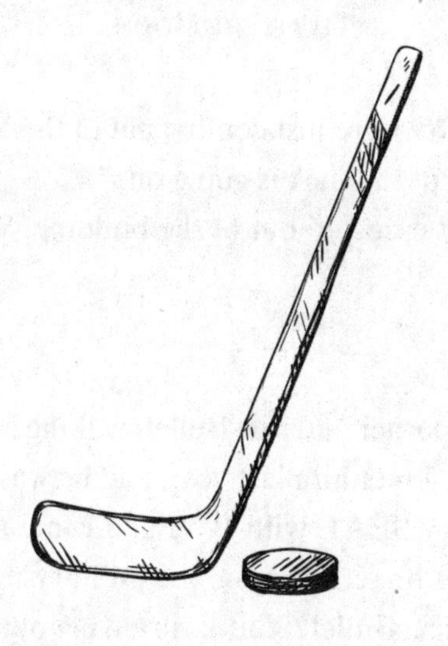

31
Clark

"Dude," Weston said, as he came into the locker room where I was talking to Scotty. He was feeling down on himself after his showing on the ice today.

I looked up at Weston and immediately moved to my feet. He looked pissed off, and he was not a guy who reacted unless something was seriously wrong. "You all right? What happened?"

"Doc just got escorted out of the building."

"What? By who?" I was already moving, and he was right on my ass.

"Bullet just escorted her to her car. Her face was swollen, and she was obviously crying and upset."

"Motherfucker," I hissed, and I was jogging now.

Wizz and Lefty were just coming out of the lounge, and they followed us. "What the fuck is going on?"

"Doc just got escorted out of the building. We don't know," Weston said.

But I knew.

I fucking knew.

I turned the corner and saw Bullet walking ahead of me, and I shouted at him. I met him last year, and he was a good guy. He used to be a Navy SEAL with Wolf and came to work security for the team after he retired from the military.

"What the fuck, Bullet? You escorted her out of the building? Are you fucking kidding me right now? She's a part of this team."

"Do not come at me, Chadwick. This was not my choice. I was called up to Sebastian's office and asked to take her to her car. That's all I know," he said, his hands up as if he had no choice.

He was clearly just doing his job.

I gave him a nod and started jogging toward the elevator. Toward Sebastian's office. Weston, Wizz, and Lefty were right beside me.

"What's going on, brother?" Weston asked when it was just the four of us on the elevator.

"Too much to explain right now," I said, as the doors opened, and I moved right past Sebastian's assistant, who was probably still processing that we'd run right past her without stopping.

I pushed the door open to find Coach Gable, Randall, and Scarlett all sitting in chairs, with Sebastian behind his desk. Randall was seated on the other side of the office, which was odd. There were papers on the floor, and I quickly realized that they were copies straight out of our notebook.

My eyes found Randall. "You petty motherfucker. You couldn't help yourself, could you?"

He moved to his feet and stepped toward me. "You are fucking an employee, Chadwick. And she happens to be your coach's daughter, you dumb motherfucker."

I pulled my arm back on instinct, ready to knock him through a wall, when Weston and Wizz both grabbed me, holding me back. Sebastian came around his desk and moved between us. John was there now, standing beside me, as well.

"Chadwick, that is not going to help anything," Sebastian said.

Scarlett was on her feet, looking pale and stressed out, and it was apparent that this had been a heated meeting long before I arrived.

I turned to look at Coach, dreading the look that I was going to see there.

He just stared at me.

Disappointment and hurt were easy to read.

"I'm sorry, Coach," I said. "I wanted to talk to you. *We* wanted to talk to you."

"Yet you didn't." His voice was low, and he sounded exhausted.

"What was he going to tell you? That he was banging your daughter?" Randall said from behind me, and I whipped around again, dying to lay into the fucker.

Lefty moved to stand in front of Coach, while Weston and Wizz held on to me.

"Clark, you need to calm the fuck down," Weston hissed.

I scrubbed a hand down my face, turning to face Eloise's father. "We were afraid to involve you. This is not something casual. I love her. She loves me. We want to be together. But this fucking contract had her nervous that she would lose her job, that she would embarrass you."

"Well, she's correct about that," Randall said.

This fucking guy.

"Listen, if you want to fire her, then you should be cutting me from the team, as well. We both broke the contract. And I promise you, if she leaves, I will not be signing with this team next year. I'm a free agent after this season, and I will not stay here if you choose to fire her because we fell in love. I'm not the first person on this team to meet the woman he loves," I said, still facing Coach.

"You should have come to me," Sebastian said, and I turned to look at him.

"We were going to. We haven't been back that long. We were trying to figure it out. Her father is the coach of this team, and she was concerned about how this would affect him."

"You'd leave this team for a fucking woman?" Randall got in my face, and Lefty stepped so close to Randall that it forced him to step back.

Sebastian groaned and picked up the phone, requesting security again.

"You don't have to have me escorted out of this building, Sebastian. I will happily walk out on my own, as Eloise would have done, as well." I turned to look at him.

He moved to the door just as there was a knock, and Bullet stood there, looking between us.

"Please escort Randall to his office for his things, and then walk him to his car. He is not to stop and speak to anyone. Randall, I'll be in touch."

"Excuse me? You're escorting *me* out of the building? Your father will have your ass, kid." He moved toward Sebastian, squaring his shoulders.

"I don't think so, Randall." Sebastian arched a brow. "Not

with all the people who have come forward about the affair that *you're* having with a staff member, not to mention the fact that I'm fairly certain you went through Eloise's desk and took that notebook, taking the time to make copies of something that wasn't your property. You've broken a dozen violations all on your own. So I'd stay very quiet right now and walk away before you make this worse for yourself."

I was surprised that Sebastian had put Randall in his place.

Randall glared at him and then did the same to Coach and me, before storming out of the room, bumping his shoulder aggressively into Bullet.

"You touch me again, and we're going to have a problem," Bullet said as he left the office with Randall.

"Weston, Wizz, Lefty, you can all leave. I appreciate you coming here with Chadwick, but I need a few minutes alone with him and Coach. I'd appreciate it if you'd keep what's happened between us," Sebastian said.

"Just know, if he goes, we go," Wizz said.

"Damn straight. We're a team. And Doc is part of that team now, too. Remember that." Weston winked at me.

I nodded before staring down at my hands because I fucked up royally by not coming forward. I should have insisted. I should have been a man and handled this.

Eloise had been in this room dealing with all of this without me by her side.

When the door closed, I glanced over at Coach, but he just stared straight ahead. No emotion on his face.

"Listen, this is a mess. I need some time to figure out how to handle this. Randall is not going to drop this, and rules were broken," Sebastian said. "Let me speak to Wolf, and I'll let you know how we want to proceed."

"Wolf, the man who is married to our chief legal?" I said, leaning back in the chair and crossing my feet at my ankles because how could they have a problem with something they'd already done?

"Yeah. That's the one." He chuckled. "So, what are you going to do? Marry Eloise to prove your point?"

I leaned forward, resting my elbows on my knees, offended by the question. "I wouldn't marry anyone to prove a point. But I'd marry the woman I love if she said yes, so sure. I'd marry her tomorrow if she wanted to. I'd walk away from this team to protect her. So you best realize that this is the real deal, and I'm not walking away from her for you, for this team, or for anyone. I'll play somewhere else if I have to. She's my priority. Got it?"

"I believe I understand now." Sebastian nodded, pushing to his feet and motioning for me to do the same. "You can leave. I just need a moment with Coach first, and then I'll reach out to my brother."

I turned toward Coach Gable. "I'm sorry, Coach. I should have come to you. I respect the hell out of you. I just love your daughter, and she was not ready to tell anyone. She knew this would fall on her, which in turn meant it would fall on you. But I owed you more, and I apologize."

He looked up at me, narrowing his gaze, and then gave me the slightest nod. He still didn't speak, and I couldn't tell what was going through his mind.

I left his office and dialed Eloise at least a dozen times as I drove to her apartment.

It went to voicemail every damn time.

When I pulled up in front of her building, I jogged to her door and knocked several times.

"Open up, Weeze."

When the door pulled open, my chest squeezed at the sight of her.

Eyes swollen.

Nose red.

Lips trembling.

I wrapped my arms around her and held her close. "I'm so sorry I wasn't there when you got called in. I didn't know that was happening."

She broke down, sobbing, and I just held her there.

And then she pulled back and looked up at me.

"Randall found our notebook. He printed it up for everyone to read," she said. Her words broke on a sob, and she placed her hand on her chest. "My father read it. He couldn't even look at me."

"Randall is a fucking asshole. Your dad will be okay. I briefly explained that this is not some casual fling." I reached for her hand.

"Did they call you in after me?" She moved to sit on the couch and buried her face in her hands.

"No. Weston told me that he saw you, and we found out you'd been in Sebastian's office. I went there to straighten this out and find out what happened."

Her eyes were red and puffy, and she shook her head. "Randall accused me of trying to ruin your career. He also accused me of sleeping with other players on the team. I told you that this would be different for me being a woman."

"Baby, we're going to figure this out." I tried to pull her onto my lap, and she pushed to her feet.

"I'm going to lose my job. My father can't look at me. We are not going to figure this out, Clark." She shook her head. "They didn't even call you in. You aren't the person everyone is mad at. And trust me, I'm relieved that you aren't in trouble. I really am."

She cried. "But right now, I am in this alone. I need to figure out how to walk away from this without taking my father down and without hurting your career."

Tears streamed down her face, and I felt completely helpless. I pushed to my feet and moved toward her. "Weeze, I'm in this with you. You aren't alone."

"What if my father loses his job? What if I have to leave, and you remain on the team? How will you work with my dad now? Everyone read our letters. There were intimate things in there, Clark," she said, and she was crying so hard that she was gasping for air as she rambled off every fear that she had.

I tried to wrap my arms around her, but she pushed me back. "I need you to go."

"What? I'm not leaving you." I reached for her hand, and she pulled it away. "I want to be here for you, Eloise."

She looked up at me, swiping the tears from her face. "Randall probably has someone watching us right now. We're making this worse. If you really want to help me, you need to leave. I want to be alone."

"Weeze," I whispered. "Don't do this."

"Please, Clark. You need to go. Even being associated with me right now is not a good idea. I'm sure they are packing my desk as we speak. We need to take some time apart." She sighed, lifting one shoulder as if it were the only option.

"Fuck them. I'll leave. I'll quit," I hissed.

"And that helps how?" Her voice was hoarse, and she sounded exhausted. "That hurts you. That hurts my father. Hurting the two men I love most in the world is not something I strive to do. Just go home, Clark. I need to figure out how I salvage my relationship with my father and hope I can find a job somewhere else after all of this."

"You're not going anywhere." My gaze locked with hers, and I saw it there.

She'd made her decision. She wasn't going to change her mind, at least not tonight.

She wanted me gone. She was hurt and humiliated, and I'm sure it didn't feel good that I hadn't even been called in. I just happen to walk in all on my own.

No one had called me out or humiliated me.

They saved it all for her.

"Please, baby. Tell me what I can do to fix this, and I'll do it."

"You can give me the space I need right now. That's all you can do for me." Her bottom lip trembled. "I'm asking you to respect that. I can't talk about this anymore tonight."

Fuck. The one thing she needed from me was the one thing I didn't want to do.

"All right. Yeah, if that's what you want." I took a step back, trying not to sound wounded. She didn't need to worry about me on top of all she was dealing with.

"It's what I want." She walked to the door and pulled it open.

"I love you, Weeze."

But she didn't say a word. She just closed the door the minute I stepped outside.

As if she couldn't wait for me to be gone.

I basically just ruined her life.

Who could blame her for wanting me gone? But I couldn't do nothing. If she didn't want me there, she needed to have someone there.

I climbed into my truck and pulled out my phone.

Because I was determined to fix the mess I'd made.

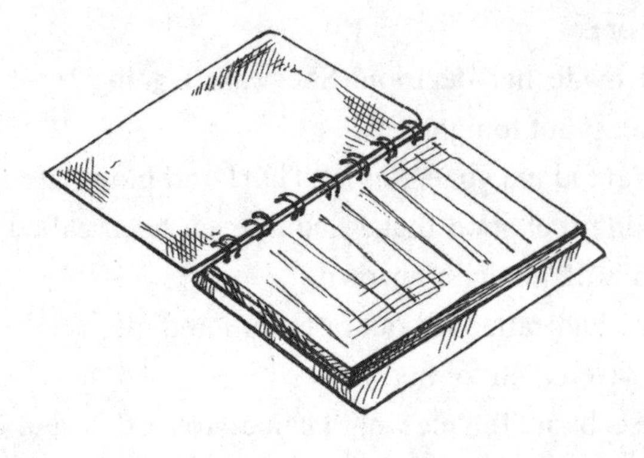

32

Eloise

I sat in the tub and cried until my fingers pruned and there were no tears left.

I was physically sick to my stomach.

My head was pounding, and I just kept playing the conversation over and over in my head.

Who knows who else she's sleeping with on the team?

Your daughter is having an affair with our most valuable player at the moment. She could cost him his career because she couldn't keep her legs closed.

I shook my head and dragged myself out of the lukewarm water and dried off. I slipped on a robe and stopped to look in the mirror. My hair was tied up in a scrunchie, my skin looked pale, my eyes were swollen and bloodshot, and my lips were chapped.

I padded out to the kitchen to make a cup of tea when there was a knock on the door.

I groaned and moved to the door, looking through the peephole as my father stood on the other side of the door.

I started crying all over again at the sight of him.

"Ells bells, open the door," he said.

I pulled the door open and fell apart when he pulled me into his arms. "I'm so sorry, Dad."

I said those words over and over as he held me in his arms and rocked me slowly before pushing the door closed.

"Come on, let's sit on the couch. Everything is okay."

I sat down beside him, using the sleeve of my robe to swipe at my face. "Everything is not okay. I've made a mess of things, and I let you down."

"Hey, hey," he said, his voice harsh now. "Don't you put words in my mouth, Eloise."

My dad rarely called me by my full name unless he was being very serious.

He turned my chin, forcing me to face him. "You're wrong about several things. First off, everything is okay. Because what is most important is that you are here on this earth with me. You and I have survived a hell of a lot worse than you falling in love with Clark Chadwick."

I blinked a few times, wondering how he knew that little tidbit as I'd barely spoken in the meeting.

"I know this isn't casual. He busted into that office, declaring his love. Saying he'd marry you today if you agreed to it. Hell, he threatened to leave the team if they let you go. He looked me in the eye and told me that he loved you. I assume you feel the same way, because I know you, sweetheart. You wouldn't risk all of this if it wasn't something real. And that's all I've ever wanted for you. To experience what I had with your mom. And the fact that it's with a man who I happen to respect and admire, that's a good thing."

"He said all of that?"

"That and more. He called out Randall and brought up the fact that other couples have had relationships on this team, including Wolf Wayburn and our chief legal, Dylan Wayburn."

"I know. But we don't own the team. And I've been having a relationship with a man who's on the team, a team that I work for, so there's that." I shook my head and shrugged.

"Yep. There is that. But loving someone is never a bad thing." He took my hand in his and smiled. "I couldn't look at you in that office because I was not there as your father. I was there as the coach of this team. I was also blindsided and processing what I was hearing. I did not read the letters that you and Clark wrote to one another, and no one in that office did, aside from Randall. Yes, he read two short passages, where you both shared how much you loved one another, so I think Sebastian and Scarlett were in the same boat of feeling really bad that it came out this way. No one is upset with you."

Relief flooded. I imagined them all sitting around, reading our most intimate words.

The tears started falling again. "Dad, is this going to affect your job?"

"No. But I wouldn't care if it did. You are my priority, Ells. I'm very angry at the way that they handled this situation. I knew Randall was a petty bastard, but this… This is unforgivable." He shook his head.

"Dad, you love this team. I will not be the reason that changes. You have to work things out with Randall. You're the coach, and he's the trainer. Sebastian didn't do anything other than react to what was reported to him. But I do need a favor from you."

"Of course, sweetheart. There isn't anything that I wouldn't do for you."

"I need you to talk to Clark. He loves this team. They're his family, too. When they terminate me, you have to promise me that you'll make him stay. I'll figure it out and land somewhere else. But he can't just start over with a new team at the height of his career. This city loves him, his teammates love him, and you love him. You have to help him do the right thing."

"If they fire you for this, I don't think he or I will be okay with that. So that is not a promise I can keep, sweetheart. I'm sorry." He pulled me close and wrapped his arms around me. "It's always been you and me against the world, and now, apparently, it's you, me, and Clark Chadwick against the world." He chuckled.

I just rested my head against his chest and listened to the sound of his heart beating. "Clark came here, and I told him to leave."

"It's normal to be upset about this. The things Randall said to you… I won't ever be able to look at that man again. I'm sorry I couldn't stop it. But this is not Clark's fault, honey. Don't push him away."

I lifted my head. "I'm not pushing him away because I want to. I'm pushing him away for his own good. Being seen with me right now is not a good idea. I'm about to get canned from my first job. He can still save himself. And he can't do that while he's sitting here, wallowing with me."

"When did you get so cynical?" he asked, as the corners of his lips turned up. "Come on, no one has decided anything yet."

"I just don't see how we all keep working together after that scene in Sebastian's office. I mean, Randall is my direct boss. He clearly hates me. I can't very well work for him now, nor would he tolerate that. So, there is no doubt that they will ask me to leave. And I am not taking Clark or you down with me when that happens."

He pulled me close to him again and hugged me. "This is hockey, Ells. People beat the shit out of each other one day and then high-five one another the next. Let's not jump the gun, all right? Just hang tight and see what happens."

"Okay," I whispered. "I'm really sorry if I embarrassed you, Dad."

"There has not been one day, one single moment in your lifetime, that I have been embarrassed by you. You are the light of my life. And I've failed you if you feel differently." He pulled back to look at me. "The only thing that upset me is that you didn't think you could come to me with this. I would have been happy for you. For both of you. I would have told you and Clark to go to Human Resources and be upfront with them about it. We're all human, sweetheart. It happens. But you can always come to me."

"I should have. Clark wanted to. I was afraid it would put you in a bad position, being the coach of the team. I thought if we waited a little while, it would get easier. I didn't expect to fall for him this hard," I finally said, swiping at my eyes again. "I love him so much, and it's scary enough to feel that way, but involving my father, my employer, and all the people I work with… I was scared to put that kind of pressure on us."

"I get it. But from now on, you come to me for anything. It doesn't matter if it involves work. I love this team, there's no doubt. But I don't love anyone or anything the way that I love you. I'd walk away from this team in a heartbeat if it meant protecting you, all right?"

I nodded. "You shouldn't have to."

"Well, neither should you."

I sighed. "Okay. It's late, and you look exhausted. Go get some sleep. Tomorrow is a new day. Go to work, and I'll take the next few days and wait to hear from Sebastian."

"Randall is on leave, as well, so it might be a good idea for me to go to work. I can have my ears open and find out if anyone knows what's going on. Maybe I can talk to Sebastian and see where his head is at."

"Yes. And will you make sure Clark goes to practice tomorrow?" I asked, putting my hands together. "Please, Dad. Can you do that for me? Tell him it's important to me that he goes."

"Why don't you tell him yourself?"

"I will. I just—I need to see how this plays out so I don't pull him down with me. If I call him right now, he'll want to come over, and he'll refuse to go to practice while I'm being forced to stay away. I need to do this for him, okay?" My bottom lip trembled.

"Okay. I'll make sure he goes. I'll tell him that you want us both to be there tomorrow, and we'll reassess once the decision is made." He forced a smile. "But I don't want you to be alone tonight."

"I'm fine. I'm a grown-up, remember?" I chuckled, but the lump in my throat made it hard to swallow.

"You're still my little girl," he said, and we both turned when there was a knock on the door.

It was almost 11:00 p.m. now, and I couldn't imagine who it would be. If it was Clark, it would be difficult for me not to fall into him right now. Because that's what I wanted to do. But I needed him to stay focused on his team right now. He worked so hard to recover from his injury and get into the best shape of his life. I wasn't going to derail that.

Dad moved to the door and pulled it open, and my mouth fell open.

Emilia, Lulu, and Henley wheeled in their suitcases, and Lulu held up two pints of ice cream.

"We heard our girl needed us," Emilia said, and I rushed toward her.

I hugged her before turning to Henley and Lulu and doing the same thing. "What are you guys doing here?"

"Clark called us and told us what happened, and we came immediately. If our girl needs us, we show up," Lulu said.

I gaped at them. "I can't believe you're here."

"Yep. We're all taking off work tomorrow, so we'll be here with you," Henley said. "And I'll be reading that contract of yours and giving you all the legal advice."

"Those bastards can't treat you this way," Emilia said, before turning to my dad and wincing. "Oh, sorry, Mr. Gable. It's great to see you. You're not one of the bastards, of course."

My father chuckled. "Thank you. I'm not happy with how this was handled, but I do believe this is all coming from Randall. I have faith that the owners will do the right thing."

"Men love to hate on women." Lulu quirked a brow. "I mean, not you, Mr. Gable. But this Randall dude, he's been jealous of our girl since the day she started."

"Agreed." Henley sighed. "Let's have ice cream and talk about all the ways we hate him."

"And that's my cue. I'm going to let you have your time. Thanks for showing up for my girl," he said, pulling me into a big hug.

"I love you, Ells. I'll call you tomorrow. Try to get some rest."

"I will. Love you, Dad." I closed the door after he left and padded back over to the couch.

"Clark sounded pretty desperate when he called," Emilia said, as she sat down beside me.

A deep lump sat in my throat, making it hard to swallow. Clark knew what I needed, and even though I asked him to leave, he made sure they were here for me.

He loved me, and that meant everything to me.

I didn't know what our future looked like, but I knew without a shadow of a doubt, that he loved me.

Lulu brought over the ice cream, and Henley grabbed four spoons.

"Okay, tell us everything," Henley said.

I started from the beginning, when I'd just been called to Sebastian's office. They listened to me, they cried with me, and they were angry on my behalf. I never had friends like these three. They didn't judge; they just supported me.

"Listen, this is bullshit. And if they let you go, you can come work at MSL with me until you figure out what you want to do." Lulu wrapped an arm around me. "And if I see Randall ever again, I will kick him in the balls for what he said to you."

"I mean, the fact that he went through your desk and took your notebook. How is that not a violation of the contract?" Emilia asked.

Henley had the contract on her lap as she read it in detail. "That would certainly be cause for termination, but you'd have to prove that he took it, as he's claiming he found it."

"I'm so sorry this happened, Elle." Emilia leaned her head on my shoulder. "Love hurts, huh?"

"Well, I don't know about love hurting, but this pint of ice cream is not sitting so well in my stomach. I think I'm lactose intolerant," Lulu said, leaning her head against my other shoulder.

"You are not lactose intolerant. You just ate an entire pint of gummy bear ice cream, and that would make anyone sick." Henley laughed.

"Agreed. Gummy bears don't belong in ice cream," Emilia said, peeking up at me. I forced a smile. It helped that they were here, but this deep sadness was still sitting on my chest.

I missed Clark. I couldn't imagine how this would work if I had to move somewhere else for a job. He traveled with the team all the time. We'd never see one another.

A sob escaped my throat, and they all startled.

"Damn, you guys. The gummy bear ice cream distraction did not work. Our girl just needs to be sad." Lulu wrapped her arms around me. "We're here for you. Cry as much as you need to."

And that's exactly what I did.

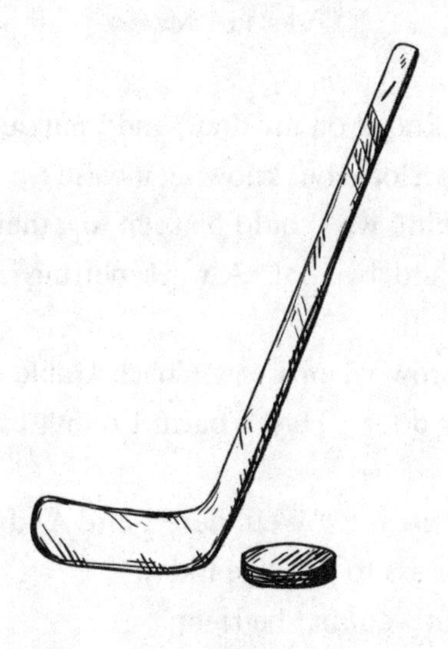

33
Clark

I respected Eloise when she asked me to stay away, but I'd barely slept. I was grateful that Henley, Lulu, and Emilia were with her, and they sent me a few texts, letting me know she was doing okay.

Nothing about this was right.

I should be there with her.

I was not going to practice today. I didn't see how it made sense that I was allowed to go to work, and she wasn't. I poured myself a cup of coffee and glanced down at my phone to see texts from my brothers, my sister, my cousins, and my teammates.

I scrubbed a hand down my face.

I didn't feel like talking to anybody right now, aside from the one person who didn't want to talk to me.

There was a knock on my door, and I hurried over, a part of me hoping it was Eloise but knowing it wasn't.

She didn't think we should be seen together right now, and I knew she'd stand by that. Always putting everyone before herself.

I arched a brow when I saw Coach Gable standing on the other side of my door. "Hey, Coach. I didn't expect to see you here."

He walked past me. "Well, here I am. And I came to make sure you get your ass to practice today."

"Not going. It wouldn't be right."

He made his way to the kitchen, helped himself to a cup of coffee, and then motioned for me to take a seat at the table. He held up the pot, offering to top me off.

"I'm good. Thank you," I said, taking a seat as he sat across from me.

"So, what wouldn't be right about you going to practice?"

"Well, my girlfriend isn't allowed to go to work because we've been in a relationship, and she's being punished for that, so why am I allowed to go to work?" I shrugged, taking a sip of my coffee.

"Because the world isn't always fair," he said.

"That's your answer?"

"It's the truth." He set his mug down. "Listen, I agree with you. It's not right. That's why we're going to go to practice together. So we can see what's going on. Randall shouldn't be there. Maybe Sebastian will call you back in and give you an update."

"He can call me, just like he can call Eloise."

"Listen, Clark, I appreciate the show of loyalty. I'll be marching my ass out of that place, as well, if they terminate her.

But right now, she asked me to go to practice, and she asked me to make sure that you go, too. So that's what we're going to do. Because she loves us, and she wants us to do this."

"At least she's talking to you," I said.

"Oh, don't start feeling sorry for yourself. You're one of the best hockey players in the league right now. It doesn't look good if you're acting like a mopey little baby." He smirked. "It really ruins the bad-boy pro-athlete image, you know?"

I blew out a frustrated breath. "I don't give a shit about that."

"I know you don't, son. But we're not doing this for us; we're doing this for her. Let's go see what's going on. We can't do anything for her if we're sitting at home, sulking." He pushed to his feet. "Now go get dressed, and be ready to run a few extra miles, as well."

"For what?" I gaped at him.

"For not telling me that you were in love with my daughter. You should have come to me." His gaze met mine.

I nodded. "I fucked up. I owed you more."

"Correct. And now you owe her this. She doesn't have the option of going to work today, but you do, and she wants you there. So pull up your big-boy pants, and get your ass moving."

I jogged to my room and quickly changed before grabbing my gym bag and following him outside.

"You're riding with me today," he said, unlocking his car doors with his remote.

"How come?"

"Because everyone on this team will know that we are united on this. Until they make a decision, we show up. If they terminate my daughter, we can both walk if that's what we want to do. But we do it together. Randall sees it. Sebastian sees it. Human Resources sees it. Your teammates see it. And most importantly, our girl sees it. She knows we've got her back and one another's back. That's what family does," he said, as he slipped into the driver's seat.

"Damn straight, Coach."

We drove to the practice facility and made our way inside.

My teammates were all looking at me and Coach with this pitiful look on their faces.

Word travels fast on this team.

I glanced at Coach Gable, and he quirked a brow as if I should know what to do.

"Huddle up," I said, and all the guys gathered around. "I appreciate the support. But right now, we've got practice. So get your head in the game and get ready to work hard."

"I don't see Randall here today either," Lefty said. "Is he on leave, as well?"

"He's on leave, as well. I can't share more than that right now," I said, my voice void of all emotion because I felt nothing but disdain for Randall.

"How about I lead us through today's practice?" Lefty said. As team captain, his stepping up would speak volumes.

"That would be great. Let's do it." I led them to the gym, with Coach beside us.

"Nicely done," he said, keeping his voice low. "But you're still going to run a few extra miles just so I can prove my point."

I chuckled. It wasn't as loud or boisterous as it would normally be, but I was trying to do what my girl asked of me.

The next few hours were a blur.

Lefty pushed us hard, and then I ran the three miles that Coach insisted on.

We hadn't heard anything from anyone, but everyone was aware that both Eloise and Randall were missing from practice.

"You think we'll hear anything today?" I asked Coach as I wiped my face with a towel when I got back to the locker room.

"Not sure. Everyone's being quiet upstairs."

I nodded before taking a quick shower and getting dressed.

"Chadwick," a familiar voice called out, and I turned to see Wolf Wayburn standing in the locker room. He and I had gotten along well last season. "You got a few minutes to talk?"

"Yep," I said, my gaze meeting Weston's, and he nodded as if to say that everything would be fine.

He held up his hand for a fist pump and told me to call him after the meeting.

I rode in the elevator with Wolf, and we made small talk. He gave nothing away about what this meeting was going to be addressing.

And I realized in that moment that I didn't care if they were going to cut me after this season. All I cared about was if they were going to terminate Eloise.

Because if she left, I already decided that I'd follow the minute my contract ended.

I just hoped they'd do the right thing by her.

He glanced over at me and smirked. "Don't be so tense. We're not the enemy."

"All right. I hope that's true."

"Damn, you've got it bad. I get it, buddy. Been there myself." He clapped me on the shoulder when we stepped off the elevator, and he led me to Sebastian's office. When he pushed the door open, I saw Scarlett, Coach Gable, Sebastian, and Wolf's wife, Dylan, there, as well.

They brought legal here, so something was going down.

I took the seat beside Coach Gable, and he and I shared a look, reminding one another that we were on the same page no matter what happened.

"Thank you for joining us," Sebastian said. "I want to apologize to both of you for the spectacle yesterday. We did not call that meeting. Randall did. I had no idea that was going to happen until he walked in. He only told Scarlett that the meeting was urgent, but she also wasn't aware of what it was regarding. Just that it was an emergency meeting."

I nodded. "I thought it was odd that Eloise would be dragged in here and humiliated the way that she was when no one requested that I attend. We were guilty of the same crime."

"Last I checked, falling in love is not a crime," Dylan said, looking up from the file on her lap.

"Correct. The only mistake was not just coming forward with it," Sebastian said.

"Well, I won't speak for Eloise, as she isn't here, but I can tell you that I would have been hesitant to come forward, as well," Dylan said.

"Why?" Sebastian asked.

"Well, let me ask you, Scarlett. If you were in the same position, and you were in love with a player on this team, one who is also a very important member of this team, and you were newly in a position with this organization, would you have felt comfortable coming forward?"

"No." Scarlett shrugged, no hesitation. "Add in the fact that this affair was brought to our attention, yet only one person was marched into this office and treated with blatant disrespect, I stand by my answer."

"Thank you for your honesty, Scarlett." Dylan glanced at each of us, her brow arched knowingly.

"As I shared with both you and Wolf, I did not know what I was walking into. Randall called that meeting and asked me to request Coach, Scarlett, and Eloise be present. He then read us two entries from the notebook after I phoned her and requested her to come to my office," Sebastian said, scrubbing a hand down his face.

"Yes, we understand how it all played out. We can't change what happened yesterday, but we can make some changes moving forward," Wolf said, glancing at his wife before looking at me and Coach. "Randall's behavior is inexcusable."

"Correct," Dylan said, closing the file on her lap. "Listen, I've gathered all the information necessary to make a decision. But I feel the person most deserving of those details is not here today, and that's Eloise. We brought you both here to let you know that Randall's behavior yesterday was inexcusable. I feel it's only fair to discuss the information we found with Eloise first, as it involves her private property. And Clark, we brought you here to apologize for the way that this was handled. Obviously, it's not a secret that my husband and I met while we were both employed by the Lions, so you wouldn't have gotten judgment from me if you'd come forward, but I also understand why you were hesitant," she said.

"So, I'm not in any trouble for having a relationship with another employee?" I asked, my voice flat and void of emotion, because I wanted to know what this meant for Eloise.

"I'd be a bit of a hypocrite if I wrote you up for dating an employee, wouldn't I?" Wolf asked, his tone laced with humor.

"And Eloise is fine? I mean, her position here with the team, is that still hers?" I asked, and Coach leaned forward beside me, clearing his throat.

I could feel anxiety pouring from him.

"I would have called her in to speak to her today if she hadn't been put on leave." Dylan turned to Sebastian and frowned.

"Hey, I'm fairly new at this gig. I was trying to end an explosive situation, and I had Randall go on leave, as well. And for the record, I like Eloise," Sebastian said, defending himself and then throwing his hands in the air when I glared at him. "Not that way. I mean, she made it very clear early on that she wasn't interested, not that I would cross the line with an employee, of course."

Wolf groaned. "Okay, that's more than we needed to hear."

"My point is, she isn't here, so I've scheduled a meeting with her first thing tomorrow morning. I'll let her know the status of her position here with the Lions." Dylan stood. "Seeing as she's already been put through it by this team, I'd like to meet alone with her tomorrow first, if no one has a problem with that. Pending the outcome of our meeting, I'll update you, Scarlett."

What the fuck did that mean?

Coach and I shared a puzzled look, but we all nodded.

"Thanks for your time, gentlemen." Dylan quirked a brow. "Now take me home, husband. It's been a long day."

"You got it, Minx." He winked at her and gave me a nod before we all left the office.

When Coach and I got off the elevator on the same floor, we both turned to face one another.

"She's getting an apology, right?" I asked.

"I don't fucking know. I think so. They seemed to feel badly about the situation." He shrugged. "But I'm not going to say a word to her just yet, because she deserves to hear it from them. She's already had Randall make it clear that nepotism got her here, and she's clearly taken plenty of shit for loving you."

"Hey, why am I the bad guy?"

"Because I'm your girlfriend's father. I get to make you the bad guy whenever the hell I want to. And I'm still your coach, so don't be expecting special treatment." He smirked as he scrubbed a hand down his face. "I hope we read that meeting correctly and she's going to stay. Because I'd like all three of us to be here, or it doesn't work anymore, does it?"

"Nope. And I think they know that."

"I sure as shit hope so," he said.

"And how does this play out with Randall? How do we work with that guy after he spoke to her the way he did?"

"I don't know," Coach said, scrubbing a hand down his face. "But let's see what they say tomorrow. I'm guessing they are going to ask her to stay."

"Still doesn't mean she'll want to date me after all that has happened. Maybe she'll want to end things," I said, feeling a heavy weight on my shoulder.

She hadn't called. She hadn't texted.

I'd sent her several texts telling her I loved her.

Maybe the writing was on the wall.

And she didn't think we were worth the fight.

But I'd never stop fighting for her.

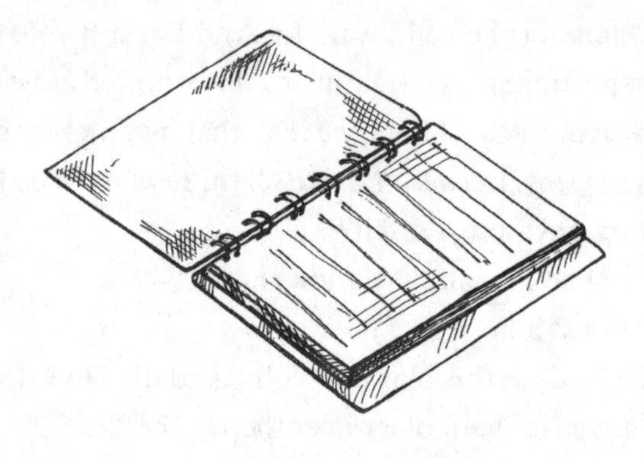

34

Eloise

"Okay, thanks for coming. I love you guys so much," I said, as they stood at my door with their bags.

My stomach was in knots because I was heading to meet with Dylan Wayburn this morning.

My father had told me that he and Clark had both attended practice and that they received an apology for the way the situation was handled. He said there was no mention of anything further. I didn't press because I already knew that Randall would be returning, and he would not want me on staff.

I was at peace with it.

Henley thought I could plead my case about the notebook being taken from my office, but I had no way to prove it, and I wasn't looking for a fight with Randall.

I couldn't work for a man who so blatantly disrespected me.

The writing was on the wall.

I would need a new job.

What I was hoping to negotiate was that I would receive a letter of recommendation from the Wayburns so I could find employment elsewhere.

My chest ached because I didn't know what that meant for me and Clark.

But I also felt relieved that Clark and my father hadn't had any fallout regarding their positions with the Lions.

I could live with this.

I couldn't have handled it if I'd been the cause of them having to walk away from a team that they both loved.

"Love you. Call us immediately after the meeting, okay?" Lulu said.

I agreed and waved goodbye.

I drove the short distance to the Lions' training center. I knew the team would all be on the ice now, which was why it was so quiet when I walked in. I rode the elevator to the top floor. My stomach twisted as I remembered being here just two days ago and not being prepared for what was coming my way.

Today, I was prepared.

They could fire me. Yell at me. Threaten me.

None of it mattered.

I wouldn't cry, and I wouldn't crumble.

I only made one mistake, and that was keeping my relationship a secret. In hindsight, I didn't care that everyone knew that Clark and I were together.

I loved that man madly.

I thought about the words my mom had said that last year of her life.

Make sure you're over the moon for whoever you give your heart to.

There was no doubt that I was completely over the moon for Clark Chadwick.

So I'd already won in the short time that I'd been a part of this team.

And I should have realized that two days ago when I thought my world was ending.

I hadn't lost the man that I loved.

What I'd lost was a job. It was just a job.

I'd find another one.

One that appreciated me.

One that wasn't snooping through my desk for leverage against me.

I blew out a breath when I paused in front of Dylan's office, and I knocked on the door.

"Come in," she called out.

I stepped inside, and Dylan Wayburn strode towards me with all the confidence in the world. I hadn't met her before, as this was my first run-in with the legal department.

"Eloise, it's lovely to meet you. I'm Dylan Wayburn. Thank you for meeting me here today." She motioned for me to sit in the chair across from her desk, and she surprised me when she didn't go around to take her chair and instead sat in the seat beside me.

"It's lovely to meet you, as well," I said.

"Okay, let's get right down to it. On behalf of the Lions team and the Wayburn family, I apologize for what happened here two days ago," she said. "I didn't fill your father or Clark in on the details about Randall, and I'm going to trust you with this information because I think you deserve to hear it. But I'd appreciate it if you'd keep it between us. Of course,

I understand that you will be sharing it with your father and Clark, but I'd like to spare the rest of the team all the dramatics involved here."

I nodded, surprised by how this meeting had started. "That's not a problem."

"I spoke to Talia, Randall's assistant, yesterday," she said, one brow arched, which told me that she knew their relationship ran a bit deeper. "She was all too happy to spill her guts and tell me that Randall did indeed go into your office, into your desk, and take the notebook out. He then proceeded to have her make copies of everything in the notebook so he could present it at his ridiculous attempt at a coup."

"I was fairly certain that had been the case, but I wasn't so sure I could prove it. Not that it matters, because how can I work for a man who is willing to stoop so low to get me fired? But I'm relieved to know that I'm not imagining this and that he really did do the things that I thought he did." I shrugged. "I wasn't after his job. I was happy to be in the position I was hired for. Sure, it is a long-term goal of mine to be an athletic trainer, as well, but I wasn't going to step on any toes to get there."

"I understand that. Sebastian tells me that you are doing an amazing job and that the team loves you. And we'd like you to stay on here at the Lions organization," she said.

I sighed because obviously, it would be the best option for me, considering my boyfriend lives here, but I didn't see how that could work. "I appreciate the offer to stay, but I work directly under the athletic trainer, and I don't think that would be a good situation for anyone on the team."

"I think you're aware that I met my husband while employed by this team, am I right?" she asked.

"Yes. I think it's great."

"Well, loving someone isn't a criminal act, Eloise, but sneaking into another employee's office and rifling through their desk and stealing personal materials is actually a crime. As is making photocopies of private property and dispersing them with malicious intent. Randall is no longer a part of this organization."

My eyes widened, and I'm sure my mouth was gaping open. "Randall is leaving?"

"He was given the opportunity to resign, which I feel was more gracious than he deserved. But we aren't here to destroy anyone's future, just to build a positive and supportive work environment, which he was not providing." She held her hands up when I started to panic that I caused the man to lose his job. "This did not start two days ago. Sebastian was not a fan of Randall, and he'd already spoken to Wolf about your credentials and qualifications before any of this happened. He witnessed some very petty behavior, and Wolf had noticed it last year, as well. It was time for him to go. This team is ready for change, which is why my brother-in-law has stepped into this new role. We would like to offer you the position of athletic trainer as well as physical therapist. We will have you interview candidates to assist you, but we'd like you to head up the entire department if you're willing."

My breath caught in my throat, and I shook my head, trying hard not to cry. "I didn't expect this."

She pushed to her feet and grabbed a box of tissues from her desk. "Let it out, girl. I've got four sisters, and we love a good cry. You've earned it. You were treated unfairly, and that type of behavior will not be tolerated on this team."

I blew my nose and buried my face in my hands and did exactly what she said.

I let it all out.

She sat right there with me until my breathing slowed, and I wiped my face.

"It's not easy existing in a man's world. Randall was threatened by you, and he went after you in the most appalling way. I am sorry about all of it. I didn't want anyone to know about Randall until I shared it with you first. I felt you deserved to know the whole story. We will let the team know that Randall has moved on, and you are stepping into this new role. I don't expect any pushback, but if you receive any, you know where to come, moving forward." She smiled.

"Thanks, Dylan. I really appreciate it."

"So, what do you think about the offer? I think it's time we get some more badass women in this company in high positions. Are you game?"

"I am. I'd be honored," I said. "But I need to make it known that Clark and I are very much together. I mean, he probably thinks I'm running away from him after how I behaved when all of this went down, but we're together. And if that's a problem, please let me know that now, because I'll find another place to work if that's the case."

A wide grin spread across her face. "I'm so happy to see that you've got it as bad as he does."

I chuckled. "I definitely do."

"It's not a problem. I'm sure you can both behave like professionals in the workplace, right?"

I had a brief flashback of the day that Clark dropped down to his knees in my office, and I could feel my cheeks heat, but I shook my head and smiled. "Of course."

"But how about this… seeing as we put you through hell two days ago. You get to be a little unprofessional for one day and go tell your man that you're staying on this team. And then you can go back to being a professional tomorrow." She winked. "I know Wolf needs me to show him a little love after I push him away when I'm upset."

My head tipped back in laughter. "All right. I'll try to remain as professional as possible when I tell him the news."

"Just know that no one is watching or judging." She chuckled. "Happy you're staying on board. I'll have your new contract sent over to your office later today. And we'll be taking out that ridiculous clause. We're all grown-ups here."

I pushed to my feet and shook her hand. "Thank you for everything. I'm so grateful."

"Of course. I'll see you later."

I hurried out of her office, my heart slamming against my chest, and I reached into my bag and pulled out the notebook. I leaned against the wall and jotted down a quick note.

Hey Chadwick,

I'm sorry the last few days have been rough. Thanks for giving me my space. But I thought you should know that I'm still working here...

I'm over the moon for you, Clark Chadwick.

I love you,
Weeze

The doors opened, and I stepped off the elevator, making my way down the long hallway and out to the ice rink.

I wasn't walking anymore. I was jogging.

Then I was in a full-blown run.

I couldn't stop myself.

I yanked the door open, just as the buzzer went off, and the guys finished their scrimmage.

I continued running down the stairs toward the door to the ice.

I couldn't get there fast enough.

I searched the ice for him.

"Hey, Chadwick, I think your girl might be looking for you," I heard Weston yell out, and I didn't even care.

I pulled the short door open, remembering I was in heels and slightly uncoordinated, so I held on to the wall and took a few steps, which was not a good idea at all. Before my ass hit the ice, I was scooped up on a whoosh. He hugged me against him, and I didn't fight him at all.

Because my boyfriend was a hotshot on the ice, and he saw me coming before I could make a fool of myself and fall.

"Hey, Weeze," he whispered in my ear. "You okay?"

I pulled back, smiling down at him. "I'm okay."

"Yeah?"

"Yep. I wrote you a note in our notebook."

"How about you just tell me?" he said, his eyes searching mine.

"I didn't handle things well. I was just embarrassed and scared that I would derail your career. And terrified that I ruined everything," I said, as a tear streamed down my cheek.

"If you go, I go. That's how this works."

"Well, we aren't going anywhere." I smiled.

"You're staying?"

"I'm staying."

"I don't want you working for Randall," he said. "Not after what he's done."

"Randall has resigned. He's no longer here. But that stays between us for now, until they announce it to the team. I'm the new trainer, as well."

"You're fucking with me."

"I am not." I chuckled. "Apparently, loving you is not a crime."

"Well, if loving you is a crime, they can lock me the fuck up. Because I love you, Weeze."

"I love you, too." I sighed as he set me on the edge of the wall and stroked the hair away from my face. "I realized something today."

"Tell me."

"What we have is rare. It's special." I shook my head. "It's everything."

"Agreed." He kissed the tip of my nose.

"This is what matters. You and me. I thought back to how my mom told me never to settle when I gave my heart away, and I get it now. Because you complete me, Clark Chadwick."

His lips turned up in the corners. "You complete me, too, baby. It's you and me moving forward. No more running."

"No more running," I said.

He took my bag from my hand and dropped it onto the ice, lifting me back up and skating past the guys.

"I got the girl!" he shouted, and they cheered. My head tipped back in laughter when I saw my father shaking his head and telling everyone to get to the weight room before he smiled and winked at me.

We just skated around the ice, kissing and laughing after everyone was gone.

I decided that tomorrow I could go back to being a professional.

But today, I was going to enjoy being in love with my hockey player.

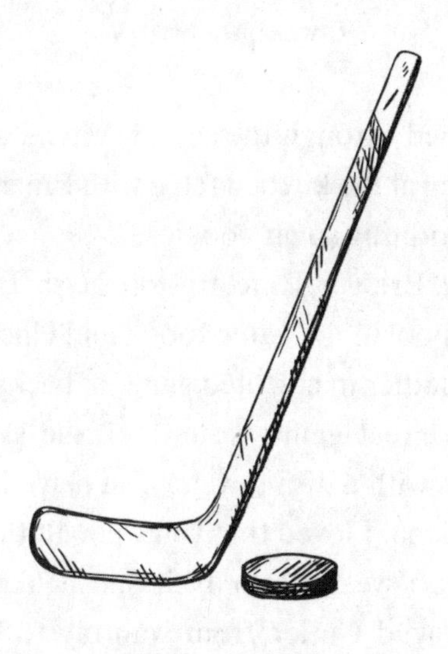

Epilogue

Clark

"How are you feeling, honey?" my mother asked, as I came up behind her and wrapped her in a hug.

I loved Thanksgiving. It was all about family and good food and football.

I was grateful the NHL never had games on Thanksgiving Day. We had a home game yesterday, and my entire family had come to the city for it.

We had a rocky start to the season, but we were finding our footing. It was a marathon, not a sprint, as we played eighty-two games over a seven-month period. We had time to build and allow our new younger players to find their rhythm.

"I feel good." I kissed her cheek before stepping back and snatching a piece of celery off the charcuterie board.

Music hummed through the sound system, and Melody and Cutler were sitting at the kitchen table with Emerson, Eloise, and Aunt Isabel, decorating sugar cookies.

Archer, Axel, Bridger, Rafe, Easton, Nash, Lulu, and Henley were all playing pool in the game room, and Uncle Carlisle sat at the bar with my father in a heated game of backgammon.

"That was a great game yesterday," she said, turning and wiping her hands with a dish towel. "You played well."

"Thanks, Mama. I loved that you were all there."

"Nowhere else we'd rather be." She winked. "Although I think you've swayed Cutler from wanting to be a boxer like his uncle Romeo to wanting to be a professional hockey player now."

"Yo, Beefcake," I said, moving to the table to sit with them.

"Yo, Uncle Clark." He chuckled.

"Word on the street is you want to be a hockey player when you grow up."

"I think it would be cool to be a hockey player, just like you." He smiled, with orange frosting on the tip of his nose. "Uncle Romeo said I shouldn't be a boxer 'cause we don't want to ruin this handsome face."

Emerson's head tipped back in laughter. "It's a very reasonable point. I love this little face of yours exactly how it is."

"Well, bad news, Beefcake. I got an elbow to the cheek yesterday, so hockey isn't necessarily the safest profession." I smirked, and the little dude looked up at me with a wide grin on his face like it was great that I had a bruise beneath my eye.

"I think you look cool." He beamed.

"And I think you want to be a hockey player because sweet Gracie Reynolds told you hockey players were cool," my sister said, her voice teasing.

"That's your friend from Cottonwood Cove, right?" I asked, remembering that's where his uncle Romeo's brother, Lincoln Hendrix, lived. He was a professional football player, and we were all fans of his. His wife had a large family that Cutler had grown close to.

"Ahhh... it's always about a girl, isn't it?" I leaned back against the cushioned banquette, as Eloise turned to look at me. Her cheeks were pink from the glass of wine she was sipping, and she smiled at me.

"I like Lolo's new necklace," Melody said. The little angel had orange and red icing all over her fingers, as she tried over and over to pick up individual sprinkles to place on her cookie.

Eloise placed her fingers over the little gold moon charm, resting just between her collarbones.

"Uncle Clark gave this to me this morning." Her teeth sank into her bottom lip.

"Had to get my girl something to celebrate our first Thanksgiving together." I wrapped an arm around her shoulder and kissed her cheek.

"You two like moons, huh? I like moons, too," Cutler said.

"Well, I'm over the moon for my girl, so it seemed fitting. And you should always be over the moon when you give your heart away." I winked at Eloise, and she leaned against me and smiled.

My mom, sister, and aunt Isabel were all swooning over the necklace, and Cutler gave me a smirk as if to say good job.

The buzzer rang on the oven, and my mom and aunt were on their feet as if it were suddenly go time. Emerson joined them, just as everyone came out of the game room and jumped in to help.

The turkey was done, the sides were all carried to the table, and we all gathered around the large dining room table, taking our seats.

My father and Uncle Carlisle were filling wineglasses, food was being passed from one person to the next, and Lulu started laughing as she held her phone up.

"Well, looky here. I just got a notification that the *Taylor Tea* did a special Thanksgiving edition, and it's all about a certain couple sitting at this table, if I'm reading between the lines."

Bridger groaned. "Now she's taking over Thanksgiving. I'd like to eat my turkey in peace."

"I want to hear what it says," Cutler said, waggling his brows.

"Beefcake, you're breaking my heart," Bridger grumped.

"I thought you didn't have a heart," Rafe said teasingly as Bridger chucked a dinner roll at him from across the table.

"Hey, knock that off. And for the record, Bridger has the biggest heart beneath that grumpy exterior." My mother blew him a kiss.

"Okay, let's hear it," Easton said, passing the stuffing to Henley.

"All right. I'll do the honors," Lulu said as she glanced down at her phone and cleared her throat dramatically. "*Hey there, Roses. It's the Thanksgiving edition because we have so much to be thankful for. Booze and Brews is doing a Thankful Happy Hour on Friday and Saturday this weekend, with line dancing and two-for-one drinks. The Honey Biscuit Café has made a big announcement… They will be bringing honey biscuits to the menu.*"

Easton fist-pumped the sky. "It's about damn time."

"This is really riveting literature," Bridger grumped as he poured gravy over his entire plate and then poured a little bit on Melody's mashed potatoes.

"Continue, I love this," Henley said.

"*But the most exciting news is that our favorite Rosewood River family seems to be very busy right now. Looks like we misread the hockey team owner and billionaire who came to town and appeared to want to sweep our favorite newcomer off her feet… because our favorite hockey star got the girl. Apparently, when she's not training him or healing his wounds, she's busy stealing his heart. Sorry, ladies, another bachelor bites the dust,*" Lulu said dramatically. "Gahhh… I love this!"

"They're talking about you two," Cutler said over a mouthful of potatoes as he pointed at me and Eloise. "They must know that Uncle Clark is over the moon."

Everyone chuckled, and Bridger folded his hands together. "Are we finished with the ridiculous gossip column now?"

"Nope. There's a little more. Continue eating, and I'll read the last paragraph," Lulu said, taking a sip of her wine before setting her glass down. "*Speaking of eligible bachelors who have flown the coop. We all know another member of the family fell hard for his lovely lady, who is famous for her style and jewelry.*" Lulu squealed. "They are clearly talking about us, Rafael."

"They sure are, baby," Rafe said, as he leaned over and kissed her cheek.

"Okay, last part." She smirked at Bridger, and then her eyes moved back to her phone. "*But word on the street is, this particular man was seen with several family members in the city at a different kind of jewelry store. From what I've heard from my sources, he purchased an exquisite engagement ring, and wedding bells are in their future.*" Lulu paused, eyes wide as she turned to look at Rafe.

The table went completely quiet.

You could hear a pin drop.

“What? You bought a ring?” she whispered.

“Un-fucking-believable,” Bridger hissed, and my mother shot him a warning look, as did Archer and Emerson, but the fact that the *Taylor Tea* had just outed Rafe’s surprise engagement was more pressing than Bridger dropping an F-bomb at the dinner table, apparently.

“I, er, I—yeah, well, it was supposed to be a surprise.” Rafe took her hand in his and shrugged.

“You bought me a ring, Rafael!” she shouted and lunged forward on top of my brother, causing his chair to fall backward and hit the floor with her on top of him.

“Well, I guess the jig is up,” Rafe said over his laughter. “And if I can live without you causing me permanent injury before I propose, it will be a miracle.”

Laughter erupted around the table.

“Someone get this man another malachite stone,” I said, pulling Lulu to her feet and helping my brother up.

“You can still surprise her with the way that you propose,” my father said.

“Eloise, did you mention to Emilia that we’d all gone with Rafe to look at rings?” Bridger asked, not hiding his anger that they just shared this in the newspaper.

“I may have mentioned it, but I can’t remember,” Eloise said, glancing between Bridger and Rafe. “But I promise you, Emilia is not writing this column.”

“I agree,” Henley said. “And anyone could have heard about it. You guys do draw a lot of attention when you’re all together.”

“We were in the city. We didn’t shop here in town.” Bridger arched a brow, glancing around the table. “Start paying attention to all the information they have about us. It’s an inside job.”

“It isn’t Emilia because if it were her, she wouldn’t want to ruin the surprise for me, so that makes me 100 percent certain it is not her," Lulu said. "And it's fine that they wrote about it. We've talked about getting engaged. I just didn't know you bought the ring yet. There's still plenty of surprises to come."

"Agreed," my mother said. "It's still a wonderful celebration, and we have so much to be thankful for."

"We sure do. Let's raise our glasses," Keaton said, holding up a glass as we all did the same. "Cheers to our growing family. To all the exciting things we have to look forward to. To love, to laughter, to making memories."

"Salut!" we all shouted at once.

I leaned over and tugged Eloise close to me. "Love you, Weeze. Happy Thanksgiving."

"Cheers to many more, Hotshot."

"Count on it." I tipped her chin up and kissed her.

Just like I planned to do every day for the rest of my life.

• • •

We were back in the city after a winning game last night. Thankfully, we had the morning off from practice, and Eloise and I were sleeping in later than usual.

"This is my favorite way to wake up," I said, as we sipped our coffee in bed.

"Which part? Sleeping in or coffee in bed?"

"You skipped over the best part. Waking you up with my head buried between your thighs. Hearing you cry out my name. Tasting you on my lips for the rest of the day." I chuckled when her cheeks pinked at my words. "I love that you can still be shy with me."

"You have a filthy mouth," she said with a laugh. "But yes, that was a nice way to wake up."

"I say we make it part of our routine," I teased as we both set our coffees down on the nightstands.

"Yeah? I could get on board with that. But only if you let me return the favor."

I tucked the hair behind her ears and stroked her jaw. "We've got all day to do whatever we want."

Her phone rang on the nightstand for the third time, and she glanced over at it. "I better see who that is."

I leaned back against the headboard, as she reached for her phone.

"Hey, Emilia," she said, before switching it to speakerphone. "Everything okay?"

A small sob came from the other side of the phone, and I sat forward.

"Emilia? Are you okay?" Eloise asked, concern in her voice.

"Yeah, sorry. I just need to vent."

"I'm here. Tell me what's happening," my girlfriend said.

"It's a busy day at the floral shop, with everyone in holiday mode, you know?"

"Yeah, that's a good thing, though, right?" Eloise asked, her free hand lacing with mine.

"Usually, yes." Emilia sucked in a few breaths, clearly trying to calm herself down. "But the flower shop was packed, and Bridger came in and basically told me off in front of everyone. He said I ruined Lulu and Rafe's engagement, and I should be ashamed of myself." She hiccupped and sniffed, and it was clear that she was crying as her voice shook with every word. "He basically insinuated that I was an awful person, and everyone in the flower shop was staring at me, and it was awful and embarrassing. I just don't know why the guy hates me so much."

I reached for my phone and texted in the group chat.

Me: *Seriously, Bridger. Did you just walk into the flower shop and go off on Emilia Taylor?*

Rafe: *Tell me you didn't do that, dude. She's friends with all the girls. This is not going to go over well.*

Easton: *Let's give him a chance to speak before we decide he's guilty.*

Axel: *Always the lawyer. <laughing face emoji>*

Archer: *All right, let's hear it. What happened?*

Bridger: *News travels fast when you're the author of an anonymous column. Did she already put it in print?*

Me: *She did not. She's on the phone, crying right now to Eloise. Dude. You yelled at her in front of a bunch of customers? You've got to let this go.*

Bridger: *So she can just print about relationships, engagement rings, or whatever the fuck she wants to write about our family, and no one gives a fuck?*

Rafe: *We're not even upset about the ring. We've talked about getting engaged, so shopping for a ring isn't a big deal.*

Bridger: *She outed you for buying a ring.*

Rafe: *The engagement will still be a surprise.*

Bridger: *I wouldn't tell the girls your plans, or I promise you, it'll end up in the paper.*

Easton: *You don't even know that it's her. I think avoiding her because you dislike her is one thing, but yelling at her at her place of business is not okay.*

Bridger: *I'm going to hit you in the dick with a pickleball next time I see you.*

Axel: *Just apologize to her and move on.*

Bridger: *Not apologizing unless she has proof that it isn't her. Which she doesn't because I'm telling you, she writes that fucking column.*

Rafe: *Not sure you're the best "reader of people." I don't think it's her.*

Bridger: *Because Lulu doesn't think it's her?*

Rafe: *Correct.*

Bridger: *Lulu also thinks gummy bears are a food group. I'm basing my assessment on facts. She is privy to every single thing that's been written.*

Archer: *So is Melody. Maybe she's writing the column. <thinking emoji>*

Bridger: *<middle finger emoji>*

Me: *You need to apologize. If she wrote the damn column, I don't think she'd be befriending everyone in the family… aside from you.*

Bridger: *Wake the fuck up, man. Of course, she is. This gives her better access to material.*

Easton: *Don't be a dick. Apologize.*

Rafe: *Agreed. I hate conflict. Make this right.*

Archer: *I'm taking Melody for some flowers today. Maybe I can apologize on your behalf.*

Bridger: *I'll shave your eyebrows off in your sleep.*

Axel: *I'd like to see that.*

"I'm so sorry, Em. Call me after work. Love you," Eloise said.

"Love you, too."

I set my phone down when she ended the call. "Is she okay?"

"Not really. She's going to talk to Henley because she wants to file a defamation of character claim against Bridger," Eloise said, throwing her hands in the air. "He needs to let this go."

"I think having Henley file the complaint is a bit of a conflict, seeing as Bridger is our brother."

"She's the only lawyer Emilia knows," Eloise chuckled. "Maybe she'll get over it, but I think he made a scene today, and it is just not okay. Can you talk to him?"

I sighed. "I was just texting about it. Everyone told him to apologize, but he's insistent that it's her. And when Bridger gets something in his head, it's hard to change his mind. But what he did is not okay, so he needs to do something to fix this."

Eloise slipped back down, resting her head on my chest. "Emilia wouldn't have written that about Rafe buying the ring because she adores Lulu. She wouldn't do that to her."

"Listen, Weeze, I don't think it's her. I don't think anyone in the family thinks it's her anymore, now that we've been around her more. But Bridger is all about family, and in his mind, he thinks he's protecting the family by calling her out."

"She was crying pretty hard. I feel bad for her. I want to send her flowers, but I'd have to order them from her." She chuckled. "We need to make this right."

"I'll talk to him about it one-on-one and see if I can get through to him," I said, moving quickly and flipping her onto her back and settling between her thighs. "But right now, I want to have my way with my woman."

"You're such a caveman." Her teeth sank into her bottom lip. "How about you have your way with me in the shower?"

"Ahhhh… a naked, sudsy Eloise is my favorite." I leaned down and kissed her.

"You're my favorite, Clark Chadwick," she whispered.

I moved to my feet, flipping her over my shoulder fireman-style, and smacking her on the ass. "You're my favorite, too, Weeze."

Laughter bellowed from her sweet little body as I carried her to the bathroom.

I couldn't remember a time in my life when I'd been this happy.

This content.

I was definitely over the moon for this girl.

Hockey was no longer my first love. I hadn't even known what love was before.

Hockey was my passion.

Eloise Gable was my first love.

My only love.

Acknowledgments

Greg, Chase & Hannah, I love you endlessly!

Mom, thank you for reading everything that I write the minute I finish it! It means the world to me. Love you!!

Willow & Catherine, so grateful for you both, and your friendship means the world to me. Love you endlessly. #lovechainforever

Kandi, thank you for being YOU. Love you!

Pathi, endlessly thankful for you! Love you so much!

Nat, I am so incredibly grateful for you! I love being on this journey with you! I would truly be lost without you! Love you!

Nina, I'm so grateful for you! Thank you for believing in me and being such a support to me! Love you so much!

Jessica Turner, I'm so grateful for you! Thank you for believing in my books! Seeing them in bookstores is a dream come true, and I'm so thankful for you! Xo

Kim Cermak, so thankful for you! Thank you for having a thick skin on my behalf and for the Bravo chats and the endless support! Love you!

Christine Miller, Kelley Beckham, Tiffany Bullard, Sarah Norris, Valentine Grinstead, Meagan Reynoso, Amy Dindia, Josette Ochoa, Ratula Roy, Jill McManamon, Jaime Guidry, Megan Cermak, and Emma Walczak, I am endlessly thankful for YOU!

Tatyana (Bookish Banter), thank you for being such a support, and teaching me your savvy tricks! Love you!

Abi, thank you for beta reading and for going back through each series to help me create new bonus material! Love you so much!

Janelle (Lyla June Co.), thank you for your support and friendship! I'm so grateful for you!

Paige, you make mother proud. I love you so much and I'm so grateful for your friendship!

Stephanie Hubenak, thank you for always reading my words early and cheering me on. Our daily chats are my favorite.

Kelly Yates, so thankful for your friendship! I love our chats and I'm so thankful for the endless laughs!!

Logan Chisolm, thank you for being the best booth babe at the signings, and for creating the most gorgeous videos for me! I'm so grateful for you!

Kayla Compton, I am so happy to be working with you and so thankful for YOU!

To all the talented, amazing people who turn my words into a polished final book, I am endlessly grateful for you! Sue Grimshaw (Edits by Sue), Hang Le Design, Sarah Sentz (Enchanted Romance Design), Christine Estevez, Ellie McLove (My Brothers Editor), Jaime Ryter (The Ryters Proof), Julie Deaton (Deaton Author Services), Kim and Katie at Lyric Audio Books, thank you for being so encouraging and supportive!

Crystal Eacker, thank you for your audio beta listening/reading skills and for always coming through for me when I'm in a state of panic! So grateful for you my sweet friend!

Erika Plum, thank you for the adorable bookmarks! You nail it every time!

Jennifer, thank you for being an endless support system. For running the Facebook group, posting, reviewing and doing whatever is needed for each release. Your friendship means the world to me! Love you!

Rachel Parker, so incredibly thankful for you and so happy to be on this journey with you! My forever release day good luck charm! Love you so much!

Gianna Rose, Diana Daniels, Rachel Baldwin, Sarah Sentz, Ashley Anastasio, Kayla Compton, Tiara Cobillas, Tori Ann Harris and Erin O'Donnell, thank you for your friendship and your support. It means the world to me!

Dad, you really are the reason that I keep chasing my dreams!! Thank you for teaching me to never give up. Love you!

Sandy, thank you for reading and supporting me throughout this journey! Love you!

To the JKL WILLOWS… I am forever grateful to you for your support and encouragement, my sweet friends!! Love you!

To all the bloggers, bookstagrammers and ARC readers who have posted, shared, and supported me—I can't begin to tell you how much it means to me. I love seeing the graphics that you make and the gorgeous posts that you share. I am forever grateful for your support!

To all the readers who take the time to pick up my books and take a chance on my words…THANK YOU for helping to make my dreams come true!!

Doubling the Trees Behind Every Book You Buy.

Because books should leave the world better than they found it—not just in hearts and minds, but in forests and futures.

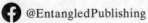

Through our Read More, Breathe Easier initiative, we're helping reforest the planet, restore ecosystems, and rethink what sustainable publishing can be.

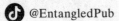

Track the impact of your read at: